D0919712

THE LARAN GAMBIT

♦♦♦♦♦♦

THE LARAN GAMBIT

♦♦♦♦♦♦

A NOVEL OF DARKOVER®

♦♦♦

MARION ZIMMER BRADLEY

AND

DEBORAH J. ROSS

Also by Marion Zimmer Bradley and Deborah J. Ross

The Clingfire Trilogy

The Fall of Neskaya
Zandru's Forge
A Flame in Hali

The Alton Gift
Hastur Lord
The Children of Kings
Thunderlord
The Laran Gambit
Arilinn (forthcoming)

Edited by Deborah J. Ross

Stars of Darkover
Gifts of Darkover
Realms of Darkover
Masques of Darkover
Crossroads of Darkover
Citadels of Darkover
Jewels of Darkover (forthcoming)

Jacket art by Matthew Stawicki
Jacket design by Dave Smeds
Edited by Judith Tarr

ISBN-13 978-1-938185-72-4
ISBN-10 1-938185-72-2

A publication of
The Marion Zimmer Bradley Literary Works Trust
PO Box 193473
San Francisco, CA 94119-3473
www.mzbworks.com

Notes

The *Laran Gambit* had a long, convoluted path to publication that began in 2013, when I submitted proposals for the next three Darkover novels. When I developed the concepts and plot for *The Laran Gambit*, I wanted to return to the "modern" timeline envisioning Darkover as no longer vulnerable to exploitation, as it had been in earlier novels such as *The World Wreckers*. I wondered what the Terran Federation, now the Star Alliance, could want so desperately as to reach out to Darkover. The Powers-That-Be on Terra might not be the ones in need. In fact, they might be the problem. In *The World Wreckers*, Regis Hastur negotiates for Darkover's independence using Comyn psychic powers as a bargaining lever. What if the Terran leaders had developed a technological form of telepathy? Or, better yet, of mind control? Soon I had the basic conflict of machine-based mind control versus natural Darkovan *laran*. I wanted a protagonist whose strengths were compassion rather than brute force. As I wrote, child psychologist Bryn spoke to me about her young patients, traumatized as a result of the Star Alliance's brutal tactics, and I knew I had the right voice.

Meanwhile, the real world moved on. The 2016 United States presidential election increased the polarization of the nation, and social media turned into a hotbed of contention. Mass shootings at schools, houses of worship, and other public places left communities stunned and grieving. The #MeToo movement highlighted the prevalence of sexual assault. Humanitarian crises deepened across the world, and the effects of climate change accelerated. Wildfires raged across the West, and hurricanes devastated other parts of the country. A pandemic struck, leaving tens of thousands and then hundreds of thousands, and then millions of people dead. A violent insurrection threatened to topple the government. Just when we thought things could not get any worse, Russia launched a war with Ukraine, still raging as I write this. More than once I've wondered if my vision of a ruthless, totalitarian Star Alliance was not becoming reality.

I didn't write *The Laran Gambit* as a prediction of the future or a commentary on our modern world. I wrote it as an entertaining story. Yet as I worked through the editorial revisions, I remembered these words from J.R.R. Tolkien's *The Fellowship of the Ring*:

> "I wish it need not have happened in my time," said Frodo.
> "So do I," said Gandalf, "and so do all who live to see such times. But that is not for them to decide. All we have to decide is what to do with the time that is given us."

This is the decision that Bryn faces in *The Laran Gambit.* What will she do with the time that is given to her? How will we all face the crises of our times? In the end, my personal response is to tell stories. I believe that stories can heal us, strengthen us, and inspire us. They can create bonds of understanding and join us in communities. Darkover is a special place for so many readers, one in which characters come to know one another deeply. We all crave that connection, especially in troubled times.

Welcome, dear friends, to this marvelous world. May it ease your sorrows and give you hope.

Deborah J. Ross

Acknowledgments

Special gratitude to All The Usual Suspects: Ann Sharp and Elisabeth Waters of The Marion Zimmer Bradley Literary Works Trust encouraged me every step of the way; my agent, Russ Galen, and my editor at DAW, Betsy Wollheim. The Word Dragons—Juliette Wade, Janice Hardy, and Kimberly Unger—kept me sane during publisher musical chairs. Judith Tarr did an amazing job editing this version, and copy editor Michael Spence caught many oopsies. My cover artist, Matthew Stawicki, created the gorgeous painting of Bryn crash-landing on Darkover, and Dave Smeds transformed it into a stunning design. My spiritual sisters and occasional walking buddies, Karie, Chris, Lee, Antonina, Francesca, Janet, Janyce, and Noelle, sustained me with candles in the dark and hikes along the coast.

My family made it all possible. I love you more than I can express in words.

For the children—
the ones who didn't make it and the ones who did.

The sky was on fire.

Bryn Haslund halted outside the thirty-story tower housing the psychiatric clinic where she worked, glanced upward, and forgot to breathe. A glory of orange and violet bathed clouds was piled high like mountains. She felt as if she were gazing into a faraway country, a land of fjords and rolling plains, of hidden valleys and breathtaking peaks. A planet circling a ruddy sun. A place where anything could happen.

The light shifted, muting the sunset colors. The mountains sagged into formless, gray-bellied shapes. A wind whipped through the corridor of the street, laden with eye-stinging dust. Although the layers of her coat and bodysuit provided sufficient insulation for a brisk autumn day, goosebumps sprang up on her skin, not from physical cold but one of those odd premonitions she'd had since her teen years. She'd been working too hard and seeing too many children, she told herself.

On the windows of the tower across the street from hers, ad panels flashed the crest of the Star Alliance. In the center, wreathed by the stylized emblem of the member planets, First Minister Arthur Nagy beamed his paternal smile above the motto, *Together the Future*. Almost every building large enough bore a similar message: *Together the Stars. One Alliance One Hope.*

The vacant eyes of Bryn's young patients told a different story.

Bryn hurried down the street, noticing more uniforms than usual: city police in traditional navy and StarGuard troops in gray camo, blasters prominently displayed. She frowned, wondering why the interstellar infantry was patrolling the streets of Terra Central.

Weaving between the other commuters, she reached the tram stop. The next car was so densely packed, there was no possibility of squeezing onboard. The one after that was equally full. Bryn had never seen them so crowded. There was nothing to do but wait unless she wanted to walk. As it was, she'd be cutting the time short, joining her sister's family for dinner before their father's televised speech.

Voices rose and fell around her, the conversations shifting from heated to subdued. Ordinarily, she would have tried not to listen, but today she could not shut the words out. The woman to her right was talking with her companion about the planet Renney, complaining about the embargo.

"I don't for a minute believe this business about terrorists. For heaven's sake, it's an artist's colony!"

"Not the whole planet, surely. Even if those creative types are eccentric, even revolutionary—"

"Hsst!" A man in a worn coat snapped at the two women. "You don't know who might be listening!"

A pair of students, university by their striped scarves, pushed their way past Bryn, cutting off the rest of the conversation.

The next tram approached without slowing. All four cars looked full. Bryn decided she couldn't wait for the next one. Spotting a gap in the line of passengers on the running board, she leaped for it. She grabbed the outside pole to avoid being thrown off. Just as she caught her balance, the movement of the car caused her to collide with a passenger riding on the outside.

"Hello, there!" The man steadied her with his free hand. He looked ordinary enough—neither young nor old, medium height, medium weight, unremarkable clothes, no distinguishing features except for his almost colorless eyes.

"Sorry, I didn't see you, although I can't imagine how. Here—" He moved to create a narrow opening into the interior of the car for her and guided her inside.

Bryn was used to drawing attention. She was thirty but looked younger, with striking, red-auburn curls. Suddenly uneasy, she pulled away from the man as far as the packed interior would allow.

"Are you all right?" he asked. "Not shaken up?"

"Think nothing of it."

"I've been terribly rude." He leaned closer, dropping the pitch of his voice. "Please allow me to make amends by buying you dinner."

"I am expected elsewhere," she replied stiffly. "And we don't know each other."

"A drink, then? Just one, no strings attached?"

The stranger's smile provoked a crawling sensation in Bryn's gut. If he wasn't lying outright, he was certainly hiding something. She'd had such feelings from time to time, perhaps intuitive leaps or hunches. As a therapist, she'd learned to trust her instincts about when a child was lying.

She recognized his type. If she said anything else, no matter how definite a refusal, she'd only encourage him. There must be a way to keep him from following her.

The tram slowed as it entered a crowded pedestrian plaza and began a turn. Although it was still in motion, Bryn tightened her grip on her shoulder bag, yanked the door open, and jumped.

She landed awkwardly but then caught her balance and straightened up, trying to get her bearings. This wasn't her usual stop on her way to her sister's apartment, so she didn't recognize the neighborhood. She didn't relish the prospect of elbowing her way through a milling throng in search of a landmark, but she didn't seem to have a choice.

More people were streaming into the already congested plaza from the surrounding streets. She tried to push behind a man with a grizzled, half-grown beard, wearing the overalls of a laborer. Someone on her other side shoved her. She collided with the laborer.

"Watch it!" His scowl lightened as he turned to look at her. "Pardon, lady, but this ain't no place for the likes of you. I've a daughter your age, and I surely wouldn't leave her out here at a time like this. Come on—" He moved to take her arm.

In a moment of panic, Bryn jerked away, almost falling over the feet of a pair of younger men, also in worker's garb and knitted caps. She scrambled away, putting them between her and the older man. His intentions might be benign, only to help her out of the crowd, but her heart was pounding so hard she couldn't think clearly. A tang like adrenalin hung in the air.

Something's wrong. This isn't normal after-work traffic.

Some distance behind her, a man shouted something about Vainwal and independence. She couldn't make out more through the racket. She'd lost track of the burly man in workers' clothing, the one who'd tried to get her to safety.

"Freedom for Vainwal!" came more voices from the periphery of the plaza. "Freedom! Freedom!"

A moment later, someone else took up the cry, and then another and another. "Smash the Alliance!"

"Watch out—stop shoving!" someone nearer to Bryn shouted.

"Down with Nagy! Nagy the Tyrant! Nagy the Butcher!"

The voices rose, blending into such a roar that the individual phrases became unintelligible, only the repeated name *Nagy! Nagy! Nagy!*

"THIS GATHERING IS ILLEGAL!" a mechanically-generated voice blasted from speakers on top of the surrounding buildings. "DISPERSE AT ONCE OR FACE ARREST!"

Bryn searched for a way out of the mob. She couldn't move more than a few steps. Around her, men and women, some with children in tow, were also trying to get free of the commotion.

"Watch who you're shoving!" a stout, middle-aged woman snarled as Bryn stumbled into her.

"Sorry—" Bryn began, but the woman was already elbowing past a man in a business-cut tunic. Beyond them, another man pleaded for order, hands raised, but his voice was drowned in a volley of cries.

"Justice for Ephebe!"

"Down with Nagy!"

Bryn managed to push between people here and around others there, gradually making her way toward the periphery. The next moment, half a dozen young people carrying placards cut off her path. They ignored Bryn as they rushed past, except for one young woman in a university scarf and cap.

"Whose side are you on?" the student demanded. "Get off the street if you're not with us."

"Free Vainwal!"

"Remember Campta!"

"Out of my way!" a man yelled.

"Down with Nagy! Down with the Tyrant!"

Just then, a gap opened in front of Bryn. Through it she glimpsed a line of gray camo uniforms behind shimmering force shields. A fist-sized rock hurtled over her head toward the uniforms. She flinched reflexively. The rock hit the force shields in an explosion of dust. Another went sailing, then a handful more.

The crowd surged forward. Heart hammering in her ears, Bryn struggled to hold her position. The mass of bodies carried her along like a tide in flood. She pushed one way and then the other but could not free herself. People pressed in on her from both sides. It was all she could do to stay on her feet and not get trampled.

"Down with Nagy!" roared from a hundred throats. "Death to the traitor!"

"Free Vainwal!"

The mob neared the edge of the plaza, and the Boulevard of the Planets came into view. Bryn's gut churned when she realized the boulevard was just as crowded and the whole combined mass was now headed toward the Alliance Headquarters. No matter which way she turned, more people blocked her path.

"DISPERSE AT ONCE!" The mechanical commands seemed to be coming from everywhere, echoing off the sides of the towers. Overhead, she caught the distinctive swoosh and whine of a police hovercraft.

Someone—a woman, very close—let out a shriek, high and wordless, and was suddenly silenced.

Calm. Stay calm.

The mob picked up its pace as it surged into the Boulevard of the Planets. The hovercraft sounded nearer now. Bryn glanced up to see a dozen of them forming a half-circle over the leading edge of the crowd.

She heard, "—LAST WARNING—" and the rest of the announcement was lost in a deafening uproar. Flashes of orange light appeared along the cargo compartments of the hovercraft.

A round, metallic object catapulted toward her. It missed her and struck a man on the shoulder. The casing flew into pieces. Orange-tinged smoke billowed forth.

Around Bryn, people started screaming. The crowd shifted into a stampede. A person slammed into her, knocking her off-balance. Before she could regain her footing, another pushed her hard in a different direction, and then another. Her shoe caught on something soft. She tripped and slammed into the pavement. There was no possible way of getting to her feet in the confusion.

Bryn curled into a ball, drawing her knees tight to her body and covering her head with her hands. She felt blows against her back—feet, lower legs, she couldn't tell. The impacts were glancing and not aimed with any force. These people weren't trying to hurt her, but an unlucky impact—on her skull, on her spine—

Just stay calm...breathe...let it pass... There will be an opening...a chance to get away...

Something hard and sharp struck her lower spine. Her vision went white and her muscles locked. Pain raced down her back like an explosion of fire. For a terrifying moment, she couldn't move, not even to draw breath. She was hit again, this time on the shoulder. She heard someone screaming, then realized it was her own voice. A rushing, roaring sound like storm-whipped waves echoed weirdly, filling her skull. The world went gray and then cold.

◆◆◆

Bryn's next conscious thought was that she had been ill. Her tongue was coated with sour-tasting mucus, her muscles trembled uncontrollably, she felt cold but not feverish, and her eyes wouldn't focus properly. A thin, antiseptic smell tinged the air. In the distance, things clanked and rattled and jingled. She heard muted voices, then a man speaking, although she couldn't make out the words, then shouting. The cadence sounded like swearing. This place was far too noisy for anyone to rest. She must be in a hospital.

She wanted more than anything to go back to sleep and for the world to make better sense when she woke again, but she couldn't get comfortable. The bones of her hip and shoulder ached. To make matters worse, the more awake she became, the thirstier and more nauseated she felt.

"Hello?" she called or tried to because her throat was so raw, the word came out as a croak. She doubted anyone could hear her over all the noise.

Where was she, anyway? She remembered leaving her office, then the crowds on the tram. Getting off...the protest building into a riot...being unable to escape, almost as if she were being herded along...the hovercraft blaring out orders to disperse...canisters tossed onto the crowd. Knockout gas? That would explain the nausea and thirst.

Bryn lifted her head and looked around. She was lying on a railed bed in a narrow room. The walls, what she could see of them, were the color of a rainy day, making the place seem even colder and bleaker.

"Hello!" she called again, louder this time. "I'm awake!"

Again, there was no response, but the worst of the nausea seemed to be wearing off. There was nothing to do but wait and try not to think too hard about missing Father's speech. Leonin would be anxious when she didn't arrive on time, Saralyn would be trying to keep everyone cheerful, and as for the speech itself and the reaction to it—

Breathe, just breathe. The police probably have a hundred people to process, and they'll let us all go... Yes, surely they would. She'd committed no crime, broken no laws.

She remembered how the shouted slogans—*Down with Nagy, Smash the Alliance*—had arisen in the periphery of the crowd as if they were being *herded.*

Lying back, she focused on taking deep, slow breaths. Sure enough, only a short time later, she heard a burst of louder metallic clanging and then the tap-tap-tap of shoe heels. They stopped at the foot of her bed. Lifting her head, she saw two women, one in medical garb, the other in a severely tailored dark suit.

"Bryn Haslund?" asked the woman in the dark suit. Her hair hung in soft white curls around a face so smooth and unwrinkled as to give no hint of her age.

"Yes?" Bryn answered.

"Very good. You're to come with us."

"Sit up slowly." The medic slid an arm under Bryn's shoulders and helped her to rise. "The antidote's cleared the knockout gas from your system by now, but there can be residual lightheadedness. Wouldn't want you to faint on us now, would we?"

The edges of Bryn's vision went fuzzy and her knees threatened to give way under her, but she managed to walk with a measure of dignity down a corridor lined with barred windows and into a smaller room furnished with a table and chairs.

Sitting on the other side of the table was the man who'd tried to pick her up on the tram. "Please be seated," he said in a pleasant voice.

She complied. "Who are you, and why were you following me on the tram?"

"If you had come with me, all of this—" he hesitated, and a faint expression of disgust came over his face, as quickly disappearing, or perhaps Bryn had imagined it, "—could have been avoided."

She glared at him. "You were *stalking* me. Why?"

"In general, a person in your position is wise to be guarded. Especially, if I may say so, a woman as young and attractive as yourself. But in this instance, your suspicions placed you beyond my protection. Fortunately, that difficulty has now been remedied."

"You—you tried to hit on me like a gormless adolescent and now you're saying that this—my getting gassed and thrown into this place—is somehow *my fault* for not falling for your ridiculous pick-up line? What's your name, anyway?"

"That is truly not something you need to know," he said, his expression remaining mild, "but you may call me Black."

Her skin prickled. "Black? Is that a first name or a last name? Or black as in the color of your uniform?" It was a wild shot, guessing that he worked for StarOps, but she knew in an instant that it had hit home.

"Please try to moderate your antagonism, Ms. Haslund. I regret any discomfort occasioned by our previous interaction."

Bryn opened her mouth to let him know exactly how insincere he sounded but then thought better of it. In all likelihood, he couldn't help being obnoxious or a nuisance. A nuisance who just happened to work for StarOps. If she stopped to think about it, she'd be properly terrified instead of still queasy from the knockout gas.

"Apology accepted," she said, "but I would appreciate an explanation. You were following me and then you tried to take me aside, presumably so I wouldn't get caught up in the demonstration—*and how did you know there was going to be one, anyway?* What are you after? And who sent you?"

"I have been assigned to your protection, and I thought if you accompanied me of your own volition, there would be less public notice taken."

"If I'd come along quietly, you mean?"

His face tightened, and in that fraction of a moment, she realized he was not as inexperienced as she'd first thought. In fact, he gave off the fragrance of danger, and that made her even more angry.

"As for the incident," he said, "my superiors had received intelligence that something of this sort was impending. As a family member of Senator Haslund, we could not allow you to be injured. In this duty, I failed. For that, I am profoundly sorry."

"Isn't it unusual to provide protection for the families of Senators? You never have before. I've come and gone from my office for years now without anyone trailing me." Her work with refugee children had never been controversial. Even those who supported the Star Alliance's military actions sympathized with its young victims.

Black's features remained as composed as before. "You are correct. In the past, it has not been necessary. But now, with the current political situation as it is, we cannot be too careful."

Bryn felt cold. StarOps had known about the demonstration and might well have placed provocateurs to turn it into a riot. Which meant they'd also known about the Vainwal declaration ahead of time. Which meant Nagy himself had known and had planned to discredit Vainwal's supporters.

Nothing Black had just said was an overt lie, and yet she didn't believe him.

"I'm tired and not feeling very well. The gas, I suppose. I'd like to leave now, if you please." She pushed away from the table and stood up.

"Certainly. You are not a prisoner." Black rose and rapped on the door. An instant later, the dark-suited woman opened it and stood back for them to exit. "I will ensure your safe arrival to your sister's residence in good time for Senator Haslund's speech."

"I've missed it, thanks to you."

"On the contrary. The speech has been delayed. Please allow me to convey you much faster than possible on your own."

Bryn nodded, a sharp jerk of her chin. It wasn't unheard of for events like her father's speech to be postponed for one reason or another. If Black was willing to use StarOps privilege, a private vehicle, for example, to cut through traffic, she wouldn't say no. But that didn't mean she trusted him.

Black escorted Bryn into an underground parking area, deserted except for a line of armored vehicles and a long, sleek car waiting at the curb. It was the same size and general appearance as the one provided to her father on official occasions. He opened the back door and gestured her inside. She complied.

Black slid onto the front passenger seat and they drove off. Bryn couldn't see much of the driver through the light-distorting barrier, other than the back of his head. The windows, although dark, were not entirely opaque. Craning her neck, she made out high-intensity security lights overhead.

Although Bryn could barely feel the vibration of the car, she sensed its upward movement. They were ascending a ramp, then. Now and again, she felt a change in acceleration, either slowing or turning, but since she didn't know the location of the compound, remembering the route would do her no good. A couple of times, Black glanced back but made no attempt to strike up a conversation. At first, she felt relieved she wouldn't have to make small talk with him. Then she wondered if she wasn't being too harsh. He didn't set the policies, after all, and he'd been scrupulously polite to her. It was natural after an ordeal such as hers to lash out, to look for someone to blame. She knew how to handle these reactions in her patients.

The limousine halted, its deceleration so smooth that it took Bryn a moment to realize they were no longer moving. On exiting the car, she found herself in front of Saralyn's apartment tower. Everything she could see, building and street and pedestrians and the tram stop on the next corner, looked perfectly normal. For a heartbeat, she wondered if she'd been ill and had dreamed up the riot.

Black waited while Bryn placed her hand on the building's security sensor. When their first child was born, Saralyn and Tomas had added

Bryn to the family's account, "just in case." They entered the building and crossed the tiny foyer. The elevator door whispered open and Black gestured for Bryn to wait while he checked its interior. He followed her until she reached Saralyn's apartment.

The door flew open and Leonin stood there. A dusky flush darkened his face. His brows were drawn together and his lips, full and expressively mobile, parted just before she rushed into his arms.

"You're here—you're safe," he said as he drew her inside. Just before the lock chimed shut, she caught his quick glance over her shoulder at Black.

Bryn leaned into Leonin's strength as his arms enfolded her. Until that instant, that moment of letting go, she had not felt the effort with which she'd been holding herself together. As long as Black was there, she had not dared to let her guard down. Now her eyes stung and her throat closed up. The numbness inside her gave way.

"You're all right. It's over now," he murmured, his breath warm against her hair.

I should be stronger than this, she thought.

Wiping away tears, she pulled away. He handed her a handkerchief from his pocket. The fabric was warm and smelled faintly of the almond soap he favored.

"I feel like such an idiot for breaking down," she said as she dabbed her wet cheeks.

"No, not an idiot at all," Leonin said. "A strong person who's been overwhelmed. Whatever you've been through— That man outside was StarOps, wasn't he?"

"What happened?" Saralyn stood at the entrance to the kitchen and dining areas, hands twined together over her breastbone. It was an old posture, one she used to sleep in when she'd had bad dreams as a little girl, and seeing her baby sister like this brought a fresh sting of tears to Bryn's eyes. "Why are you so late?"

"I got caught in a riot—or protest—or something," Bryn said. "They used knockout gas on us. I woke up in a clinic." She stumbled through the rest of her story.

"How terrible." Saralyn put her arm around Bryn, and together they sat down on the sofa.

"I heard about the riot on the news vids but had no idea you were there." Leonin lowered himself beside Bryn. "It sounded like a demonstration that began peacefully until provocateurs forced a confrontation with law enforcement."

"*Provocateurs*?" Saralyn said. "Leo, really! You and your conspiracy theories!"

"The people of Vainwal—and Renney and Ephebe and a dozen other planets, not to mention the Class D Protected Worlds—have legitimate grievances. That truth is hardly a *conspiracy theory*."

"We *need* to stand united—"

"We *need* to stop silencing people—"

"Stop it, both of you!" Bryn surged to her feet and whirled to face them. "There's no good in turning on one another!"

"Love, forgive me for adding to what you've already been through," Leonin said. "And Saralyn, my apologies. My temper got the better of me, and I spoke without thinking. Bryn is right: this is not the time for yet another political discussion. We know where we each stand, we don't agree, and for now, it's better to just let matters rest. After all, supporting Bryn is one thing we *can* agree on."

Saralyn turned to Bryn. "I'm such a booby! Anyone with half a brain can see you've been through a terrible ordeal. Forgive me, please, and chalk my bad behavior off to fretfulness. You were late and we couldn't *imagine* what had happened to you!"

Leonin looked as if he'd like to say, *I could imagine a great many things happening to innocent people today*. Bryn loved him for his silence. She could always tell when he stopped himself from being confrontational.

"Is something troubling you?" Bryn said to Saralyn. "Has anything worrisome happened?"

"Oh! Nothing, really. For a little while now, I imagined someone was—well, not exactly following me. More like keeping an eye on me. When I'd look, though, it was all different people on the street, in the cafe, at the park. Everything was fine. I must have been making it up, or it was just nerves, I suppose."

Before any of them could say more, Tomas poked his head out from the hallway. "Is it safe to bring the kids out? They're about to die from curiosity."

"Yes, please. I'd love to see them." Bryn took another swipe at her eyes. Rhys and Bettony were loving and energetic and resilient. They lifted her spirits, reminding her what normal children were like, not hollow-eyed survivors with nightmares so terrifying, they'd lost the ability to scream.

The children flew down the hallway like a pair of romping puppies. Bryn dropped to her knees, for Rhys was only two to his sister's eleven years. His joy at seeing her was so pure, so unfeigned, her heart gave a skip. He smothered her in hugs.

"Goodness, you have grown!" Bryn exclaimed. "And you, young woman," for Bettony had been born with a full complement of self-assurance, or so the family joke went, "you grow more poised every time I see you."

"Silly aunt," Bettony said with a giggle, "you see us practically every week. And Uncle Leo, too." She planted a kiss on each of Bryn's cheeks. With that, the greetings concluded. Rhys returned to the pile of toys in the middle of the living room and Bettony to her reader.

"Shall we eat now?" Saralyn asked. "Father's speech isn't due to begin for another hour."

Bryn still felt queasy from the gas, but food would help settle her stomach. One of Saralyn's enthusiasms since she had become a mother was bland food. One of the many celebrities offering nutritional and child-rearing advice with neither personal experience nor professional training had made several fortunes with a series of vids and heavily advertised products that supposedly developed a child's taste by avoiding strong flavors. Or, in Bryn's mind, any flavors at all. At least, the meal would be hot.

They proceeded to the dining area, with Saralyn handing out bowls of stuff that looked as if it had been blanched and then pureed. Bryn spooned a portion of what she thought might be creamed rice onto her place just as Saralyn scowled at Rhys.

"Not with your fingers! Tomas, can't you keep him in better order? At least when we have guests?"

"Rhys," Tomas addressed his young son in a perfectly serious tone, "would you prefer to eat here with your spoon or in your room with your fingers?"

"No!" Rhys cried, scooping up something that had lumps and flecks of green. "With Auntie Bryn!"

In the past, this would have been Bryn's cue to coax her nephew into better table manners. She searched within herself for the energy to deal with a two-year-old who was clearly hungry, tired, and overstimulated.

"Rhys—" she began, but Leonin had already swept the boy up in one hand, dish and spoon in the other, and headed toward the bedrooms, chanting, "Crocodile, crocodile, who's got the monkey?"

He's wonderful with them, Bryn thought. The joy Leonin found in children was the first thing that drew her to him. They had met as volunteers at a refugee family center that referred some of Bryn's patients. She'd had to drop the unpaid work as her professional load grew and he'd spent more and more time on political causes, but they had stayed in touch and eventually fallen in love.

For the next several minutes, Bryn faced no greater challenge than managing a few mouthfuls of mush. The stuff wasn't creamed rice. She didn't know what it was, and she didn't care. It was smooth and warm, and she could swallow it.

"*Anyway*," Saralyn said, as if continuing a previous conversation, "there was no call from Father, no ping, nothing. Just an announcement on the vid saying the speech had been rescheduled. Tomas, didn't they say they'd been having technical difficulties?"

"That's what they say when they don't want to say," Bryn said.

"Someone on his staff would inform us if he were ill, wouldn't they?" Saralyn said, fork poised halfway to her mouth. "It's nothing to worry about."

Bryn set her own fork down. Saralyn was determined to believe whatever the Alliance representatives said, or whatever they fed the media.

If I had not met Leonin, I might have been the same.

"Something's going on," Bryn said. "That man, Black, was following me even before the riot."

"Following you?" Tomas said.

"Assuming he was telling the truth, he'd already been assigned as security for us as Father's family."

"Well, of course. Father's an important man," Saralyn said, as if that explained everything. "Important people often have enemies. He shouldn't have to worry about the safety of his family. It's the government's responsibility to make sure no harm comes to us. We *deserve* protection."

"We've never needed bodyguards before, let alone StarOps," Bryn said.

Saralyn stared at her half-eaten meal, a flush rising to her cheeks.

"We live in tempestuous times, and transitions are always difficult." Tomas broke the uneasy pause in his soft, easy voice. "Like other changes that have come before, this one will pass and the Alliance will be stronger for it."

Once we were only one world, Bryn thought. *And then two and five and more.* But, as Leonin had pointed out a hundred times, the Alliance was inherently unstable because it was based on coercion, not voluntary cooperation. Worlds like Ephebe and Thetis ended up under martial law. Campta had been carpet-bombed, uninhabitable by any living things more complex than algae.

Leonin returned, leading a smiling and cleaned-up Rhys by the hand. He winked at Bryn as he lifted the little boy onto his seat. Everyone finished the meal without friction. The conversation centered around the daily events in the children's lives. Bryn found it far more pleasant to think about what a wonderful father Leonin would be than to ponder the fate of the Alliance.

The door chimed and Tomas went to answer it. Leonin turned his head to brush his lips against Bryn's cheek. Bryn tipped her head back, then caught sight of Bettony staring at them.

Tomas stepped back to admit a young woman carrying a book pack. She had the slightly distracted look and striped scarf of a university student. Apparently, she was their usual babysitter, picking up an extra evening's work to help clean up after the meal. Bettony loudly insisted that she was old enough to watch Grandpa's speech.

"Then you can *also* help in the kitchen," Saralyn said. In response, Bettony grabbed her brother's hand and hurried off toward their bedrooms.

"You don't mind missing the speech?" Leonin said to the young woman, who was already carrying piles of plates into the kitchen.

"Not really." The young woman began loading the dishes into the ultrasonic cleaner.

"What are you studying?" Bryn asked. "I'm sorry, I didn't catch your name."

"Erica. Historical Fashion. Look, I'm just here to do a job. I get enough politics on campus. This has nothing to do with me."

Tomas said, pointedly, to Leonin, "Not all students are activists."

"We were, in my day," Leonin said.

"*I* wasn't." What Bryn meant, and he understood, was that she'd been determined to follow any path except her father's.

"And yet here you are," Leonin said to her, "helping refugee children recover from the atrocities of the Alliance."

"Healing isn't the same as activism."

"Isn't it? Both challenge the *status quo*. Every day, you see first-hand the results of Nagy's willingness to use military power—"

"Not here, Leo," she pleaded. "Not now."

"If you'll excuse me, I have work to do." With a nod in Saralyn's direction, Erica strode off down the hallway.

Tomas picked up the conversation. "After today's riot and the effectiveness with which it was put down, I'm not at all convinced that popular activism is the answer. Your father and his colleagues, on the other hand, stand a very good chance of influencing the course of events in a positive direction. But not ordinary people."

"We can all agree on that." Saralyn's scowl eased. She might be temperamental, Bryn thought, usually because she was trying to do too many things perfectly at once. And it was entirely possible Saralyn was correct that she was under surveillance.

While Saralyn set up the vid and rearranged the chairs, Leonin muttered to Bryn, "That attitude—" nodding in the direction Erica had gone, "—is like handing victory to Nagy without so much as a whimper."

"People will listen to Father, you know they will," Bryn said. "The two of you may not agree on every detail, just as you and I don't, but he has tremendous influence, not only in the Senate but in popular opinion."

"Spoken like a politician's loyal daughter."

"You know me better than that!"

"Love, I meant only that you've grown up as an insider, trusting the system. Thinking in terms of influence and the balance of power. Me, I'm an *outsider*."

"A gadfly," Bryn said with a smile. She pinched her fingers and waved them in a circular pattern. "Zzzz…."

"An external conscience, if you will. Just as your father is an internal one."

She stood on tiptoe to plant a kiss on his nose. "Which is why the world needs both of you. I wouldn't have you any other way."

"Are you two lovebirds finished?" Saralyn said. "They're introducing Father now."

In a considerably better mood, Bryn settled on the living room sofa. She felt sore in every joint and muscle, but good news and a good night's sleep would help. Leonin sat beside her, and Saralyn and Tomas took the two free-standing posture chairs. Bryn leaned into Leonin's warmth, as she so often had in the four years they'd been together.

Saralyn's vid system was a newer model, capable of displaying holographic images, and now those images overlaid the walls of the living room. The Senate chamber was constructed in the old style, with an audience section, side wings for press and security, and a podium on a raised dais at the end of a long center aisle. Senators, many of whom Bryn had met personally on one occasion or another, and their entourages jammed the lower sections. Quite a few were engaged in animated conversation. Saralyn turned down the volume so it wasn't deafening. It wasn't possible to make out individual voices in the general clamor.

A dozen chairs were arranged behind the podium, all more ornate than those below. Bryn had seen the chamber many times since her father had taken office, in person when she cared to attend, and via vid on occasions like this. She hadn't noticed before how the center chair, the one directly below the Star Alliance banner—the First Minister's Seat—dominated the dais. Had she misremembered, or was it now noticeably the largest? She decided she must be imagining things, perhaps as an aftereffect of the knockout gas.

"You okay?" murmured Leonin.

She rubbed the bridge of her nose. "A bit of a headache from the gas."

"They had no business—" he said tightly.

"Please, Leo. I love you, and I love that you're so intense. Most of the time, anyway. For right now, let's just be with my family and listen, okay?"

"I get carried away when your welfare is concerned. Forgive me?"

"This time."

One eyebrow lifted. "Just this one time?"

Bryn's answering smile eased the tension in her skull, although she could not resist saying, "Don't press your luck."

A line of dignitaries filed onto the dais from a side door and took their places in front of their seats. Ernst Haslund was not among them.

"*Where is he?*" Saralyn said, her voice rising in pitch. "He's supposed to—where is he?"

"Easy, my darling. I'm sure there's an explanation." Tomas spoke reassuringly as he reached out to take Saralyn's hand. "It'll be fine."

The assembly below the dais quieted. From the loudspeakers above the wings came a fanfare, a variation of the "Star Alliance March." Bryn had never liked the piece, and this arrangement was even more overblown than usual. Her stomach clenched.

Father's fine. He's got to be.

The fanfare shifted into its final cadence and ended on a sustained chord that made Bryn's scalp muscles tighten again. Arthur Nagy entered. The entire live audience burst into applause. As the vid cameras zoomed in, Nagy's figure swelled to superhuman size. He beamed as he accepted the acclamation, his expression gracious and fatherly.

Leonin's hand-held link vibrated. He scanned it, scowling.

"Must you do that *now*?" Saralyn said.

"Sorry, very rude of me." Leonin tapped the link and slid it back into his shirt pocket. To Bryn, he added, "It's Rashid, wanting to make sure I haven't been arrested."

"Your brother's being unusually paranoid." Bryn kept her tone light. "Better for you to worry about *him*."

"Better to worry about neither of you," Tomas said. "Better to not have *cause* to worry."

Meaning, Bryn supposed, that the brothers had been openly vocal in their criticism of the dynastic regime, although Leonin was restrained while in the company of Saralyn's family. Neither one had kept secret their belief that Arthur Nagy was the greatest threat to the freedom and self-governance of the Alliance worlds since his mother, Senator Sandra Nagy, had seized control. They insisted the present Senate was a joke, circus trappings to convince people they had a voice. Ernst Haslund had not been offended the first time the man who was dating his younger daughter threw that opinion in his face; instead, he had patiently explained the need for slow but peaceful evolution of political systems.

In the vid, the Senate took their seats and First Minister Nagy delivered his formal welcome. Bryn's attention wandered, for she had heard the identical speech a dozen times. Nagy must have memorized it, and the text was so bland and nonspecific as to be suitable for almost any public occasion.

In mid-sentence, the visual transmission wavered. Pixels replaced the solid-looking three-dimensional images, whirling into a cylindrical blizzard. Nagy's voice gave way to an ear-splitting squeal. Saralyn clapped her hands over her ears, and Tomas lunged for the controls. Bryn covered her ears, although it did little to shield her from the pain flaring in her skull. Her headache returned, more intense than before.

The squealing died as Tomas muted the volume, but the roiling visual static remained. Over the next few seconds, it resolved. The image was flat and grainy but clearly showed a human head and shoulders. Between the poor quality and the mask and hood covering head and neck, the person was unrecognizable. Bryn could not have determined the gender, age, or race. The voice, when it came, had been mechanically distorted, but the words were clear enough:

"Citizens of all worlds, your government has been lying to you! The Star Alliance is not and never has been a benevolent fellowship of planets, devoted to order and prosperity. It is a brutal tyranny, bent on hammering down anyone who dares to protest. Its order is the rule of the iron fist. Its prosperity means the pillage of all worlds except the select few—"

The voice might be distorted and the speaker's features cloaked, but Bryn recognized Rashid's oratorical style.

"*For a generation now,*" Rashid's words rolled on, "*the Nagy dynasty has used the power of Spaceforce to silence any planet that dares to protest unfair trade practices and military law. Wake up!*"

"How dare they?" Saralyn said. "What next? Anarchy in the streets? The Alliance falling apart—"

Leonin, please don't say anything.

"It's all right, sweetheart," Tomas said. "They'll have it under control in a moment."

"*Stand with Vainwal!*" Rashid shouted. "*Remember Campta and Ephebe! Rise up—*"

The transmission cut off abruptly. In the silence that followed, Bryn found it difficult to breathe. The muscles of Leonin's jaw contracted visibly, but he said nothing. His fingers closed around Bryn's.

"Thank goodness that's over with," Saralyn said.

With a burst of static, the vid resumed. The image of Arthur Nagy leaped into focus. Every silver-gray hair was neatly in place, and his expression was grave but poised. The Senators seated behind him looked stony-faced and shocked. Nagy held a palm-sized link. He glanced down at it, then folded it in his fist.

"Friends and citizens, please remain calm," Nagy said. "As you can see, normal communications have been restored. We expect to hear shortly that the perpetrators have been apprehended. Rest assured, the consequences for those who have committed this outrage will be grave."

The assembled Senate applauded with the correct combination of relief, enthusiasm, and sober restraint. Nagy acknowledged them with a nod. He did not smile.

"In the difficult days to come, I shall call upon your loyalty and sound thinking. We must all work together for the greater order and stability that is the bedrock of our modern society. Once we were confined to a single planet, and then a single system, but it is the nature of our species to push ever outward. Not to scatter but to create an expanding sphere of resiliency, prosperity, and security. The things we hold dear, and all our hopes for the future, depend on maintaining a cohesive, well-ordered system." He paused as applause swelled.

"Cohesive," Saralyn repeated with a sideways look at Leonin. "That doesn't sound so bad."

Where's Father? occupied Bryn's thoughts. And *What's on Nagy's link? He's leading up to something.* The fine hairs on the back of her neck prickled.

The applause died down. Nagy continued in the same vein, implying that the Star Alliance was the only thing preventing all civilization from coming to a flaming halt. He included praise for his mother and her pivotal leadership role in preventing such a catastrophe when the old Terran Federation fell apart.

"To each generation, a new challenge arises," he said, zeal building with each phrase. He wasn't shouting, but his voice seemed to fill the chamber.

Despite all her reservations about the man, Bryn held her breath, waiting for what he would say next. She had the sick, fascinated feeling that something terrible was coming, something that would change her world but not in a good way. It reminded her of waiting in the hospital the day her mother had died from a cerebral aneurysm. As long as the doctor had not said the words, there was a chance her mother might live. Now, as then, she desperately wanted her life to go on as before. Her work with children from war-ravaged planets. Family dinners with Saralyn and her family. Moments of sweetness and passion with Leonin.

She had rarely been so grateful for Leonin's steadiness. No matter what happened now, they would face it together.

"Friends and citizens," Nagy said, "it is with sadness and determination that I make the following announcement." He paused, drew breath, and glanced at the link in his hand.

Here it comes, Bryn thought, and held tightly to Leonin's hand.

"I have here an official communiqué from the Planetary Parliament of Vainwal. They have just passed a resolution of autonomy. All military, administrative, and economic ties are hereby severed. In other words, my friends, Vainwal has seceded from the Star Alliance."

"Well," Tomas said, talking over Nagy's next remarks. "They've gone and done it."

Leonin shook his head. "I can't say it was unexpected. All the signs pointed to this happening soon."

"Where's Father?" Saralyn's face was flushed, her eyes too bright. "He was supposed to address the Vainwal question."

"Try him on his link," Leonin urged.

"I already tried!" Saralyn wailed. "Just before the broadcast—and my call wouldn't go through. I can't understand why he would turn off his link *now*. It doesn't make sense. He *always* calls before a big speech. He says I bring him *luck*—well, maybe not luck, but he says that having a family keeps his political work in perspective. Talking to the kids reminds him that these decisions affect real people."

"Let me see if I can reach him." Bryn dug her link out of her bag and touched the key for her father's private line. Instead of a search signal, she saw only the pattern that indicated that his link was inactive. She canceled the call, wondering for a moment if the difficulty was on her end. Even if her father were tied up in a meeting, he was never completely unreachable, not by his family.

"Problem?" Leonin stood at her shoulder.

"I should have been able to leave a priority message. I'll try again in a little while."

"Vainwal *can't* secede," Saralyn was saying to Tomas. "They're a core Alliance member. It's just not possible. There must be some mistake."

"They've already done it, my dear," Tomas said. "The First Minister would never have announced it unless it had been verified."

"Father was going to appeal to them, bring them to their senses—that's what his speech was to be about, he told me—but it's too late now, isn't it? It's official. Oh, this is terrible!" Saralyn scrambled to her feet and dashed out of the room. Bryn watched her go. Tomas gripped the arm rests of his chair until his knuckles went white.

"The Alliance needs Vainwal much more than Vainwal needs the Alliance," Leonin said after a moment. "Rich tourists aren't going to stop spending their money on Vainwal. Vainwal will now keep all the revenue. But the Alliance badly needs the income. It won't let Vainwal leave without a fight."

"A fight?" Tomas repeated. "You mean civil war."

"The news sounds bad, I admit, but it's not over yet," Bryn said, trying to sound more hopeful than she felt. "I still believe Father can find a peaceful way through this crisis. At the very least, he can persuade both sides to take a step back and talk things through. We all know how convincing he can be."

"I—" Leonin broke off as the vid cameras shifted to the figure of the hosting newscaster.

"And now we go to Ernst Haslund, one of the most revered members of the Senate, known as a long-time advocate of greater autonomy for the planets through reciprocal trade agreements, guarantees of civil rights, and legislative representation. Senator, what is your view of the breaking news from Vainwal?"

"Sara!" Tomas called. "Your father's on now."

"At last! What a relief!" Saralyn hurried back in and took her place, her face still flushed.

The image of Ernst Haslund came into focus. Bryn didn't recognize the background, just a wall of uniform gray. It wasn't the Senate chamber, that much was certain. He was wearing an apparatus that covered his temples, perhaps a specialized headset to amplify his voice in a difficult acoustical environment.

"My fellow citizens of the Star Alliance," he began. "A generation ago, the civilized worlds of the Terran Federation stood on the brink of destruction. Conspiracies and insurrections threatened the fabric of our interstellar fellowship. It was a dark and terrible and perilous time, one that might well have resulted in the obliteration of all life on planet after planet. Humanity stood at a crossroads. It took courage and clarity of vision to answer the question of whether we would disintegrate into separate worlds, many of which were capable of destroying each other and possessed the malevolent will to do so."

Bryn could hardly believe this was her father and not an automaton created in his image. The face was his, but not the tone or the words. His voice, usually an expressive, melodic baritone, sounded flat. His eyes, too, looked lifeless, although that could have been the artificial lighting.

"Thanks to the inspired leadership of First Minister Sandra Nagy," he said, "we survived this dark time."

Leonin glanced at Bryn, and she knew he was thinking the same thing. How was it possible that her father was *praising* Sandra Nagy? He'd *detested* the old bat! Oh, he'd been scrupulously polite to her in person, just as he was to her son, Arthur, the current First Minister, but he had far too much integrity for outright obsequiousness.

"She and those who had faith in her vision managed to hold together our Federation. The task was neither simple nor briefly accomplished. Disorder had become widespread. Weapons of mass destruction were now in the possession of those who did not hesitate to use them for their own territorial interests."

Movement at the periphery of Bryn's vision caught her attention. The babysitter had entered the room, kids in tow. All three were staring, openmouthed, at the image of Senator Haslund.

"In the end, Sandra Nagy's goal of a united family of planets prevailed. Today the Star Alliance that the Federation gave rise to is stronger and more prosperous than ever before. We encompass worlds as diverse as Alpha Two, with its advanced scientific and technological institutions, and primitive Class D Protected worlds like Cottman IV. While respecting local customs, people everywhere in the Alliance enjoy the same freedoms and are protected by the same laws.

"Every generation faces its own test. In the time of our parents, the Federation almost disintegrated. Now the Star Alliance faces a similar challenge. Despite the many improvements in the quality of life and prosperity of the member worlds, problems remain. Even with endless resources, it takes time to address shortcomings of the magnitude of those we now face. But for some, our progress was not rapid enough. Factions wanted their own concerns addressed first. Many attempted to exploit the situation for monetary gain or their political agenda."

Bryn found it difficult to follow her father's speech, one plodding phrase after another. Sometimes she could not tell when one sentence ended and the next one began. The rhythm was wrong. She kept waiting for his words to catch fire, as they so often did when his intellect and his passion for justice fused into a stirring call for action. If ever there was a time when such leadership was needed, it was now. Instead, he droned on, echoing the same slogans she had heard from Arthur Nagy's lips.

"Although we have achieved a new era of stability and security, there are those who seek to undermine our progress. Agents have infiltrated the governments of many planets, urging secession as the only solution. Provocateurs generate discontent, often to the point of outright violence against legitimate authority. Today's clashes on the streets of Terra Central demonstrate the power of these subversive groups, whose only object is to sow discord and, ultimately, anarchy. The Alliance stands for equal opportunity for all its citizens, and we, the elected members of government, have a solemn duty to defend all citizens. We cannot allow petty dictators, anarchists, pirates, and criminals to destroy the union it has taken generations of sacrifice to create. Therefore, I urge every loyal citizen to support First Minister Nagy in his commitment to preserving the integrity of the Star Alliance."

"No!" Bryn burst out. "I don't believe it!"

Saralyn turned to Tomas, her brow furrowed and lips downturned. "Father would *never* say those things."

"Nagy's gotten to him somehow," Leonin muttered. "That's the only explanation."

The air tasted of adrenaline. Bryn's pulse raced, and she felt a burning along her nerves. Something dangerous was coming. Closer now, closer. Yet no one else showed any trace of alarm.

Meanwhile, Tomas thanked Erica, paid her, and ushered her to the door. Once they were alone, they focused on the vid once more, perhaps hoping to find out it was all a mistake. There was Nagy again.

"Vainwal has chosen the unfortunate course of separation," Nagy said. "In doing so, its misguided leaders risk disaster not only for their own world but for its neighbors. We will use every means at our disposal to prevent famine, disease, and possible planetary obliteration as the consequences of this rash action. Thank you for your attention."

The vid image flickered to the seal of the Star Alliance, accompanied by an instrumental rendition of the anthem. For a long moment, no one spoke or even moved. Bryn wasn't sure anyone was breathing. Then everyone started talking at once.

"How is this possible?"

"What the hell is going on—"

"—a computer rendition?"

"Pre-recorded?"

"He'd never—not of his own volition—"

Leonin touched Bryn's hand. "Sweetheart, I'm so sorry."

I've got to get out of here. I've got to get to Father. Something's happened to him.

"Father wouldn't give in to pressure." Saralyn's brows drew together, her mouth tight. "He just wouldn't!"

"Not against himself, that's true," Bryn said. "But if they threatened us—" She couldn't bring herself to say, *or the children...*

"You need to leave now," Tomas said to Leonin. The conversation fell into silence. "The longer you remain, the greater the chance we'll be associated with your *extreme* views. For all I know, your organization was the one that fomented the riot and is now under investigation—"

"What are you saying?" Bryn cut in. Her nerves felt scoured raw. "You can't seriously believe—"

"It's all right," Leonin said. "And Tomas is right. The Free Worlds movement doesn't condone violence, but Nagy's crew will make us into his scapegoats anyway. Tomas, I regret bringing risk to you or your family. It was unintentional, please believe me."

"I—I don't wish you ill," Tomas conceded. "But I have to protect my wife and children. The longer you're here, the greater the jeopardy you put them in."

"In the past, we've agreed on very little, but I've always respected your devotion to your family," Leonin said. "Of course, I'll leave."

An electric feeling sizzled over Bryn's skin. *The danger was coming closer—almost upon her now—*

Tomas tapped the panel beside the door to display the security views of the corridor outside the door. "It looks like the way is clear. I'll check the street."

Images flashed across the panel, showing Black and the car he had come in. And there was the babysitter, gesturing and pointing in the direction of the apartment. Had the girl been placed here to keep an eye on Saralyn's family in case StarOps needed leverage against the Senator? Bringing Leonin to dinner had been a foolish risk.

"Is there another way out of this building besides the front entrance?" Leonin asked.

"Yes, there's a back staircase down to an emergency exit," Tomas said. "You can take it to the garage or out back to the service alley."

Leonin took Bryn's hands in his. His eyes looked even darker than usual. "I'll contact you when it's safe."

Bryn's danger-sense flared into full, blinding intensity. She knew it was crazy. Black was after Leonin, not her, but she *had* to get out of there. It seemed as if her very life and the lives of uncounted other people—of her father—depended on flight. "I'm coming with you."

"It's not safe—"

"Don't argue! Just let's *go*!"

There wasn't time for proper goodbyes, not even a sisterly hug. Bryn slung her bag over her shoulder and snatched up her coat, racing Leonin for the door.

They hurried off in the direction Tomas indicated. The corridor ended in a door labeled *Emergency Exit*. Leonin pushed it open, but no alarm sounded. Beyond lay a stairwell, stark and unadorned. Bryn's heart was beating so hard, it sounded almost as loud in her ears as the clattering of her shoes on the metal stairs. Her bag swung wildly, banging against the railing until she managed to tuck it under her elbow. A couple of times she tripped, but Leonin caught her and she kept on.

From the street level, a door led to the lobby. They continued down until they reached the garage level. Personal vehicles, single- or double-passenger models shrouded in dust covers, stood in orderly rows. To one side, a ramp slanted upward toward the street. Surely Black would be watching it.

"Service entrance—" Leonin started along the perimeter of the parking area. Bryn scrambled to keep up with his longer strides. The garage was narrow, only two rows to either side of a central lane, but it was long. The further they got from the ramp exit, the thicker the dust on the vehicle covers and the fewer empty spaces.

Just as they reached the end of the overhead lights, a clanging noise brought them both alert. Leonin peered back the way they had come, listening intently. Bryn listened, too, but the sound did not return. She wasn't sure she would have been able to hear it over the hammering of her heart.

"It's all right," he said.

"We'd better get out of here," she said, sounding braver than she felt.

He took her hand and together they resumed their path along the wall, going deeper into the shadows until they reached the service door at the far end. It was the same color as the surrounding wall, and it was unmarked, bearing a shallow depression instead of an ordinary handle or latch. He fumbled inside the depression. It took him several tries, muttering under his breath, before the door clicked open.

Beyond, stairs opened to the sky. The two of them hurried up the flight and emerged into an alley. The alley was empty except for stacked plasteel bins.

"Which way?" Bryn had gotten turned around while they were underground. The last thing she wanted was to go rushing back into Black's clutches.

"There." He pointed.

Bryn's sense of impending peril lessened slightly. "You know where this goes?"

"Hopefully, it will be far enough to put us beyond the initial field of search."

He led her down the alley and then a secondary street, and another alley, slowing so as not to draw undue attention to themselves. Bryn couldn't keep track of the turns. By the fourth or fifth street, they had passed out of Saralyn's immediate neighborhood. Widely spaced lights illuminated a street lined with bars and dancing clubs. Gambling places, too, no doubt. The businesses seemed to be doing a brisk trade, with people going in and out, cramming the pavement outside the entrances. A flitter with glowing police markings passed overhead.

Halting beneath a burned-out street light, he tugged her into an alcove outside a shuttered business. Now that she was no longer moving and the first burst of adrenaline was fading, she felt the wind gusting on her face. She shivered.

"Your coat," he said, "put it on—no, not like that. Drape it over your head."

She stared at him, for the first time aware of the rashness of running off with him. Why, why had she done it? Sheer panic? The trauma of the riot and being gassed? Instinct propelling her into flight? Was this truly the best way to find out what had happened to her father? *Why, why had he said those things?* If she'd stayed, she could have talked to him—

"Hide your face," Leonin said, misreading her hesitation.

Mutely, she pulled the folds of the coat into a hood and tucked her bag under her armpit.

He pulled up his jacket collar and raked his hair forward over his brow. "Not an effective disguise for either of us, but it's the best we can do. Don't speak unless you have to. Your accent will give you away."

He meant that she talked like an educated person. She nodded in agreement.

Leonin ducked into a bar a few doors down, Bryn following silently at his heels. The place smelled of beer and furniture polish. There was no vid, only a music streamer blaring out tunes from several decades ago. None of the patrons paid them any notice. Half of them seemed to be drunk, holding loud conversations, laughing at their own jokes, or staring at their drinks.

The bartender glanced their way. "You see that crazy brother of yours, he owes me forty."

Leonin tossed the bartender a chip. Bryn started to protest that the payment could be traced back to him before she caught the blue-green stripe of universal tender. *Of course, a place like this must deal in untraceable transactions.* She had no such currency, nor could she obtain any without the withdrawal appearing on her account. Until that moment, she had never considered how hard it would be to disappear, and how ill-prepared she was to do so.

"I was never here." Leonin said.

The bartender pocketed the chip with a grin.

Leonin guided Bryn toward an unmarked door behind the bar. It was the old-fashioned kind, as heavy as a fire barrier, with a pressure damper that prevented it from swinging freely. Just as they slipped through, the sounds of crashing furniture and raised voices came from the bar.

"Stop! Police!"

"Leonin Vargas, you are under arrest!"

Leonin braced his shoulder against the door, using his weight to overcome the resistance of the damper. Bryn placed her hands on it and pushed. The door closed, cutting off the racket, but there didn't seem to be a lock on this side. Bryn looked around for something to wedge the door shut. The room around her appeared to be used for storage, what she could see from the cheap, motion-activated overhead light. There wasn't much except a couple of broken chairs, a table like the ones in the bar, plastic crates, and what looked like a dress mannequin with half its torso splintered off. A spare door that did not match the others in paint color was propped against one far corner. She picked up one of the chairs.

"Don't bother," Leonin said. "Our friends will keep the cops busy for a while, and we don't want to leave evidence of having passed this way if we can help it."

Bryn set the chair down. "There's no way out. We're trapped."

"No, we're not." Leonin gave her a lopsided grin. "Welcome to the Free Worlds underground."

He shifted the mismatched door to one side. Behind it, another door led to a passageway that was so narrow, they had to turn sideways to fit through. After they slid inside, he moved the inner door back into place. It fitted so tightly that no light penetrated. A moment later, he clicked on the pocket light. They stood on a narrow landing that gave way to a vertical shaft. Rails for hands and feet disappeared into its depths on the near edge.

Ordinarily, Bryn wasn't afraid of heights, but a chill crept along her spine at the prospect of descending that shaft. To go down there would change her life forever. No matter what happened now, she could never go back. As if getting caught in a riot, gassed, and then having StarOps on her trail wasn't *irrevocable* enough.

"Let's go," she said.

Grasping the pocket light between his teeth, Leonin descended the shaft. Bryn followed. The icy, pitted metal of the handrails dug into her palms. It smelled of rust. Step by step, she felt for each foothold before transferring her weight. She tried not to think of the metal giving way or the bolts that anchored the ladder breaking. Or how deep the shaft was. Or what lay at its bottom.

The light seemed dimmer now, and she realized that he had outstripped her. She tried to go faster, but that only resulted in one foot slipping because she had not taken care to place it securely. With a shriek, she scrambled to grab on. Her weight went onto her hands and her skin stung where the rust bit deep. She clung to the ladder, panting. She couldn't move. Not down but not up again, either.

"You all right?" His voice seemed to come from the bottom of a well. Too deep, too far for her to follow.

I can't do this.

It was just a ladder in the dark, nothing to be afraid of. If she closed her eyes, she could imagine it was daytime in a park. She was climbing down a tree, that was all. She'd done it a hundred times, although her father had always been there to catch her. Now it was her turn to save him. Whatever it took.

She drew in one breath, and then another, deeper and easier this time, and then her heart did not pound quite so loudly in her ears.

"I'm okay," she called. "Just lost my footing."

"We have to keep moving."

Cry later, she told herself.

Before she could take another step, her danger-sense flickered to life again. She froze on the ladder.

A percussive *whump!* rocked the shaft. The shock wave slammed into her. Her teeth vibrated with it, and her muscles locked so that she could not draw in a breath. Debris—dust and chunks of brick and crumbled mortar—rained down the shaft.

Grabbing for the bars, she missed her hold and plummeted into darkness. A moment later, she landed at the bottom of the shaft. The fall wasn't long, but the impact jarred every bone in her body. Acrid powder stung her nose and set off a paroxysm of coughing. Her eyes smarted. Through streaming tears, she saw that Leonin had dropped his pocket light, although it had not gone out.

All right...we're both all right.

The world had gone silent. Her ears felt as if they were stuffed with cotton. She wondered if they should go back up, see if anyone was hurt—*of course, they were hurt, those who weren't killed outright, do you think anyone could have survived a bomb like that?*—and then even more confused thoughts—*who set the bomb, it* was *a bomb—don't be naïve, it was StarOps—my god, they want me dead—no, they want* Leonin *dead, I'm just collateral damage—collateral damage like the people in the bar—*

Then she was shaking, crying uncontrollably. She couldn't hear her own cries, and that frightened her even more. Strong arms went around her, holding her tight. Heedless of the dust, she buried her face against his chest. He stroked her hair over and over again. Her shudders subsided. He kept up his soothing touch, and after a time she could make out his voice, although it sounded muffled and far away.

"Okay, you're okay..."

I'm not okay, she wanted to scream. *And I won't be until this is over.*

When she took a deep breath, it sounded like a sob. "I'm better now."

Leonin bent to pick up his pocket light and glanced up the shaft.

"I'm so sorry," Bryn said. "Those were your friends upstairs."

"Love." His eyes were pools of darkness in the oblique illumination from his pocket light. "There will be a time to honor their memories. That time is not now. *Now* the only thing I can do for them is to make sure those responsible do not get away with it."

He must work through his anger and grief in his own way. Bryn squeezed his arm, as much in comfort as in agreement, and let him interpret it as he would.

The truth was that she didn't want to be a revolutionary; she just wanted to make sure her father and Saralyn and Tomas and the kids were all right. Then she'd go home and sleep for a week. No, she'd help her young patients, as always. Her morning appointment was a ten-year-old girl who slept with the lights on and screamed when she was touched—she was going to show up—and Bryn wouldn't be there—

Breathe. Just breathe.

Leonin walked up to the oval metal door at the bottom of the shaft. The door looked old, with a central wheel and a system of levers. Handing her the pocket light, he grasped the wheel. It resisted at first, although he braced his feet and put his strength into turning it. At last, with a sound like pitted surfaces dragging over one another, the wheel turned and the door opened.

A tunnel yawned ahead, dark and still. Her skin crawled, but this was the way forward. Ducking inside after him, she felt as if she had entered another world. The curved walls appeared to be porous stone that had crumbled along its edges.

"What is this place?" Her voice echoed weirdly.

"Pre-spaceflight public transportation system. See the rails?"

Dust-covered metal lines ran straight down the center of the floor.

"Rashid discovered this system in the old records," he said. "I hoped we'd never need it."

She followed him down the passage. The floor slanted down to an intersection. She tried not to imagine Black and his men tracking them silently, coming closer and ever closer.

"That way," he said, his voice echoing.

They went on, continuing downward and then flat. The air smelled stale. After a time, she noticed that the walls glistened in places. Condensation ran in rivulets to pool between the rails. Her skin felt clammy.

The passage narrowed and the ceiling slanted lower. They seemed to be going even further down. The temperature dropped, and she was glad she'd grabbed her coat.

"Where are we?" Bryn found herself whispering.

"Under the river. Do you need a break, or can you keep going? I'm sorry I don't have any water for you."

Under the river. Yes, that made sense, given the chill damp. She imagined all that water over their heads, the crushing weight of it, tons and tons, and then thrust the vision from her mind.

Bryn felt as if she had been walking all night. Her legs had gone numb and her mouth, dry. When Leonin called a halt, she slid down against the tunnel wall, heedless of the wetness. She was so thirsty, she considered licking the moisture off the rock face, but she wasn't that desperate yet. She closed her eyes, folded her hands in her lap, and waited for sensation to return to her muscles.

Leonin lowered himself to the ground beside her and switched his pocket light to low in order to save its power. In its subdued light, he looked haggard.

He took her hand and raised it to his lips. "I'm sorry to have dragged you into this."

"I doubt you had much say in the matter."

"Yes, I distinctly remember trying to talk you out of it and failing. You were unusually determined, even for you. Love, why *did* you insist?"

Bryn hesitated. She'd never discussed her danger-sense with anyone. Sitting together in this dank tunnel, it seemed a flimsy motivation. To risk her career, her freedom, maybe even her family's safety, for an intuition?

"I'm not sure," she said. "Maybe I panicked. Or maybe I'd had enough of the StarOps version of hospitality."

"I'm glad you came, for both our sakes. The thought of you in the hands of that StarOps agent would drive me crazy. What was he called, Black? An apt description."

"I doubt it's his real name, or if I was his primary target. I think everything hinges on my father."

"Your father, exactly. Why did he change his mind so radically? And at a time when so many of us were looking to him as a voice of sanity? Do you think Nagy got to him?"

Her father had always maintained an unshakable faith in the ability of sentient beings to work together. Then why had he come out in complete support of Nagy? What lies had Nagy told to persuade him? Lies...or threats?

"It's possible that Nagy convinced him that if he didn't support his agenda, something terrible would happen to Saralyn and me, or maybe his grandkids," she said. "That would explain why Black was following me, so he'd know my whereabouts. Saralyn suspected she was being watched, too."

"You may be right, but there's nothing we can do about it now. We've got another, much more pressing problem. Rashid and I have made no secret about our political views. We've known we've been under surveillance. I just never thought it would affect you, too. I'm so sorry I dragged you into this."

"I *chose* to be here with you. And it's too late to turn around, even if I wanted to."

"You win. End of discussion."

"Thank you."

"I've been thinking about the demonstration," Leonin went on after a pause. "The violence was provoked by a small number of people. Now Nagy is trying to discredit anyone who disagrees with him. His next move will be to declare martial law. That means my brother and I, and our allies, can no longer settle for peaceful demonstrations. If we are to stand a chance against Nagy's regime, we'll have to fight fire with fire."

"Resort to violence? Leonin, no. *No.* It goes against everything we believe in. Think of the children I work with and how their lives—their families, their entire worlds—have been devastated. I *know* you'd never be a party to that. There must be a better solution."

Leonin drew a ragged breath. "We will use nonviolent means whenever possible, I promise. But we have to take a stand. We can't stand idly by when our friends are arrested or killed."

That was as much a concession as she was going to get. They were both too stressed to think clearly. She'd have to wait for a better time to press the issue. Taking her silence as the end of the discussion, he got up and held out his hand to help her to her feet.

"We have to get to my father," she said. "He's our best chance of finding a peaceful way through this crisis."

"And so we shall. But for that, we need safety and resources. Information. Contacts. My brother and his people will have both at the safe house."

"I suppose that's as good a place as any to start."

For a time, they walked along in silence. Bryn's bag bumped against her hip, and she tried to adjust it to a more comfortable position. Soon she had gone beyond the annoyance of mild thirst and fatigue. She did her best not to entertain thoughts of dehydration, focusing instead on putting one foot in front of the other.

The tunnel debouched onto a huge underground chamber. By the limited pocket light, she made out that they were standing in a trough partly filled with debris. Other than *across the river*, she had no idea where they were.

"That way," Leonin said, indicating a raised walkway. They headed along it, reaching a set of stairs with the rusted remains of handrails.

Bryn hurried up the stairs. She was panting by the time they made it to the first landing and turned back in the opposite direction. As they reached the next level, a cramp in her side threatened to fold her over, but she refused to give in to it. She kept her head raised and her eyes focused upward. Soon she'd be out of that dank, confined space.

She almost wept when they came up against a metal barrier. She pushed against the corrugated surface as hard as she could, with no result. She might have been trying to lift a mountain. Leonin made a couple of attempts, grunting with effort as he braced himself against the side of the stairwell.

"This place must have been sealed up when it was abandoned," he said, stepping away from the barrier. "It's my fault we're in this mess. I never should have used an escape route that wasn't fully mapped."

"We didn't have a choice." This whole wretched day—from her first encounter with Black to the demonstration to Father's inexplicable support of Nagy to their flight underground and the bomb that had trapped them here—had been unplanned, beyond her control. She felt like a puppet whose strings had been yanked and tangled by an immensely powerful, capricious, and delusional power. Her temper flared at the thought. She wanted to lash out, to give whoever had set all this up a piece of her mind. There was nothing she could do and no one she could vent her vexation upon except Leonin, who deserved none of it. But the rush of adrenaline cleared her mind.

"The city planners blocked the entrances to the stations," she said, thinking aloud, "but logically those can't have been the *only* ways in and out. I don't believe the people who built this system were incompetent—it's too well-built. Look, we didn't use stairs like these when we came in through the bar. It stands to reason that there must have been emergency exits and that one of them became that shaft."

"I do believe you've missed your calling," he said. "Instead of a child psychologist, you should have been an archaeologist."

"Some days, I'm not sure there's much of a difference. It's all a matter of digging below the surface." She got to her feet. "So, where would you likely find an emergency exit, and what would it look like?"

"Not at a station like the one we just left, because you already have the regular entrances. Maybe between stations?" He shone the light along the trough in the direction they'd been traveling.

"All right, let's try that."

They went back down into the tunnel and eventually came to another set of stairs leading upward. She felt the stir of air on her face, fresher and colder than in the tunnel.

Leonin directed his flashlight upward, but there was no visible ceiling. "I think this leads to the surface."

Night must have fallen while they were belowground. No wonder she was so tired. She set one foot on the first step and began to climb. It was becoming more difficult just to lift her legs. He caught her just as she stumbled and was about to fall. She regained her balance and took another step.

Near the top of the stairs, she glimpsed a dim orange light. It brightened and then dimmed, as if from a variable source. *Fire*? The skin along her spine prickled, but she took a deep breath and followed him up the last few steps.

The exit was bordered on two sides by crumbling concrete and on the third by a rusted metal gate. When she touched the gate, the porous metallic surface bit into her skin.

Bryn moved back down a couple of steps while Leonin wrapped his hands in the folds of his jacket, took a firm, two-fisted grip on the grate, braced himself, and jerked. The metal resisted him with a high-pitched shriek. Flakes of rust went flying. He pulled again, and again, and this time the metal bar snapped. The grate came loose. He set it down and it tumbled down the steps, barely missing her.

Bryn followed Leonin up the stairs into the open night. The blur of light pollution blotted out the stars. Wind, bearing a smell like rotting seaweed, hit her in the face. Her coat kept out the worst of it, but the adrenaline that had kept her moving this far was now almost gone. She shivered, as much from emotional exhaustion as cold.

Half-ruined buildings bracketed an open space. In the center, she spotted a group of people standing around the fire that was the source of the orange light. It was contained in a metal barrel, and now and again the wind fanned the flames above their heads. The veil of smoke made it difficult to ascertain their numbers or whether they were men or women. The two largest turned in her direction. She read curiosity but also menace in their posture.

"Come on," Leonin said, keeping his voice low. "They know where we are, more or less."

"Couldn't we just…" Another bout of shivering shook her. "...go back?"

"The fire isn't much, but it's warmth," Leonin said. "If it's any reassurance, I very much doubt anyone we meet out here will go running to the police, let alone StarOps. Just the same, be careful. Don't say anything that might be interpreted as hostile."

"Just pretend we belong here?" Was that her voice, on the ragged edge of panic? She sounded like one of her patients.

"Better let me do the talking." He took her hand and headed toward the fire. Her danger-sense, still active, nudged her. There was nothing to be done, no choice but to go on.

As they neared the fire, the people huddled there dispersed to either side as if preparing for a flanking maneuver. A large, bearded man remained in the center, his body language belligerent. Two others took up positions diagonally behind him.

"Evening." Leonin's voice sounded lower in pitch than normal, and gravelly.

"Strangers," muttered the bearded man. One of the others added, "Not safe."

"We mean you no harm." Leonin held one hand out from his side and with the other pulled Bryn closer in an unmistakable gesture of protection. "We're lost."

The bearded man again: "You came up through the tunnels?"

"That we did, friend. And if you'll—"

Bryn knew instantly that it was a mistake to call these people *friends*. She and Leonin might be haggard from lack of sleep and their clothes might be stained from their journey, but the two of them were clearly well-nourished and well-clothed, people who had things worth stealing. Outnumbered and unarmed, they would be easy prey.

As if in answer to her thought, a woman clad in layers of patched, dark clothing sidled closer, eyes fixed on Bryn's bag. Bryn imagined the tension in the air like a supersaturated solution. All it would take was a single mote of dust—a word, a movement—and the people surrounding them would crystallize into a mob.

She slipped the strap over her head and thrust the bag at the woman. "Take it!"

The woman stumbled backward, eyes flashing and pale-rimmed. As she grabbed the bag, she lost her balance and went down. The next instant, a half-dozen of the others rushed the fallen woman, howling. Someone screamed above the sound of mindless howls. The bearded man shouted, but Bryn couldn't make out his words.

"Come on!" Leonin grabbed her hand and sprinted away.

Bryn raced through the darkness, following Leonin on an oblique path away from the fire but not back toward the tunnel entrance. She stumbled over the uneven, weed-laced pavement, scrambled for balance, and pushed herself for more speed.

They reached the edge of the open area and plunged into the labyrinth of tumbled-down buildings. Slabs of paving shifted under her, and she slipped on puddles of greasy liquid. Once her feet went out from under her. She caught herself against a wall and then wished she hadn't. Something slimy and rank-smelling covered her palms. She didn't want to wipe her hands on her coat, but leaving that noxious, reeking stuff on them would be even worse.

"You okay?" He touched her sleeve.

She shuddered, rubbing her hands together. "Ugh."

"I think we've gotten away." He glanced up. "Dawn's coming, and then we can orient ourselves and make our way—"

"Not so fast!" came a harsh, accented male voice, not from behind them but ahead along the ramshackle street.

She made out the bulky outline of the leader of the gang. Her heart sank. They were never going to get away. This man knew these ruins and they didn't. His confederates would surely be hiding in the shadows, waiting for his signal.

What does he want with us? I gave that woman my bag— She realized how much more she and Leonin had to lose.

The bearded man took a step closer. He was armed with a metal bar as long as his arm, carried as if he'd had plenty of experience using it. Maybe Leonin had an idea how to fight it, maybe not.

Ever since she'd left her office—yesterday, was it?—she'd been off-balance, taken by surprise with every new event. Without useful experience and survival skills, she now faced a man who might be twice her mass and capable of killing her. She couldn't stand against him physically; she'd fold like paper under the first blow. She'd never held a weapon in her entire life. But she *wasn't* helpless. She'd walked through far worse nightmares than this with her young patients, and they'd trusted her to bring them safely through. Trusted her because she had established that relationship, built it step by step, moment by tentative moment.

Her pulse quieted. She envisioned the man before her as not a hoodlum but a leader of his rag-tag community, a man forced by circumstances to be tough.

She slipped off her coat and held it out to him. "You already have my bag. Take this, as well."

The bearded man did not move. From behind, she heard Leonin's quick breathing. She sent him a silent plea to remain still, to let the encounter play out.

Bryn kept eye contact with the man. "Take it. Put it to good use for your people."

With each passing heartbeat, she dared to hope that her offer would be accepted and that truce, if not cooperation, would follow. As for the coat, she would manage without it; at the moment, she was too keyed-up to feel the cold, although she would soon.

The man lowered the bar as he took a step toward her. Just then, Leonin hurled himself between them.

"No, don't—"

The two men slammed into the ground, swinging punches and grappling with one another. The bar clanged as it skittered across the broken paving and bounced off a stone wall.

Bryn couldn't think what to do. The fight was too fast-moving, the blows too strong.

"Stop!" she cried. "Please stop!"

Shadows cast pools of near-darkness at the foot of the walls but there—where the light made its way past the buildings—she spotted the metal bar.

Grunting, the two men tumbled one over the other. Their bodies rolled over the bar. She jumped aside, barely avoiding getting pinned against the wall. Seizing the opening, she lunged for the bar. A boot collided with her ankle as she passed. Her foot skidded out from under her, and she dropped to the ground. The impact shocked the breath out of her. For a panic-laced moment, she couldn't breathe.

Eyes streaming tears, she forced herself to crawl toward the bar. Her fingers brushed the tip. She tried to grasp it, failed, pulled herself closer by digging her other elbow into the gritty paving, and finally got her fingers wrapped around the metal. She scrambled to her feet, her ankle shrieking in protest, and took firm hold of the bar with both hands. Lifting it overhead, she screamed as loudly as she could, without thinking about what she was saying, only that she had to do something—*anything*—to bring the two men to their senses.

Someone came up behind her and grabbed the bar. She struggled to hold onto it, but it was no use. The man behind her was too strong, his grip like stone. The bar slipped from her grasp. The next moment, she found herself restrained. One arm held her firmly, crushing her ribs so she was barely able to breathe. With the other hand, her assailant twisted one of her arms behind her. He was tall enough to lift her into the air.

"Got her!" he shouted.

A handful of people rushed out from behind the broken walls—women among them—instantly recognizable as those who had huddled around the fire.

In that brief time, the man behind Bryn had wrested the bar from her, the bearded man had rolled on top of Leonin. He now knelt, straddling Leonin's hips and pinning his shoulders to the ground. She struggled as hard as she could, clawing with her free hand and lashing out with her feet, but she only succeeded in choking herself. She stopped fighting, hoping that her captor would relax the pressure on her ribs. When he did, she sucked in a lungful of air.

"What do you want?" she managed to say. "Why are you doing this?"

"Quiet—"

A fist-sized object came hurling through the air and landed beside the two men still scuffling on the ground. It trailed red-tinted, glowing smoke and emitted a hissing noise. The next instant, it exploded with blinding white light. One of the attackers howled. The world went gray-white and featureless in Bryn's sight. She blinked hard but couldn't tell up from down or wall from open space, although she could hear the men in front of her. And footsteps, approaching rapidly.

"Get them going!" came another man's voice.

Rashid?

Bryn heard the sounds of cloth rustling, then a man grunting. "Leo."

"Here—just can't—see." He was breathing hard, but at least he could talk.

The man holding Bryn whirled away, sending her staggering. She managed to catch herself on both hands. The next moment, someone hauled her to her feet.

"R-Rashid? How did you find us?"

He wrapped one arm around her waist and another under her elbow. "We've got to move fast, before the scavengers regain their sight. Don't fight me, just follow along."

Propelled by Rashid's grip, Bryn stumbled along the uneven paving, taking one turn after another. Her shoulder burned where the scavenger had twisted it, and her head still throbbed from the explosion. The glare-blindness began to fade, and she made out the outlines of disintegrating buildings. They halted before one of them, not visibly different from its neighbors. All were equally dilapidated, eroded by weather, and had been looted many times. Such places contained valuable metal and plastic, as well as old furnishings. What remained were husks, their broken windows sightless eyes.

Behind her, Leonin was barely on his feet, sagging between two of their rescuers. The light was now strong enough to reveal bloody abrasions on his face. A swollen, purpling bruise almost shut one eye. Two of the rescue party linked arms to create a chair carry for him.

"Leo!" Bryn cried. "He's hurt—he needs medical care—"

"No talking!" Rashid sounded angry. "Not out here!"

Rashid tapped on the weather-beaten door. Bryn would not have been surprised if it had fallen to pieces, but the resulting sound was solid, not hollow. As the door swung open, she saw that it had been disguised to look broken but was reinforced on the inside with metal bands. A man holding a blaster rifle stepped back for the party to enter. As he passed, Rashid clapped the man on the arm.

"Stay strong, Jess."

"Stay strong."

Bryn's first impression of the interior was a poorly illuminated labyrinth of corridors. Then Rashid threw open another door and they all went in. He passed his hand over a sensor plate just inside the door, and light filled the room. It accented his features, a leaner, harsher mirror of

Leonin's: arched cheekbones, prominent nose, straight brows, and glossy black hair.

The two men supporting Leonin laid him on a crude bed along the far wall. Other furnishings included a worn, comfortable-looking sofa, a stack of folding chairs, a side table laden with bottles and dirty glasses, and a plate of broken flatbreads.

Rashid propped Leonin's head up on a pillow, loosened his clothing, and eased off his shoes. Leonin winced, smothering a groan. Bryn clapped her hands over her mouth to keep from crying out. These people were trying to help him; the last thing they needed was a shrieking woman. Or a fainting one, she thought as her vision went gray around the edges and the room tilted sickeningly. She looked around for a place to sit and ended up dropping onto the sofa. An older man, leather case in hand, burst through the door. Then she could no longer follow what was happening, it was all too confusing in her current state and her view was blocked. She heard the men's voices—the snick as the leather case opened—the sound of ripping fabric—Leonin groaning—

He could have been killed. We could both have—

Shivers racked her. She looked around for a receptacle in case nausea overwhelmed her.

The next moment, the older man was leaning over her, instructing her to lie down on the sofa, where he performed a brief examination, then placed a pillow under her knees and covered her with a blanket. "She'll be fine," he said.

Bryn settled back against the pillows. Her lips were dry, and her mouth tasted like paste. She drifted off for what felt like only a moment. When she jerked back to consciousness, Rashid stood beside the sofa, holding out a bottle. She gulped it down. It wasn't water, most likely an electrolyte drink.

"How is Leonin?" she asked.

"My brother prides himself on being indestructible," he said, sitting beside her, "which we both know to be not the case. It looks like most of the blood isn't his, and he came away pretty well from what could have been a nasty beating. From the shape of his knuckles, I suspect he gave as good as he got."

"But his eye, it looked so bad—"

"Our medic is ex-Spaceforce and has seen worse. Says the blow caught the rim of Leo's eye socket at just the wrong angle. The skin will turn black, then green and yellow, but there's no risk to the eyeball itself. He's likely got a couple of cracked ribs, which just need strapping. So *do not worry* about him. No—" when she tried to sit up, "—you were suffering from shock. Exposure and exhaustion are a bad combination. Look, Bryn, you and I have never seen eye to eye on politics, and your father is the last person I'd ever want as a relative by marriage, but I've never wished you harm personally. Understand? Leo would never forgive me if I let anything happen to you. So please sleep if you can. Medic says it's the best thing. We'll talk once you've rested."

"But Leonin—"

"—is not going anywhere, and neither are you. No more arguments. I have too much to do besides browbeating you into taking care of yourself. For the moment, you're safe."

Safe, she repeated to herself. And Leonin wasn't badly hurt. *Safe, both of us.*

When drowsiness weighted her eyelids, she didn't resist.

◆◆◆

Bryn downed the soup and pills offered wordlessly by a thin, dark woman in a spacer's jumpsuit, and slept again. Woke, drank, swallowed, slept. When she came to herself the next time, she felt surprisingly well, although in need of a wash. She found a lavatory in the adjacent room. Feeling considerably refreshed, she went in search of Leonin.

The corridor ended in an unlocked door and beyond it, a large chamber, easily the size of a university conference room, dominated by a huge table. Before she could take a step inside, a wiry, gray-bearded man unholstered a blaster and aimed it at her. She froze, half expecting her danger-sense to engulf her, but it stayed quiescent. She was in no immediate jeopardy, then. After a moment that seemed to go on for an hour, the man lowered the blaster.

"Good to see you on your feet." That was Rashid, sitting on the other side of the table.

Beside his brother, Leonin looked battered but alert. Strip sutures closed the cuts on his face, and bruises darkened the skin around one eye. He started to smile, then grimaced. Bryn embraced him as gently as she could.

"It looks a lot worse than it feels," he said, his words slightly distorted by the swelling in his lower lip.

Bryn spared a glance at their surroundings. Banks of equipment lined two sides of the chamber. Although she was more knowledgeable about research computers, she recognized these as military-grade equipment. Like the blaster, much of this technology was illegal for private ownership. A half-dozen men and women, all in dark clothing, undistinguished by emblem or badge but suggesting a uniform, sat at the stations. Their eyes flicked in her direction but they did not pause in their work. They wore cybernet headsets that allowed interfacing with computing systems without brain implants.

It's a command center, she thought. *A war room.* She'd known the Free Worlds Movement was organized but had no idea they'd managed anything like this.

The gray-haired man brought a chair for Bryn, and she eased herself into it.

"Everyone," Rashid said, "this is Bryn *Haslund*. That's right, Haslund."

At that, the entire room fell silent. The computer workers swiveled their chairs to face her. By the shift in their expressions, they'd disengaged from the nets.

In the past, Bryn had felt uncomfortable being known only for her father. It had happened so many times in her life that when she was a teen, she'd considered legally changing her name.

Rashid made introductions, referring to the others only by first names, and undoubtedly not real ones at that, names like Styx, Jax, and Mode. She couldn't keep track of the others. Styx, the woman who'd brought her the pills, offered a nod.

Rashid looked pointedly at Bryn. "Leo told us how a StarOps agent going by the name of Black stationed himself outside your sister's apartment and then tailed the two of you. He was likely the one who gave the orders to bomb the bar. They'd had it under surveillance for weeks and were probably waiting for an excuse to get rid of it."

"The owner, did he survive?" she asked.

Rashid shook his head. One of the others made a sound that could have been a growl. These people had *known* the owner. Perhaps they'd been friends.

"We never intended to use the old subterrane as a passageway," Rashid said, already moving ahead. "Too many of the sections are buried or blocked off. This side of the river's not safe for city folk."

"Believe me," Leonin said in a grim voice, "if there had been any other way, we would have taken it."

Bryn flinched at the edge in his voice. This wasn't the first time the two brothers had disagreed about tactics, sometimes quite vociferously. During the four years Bryn and Leonin had been together, she'd found herself in the middle of one shouting match after another.

"We're grateful for your help," she said. "How did you know we needed rescuing, let alone where to find us?"

Rashid shot her a grin that on Leonin would have been charming but now struck her as not entirely sane. "Planted a locator in one of Leo's buttons."

Leonin's expression told Bryn he hadn't known.

"It was a precaution in case things went bad," Rashid explained.

"I wish you'd asked first," Leonin said, "but I'm glad you did it."

"What are brothers for but to annoy each other?"

"Your rescue was most welcome," Bryn said. "But now I must appeal to you again, and just as urgently. I haven't been able to contact my father. Neither has my sister. It's never happened before that he's been out of touch this long. I'm afraid something's happened to him. I hope that with your resources you can help me find him."

"Something's *happened* to him?" Rashid turned to her, all friendliness gone. "You could say that. You could *also* say that after all his fine words, Ernst Haslund has shown his true colors as Nagy's pawn."

"In that single speech, he did our cause immeasurable harm," Mode said.

Heat swept Bryn's cheeks in a flare of anger. "My father would *never* voluntarily say those things. He'd *never* throw his support behind Arthur Nagy."

"Did we hear the same speech?" Rashid shot back. "Or was one of us hallucinating? He backed Nagy right down the line. Now any hope we had from that so-called *voice of reason* is gone. And all the time those *good, reasonable* people waited around instead of taking real action has set us back all the more."

"To give him credit, in the past the Senator spoke out for many who believe in independence for the Alliance worlds," Leonin said. "He's been a powerful influence and advocate until now. We had every reason to hope he could accomplish what he said."

"Who's the more fool, brother? You for putting faith in a politician, *any* politician? Or me for listening to you?"

"My father *is* your ally!" Bryn said. "He has never condoned violence. He *hates* what's happening!"

The room fell silent. Everyone stared at her.

"And yet he gave that speech," Mode said quietly.

"But something's wrong," Bryn insisted. "I can't believe he acted of his own free will. If he had been himself, he would have given a very different speech, I can assure you. He would have argued *against* retaliation for Vainwal's secession, not allied himself with Nagy."

"People change their minds," Rashid said over the muttering in the room. "Or they throw away their so-called principles when things get tough. Politicians think of their careers first and their consciences afterward. Talk is cheap."

"Not. My. Father's." Bryn bit off every word.

"I don't believe it, either," Leonin said.

"Believe what you like," Rashid exclaimed, throwing up his hands. "Believe it until the sun turns into a red giant and then goes dim. That won't change what the Senator said or how he played into Nagy's hands. That one speech set our cause back by decades, and that's if we're lucky."

"Nagy must have gotten to him, threatened him," Bryn said. *Or Saralyn and her kids. Or me. One life, a few lives, against so many...*

The sacrifice would be unendurable. It would tear him apart.

In that brief moment, the room had fallen silent. Rashid was staring at her with dark, unreadable eyes.

"Rashid, take a look at this," said one of the techs sitting at the bank of computers. "Just now coming across."

Everyone at the table turned to look, Bryn included. A vid flared to life on the screen. The image was flat, from the kind of distance field cameras used in news stories. A woman stood on the front steps of a building, the half-glimpsed pillars of a Star Alliance center. She was flanked on either side by men who could have been Black's twins.

Saralyn. The image was too small and grainy for Bryn to be certain, but she sensed her sister's terror in her posture, the paleness of her cheeks except for two spots of hectic color, and the way she looked straight ahead instead of how she usually swept a crowd. She'd always had an instinct for where to stand to make the best social impression. Now she looked as if she desperately wanted the pavement to open up and swallow her up.

As Saralyn lurched from one stilted phrase to the next, Bryn had the same feeling of disorientation as when she'd listened to her father's speech. This could not be her sister's voice, her sister's words. Saralyn had always been the more conventional of the two, but she had always defended their father's positions. Here was Saralyn, praising their father's support for Nagy and urging all citizens to stand united against terrorism.

"Finally, I want to appeal to the public for help in locating my sister, Bryn. She disappeared shortly after our father's speech on the Vainwal situation. I have been informed the authorities have incredible, I mean *credible,* evidence that she's been kidnapped by insurrectionists of the Free Worlds Movement. Bryn, if you can hear me, we're doing everything we can to bring you home. The kids miss you. *I* miss you. We're all safe here. We're well protected. Just please—you stay safe, too."

The speech ended with Saralyn being rushed away. Mode flicked the broadcast off as Bryn sat, stunned. Leonin placed one hand on hers. His skin was warm, his touch firm.

"Looks like they got to her, too," he said.

"Saralyn must have been threatened, or her husband or children," Bryn said.

From the time they were children, Bryn had been the more adventurous, the risk-taker, while Saralyn preferred observation and quiet play. As a young woman, Saralyn had become enamored of fashion.

I fled to psychology, Bryn thought, *and she buried herself in fancy clothes.*

Yet Saralyn would never stumble over a word like *credible.*

"We're well protected," Saralyn had said. Had she meant *guarded? The bait in a trap!* To approach her would amount to walking into the clutches of StarOps.

Thank you, Saralyn.

"It's time to cut our losses," Mode said.

"No," Bryn said with such firmness that the others jumped. "I don't know how many times I have to say it: something is wrong with my father, something that Nagy or his agents have done. We can't abandon him."

"What exactly do you expect us to do?" Rashid asked.

"We have to find him," she said. "We have to get him out of wherever he's being held and undo whatever hold Nagy's got over his mind."

"That's a pretty tall order," Jax said.

"We're already stretched too thin," added one of the others. "We can't spare the personnel."

"You want us to hold off on our mission until Vainwal has been hammered flat, or worse?" Rashid said.

"If my father were here, he'd be the first one trying to avoid military retaliation."

"What's the point of arguing the impossible?" the white-haired man asked. "As far as the public is concerned, the Senator has thrown his weight behind Nagy, with everything that means, and Nagy won't hesitate to exploit that at every opportunity. Every moment Nagy goes without real opposition is another moment he's solidifying his power."

"But if she's right, if there were some other way, isn't it worth the gamble?" Styx had been quiet until this point. "It's worth considering, at least."

"I don't think you understand what's at stake here," Rashid said, addressing Bryn. "The resources involved—do you even know where your father is?"

"That's the first thing we need to find out," she answered. "It will happen a lot faster with your resources than if I have to search on my own. I've asked for your help and I still want it, but I am going after my father even if it means going alone. I know it's a risk. Black is out there, hunting for me. I don't have your skills or equipment. This is something I have to do—I *will* do—no matter what."

"It's a fool's mission," someone said.

"You'll get nabbed by StarOps before the day's out," Rashid said.

"And then she'll give us away," Jax said.

"That's not going to happen," Leonin said, squeezing Bryn's hand. "I'll do whatever I can to help. You know I will, no matter what my brother decides."

"Whose side are you on, anyway?" Rashid said.

"We've been planning what to do in the event of a planetary secession," Styx said temperately. "We knew that one of the member worlds was going to break away. We just didn't think it would be this soon."

"But," Jax added, "we thought we'd have Senator Haslund's influence to smooth the way with Terra."

Rashid was the leader, the one Bryn must convince. The others had their opinions, but they'd go along with whatever he decided.

"Every day in my work I see the results of one brutal Alliance action after another," she said, speaking directly to him. "I treat children whose lives and families have been destroyed on Ephebe and Remy and half a dozen other worlds. We're on the same side in this fight. I don't have any illusions that it will be easy to track down my father on my own. But if I have to, *I will*."

"Good god," the white-haired man said. "She's a maniac."

"What are you going to do?" Leonin shot back at him. "Lock her up? Become just as bad as StarOps?" After a half-second's pause, he said, "She's right about how much we need your help, Rashid. And she's twice as stubborn as you are."

"Okay, you've made your point. And no, of course we won't hold you against your will, Bryn. We're not monsters." Rashid raked his fingers through his hair, a gesture that reminded Bryn of Leonin when he was trying to make up his mind. "I've got to think on this. If we were to track down your father... What about his speech? Did you recognize anything in the background? Did he give any clues in his word choice or manner of speaking?"

"Just the blank wall behind him," Bryn said. "It could have been anywhere on Terra."

"Or off-world," Styx said.

"The way he sounded," Bryn said, "he was so unlike himself. I don't know any psychotropic medication that would produce exactly those symptoms, but my expertise is limited to therapeutic agents."

"We'll see what we can find out," Rashid said. "That's as much as I can promise right now. Depending on what we discover, we'll decide what else to do. This might be the end of it, you understand?" She nodded. "And now, as my brother looks like he's about to pass out, you two ought to rest. Or at the very least, stay out of our way. I'll let you know when we've learned anything."

Leonin looked even paler except for the livid bruises, but he hauled himself to his feet. Mode took them back down the corridor to the room with the bed and set up a hand-held with the Senator's speech. Bryn took one of the chairs, switched on the hand-held, and began going over her father's recorded statement, word by word, syllable by syllable, one expressionless moment at a time.

Bryn fell asleep while watching the recording of her father's speech on a hand-held viewer for what seemed like the twentieth time. The combination of the featureless background, flat expression, and monotonous delivery was soporific. She woke, her cheek aching from where it had rested against her folded arms. Leonin was still asleep on the bed.

The hand-held had returned to idle mode. She stared at it, unable to escape the feeling that she'd missed something. She consulted her notes. After a number of repetitions, she'd noticed an odd shift in her father's pronunciation of certain vowel sounds, but it wasn't consistent. She had no idea if it was deliberate on his part—was he trying to send a coded signal?—or an artifact of transmission. Her training didn't include the linguistic analysis necessary to make a determination. Whatever the explanation, it was the only anomaly she had been able to detect.

She got up quietly so as not to disturb Leonin. The door wasn't locked, nor was anyone stationed outside. Rashid had meant it when he'd said they weren't prisoners. She made her way back along the corridor to the command room. Images flickered across the screens, and read-outs were piled on the central table. Rashid and Styx bent over the table, studying a star map. When Rashid glanced up, Bryn noticed the shadows beneath his eyes. She felt a twinge of sympathy for him and wondered if he rested.

"I haven't found anything useful," Bryn said in answer to his greeting. "Except possibly this." She explained about the distortion.

"That's actually helpful," he said. "Good work. We've been analyzing the transmission to determine its origin. You've verified this isn't your father's natural speaking rhythm, so it's likely an artificial distortion. Signal delays were one of the parameters we used. We were able to combine them with parallax computations."

Something hot and bright rose in her throat. "Where did it come from?"

Styx said, "Our best guess—and it's only a guess, mind you—is that the signal arose on Alpha."

"Alpha!" *Alpha, of all worlds?*

"You know it?" Rashid asked.

"Yes, of course. I did my residency there." Alpha was the Alliance's center for scientific and medical research. None of the clinicians she'd studied under had cared that she was a Senator's daughter. Their focus on rigorous science in the service of humankind had been a refreshing balm after Terran politics.

"I've heard that the Alliance has its own government-funded labs, hidden away on different worlds, working on classified projects," Rashid said.

Bryn nodded. "Some of those labs are on Alpha, but the researchers operate under the strictest security. At the university, we tended to regard them as prostituting their scientific ethics for funding and advancement. There wasn't exactly an easy fraternization between us."

Styx snorted. Bryn ignored her.

"That may be so," Rashid said. "Nagy wouldn't risk a scientist sighting the Senator and then blabbering about it. He'd have to keep him hidden, and Alpha doesn't have extensive prison facilities."

Alpha had deserved its reputation as being law-abiding when Bryn was a grad student. Huge areas of the planet were undeveloped or parkland, with the inhabited areas devoted to science and technology, or support services. Felicity Sage, the professor who had been her mentor, was a staunch advocate of nonviolence.

"Alpha's a center of neurological research." Bryn got up and began pacing to help her think clearly. "Its facilities are the most advanced in the Alliance. For many kinds of research, it's the only place to go."

"You mean mind-control drugs?" Rashid asked, his tone grim.

"I know of a dozen drugs that might be used to control people, everything from anxiolytics to antipsychotics," Bryn admitted. "The problem is that to overcome volition, they impair so much central nervous system function that the patient—the subject—clearly cannot think or speak normally. My father's affect was flattened, but he didn't seem disoriented. He used complete sentences. However much we may object to the content of his speech, his arguments followed logically."

"That's just the drugs you know about," Styx said. "Who's to say they haven't developed new ones?"

Bryn paused in her pacing. "As much as I hate to admit it, that is entirely possible. I wish I could say for sure, but my specialty wasn't psychopharmacology. It's too risky to use mind-altering medicines in children. I focused on technologies like corticator devices to normalize brain function after trauma."

"We're not talking about helping children," Styx said. "We're talking about— Look, you just admitted that Nagy might have used a drug created by Alphan scientists to turn your father into a puppet, spouting whatever words were put into his mouth."

"Anything is *possible*," Bryn said. "If such a drug were developed, it would most likely be on Alpha. But that's not the only way to think about the problem. A moment ago, I mentioned the corticator devices I use in my work. They were developed on Alpha, too. A century ago, the labs created models for sleep learning. Updated versions are widely used to acquire languages and cultural information during interplanetary flight."

Rashid nodded. "Our agents use them to prep for off-planet missions when they're setting down away from urban centers. We use older models, as they're cheaper and less easily traced, but they still do a fair job at instilling local dialects. You think such things can be used to force a person to say things he doesn't believe in?"

"Not the devices I'm familiar with, no. They're designed to normalize brain function that's been disordered by trauma. As an analogy, the D-Alpha series gives you access to a new language but doesn't dictate how you use it. Maybe there's a new version I don't know about that might impair free will and judgment. But there are other technologies. At one time, the Alpha labs experimented with a psychic mind probe."

"A mind probe?" asked Styx, who had been looking progressively more disgusted as the discussion progressed.

"It was designed to extract information for espionage purposes, but it could be used to recover memories in a therapeutic or legal context," Bryn said.

"You mean when someone wants to remember but can't?" Mode said.

"As far as I know, yes, but the project was abandoned as too crude and too damaging to the subject's neuroarchitecture."

"You *think* it was abandoned," Styx said. "But you don't have proof. How do you know Nagy didn't continue the program in secret?"

"I don't know that," Bryn said, trying to keep her tone calm and rational. "I *hope* it really was unworkable."

"I wouldn't count on it." Rashid frowned. "A working psychic probe would be disastrous in the hands of Nagy's enforcers. There would be no way of keeping anything secret from his people. Anyone who got captured could be forced to reveal everything they knew. We can train ourselves to withstand torture, but I have no idea if it's possible to hold out when your brain's being manipulated."

"I don't know if such a probe exists," Bryn said. "I meant only that *if* it were fully developed, that work would almost certainly take place on Alpha."

"Nagy wouldn't hesitate to use it on your father."

Bryn suppressed a shudder. "The old psi-probe was supposed to be read-only, at least the original version. The only way to be sure the program hasn't been restarted with a new version is to check what's in the literature. I can research that for you from your computer."

The gray-haired man frowned. Styx said to Rashid, "Not a good idea. Our exposure might be compromised by such a targeted search. Her credentials are sure to ping StarOps."

"Really?" Bryn rounded on the other woman. "You think StarOps will be priority scanning for a search of psychotechnical literature? Isn't that a bit far-fetched? And isn't information, even a little, better than running on blind fear?"

"Enough!" Rashid cut in. "Bryn has a point. The more we know about what we're up against, the better we can plan. Bryn, can you search anonymously? And can you get in and out fast?"

"It'll restrict my access, but I can still get a rough idea of whether there's been any published research in the last decades. As for fast, you do know I was a graduate student on Alpha? Fast was the only way to get anything done and still have time for sleep."

"All right, then." Rashid's fleeting smile looked very like his brother's. "Styx, set her up." Styx didn't look happy, but she complied.

Bryn logged into the psychotechnology literature database under a limited guest account and began a search for the prototype psychic probe. A list appeared, barely enough to fill a single screen. The items were abstracts only; the papers themselves had been marked *Archived, Unavailable.* Only one of the papers was less than twenty years old, and that one was a review of the previous studies. The theory and engineering behind the device were mentioned in the sketchiest terms. The authors concluded the psychic probe was inherently flawed.

It wasn't unprecedented for research to be abandoned. After so much time, a graduate student desperate for a dissertation topic might make another attempt. The Alliance might fund a small grant because of the potential significance of a working mind probe. But for there to be *nothing* in the record strained credulity. That meant either the studies weren't being published or they had been censored.

Someone didn't want this tech duplicated.

She tried searching the authors of the previous papers. Two of them had gone into other fields and the others had not published anything since, which she deemed another questionable finding. Had they been dissuaded from following up on the probe? Or had they continued in secret Alliance-run facilities? *Were* there such things, and more to the point, were they on Alpha? A month ago, before the riot and everything that followed, she would have found the notion ludicrous, but now she was not sure.

She keyed in *mind control* and *thought control*, but neither phrase yielded useful results. Then, on a whim, she entered *telepathy*. Much to her surprise, that brought up not only the definition and folkloric entries but one under Anthropology: *Project Telepath. Darkover.*

A tap on her shoulder broke Bryn's concentration. "Time to log off," Styx said, "before we pick up an echo." Leaning over Bryn's shoulder, she touched the keypad, breaking the connection.

"Tell me you got something useful enough to justify the risk," Rashid said, entering.

Bryn told him what she'd found. "If the publications are sufficiently obscure, I'll have to use a university access to technical journals."

"If it's there, you'll find it." Leonin stood in the doorframe.

Bryn faced Rashid. "The Free Worlds Movement operates on a number of planets. You must have contacts that aren't closely monitored. Please help me get to Alpha. There's no time to lose."

"Help *us*," Leonin reminded her. "I know some of the Free Worlds people there, in case anything goes wrong."

"You always were a sucker for lost causes, Leo," Rashid said.

"I sure hope so. After all, I still have faith in you."

Rashid made a rude noise and then turned back to Bryn. "How do you propose to find your father? A planet's a big place."

"Alpha may be the center of the Alliance's psychotechnology," she replied, "but the labs capable of making a working probe aren't located on every street corner. The most advanced research facilities are in Alpha City. Likewise, the handful of scientists with the expertise to develop, test, and apply them. Felicity Sage, my old mentor, knows them all."

"All right, I'll help you, if only to get you out of my hair. I can get you to Alpha, but after that, you're on your own."

"The fewer people involved, the better," Bryn said.

"That's good, since we just got word that Spaceforce is on its way to occupy Vainwal. It's only a matter of time before the Alliance puts down the secessionist movement there, executes the planetary leaders, proclaims martial law, and then uses that as an excuse to do the same to any other world that dares assert its right to self-rule."

Leonin clapped his brother on the shoulder. "I knew we could count on you."

"Which you may live to regret. The ship's third-rate and pretty rough. On the other hand, the captain's one of our own. He won't sell you out."

"Thank you." Bryn resisted the impulse to throw her arms around him.

"I don't have much faith in this crazy scheme of yours," Rashid said. "If you can pull it off, I'll be the first one to cheer. But I won't be holding my breath waiting to hear from you."

◆◆◆

Bryn, Rashid, and Leonin emerged from the Free Worlds headquarters, followed by a pair of Rashid's men, blasters at the ready. Outside, a chill wind whipped down the street, tasting of chemicals and rain. A rust-colored sunset tinted the massed clouds overhead. She clutched the satchel Rashid had given her, containing a spare set of underclothes, a fake identity card, and a few essentials like tooth cleaner and antiseptic. Styx had given her a clean set of clothes, a knee-length tunic, loose pants, and knitted jacket, since her own were torn as well as soiled.

They moved through the streets, keeping to the shadows. Bryn tried not to think what might happen if the scavengers rushed them, pitting bare hands and lengths of wood against blasters. It would be a foolhardy move, one that only desperate people would undertake. *Something ought to be done to help those people*, she thought before reminding herself that she was in no position at the moment to help anyone. But no attack came, nor any sight of the ragged folk living there; they must have learned to leave the Free Worlds contingent alone.

They emerged from the maze of streets and alleys to an open space. Derelict vehicles stood in rows on the cracked, eroded pavement, most of them deteriorated with age and broken up by looters.

"What is this place?" Bryn asked.

"Parking lot," Rashid replied. "At least, that's what we call it. We hide our transportation in places like this. When the authorities fly over, they just see a junkyard."

"Junkyard is right," Leonin said. "Don't tell me we're going to use one of these."

"That's exactly right. And there's our ride." Rashid indicated a vehicle that looked very much like the others. The exterior was battered and dented, the windows coated with dust. The wheels did not rest on bare rims, however. The tires looked solid. When Rashid grasped the door handle, the door swung open soundlessly. Inside, there was seating for eight on benches with ratty, half-rotted upholstery.

They piled in, one guard in the passenger seat and the other in back, with Rashid driving and Bryn and Leonin on the forward bench. Lights sprang up across the display panels.

"Don't let the dust fool you," Rashid said. "It's a solar particulate, and it keeps this baby fully charged."

"Solar particulates are advanced tech," Leonin said. "I've never heard of them in civvy use."

"I didn't say we'd come by it honestly." Rashid released the brake and the vehicle moved forward. Although it was nearly full night, he didn't switch on the head lamps.

The vehicle reached the end of the lot. Beyond lay strips of weedy green, stunted trees, and rows of windowless modular buildings. Bryn spotted automated surveillance towers on the rooftops but no human guards. As they went on, they passed intersections and increasingly frequent piles of rubble.

Night closed in, draping the ruins in shadow. Eventually, the broken paving of long-deserted roads gave way to bare earth gouged by deep ruts and sinkholes. Rashid slowed as he steered around the holes, although the vehicle still jerked and rocked over the uneven terrain. Bryn grabbed a bar on the inside door and tried to breathe evenly.

Mile after mile passed, and the furrows grew shallower and more sparse. They entered a wooded area, following a trail barely wide enough to pass. Dense blackness engulfed them, broken only by the light cast by the head lamps and a faint, ghostly shimmer of the road.

"Almost there," Rashid said after they had traveled for some distance.

A stretch of pavement, cracked and blackened, came into view. A half-dozen surface-to-orbit shuttles, at least a generation out of date, perched on their landing pads. The outbuildings surrounding the poorly lit central area looked in shoddy repair.

Rashid halted at the edge of the field. "Here we are. Follow me."

They all exited the vehicle, with one of the Free Worlds men bringing up the rear. As they walked out onto the field, Bryn's courage almost failed her. She'd traveled to several worlds, to Alpha for her residency, also to Vainwal and the watery world of Thetis for vacations. The ships she'd taken had always been top of the line. These, on the other hand...

A ship doesn't have to be pretty to be safe, she reasoned, trying to quiet her fears. *It's what's inside that counts, like people. All this—the scoring, the discoloration—that's cosmetic.*

Nevertheless, she stifled a groan when Rashid led them up to the most broken-down looking of the shuttles. A man in spacer's overalls who'd been lounging beside the landing struts straightened up at their approach. A captain's winged pin glinted from one breast pocket.

Of course, it had to be that *one.*

Rashid and the captain exchanged a few words. Bryn caught the warmth with which they grinned and slapped one another's shoulders. Rashid gestured to her and Leonin to come over and made introductions. The captain's name was Wie or Whee, or possibly We. He was as battered-looking as his ship. A scar ran along one temple and across the arch of his cheekbone. Bryn thought he looked like a crook, a smuggler most likely, and she suspected that was exactly what he was. Who else would work with the Free Worlds party?

Or, she added silently, *who would know how to slip through Spaceforce patrols?*

The captain's eyes narrowed as he regarded Bryn. "Don't normally take passengers, you kien?"

"We're grateful for your help, nonetheless," she said.

"This whole daft idea's on Rashid's head. He thinks it's important, nothing. Get onboard. Sooner off-dirt, better for everyone."

To Bryn's relief, the safety webbing in the shuttle cabin looked in good repair and the engines purred to life without a hitch. She exchanged glances with Leonin, in the seat beside her. He grasped her hand, and she managed a smile in return.

Although the shuttle took off smoothly, Bryn's stomach lurched as it always did when they entered the microgravity of orbit. She focused on breathing regularly, *in...out...* during the trip to the spaceship. It was uglier than she'd expected, a bloated teardrop as space-scarred as the shuttle. Wie unbuckled them and handed them out the hatch as if they were freight. Bryn knew the principles of maneuvering in microgravity but had never had much practice, so she tried to relax and let the captain do his job. As they went through the airlock, she realized that, like the shuttle, it did not generate its own gravity.

All the way to Alpha in micro-gee? She swallowed sour-tasting saliva and tried to ignore the rebellion in her belly.

When they emerged from the airlock, a static-blurred voice issued from an unseen speaker. The distortion was so bad, Bryn could not even identify the language. Captain Wie replied in the same tongue.

"Ship-speak," Wie told Bryn, and now she detected a faint, mischievous twitch in the muscles around one eye. "Mate's nervy to get underway. Too damned much Force patrolling, ye kien?"

"I kien."

That brought a deepening of the crinkles.

Captain Wie shoved Bryn and Leonin into a narrow chamber with bunks on either side, hand grabs, and hatches at either end. The bunks resembled shelves covered with tattered old mattresses over frames. Bryn grabbed onto the bars and pulled herself to one of the bunks while Wie got Leonin settled.

Bryn inhaled deeply as the captain fitted a breather mask over her nose and mouth. The device would provide the correct oxygen mixture, a less costly method than filling the entire interior. The gases coming through the filter didn't smell right. Didn't *taste* right.

"You'll be a bit space-sick on re-entry," the captain said, tightening the straps of the mask. "Sorry, don't carry the drugs. No passengers to need 'em, ye kien?"

"I don't want to sleep!" Her voice sounded tinny and distant, as if she were speaking from the end of a tunnel. *But Rashid trusted this man.*

"Ye do, believe me. The trip's mickle rough on civvies."

"I don't care!"

"*Really* rough."

From the other side of the compartment, Leonin mumbled, "I think we'd better do...as the captain suggests. If he...won't matter...if we're... awake."

Each gasp brought the sleeping gas deeper into Bryn's lungs. Her body felt as if it belonged to someone else. Her mouth went numb, her lips unresponsive. A fearful thought seized her, that if she succumbed to the gas she would never wake up. Then it came to her, as if someone were whispering in her ear, that not once since meeting Captain Wie had her danger-sense stirred. With that thought, she slipped down the long, dark slope.

Pounding rattled through Bryn's skull. She tried to rub her temples, but something restrained her hands. The next moment, they came free. She felt the cool, wet slap of a patch applied to the side of her neck. Her mouth filled with the taste of something burned, like charcoal. The next moment, the taste faded and her vision steadied. She focused on the man leaning over her.

"Captain...Wie...." Her throat hurt when she tried to swallow. The inside of her mouth felt papery.

The captain handed her a bulb drink. Sipping, she discovered a lukewarm, slightly bitter liquid that wet her throat and left her feeling more alert. Her stomach felt steady, although she was still in a microgravitational field.

With a satisfied nod, the captain floated away. The restraining nets took a few minutes to figure out, but at last, she freed herself. Leonin was sitting up on his bunk, webbing across his thighs to anchor him in place, rubbing his sides.

"You okay?" she asked, thinking of his injuries.

"Better than," he said. "Space sleep must be restorative."

"Space sleep shot up with healin' juice sure is." With a nod, Captain Wie swung each of them through the compartment door and the airlock, and strapped them into the shuttle, then took the pilot's seat himself.

The shuttle was soon away, with only a passing sight of the planet below as they crossed the terminator into night. Compared to Terra, where light pollution was so extreme that it shrouded the entire dark side of the world in a luminous haze, only a sprinkling of pinpoints marked the major cities of Alpha. The shuttle made a bumpy re-entry in an open space bounded on three sides by yellowed scrub. The three disembarked, and Bryn was glad of the steady pull of planetary gravity. The ground underfoot was churned and blackened, but a breeze carried the smells of crushed greenery. The sky was clear, deep blue.

"This isn't the spaceport at Alpha City," Bryn said.

The captain responded with a snort. "Not likely I could set down there 'thout being arrested, ye kien? Folk like me use this improvised field instead." He gestured toward the end of the field. "You catch a public tram about three klicks that way, and it will take you right into the city."

"Thank you for your help," Bryn said.

The captain unholstered a blaster and offered it to her. She stared at the weapon, appalled. She knew the basics of how to aim and fire, but she'd never held one. Force weapons like blasters were legal only for law enforcement, military, and certain other, licensed personnel. When she shook her head, Wie handed it and a palm-sized, flattened plastic oval to Leonin.

"What's that?" Bryn said. "Another weapon?"

"Call booster set for the ship's frequency." At her startled expression, Wie added, "Did ye give no thought as to how to get *off* this planet? Or d'ye think smugglers' ships fall from the skies? Told Rashid I'd hang around for three days. If you can get a message to me, I'll meet you here, but don't be leisurely-like about it. If I haven't heard from you when it's time to go, you're on your own."

"I'll guard them well." Leonin tucked both items inside his jacket.

Wie offered Bryn some local paper currency. "At least, take this."

Bryn thanked him and put the bills in the satchel Rashid had given her. Without further ado, the captain hurried back up the shuttle ramp, eager to be gone. She and Leonin moved away from the blast radius as the shuttle's engines purred to life. From the edge of the field, she watched the shuttle take off.

Three days, Captain Wie had said. That wasn't much. Everything depended on her being right about her father being here in Alpha City, and whether Professor Felicity Sage still had her finger on the pulse of cutting-edge neurocybernetic research.

◆◆◆

When the sun was full up, Bryn and Leonin were tramping through fields of overgrown weeds and bushes. Wildflowers grew in profusion, evoking memories of a time when she'd faced nothing more terrible than

Professor Sage's final exams. Bryn picked a handful of flowers and inhaled. Their mingled fragrances filled her head, pungent and poignantly familiar.

"Place feeling familiar?" Leonin asked.

"More like *smelling* familiar, but yes." She tucked a flower behind one ear.

They had not been walking for more than a couple of hours when the landscape opened out into gentle hills covered with grasses genetically engineered to grow soft and low, never needing fertilizer or more irrigation than the weather satellites delivered. A short distance away sat a sprawling building topped by solar panels. A covey of preteens was playing a game with a giant, brilliantly colored ball on the lawn. They spotted Bryn and Leonin, and waved.

Such a safe, manicured landscape, Bryn thought, *nothing like the blasted settlements of Campta.* The sunlight dimmed, or perhaps that was the moment of unexpected tears, quickly blinked away.

Eventually, they came upon a well-paved pedestrian path running parallel to tram rails and a flat road for vehicles. The road led them to a small station on the outskirts of a residential area. The building was constructed of wood, treated to endure for decades yet maintain an artfully rustic elegance. No one was at the small window, but there was an automated payment kiosk configured to accept cash.

While Leonin purchased tickets to Alpha City, Bryn located a public link and entered the identification code for Dr. Felicity Sage. Even after all these years, she still knew the number by heart.

"Hello?"

Bryn's knees felt as if they had turned to jelly. She closed her eyes, too unexpectedly overcome to speak.

"Hello? Who is this?"

"Fe-Felicity. Dr. Sage, it's me, Bryn Haslund."

"Bryn! My dear, I'm delighted to hear from you. You must be on-world, judging by the clarity of this transmission. Are you here on a professional excursion—although I confess, I'm not cognizant of any impending conferences pertaining to the research we did together, but then, clinical work does take one far afield—and might you be able to work in a bit of pleasure in the form of a personal visit?"

Bryn's eyes stung. The little speech was so exactly like Dr. Sage. Empires might rise and fall, but academics remained stubbornly verbose.

"It's neither, I'm afraid," Bryn said. "I need your help. My father—"

"Hush! Not over a public link!"

Bryn's danger-sense roused, not full-blast but an unmistakable ping. Clearing her throat, she tried to sound as if she were here on innocuous business. "I'd like to see you if you have time for a visit. Perhaps we might have dinner together."

"I'm always happy to see an old student. I have advisory hours this afternoon but can join you afterward. We can meet at the university coffee shop, just the way we used to."

"Has the coffee improved any since I was a student?"

Felicity laughed. "Indeed not. But we survived it then, and we shall survive it now. I look forward to seeing you." With those words, she closed the link.

The tram arrived a few minutes later, moving smoothly and almost silently along its rails. Bryn and Leonin boarded and settled into their seats. There was only one other passenger in their car, an old man who appeared to be asleep. The next stop came a few minutes later and a group of a dozen teenagers got on, chattering and joking.

The outskirts of Alpha City looked calm and orderly, just as Bryn remembered. Gardens and strips of parkland surrounded building complexes. Every vista exuded reassurance that this was a safe, planned, *protected* place. But no place was truly safe, no place within the confines of the Star Alliance and the reach of Arthur Nagy.

Finally, the tram glided to a halt at the university complex, a few stops before the terminus at the center of the city. A wide, brightly colored canopy ran the length of the platform. Announcements of a variety of cultural and academic lectures flanked a large sign advising travelers to be on the alert for suspicious activities and seditious speech. Once Bryn would have laughed at such a sign as a student prank, but now it made her uneasy. At least there were no police in sight.

Across the boulevard from the station, people sat reading or talking in open-air cafes. Bryn inhaled the mingled aromas of pastries and coffee. Her mouth watered.

"Mmm, that smells wonderful," she said to Leonin. "Are you hungry?"

"I could eat, and I'd never say no to real coffee, but it would be foolish to spend our remaining cash on a snack. We might need it later."

"You have a point. I expect once she hears our story, Dr. Sage will not only feed us but offer us a place to stay. There are still a couple of hours remaining before I'm to meet with her. How about we check out the university library? I want to get started checking the current status of the corticator technology and psychic probes."

Leonin shook his head. "I'd be no help at all with scientific journals. Besides, I should make contact with local Free Worlds fighters as soon as possible. We can meet up with your professor afterward."

She didn't protest. He'd likely be bored while she did her research, and she wouldn't be of any use to him. "I'll see you at the university coffee shop, then."

They parted with a brief kiss, and Bryn made her way to the university library. She passed through the foyer into the dense quiet of the main room, two stories high and filled with natural light. Tables with computer access points were available to anyone and many were in use, but the restricted stacks with their shelves of physical books contained the library's real treasures. Many volumes dated back to the early years of space exploration, when ships filled with sleeping colonists ventured into unknown reaches of the galaxy. Some of these never reached their destinations, and those few that had been rediscovered centuries or even millennia later had often evolved in strange directions. These were the Class D Protected Worlds, once carefully buffered against the worst of industrialized commerce, now abandoned as the Star Alliance focused on its internal struggles.

And here I am, not five minutes in the library, thinking like a scholar again!

A flicker of movement, someone moving quickly and silently at the far end of the room near one of the corridors leading to the stacks, caught Bryn's attention. She hurried toward the figure, who turned to wait for her, a woman holding a stack of printed books wrapped in archival plastic. The librarian, Madame Marian Postlethwaite, didn't look a day older than when Bryn had been a student here. The title *Madame* had been given in jest by students of previous classes and had stuck. Now Madame Postlethwaite smiled as she gestured for Bryn to follow her. A few moments later, they arrived at a tiny office, immaculately neat and smelling of book ink and dust.

With the door closed behind them, the librarian exclaimed, "Bryn Haslund, as I live and breathe!"

"I didn't think you'd remember me."

"Pish!" Madame Postlethwaite set the books on her desk. "Sit down, let's chat for a few minutes. I never forget a book or the face of a student who fails to return it."

Bryn assumed a suitably guilty expression, although she could not remember any outstanding book loans.

"I'm joking, dear girl. Tell me, what have you been up to since you left us?"

"I went on to a clinical certificate, treating traumatized children."

"I always knew you were not destined for a purely academic life. You could have done so, you know. You certainly had a good analytical mind, but it does not necessarily follow that such a life would have made you happy. I have no doubt your patients thrive...and also that your expertise will be in demand in the future."

Bryn commented that she expected no shortage of young patients any time soon. "I don't have a current library account, so might I use a researcher access? I have a few hours to spare and it would help to be able to bring up the technical subscriptions."

"I'm sure it would, but that requires authorization." The librarian's friendly expression did not waver as her voice took on a tone that granted no exceptions for personal reasons. "If you'll be in residence—" meaning officially registered for a seminar, "—that's another matter. Or you can apply to the Dean for an exemption."

"Oh—" Bryn made a dismissive wave as if she did not want to bother such an important person. The fewer people who knew of her presence here, the better. "I'll use the public access, then."

"I said I couldn't give you research access, but there's no need to expose yourself to undergraduate hoi polloi. As an alumna, you are still entitled to certain privileges. Come along, then, and I'll set you up where you can work undisturbed."

Madame Postlethwaite led the way briskly along the corridor to the private computer carrels and indicated an unoccupied cubicle. Somewhat to Bryn's amusement, an old-fashioned ink stylus and pad of paper were also provided. Academic habits changed slowly when they did at all.

"I'll leave you to it, then. Just leave the door open when you're done, as it locks automatically from the outside. I have a key, of course, but it's an unnecessary bother if you've left behind any personal items."

"Madame Postlethwaite, I would not dream of doing such a thing."

Alone behind the locked door, Bryn set down her satchel, settled herself at the desk, and performed a quick search for corticator and psychic probe technologies. There was nothing beyond what she had already discovered from Rashid's access. She next turned to the heading, *Project Telepath.*

Department of Alien Anthropology: Darkover

To all Empire Medical Services on Open and Closed planets: You are directed to seek out any humans bearing telepathic or psi talents, preferably those latent or undeveloped. You are empowered to offer them Class A medical contracts...

At first, Bryn suspected a hoax site, but the link led her to a summary of published reports. They were old, from the Terran Empire that had predated the Federation that had itself given rise to the current Star Alliance. Within a few sentences, she was thoroughly intrigued. Following an abortive attempt on the part of World Wreckers, Incorporated, to disrupt the ecology of Cottman IV, a Class D Protected World also known as Darkover, the ruling aristocrats had launched an Empire-wide search for humans with psychic powers with the twin objectives of screening and training for useful purposes.

Psychic powers? Bryn felt an odd, atavistic shiver. Apparently, they weren't a myth.

Reading on, she learned that the inhabitants of Darkover appeared to be one of the very rare races with widespread natural telepathy. Eventually, however, the project was abandoned and contact with the planet was lost in the early years of the Alliance.

Telepathy. Reading another's thoughts...or influencing them? She saw nothing in the reports either way. Some of the participants were able to sense emotions or manipulate small objects with their minds, although the only documentation came from the Darkovans themselves, so there was understandable skepticism from Terran scientists. After the natives closed down the project, no one on Terra had investigated further. She wasn't surprised, as telepathy sounded like wishful thinking augmented by a healthy dose of native superstition. As much as she would have liked to peer into the thoughts and memories of her traumatized young clients, the reality was that such mental contact was scientifically impossible. In all likelihood, if telepathy did exist, it was so unreliable as to have no significant practical application.

Having wasted more time than she'd intended, Bryn realized it was time to get going for her rendezvous with Felicity Sage. She deleted her search history from the access, gathered up her coat, and headed for the university coffee shop.

Along the way, she passed a stand that offered news flimsies and screen displays where pedestrians could stand and view the feeds. As she approached, her gaze was captured by a headline that Spaceforce ships had made orbit around Vainwal. A story from later that same day focused on planet-wide martial law. There had been riots on Renney and several other worlds, with footage of protesters being loaded into police vans.

Her spine stiffened as new video images flickered across the screen. The first few moments were chillingly familiar: a demonstration in a mall or plaza, numbering in the thousands. She didn't recognize the place, but the architecture in the background looked typical for a medium-sized city on any of a dozen Alliance worlds. Nausea washed over her, and with it flashes of memory. She tasted the gas at the back of her throat.

This was Alpha, she told herself sternly, that most civilized of environments. But she did not feel safe and wondered if she ever would again.

On the screen, the crowd had fallen still, all at once, or so it seemed. Raised fists lowered. Signs dropped to the ground. Movement ceased. The people, as far as she could tell, just stood there. They gave no sign of paying any attention to one another. They barely seemed to be breathing. Bryn had never seen anything like it outside of a horror vid.

Then, without any visible signal, the people began emptying the plaza, individual participants staring blankly ahead as they shuffled along. Below the image, the newscaster's commentary scrolled across the screen.

Following orders to disperse peacefully, the citizenry of Renney City return to their normal, productive lives...

"What the hell?" someone behind Bryn muttered. A group of pedestrians had gathered to watch the newscast. In their faces, she saw the reflection of her own consternation.

"They all decided to give up and go home?" a young blonde woman murmured to her companion. She was clearly a student by her satchel covered with irreverent patches.

"What?" another viewer said, from near the back of the group. "Just because someone in authority asked them nicely?"

"Well, I know *you* wouldn't be so meek."

"How is this possible?" the young woman's friend said. "All of them? At the same time?"

"It *isn't* possible," Bryn replied. *Groups can be dispersed by various methods, some more coercive than others, but none of those methods work for everybody at the same time. There should be a mix of compliance and resistance. Some people would withdraw, but they would talk about why they were leaving—what happened—whether the demonstration was successful, even where they were going to have dinner*—something. *Not this—this mute, unquestioning obedience.*

"I don't believe it," said an older man in a professor's quintessential tweed and shaggy gray hair. "This footage must surely be a hoax."

"Whose side are you on, anyway?" one of the students demanded. "Attacks on the free press are the hallmarks of an emerging totalitarian state."

"That's hardly the point," the young woman said. "Consider the objective of publicizing such an event, whether real or fabricated."

"Clearly, it's to discourage dissent by advocating by example the peaceful dissolution of protest assemblies," her friend answered. The two of them went off, debating the matter in an animated fashion. The professorial type had faded into the stream of foot traffic.

Bryn glanced back at the screen. While she and the other viewers had been talking, the crowd on the plaza had thinned noticeably. Still, there was almost no noise. She searched for police presence in the scene and after a few moments found it. They were clustered around a platform several meters tall that was surmounted by an apparatus. It didn't look like either surveillance or sound projection equipment, although she could not think what else it might be. The matte, unreflective black box-like structure bristled with antennas.

The devices remained in Bryn's memory, menacing and enigmatic, as she hurried to her rendezvous.

◆◆◆

The university coffee shop spilled onto the wide pedestrian boulevard beneath bright awnings with designs of fanciful flower dragons that screened out ultraviolet radiation. Bryn found an empty table on the periphery of the outdoor seating area and settled into a chair that afforded a good view of the boulevard in either direction. A human server, young enough to be an undergraduate, came to take her order. She asked for two coffees in heated mugs, and these were delivered a few minutes later by an automated cart. She sipped hers and tried to look nonchalant, not showing the worry that increased with every passing moment.

"Sorry I'm late." Leonin took the other seat and sniffed appreciatively at the coffee. "Been waiting long?"

She waved off the question with, "A bit."

"Love, you're upset. What happened?"

Bryn tried not to look as distressed as she felt. "Footage from Renney City, a demonstration there."

"I saw the news."

Bryn heard the tremor in his voice. He'd seen. He'd understood—not only what it meant that an angry, determined crowd had suddenly abandoned their purpose, but what the images had meant to *her.*

"Do you think—" she began, lowering her voice in case anyone nearby was listening, "—these people were subjected to whatever is controlling my father? On a broader scale?" It was one thing to postulate the use of drugs or a reinvented psychic probe to influence a single person, but to administer the same to so many, in an open space—she could not imagine how that might be done.

"We don't have enough information to go on," he said.

Could manipulating a single individual be a prelude to controlling a crowd, and what then? A city? An entire planet?

A couple strolled by, arm-in-arm, their expressions relaxed and happy. "That should be us," Bryn said wistfully.

"And will be again. I promise."

Leonin held out a cheap, disposable link, the kind paid for with cash so it would not be registered to anyone's name.

"I've programmed the number," he said, with a slight emphasis on *the* so Bryn understood that he meant the one given to them by Captain Wie.

He was about to say more when Felicity Sage arrived, a small, delicately built woman with wispy gray hair. Her eyes were as bright as ever, and her smile was welcoming as she held out both hands to Bryn in a typically Alphan greeting. The strength of her grip, however, conveyed a warning.

"My dear, how good it is to see you," Felicity said. "And this is your young man." Leonin introduced himself, and Felicity unslung her shoulder bag, drew up a chair from a nearby table, and sat down.

"I'm sorry, I ordered coffee for only two," Bryn stammered. "Shall I get another, or would you prefer tea? Or something else?"

"Tea, but I don't want any now. I drank an ocean of the stuff to get through the afternoon. Advising students is a necessary evil requiring gallons of it."

"Was I that tiresome?" Bryn said, unable to resist a smile. "If so, a thousand apologies. You were always patient with me."

"No apologies required. You were so self-directed you practically advised yourself. You came to us already knowing what you wanted from your education, so my task was primarily to sign off on the coursework you'd already determined—accurately, I might add—to be necessary to achieve your objective."

"I didn't know that about you, love," said Leonin. "I mean, your determination has always impressed me, but to not even have had normal student doubts is extraordinary, even for you."

"You must remember that I'd already had those 'doubts' thrashed out of my system. But Dr. Sage—"

"Felicity, dear girl. You're no longer my student, and we are friends now, I hope."

"—*Felicity*, then, does have a point. I'd decided on psychology when I realized that what my father did was *politics*. I never had any doubts that I wanted nothing whatsoever to do with it. It seemed to me that the only way to be a separate, individual person was to do something else entirely. Until recently, I was successful."

"We shall have more than enough to catch up on, but let's do it in a more comfortable setting," Felicity said brightly. "How long are you here for, and will you need a place to stay?"

Bryn lowered her voice. "I'm grateful for the invitation, but there could be a certain amount of…risk to you."

"Risk? My dear, of course there is. I knew that the moment I watched your father's speech. I have served six terms as chair of the Department of Psychological Technology and two as Dean of the School of Social Technology. After clerking my way through budgetary deliberations and staff meetings that might as well have been populated by lava-spewing salamanders, you don't think a modicum of *risk* is going to intimidate me, do you?"

Felicity still lived in the same unit Bryn had visited during her student days, a suite consisting of a bedroom, a guest room little bigger than a closet, an office that also served as a library, and compact spaces for eating and food preparation. Although the individual rooms were small, they were elegantly proportioned and filled with natural-spectrum light. No portraits adorned the walls, only a few exquisite miniature paintings that were clearly originals.

Felicity prepared a pot of tea and a plate of sliced apples and cheese toast wedges. Oversized mug in hand, Bryn settled onto the chair facing Felicity, while Leonin lowered himself to the remaining empty chair.

"Normally I don't care for tea," he said after a sip, "but this is very good."

"Locally grown black tea, flavored with elder-currants," Felicity said.

"I could never afford it when I was a student, so I drank up whenever you invited a group of us for an evening," Bryn said.

"So you followed through with your goal of child psychology," Felicity said. "Has it proved a satisfying choice?"

"Yes, very much so," Bryn replied. "I specialize in the treatment of severely traumatized children. My patients come from some of the most chaotic and devastated areas of the Alliance, places like Renney and Campta."

"Campta? I thought that was rendered uninhabitable some years ago."

"Eventually, it was."

"Let us speak freely since we are in private. What brings you to Alpha?"

"I'm looking for my father."

"So I gathered. His speech after the Vainwal announcement was a..." Felicity hesitated, clearly choosing her next words, "...a remarkable oration."

"*Remarkable,* indeed! More like unbelievable. Outrageous. Deceitful." Bryn set her mug down, splashing the amber liquid onto the table.

"His statements were certainly out of character with everything you've told me about him, as well as his previous positions on the issues."

"You could say that," Leonin said.

"I believe something's happened to cause my father to switch his loyalty to Arthur Nagy and the worst of the Star Alliance's policies," Bryn said.

"Your solicitude for your father, while admirable, does not address the question of why you are here on Alpha—and in my living room—instead of with your father on Terra."

"He's disappeared. Neither my sister nor I can reach him."

"We have reason to believe he's no longer on Terra but here on Alpha," Leonin added. He explained how Rashid's people had traced the broadcast signal to Alpha.

"However did you come into the company of a cell of the Free Worlds movement?" Felicity said, eyebrows raised.

Bryn described her experiences the morning Vainwal had declared its independence, her first meeting with Black, the riot, and everything that followed. "Something's been done to my father to make him behave in a way contrary to all his previous beliefs. I'm afraid that Nagy used Alphan tech to control my father's mind and that's why he's here."

Felicity glanced from one to the other, lips pursing. "That line of reasoning relies on a string of assumptions. We must allow the possibility that the alterations in your father arose naturally. Certain conditions, like brain lesions, metabolic disorders, and the like can cause radical changes in personality."

Bryn had not considered a pathological explanation. Her father had always seemed in robust health.

"Occam's razor," Leonin said. "The simplest solution that fits the facts is usually the correct one. If the Senator had a brain injury or disease, why bring him all the way here when Terra has excellent facilities? And if the Senator had a stroke or a tumor, wouldn't Nagy use it to generate sympathy? No, I agree with Bryn. The reason her father is here is the *tech*. Drugs, mind-control devices, I don't know what all."

"My dear boy, do not discompose yourself. I am merely suggesting a logical approach. We must consider all possibilities based on what we know so far. The first thing is to find out if the Senator is here on Alpha. If he is anywhere in the psychomedical system, I can search for his patient records."

"Unless they're sealed or he's here under a false name," Bryn pointed out. "I wouldn't put it past StarOps. Still, we must start somewhere."

Felicity led the way to her office, where she logged in to a high-level university link. An hour later, it was clear that her research had yielded no useful results. As far as both the public and research databases were concerned, Ernst Haslund wasn't anywhere in the Alphan system. She then checked the consolidated Alliance-wide records, which indicated he was currently on Terra.

"Well," Bryn said, "we're back to my original theory, either a drug or an instrument-mediated mind control, not a medical condition."

"I don't believe we've made that much progress in psychopharmaceuticals," Felicity said. "They're systemic, for one thing, rather than targeted. And even if they were specific to a given area of the cerebral cortex, *beliefs* cannot be narrowed down to a given neurological structure."

"I don't know much about psycho—what did you call them?—psychopharmaceuticals," Leonin said, "but I do know that it's possible to get a man so drunk he can't remember his own birthday. Of course, he can't remember how to put two syllables together, either. The Senator spoke quite clearly."

Bryn said, "Not only was *what he said* out of character but *how he spoke*. There was an odd hesitation, but it wasn't the kind you see with neuropathological dysphonia."

"An activity as complex as a political speech," Felicity said, nodding agreement, "—well, I don't think that will ever be amenable to a chemical."

"Felicity, what about tech?" Bryn said. "What about the old psychic probe?"

"Years ago, I had the opportunity to speak with the original researchers. The project was discontinued when a more promising one opened."

"A more promising one?" Bryn sat straighter in her chair. "I had no idea."

"You know my field used to be alpha-cortical devices."

"Yes, I studied their therapeutic applications with you and apply them with my patients. But I don't see how they could be used to direct a person's thoughts or actions."

"The approved devices can't. We tailored them to quiet those areas of the limbic system that become chronically hyperactive in post-traumatic states. I studied how other areas might be stimulated or suppressed using similar induction techniques. The problem I encountered was the need for direct or near-direct contact."

Bryn said aloud for Leonin's sake, "Both the D-alpha corticators used for sleep learning and the therapeutic models require electrodes on bare skin for transmission. You can boost the induction signals through hair or fabric, but not much further. That limits their application."

"I'm not sure why that's a problem," Leonin said. "The sleep-learning apparatus is portable enough for use on spaceships."

"But not something you can easily carry around," Bryn pointed out. "I can only use it in my clinic, not the homes of my patients. That's a real limitation, believe me. When my kids most need the tranquilizing effect—say, when they are exposed to triggering stimuli in their daily lives—it isn't available."

"You see the problem," Felicity said. "The old psychic probe was supposed to operate at a distance. At first, only a few centimeters gap between the inducers and the patient's skull, but they'd worked it up to several meters by the time they discontinued the program."

"Several meters!" Bryn said. "That's a remarkable increase in range."

"Indeed, it is. That's why, when funding from an agency I'm not permitted to name became available to re-examine the probe, I agreed to act as a consultant."

Bryn shook her head. "I don't understand. I thought the work was discontinued. There was nothing on it in the archives."

For the first time, Felicity looked uncomfortable. "The project was all bound up in non-disclosure and confidentiality clauses. Quite different from the usual scientific grants, where the more you distribute your findings, the happier they are. I don't want to know how many contracts I'm violating by just mentioning this to you."

A silence fell over the room as Bryn struggled to take in what Felicity had said. A program bound by legally-enforced secrets, reviving old tech with new goals, goals she doubted had anything to do with healing broken minds. A lab hidden from public view and watchdog surveillance.

"At any rate," Felicity went on, "they wanted to find a way to increase the range of the corticator technology by hybridizing it with the old psychic probes. I agreed to the conditions only with the agreement that I'd be able to publish—and consult in the manufacture of—enhanced therapeutic devices. By hybridizing the psychic probe and Q-alpha corticator technologies, I and my colleagues came up with a *theta*-corticator. Initial tests were promising enough to begin preliminary human trials."

"Wait, wait!" Leonin held up his hands. "I've got the layman's version of what the alpha line is about, but what's *theta*?"

"The terms refer to types of brain waves," Felicity explained. "Theta waves occur naturally in dreaming sleep, as well as the barely conscious state—we call it *liminal*—just before sleeping and just after waking. They're associated with a state of relaxed awareness."

Being able to induce such a state in a traumatized child would be a huge benefit, although Bryn couldn't see the relevance to her father's aberrant speech in support of Nagy. He certainly hadn't seemed *relaxed.*

"Keep in mind that the theta-corticator is a hybrid based on the architecture of the therapeutic devices you are familiar with, Bryn," Felicity said. "It elicits theta in preference to alpha or other brain waves, but not exclusively. The device seemed so promising at first, I'd hoped it could be used to normalize synaptic patterns in an array of disorders. The aspects we incorporated from the psychic probe would have meant it could be used at a distance."

"Yes," Bryn said. "Many of my young clients could not tolerate pressure on the skull. They'd been too traumatized by physical restraints. And those were the ones most in need of the therapeutic alpha devices."

"About the time I left, my research group discussed re-designing the device to be implantable, thereby eliminating the need for bulky, external transmitters," Felicity said. "I had significant ethical objections, and at any rate, I had already decided to leave the program."

Leonin broke into the conversation, saying, "Could this theta-corticator be used to control behavior? Thoughts? Emotions?"

"Yesterday I would have said not," Felicity replied, "at least, certainly not for phenomena as complex as thoughts and behavior. I must confess myself naïve with regard to my colleagues' ultimate goals. I lost enthusiasm for the project when it became apparent that not only was the device unlikely to fulfill its therapeutic potential, but those same *colleagues* had quite a different objective."

"And that objective was?" Bryn said.

"The work proceeded in stages, each with its own success parameters. The first goal involved the induction of near-natural theta waves. They called it *pseudo-sedation* and developed a passivity index to quantify the effect. I was still optimistic at this point and did not quibble about terminology, although in retrospect, I should have. Sedation, real or mimicked, is not the same as *alert relaxation*, such as occurs in meditative states. My misgivings grew with the second phase, *attitude adjustment and active compliance*."

Bryn felt a rush of nausea. The use of a potentially therapeutic technology as a means of enforcing conformity and obedience—*compliance*—was a perversion. There was not the slightest doubt in her mind that StarOps and Arthur Nagy were behind it.

Felicity gave a ghost of a shrug, a brief lift of her shoulders. "After that, I returned to the alpha devices, although I never tendered my formal resignation from the theta-corticator project. Something always held me back. I told myself the connection might prove valuable at a future time. I think, though, I secretly wanted to keep an eye on what the others were doing. Where this second stage might lead."

A few taps brought up a series of password prompts, which Felicity entered. The screen displayed a heading:

Phase 3: Passivity and Hyper-suggestibility in Large Groups. Field Testing.

"Renney City," Bryn muttered. "So that's how they did it."

"To tell the truth, Bryn, when I heard about your father and how aberrant his behavior was, my thoughts ran in the same direction. Unlike you, however, I knew about *active passivity*. It sounded terrifyingly possible."

Of course, Nagy would push any research that promised a tighter, more reliable influence over the insurgents. Why use raw force to suppress dissent when you could change people's very thoughts?

"Your father may not be entered in the public health system, but that's not the only place he might be," Felicity said. "The first two phases of the program are residential. We'll have to check in person if your father's at the lab, I'm afraid. Those computers aren't networked to external systems." She furrowed her brow. "At the time, I thought it a ridiculous precaution, but now I understand. They couldn't risk the true objectives being made public."

"They didn't reckon on you," Bryn said.

"No, my dear. They didn't reckon on *you*."

Leonin shifted uneasily in his chair. "If you're right that a device was used to turn the Senator into Nagy's mouthpiece, will he return to normal if we remove it? If he's under its influence, will he leave with us? That is, assuming the lab will let us just walk out? And what about security guards?"

Leave it to Leo to consider what might go wrong.

"Getting in won't be a problem," Felicity said. "Getting *out*... I'll see what I can do about muting video and audio surveillance."

Bryn frowned. "Leo and I might pass as your junior associates, but my father's easily recognized."

"I very much doubt even the head of the project would dare to prevent me and my team from departing," Felicity said. "But you're right, your father will need a disguise. He'll be wearing research scrubs, so we should bring something he can wear under a lab coat and allow him to pass as one of my assistants. Unfortunately, I have no garments that would fit a normal-sized man. We'll have to shop on our way there."

Bryn had never seen anyone, even the president of the university, successfully stand up to Felicity. She hoped this wouldn't be the first time.

"That still doesn't address the issue of freeing the Senator's mind, whether it's from this device or a drug," Leonin said. "Sorry to harp on the issue, but even if we spirit the Senator out of there, Nagy's goons will be on the chase. We won't have time to think through our next steps. We should line up resources for what comes next."

"The effects of the alpha-corticator persist after it's removed," Bryn admitted. "Longer the more frequently it's used. I don't know about the theta device."

"Nor do I," Felicity said. "I'm not familiar with this version, including all the ways the original was modified. I wouldn't count on simply turning off the device or detaching the electrodes. If all goes well, we'll be able to bring your father to a facility where he can receive proper care."

From Leonin's expression, he wasn't counting on the rescue going smoothly. Bryn reluctantly agreed with him. This might be Alpha, but these were not ordinary times. Felicity might wield significant influence within the university, but even she might not be able to overcome the effects of Nagy's theta device. Then something nudged at her memory, a whisper: *But maybe there are others who can, those who have successfully resisted the Terran Federation and its technology...with their minds.*

"Felicity, what do you know about Project Telepath?" Bryn asked.

"Telepaths? I've never seen any scientific evidence that they exist."

"Neither had I, but the natives of Darkover seem to have developed the ability, enough to convince the old Federation to stop interfering with their affairs."

"Ancient history," Leonin said.

"You'd be surprised what's buried in ancient history, love." Bryn turned to Felicity. "Before we leave, could you copy what's known about Darkovan telepaths?"

"I hardly think it'll be useful, but it's better to have information and not need it than to need it and not have it."

Felicity located the files and copied them onto a data tab for Bryn. That completed, they left for the laboratory.

Felicity's vehicle was surprisingly roomy inside, silent and quick on acceleration. The three made a brief stop to purchase an ordinary pair of dark pants and a shirt in a loosely fitting style for Ernst. From the shop, they proceeded to the massive complex housing the university research laboratories. Bryn remembered the place well, with its architecture, much the same as the rest of the university, of light gray stone adorned with bands of geometric mosaics in muted earth tones. Carefully curated botanical gardens separated the buildings.

They parked the vehicle and proceeded on foot. Security gates, cages of heavy metal framing and scanners, framed the front entrance. Guards in university uniforms stood watch on either side. A trio of students were handing over their identification and satchels for scanning.

"So much for the vaunted freedom of academia," Leonin said.

"New Alliance directives." Felicity's tone dripped scorn. "Some gormless bureaucrat decided that the labs are a prime target for terrorist infiltration. Or some such ridiculous nonsense."

"Do we have to show identification at the checkpoint?" Bryn clutched the package containing the clothes for her father. She might not be arrested on the spot, although Leonin almost certainly would be.

Felicity turned down a paved way. "Come along."

"Do staff have a private entrance?" Leonin asked.

"*I* have a private entrance," Felicity said, adjusting the strap of her shoulder bag. "When the campus police set up the checkpoint, I informed the Dean that she faced a choice between my privacy or my resignation. I'll not have those overpriced goons rifling through my equipment. Nor will I have my movements tracked as if I were a sociological research subject. *They* must sign permission forms. I, on the other hand, do not hesitate to bully those in power into giving me what I demand. Rather mercilessly, I should add."

They reached an unmarked entrance where Felicity removed a pass card from her pocket and inserted it in the slot of the lock. The door clicked open. Past a set of glass-paned doors, they entered a hallway. The doors to either side were half-clear, revealing laboratories and offices. The entire effect was one of spaciousness, ample funding, and order. About halfway down, a sign read *Applied Corticator Sciences Laboratory*. A handful of men and women in blue science laboratory coats strolled down the hallway, carrying hand-helds or talking among themselves.

"This way," Felicity said, leading them past the conference room.

"Dr. Sage?" a male voice called from behind them.

Bryn stiffened. *Just pretend we belong here.*

Felicity paused as an impeccably groomed older man in a lab coat approached. "Dr. Boniface, I see you have not yet retired."

"Have you changed your mind about the next phase of the project?"

Felicity gestured in Bryn's direction. "I don't believe you've met Dr. Forrest, one of my brightest students. Her field is alpha devices, but I'm hoping to interest her in joining the team."

Dr. Boniface extended his hand to Bryn. "It's always a pleasure to meet someone recommended by Dr. Sage."

"I'd love to chat, but we're on a tight schedule," Felicity said.

Boniface's gaze slid over Leonin, perhaps wondering who this second stranger was, but he said nothing as Felicity continued on her way, Bryn and Leonin at her heels.

Bryn tried to think what an assistant might say about the encounter, and she decided the best course was to pretend everything was normal and ignore it.

Felicity's office was adjacent to one of the larger labs. "Lights on," she said as she opened the door. Warm yellow radiance bathed the room, adding to the light from the generously proportioned windows. Besides the standard desk and storage cases, there were two chairs. Several blue lab coats hung from hooks beside the door.

"Sit," Felicity said, indicating the two chairs. She seated herself at the desk, touched the built-in terminal to life, and began a search.

"Here we are. As I expected, the subjects for the first two phases of the theta-corticator trials are housed in a secured area of the building. They're listed by subject code number rather than by name. My biometrics should give us access if they haven't switched to a higher level of security."

"What about alarms? Cameras?" Leonin asked at the same time as Bryn said, "Won't they be observed for behavioral changes?" But Felicity had continued her search. Page after page flashed across the terminal screen.

"This should—no, that didn't work. Maybe I can—" Finally she looked up at Bryn and Leonin. "This isn't my area of expertise. The subjects are under visual surveillance, but I can't disable it."

"May I?" Leonin gestured to the terminal.

Felicity got up, making room for him. He sat down and began typing very fast. More screens flashed by. Bryn knew he had more than ordinary facility with security programs, thanks to his work with the Free Worlds movement, but the speed with which he worked surprised her. From her expression, Felicity was impressed, too.

"Aha!" Leonin's fingers paused on the keypad. His eyes scanned the lines of code. He deleted and then carefully replaced a section. "There, that should do it."

"What exactly did you do?" Felicity said.

"It's not possible to disable the cameras from this terminal. At least, not without sophisticated workarounds. But the cameras are fully functional only during waking hours; they're visible-spectrum sensitive, so they operate on a reduced frequency when it's dark, approximately ten seconds every half hour. They basically go to sleep. I was able to isolate and then reset the clock used by the cameras. As far as they're concerned, it's permanently nighttime."

"But they do turn on, if briefly?" Bryn said.

"We'll just have to move fast."

"The sooner we locate Ernst Haslund, the less chance someone detects us."

Felicity handed Bryn and Leonin laboratory coats and donned the third. They headed back toward the conference room, and finally to another elevator. Instead of a card reader, this one was secured with a biometric scanner. Felicity swiped a fingertip across the sensor, which compared the DNA in her shed epidermal cells to its memory. The status light flashed green, and the doors whispered open.

They exited the elevator into a chamber dominated by a bank of workstations and monitor displays, positioned to control access to the facility through a barred gate. Two attendants staffed the station.

"Halt! This is a restricted area," one of the guards called out as Felicity approached the barrier.

The second guard said, "Our apologies, Dr. Sage. Bose, pass her through."

The first guard did not move. "She's not on the list. Excuse me, Dr. Sage. I know who you are, but we don't have current authorization for you."

"I require access to this level," Felicity said. "Should you deem it necessary, you must of course *interrupt the Director* by verifying this for yourselves."

"Well, we..." The first guard's voice trailed off as he considered the consequences of *interrupting the Director.*

"It's all right," the second guard hastened to say. "She's already been cleared for this level." To Felicity, he said, "Sign in, please, you and your colleagues."

All three of them signed the log. Bryn couldn't remember the alias Felicity had given for her, so she made her signature as illegible as possible.

Once they were out of earshot of the guards, Felicity remarked, "It's a wonder what acting as if one possesses the authority to fire people can accomplish."

"Is the elevator the only access to this floor?" Leonin said.

"There's a ramp leading to the street level," Felicity said. "It's on the other end of the central corridor. I don't believe it's been in use since the labs here were equipped."

"Here's hoping we won't need it," Bryn muttered.

They walked past smaller offices and another conference room, this one dark. Voices sounded ahead, the words unintelligible. Two men, Bryn thought. Her pulse sped up until the voices receded.

Soon they reached a corridor where the doors were locked with biometric sensors. Felicity touched her finger to the sensor outside the first room, and the door opened. The lights were set at half, enough to reveal a wide bed fitted with sensors and restraints. A man in loose pants and shirt sat at a table. He wasn't moving except for the slight rise and fall of his shoulders, and his back was to the door. The half-light, his hair looked gray.

"Father?"

Bryn darted around the table to come face-to-face. The man sitting there, eyes glassy, face unresponsive, was a stranger.

Then she noticed the wires running from electrodes on his forehead, temples, and scalp, attached to a panel set in the table. Lights set into the contacts flickered in a slow, hypnotic pattern. Felicity leaned over the man's shoulder and studied the apparatus, although she did not touch it.

"It's a theta-corticator, but with modifications," she murmured. "Boniface's team must have made them after I left."

"What's it doing to him?" Leonin asked.

"Difficult to be sure." Felicity waved one hand in front of the man's eyes, but he did not react, not even with a blink. "He appears to be in a trance state akin to the Phase One pseudo-sedation."

"We need to find my father," Bryn said.

"Not a good idea to linger," Leonin said.

The next room was also locked but had a window of wire-reinforced duraglass, long and narrow, set high enough so only Leonin could see through it. It took him only a few seconds to report, "It's not him."

"Are you sure?" Bryn asked, remembering the fractional moment she'd been fooled.

"His hair's black."

"He's got to be here! We're running out of doors!"

"Keep your voice down!" Felicity said.

"Bryn." Leonin placed his hands on her shoulders. "We will find him. We *will*. If not here, then the next place we search."

Bryn nodded. *I have to stay focused.*

They went on. Of the next two doors, one opened on a supplies closet, the other on an unoccupied room. Then came a stretch of unbroken wall with a single door at the far end. It, too, was locked. A moment later, Felicity got it open. Lights came on, and Bryn and Leonin followed her inside.

A man had been lying on another hospital-style bed, but now he raised his head and levered himself to a sitting position. Like the others, he wore a loose, light-green shirt and pants.

She would have known that smile anywhere. Those thin shoulders, that silvery hair. Those kind eyes.

The sight of him blurred and she threw her arms around him.

"Bryn! How nice to see you!" Ernst Haslund murmured against her ear. He smelled of conditioned air, the synthetic fabric of his clothing, disinfectant, and a faint, sour odor. "You've come to visit me."

Bryn held him at arm's length, trying to compose herself. He was alive, alive and well! No wires dangled across his chest, connecting him to a bank of instruments. He wasn't physically linked to the mind-controlling technology, the way the other men had been. He recognized her, which meant he hadn't been subjected to laser lobotomy. His eyes met hers, his smile one of delight.

Then she saw, glinting beneath the wavy gray hair, the coin-sized electrodes. Not external, pasted-on, removable contacts. *Embedded.* Lights blinked, indicating activity.

They found a way to surgically implant the corticator.

She wanted to throw up.

He said, "There, there. Don't distress yourself, child. Tell me what the matter is."

"Father..." Words dried up in her throat.

Felicity put her hands on Ernst's shoulders, turning him away from Bryn. She parted his hair to uncover the electrodes, turning his head this way and that. Then she dug around in her shoulder bag and brought out a small ultrasonic probe. She took a reading, *tsk*ed in annoyance, and returned the instrument to her bag. He tolerated her handling without objection.

"I came to see how you fared," Bryn said to her father. "You disappeared—you left us so suddenly! We were all worried—me, Saralyn, the whole family."

"I'm safe, as you can see. My work often takes me... I have been doing important... I have been making sure the peace of the Alliance..." His smile faded, the muscles around his eyes tensing as if he struggled to focus.

"What am I doing in this place?" he asked Bryn. "Is it a hospital? Have I been ill?"

"No, you've—" Bryn cut herself short. "It's too complicated to explain. We've got to get you out of here."

"Yes. I must get back to work as soon as possible. Something terrible has happened."

He remembers. He's going to be all right.

He scowled. "Terrorist forces have attempted to sabotage the Star Alliance. Many are personal enemies of First Minister Nagy. They use rumor and mob psychology to stir up discontent, and have brought us to the brink of war by causing Vainwal to sever its ties with us."

"Father, no. That's not what happened. Don't you remember?" Bryn turned to Felicity. "Why is he acting like this?"

"Don't waste your breath arguing with him," Leonin said. "He's still under the influence of that infernal device."

"We'll have to do the best we can and get him home," Bryn said. "Familiar surroundings might help restore his memory."

"Home?" Ernst asked with an echo of his previous, childlike affect. "I'd like to go home now."

"Yes, home, Father dear." Bryn removed the ordinary clothing from the package. Together, she and Leonin helped her father to change. His body felt fragile, almost brittle.

Leonin took out the disposable link, glanced at it, and grimaced. "StarOps are on their way here. We've already wasted too much time."

As Felicity opened the door, Bryn felt a tremor of unease. Over the too-loud beating of her heart, she sensed a faint vibration.

"An alarm?" *In the cell door—? Or did the implanted electrodes have proximity sensors that went off when a subject passed beyond range?*

"Move," Leonin repeated. "Now. *Fast.*"

Together they hurried down the corridor as quickly as Ernst could go. Anxiety jangled Bryn's nerves.

Breathe. Focus.

The further they got from Ernst's room, the more confused he seemed and the harder it was to keep him going. Bryn wanted to scream at him that with every passing moment they were in greater danger, and would he just *move—*

Ernst came to a sudden halt, jerking free. He whirled around and started back toward his cell. Bryn and Leonin barely managed to restrain him.

"Stop it!" Ernst cried, struggling to free himself. "Just wait— I don't... what am I doing in this place? I remember a feeling of great serenity, that there was no cause for further struggle. All was right in the world. But before that, as if it happened to someone else...even greater fears about Vainwal. Yes, that was it. *That* was how I felt. Did the secession resolution pass?"

His memory was back. They must have passed beyond the range of the neural transmitter. Bryn's jitters receded a little.

"The resolution passed," she said, "and that's why—"

"Bryn," Leonin said, a note of warning in his voice. "Run now, debate later."

"I'll explain, I promise," Bryn told her father. "For now, just pretend we're all late for a—a grant funding review."

Ernst turned to her with a trace of the old humor in his eyes. "That sounds quite manageable."

A little farther down the corridor, a pair of blue-coated technicians approached them with mildly curious expressions. Felicity, in the fore, did not slacken her pace. Under her withering glare, the technicians flushed and averted their eyes as they hurried on their way.

Bryn concentrated on keeping her father moving without flustering him. He showed no further sign of bolting.

The guard station came into view, and they slowed to a more normal pace. Step by step, they neared it.

Nausea clawed at the back of Bryn's throat. She tasted sour saliva and felt the urge to vomit but managed to keep from retching. She couldn't get sick, not now, not when they were so close.

Breathe. Just breathe. Keep going—it's not far now.

"Bryn?" Leonin's voice seemed to echo from a distance.

Something terrible is about to happen—we'll die if we go on—we'll all die—

Her lungs closed up, each labored breath a wheeze. Black spots whirled before her eyes. Cold sweat laced her skin. The corridor blurred and darkened. Stumbling, she caught herself against the wall. She bent over, fighting for air. It was all she could do to keep from collapsing.

"What is it?" Her father leaned over her, his face twisted with concern. "Bryn sweetheart, what's happening?"

Bryn shook her head, unable to speak.

"Give her room," Leonin said.

"Does she have a history of panic attacks?" That was Felicity, her tone clinical.

"I don't think so," Leonin said. "And she went through worse than this back on Terra."

Not a panic attack… Bryn could not force the words through her constricted throat. *Danger-sense…must go back.*

"Back—" she managed to wheeze. "Must—go—back—" She gestured in the direction they'd come.

"Yes, yes," Ernst said. "Of course, we must go back. Back where it's safe."

"Go back?" Felicity repeated. "When we're so close? Leonin, can't you talk sense into her?"

"What if she's right?" Leonin countered. "We've triggered the alarm system. The guards at that station are waiting for us, and this time you may not be able to bluff our way through."

Listen to him…

Strong arms lifted her, half-carried, half-dragged her back the way they'd come. The first few meters felt endless. The sick feeling had wrapped itself around her guts and would not let go.

Leonin murmured encouragement. "We're almost there, love. Getting you out of there. Hang on, just a little more to go."

They had gone back a considerable distance, enough so that the guard station was out of sight. She managed to draw a gasping breath and then another. Her vision steadied, as did her balance. The floor was hard beneath her, the wall a solid support.

"Escape is madness," Ernst said. "My daughter needs proper medical care."

Leonin peered into Bryn's face. "Are you all right now?"

"Yes...no. I don't know." The feeling of impending peril was still present but less intense, more bearable. Perhaps she was beginning to adapt. She had no idea if that was even possible—she didn't know anything about this ability of hers. Until that day at the plaza, she would have denied it was even possible to anticipate danger, that it was all subliminal cues and anxiety hormones.

It's still with me. We aren't safe yet.

"We can't go back that way," she said.

"Not if you're going to have another panic attack," Felicity said. Leonin growled, deep in his throat.

"There's another way out, right?" Bryn said. "You mentioned a—a service entrance?"

"I'm not sure that's necessary," Felicity said. "The guards let us through, after all."

"I don't understand what all the fuss is about," Ernst said. "I have important work to do. I need a quiet, undisturbed place in which to compose my next speech. First Minister Nagy is counting on my support." His expression of good-natured blandness faded. "I demand to be returned to my office."

"Your office?" Leonin said. "You mean your *cell*."

Ernst glared at him.

"Father," Bryn said, taking his arm. "Your office was compromised, don't you remember? By enemies of the Alliance who'd like nothing better than to silence you."

"Was it?"

"And we've come to take you to a place of safety. That's what all this is about."

"Why yes, that makes sense. But my terminal, my writing materials, my files...you'll make certain they are secured?"

"Yes, of course." Bryn exchanged glances with Leonin and then with Felicity. "The ramp?"

"This way," Felicity said, striding away.

The ramp was generously proportioned, broad enough to accommodate a cargo vehicle. Pedestrian stairs with handrails ran along each side. As Bryn climbed, sweat beaded her face and trickled down her neck. Her father was soon red-faced and panting hard, as was Felicity. Only Leonin seemed unaffected by the exertion.

As they slowed to accommodate the two elderly people, Bryn took her father's arm, supporting him. "How are you doing?"

"Oh—" He waved his free hand in a dismissive gesture. "Other than being sadly out of shape, I'm well enough."

At least he wasn't arguing, for which Bryn was grateful.

The partial lighting of the lower ramp gave way to indirect but natural illumination from above. The ramp itself terminated in a sliding door topped by a horizontal expanse of reinforced glass. The door appeared to be secured by a lever that engaged a powered opener. Beyond lay a daylit bay closed with a gate at the far end and walled on either side. Dry leaves lay in drifts along the bases of the walls. What they could see of the street looked empty.

Bryn's anxiety took a leap when Leonin grasped the gate latch. Of course, her danger-sense was still kicking up. They'd been in danger since arriving at the university—since landing on Alpha—since she stepped out of her office building and saw the sky on fire.

The gate lifted smoothly. Felicity moved toward the opening, but Leonin put out a cautionary hand. He moved to the front as they left the shelter of the bay.

"Halt right there!" A handful of black-garbed figures emerged from behind the walls to either side. Riot shields blurred the details of their faces. Their protective clothing made them seem larger and bulkier than normal people, and there was no mistaking the menace in the way they held their weapons.

Bryn recognized one of the men holding a neural tangler. *Black! Somehow he managed to track us here.*

StarOps was like a star-spanning kraken, its tentacles everywhere. Was *any* planet beyond their reach?

She told herself furiously that she would *not* be sick. Much better to be angry.

"Freeze!" Black shouted. "Hands up, where I can see them!"

Leonin raised his hands slowly, but Felicity drew herself up and stepped forward. Indignation showed in every line of her posture. If she was intimidated by having a lethal weapon pointed at her, she gave no sign.

"You there! Young man! I most certainly will not comply. This is university property, *I* am a tenured professor and senior researcher, and *you* are trespassing. Lower those ridiculous instruments of destruction and remove yourselves from the campus before I summon security!"

From behind the sights of his weapon, Black called back, "StarOps supersedes local jurisdiction, Professor. If you have a problem with that, feel free to take it up with your governors when this is all over. Meanwhile—"

"I most certainly will *not*—"

"I will shoot you if you persist in interfering with the exercise of my duties. One more word and I'll have you arrested for obstructing a law enforcement officer. Now stand aside."

"You surely don't believe you will get away with such uncivilized behavior." Felicity's voice took on a strained, reedy quality, but she stood firm. "Regardless of what you are accustomed to, on Alpha we treat one another with respect. We do *not* indulge in the indiscriminate application of brute force or threats thereof."

For a wild moment, Bryn wondered just how far her mentor would take the confrontation.

"This is your final warning," Black said. "Nice and easy now, you ladies, and you, too, Senator, step away from Mr. Vargas. There's no need for anyone to get hurt."

Bryn's moment of paralysis broke. She placed herself between the armed men and her father. Luckily, he remained where he was. How long that would last, she had no idea.

Black and his men kept their weapons pointed at her—and her father—and Felicity, who still hadn't budged—and Leonin.

"It's all right," Leonin said. "Bryn, Felicity, Senator—do what he says."

They were at an impasse, and Bryn didn't trust Black. Gently she guided her father to the side. Felicity, outrage clear in every tense muscle, went with them.

"That's more like it." Black shifted his weight, keeping the tangler aimed at Leonin. "Leonin Vargas, you are charged with sedition and treason against Star Alliance. Ms. Haslund and Dr. Sage will be taken into protective custody. As for the Senator, he will receive the best rehabilitative care until he is able to resume office."

"You mean you'll put him back under the influence of the theta-corticator again!" Bryn shot back.

For the slightest instant, Black hesitated. Until that moment, Bryn realized, he hadn't known how much they'd discovered. Mentally she kicked herself for having revealed so much.

"Calm down, Ms. Haslund," Black said. "No harm will come to you, I promise. Everything will be made clear to you in the proper time."

Bryn's danger-sense skyrocketed abruptly. A red haze swept across her vision. Every nerve shrilled in alarm.

"Come along quietly now—" Black said.

Leonin hurled himself at Black, moving so fast that not even the other cops could react. Both men went down, wrestling, rolling. Shouting. Punching, arms and legs flailing. It was like the fight on the riverside before Rashid's people found them—fast, too fast to follow, and hard.

The StarOps cops got themselves back into formation, training their weapons on the grappling men, searching for a clear shot. Bryn wanted to scream at them not to fire, but no sound came from her throat.

The next moment, Leonin jumped to his feet, Black's tangler in his hands. Black rolled away, scrambling for the shelter of his men.

"Back inside!" Leonin cried.

Bryn grabbed her father and hauled him back inside the open gate. Felicity scrambled after them. An instant later, Leonin brought up the rear.

Blaster fire sizzled through the air before striking the walls of the bay. Puffs of vaporized rock erupted where the beams struck.

With a cry, Bryn thrust her father flat against the side wall. He was shaking so badly that she feared he would collapse. Felicity braced him, holding him upright.

Leonin thrust the tangler into Bryn's hands. Releasing her father, she took it. It felt cold in her grasp, inert but malevolent. This thing *killed* people or left them horribly crippled. She stared at it, unsure she could fire it. She'd devoted her professional career to healing children from the aftermath of such attacks. This *thing*—

Get a hold of yourself! Bryn sucked in a breath. *You can't help anyone if you're a wreck.*

Another round of fire came from the men outside, then a pause. Leonin drew his own blaster but held his fire, sticking his head out now and again to scan the area.

"We can't go back the way we came," he said. "The guards at the station will have been alerted. We'd never reach the elevator, but if we did, Black's sure to have sent a second force around that way."

"I'll surrender myself," offered Felicity. "Distract them so you can get away."

"It's me they want," Leonin said.

Bryn shook her head. "No, it's too big a risk."

The weight of the tangler dragged her hands down—its physical mass and also what it represented. After the first wave of terror, she'd gone numb inside. They would never fight their way out. They stood no chance against trained, armed StarOps. Against Black. The situation was hopeless. Their mission was over. The only choice was to surrender and hope that her father and Felicity were important enough—and visible enough—to make keeping them alive worthwhile. She herself and Leonin would face life prison terms, if they lived that long.

"You've got the right idea, though." That was Leonin, speaking now to Felicity. "One of us needs to create a distraction by pretending to give ourselves up." He pointed his blaster in the direction the StarOps cops had retreated. "I'm going to clear a path and cover you. Bryn, you take your father. Drag him if you have to, but *get him out of here*."

"What are you saying?" Bryn said. "I won't leave you!"

"Get ready to run like hell. Don't argue. It's our only chance."

Before she could reply, a blaster bolt struck the wall next to them, close enough to leave a narrow burn along her cheekbone. The pain stung, almost electric.

"We've run out of time, love," Leonin said in a soft voice.

Another round of blaster fire brought a yelp from Felicity where she had been sheltering Ernst in her arms. She didn't appear to be hurt, just startled. Leonin was right; it was only a matter of time, perhaps moments, before one or the other of them was hit.

With his free arm, Leonin pulled Bryn close. "I love you."

He kissed her, a brief, sweet moment, and then broke from their cover, firing at the StarOps men.

With a rumble and a whine of brakes, a service van skidded to a stop in the street beyond the bay. The side door slid open.

"Get *in*!" came a man's voice from inside. A second passenger sprayed Black's men with pellet fire.

Bryn aimed the tangler at the nearest StarOps location. A man shrieked, and for a moment, the rate of fire slowed.

Leonin plunged ahead, zigzagging through the diminished spray of blaster bolts. Puffs of vaporized paint marked where the StarOps fire hit the van. He reached the vehicle and knelt beside the rear end to aim back at the StarOps troops.

"Come on!" Bryn said to her father and Felicity. "Follow me." She darted out as fast as she could, her focus fixed on the open door of the van. Blaster fire sizzled through the air to either side.

The man inside the van gestured to her. "Hurry! Hurry!"

Bryn was going so fast that she slammed into the side of the van and almost dropped the tangler. Felicity pulled her father along, only a few steps behind. Bryn slipped the tangler into her pocket, then she and Felicity each took one of her father's arms. Together they half-hauled, half-shoved him into the van. Then Felicity scrambled in. Bryn was about to follow when she heard a scream from beside the rear of the van. She whipped her head around.

Leonin was nowhere to be seen.

"Get in!" the man inside the van screamed.

Bryn raced around the van to where she'd last seen Leonin. He lay beside the van's rear, partly on his side, his body contorted and one leg twitching. A blackened swathe ran diagonally across his torso and belly. The fabric of his clothing was charred, the flesh beneath it a bloody ruin. He must have taken a blast full-on, then twisted reflexively away from it as he fell.

Bryn threw herself down beside him and cradled his face in her hands. His eyes were half-open, showing glazed crescents of white. That he was alive at all was a miracle. Every breath, every movement must be agony. She pressed her lips gently to his and saw the faint reaction in his facial muscles.

She couldn't help him. No one could, not from an injury like this.

She couldn't leave him.

His mouth opened, his throat moving convulsively, but she couldn't make out what he was trying to say. He gestured one-handedly toward his front pants pocket. She found the flap, dug beneath it, and brought out the signal booster Captain Wie had given them.

Take it, he seemed to plead, *take it and go—*

His breath, which had been stuttering and tentative, now rattled in his throat. His head lolled as if whatever had kept him awake and in pain now released its grip.

Go now*!*

With Leonin's words—real or imagined—ringing in her mind, Bryn folded her fingers around the booster and gathered her feet under her.

The van was already moving off. She put on a burst of speed and sprinted for the open door. The man inside leaned out, one arm stretched toward her. In the dim interior, she glimpsed the pale ovals of faces—Felicity and her father, safely onboard. She slapped her free palm into the man's hand. His fingers closed around hers. The next instant, the van surged forward. Her feet left the paving. She felt as if she were flying. Then she landed with a thud on the floor of the van and the door slammed shut.

Bryn rolled on her back, feeling the vibration of the van's gathering speed. Her lungs ached as she tried to catch her breath.

The interior of the van had barely enough light to make out the features of the man bending over her. The next moment, he hauled her into a seat beside Felicity.

"Gratitude for the rescue," Bryn gasped. "Sorry, I don't know your name."

"Better not to use names," he said, "and we would have done the same for any comrade. Are you hurt?"

Bryn searched her memory and found no image of a blaster, but that did not mean she was unhurt. Her heart felt as if it had been crushed. "Just a scratch."

"What is going on?" came her father's voice from the front. "Who *are* you people?"

"Free Worlds Movement, local chapter," the man replied over his shoulder. "I'm truly sorry for your loss."

Bryn couldn't think what to say beyond, "Thank you."

The van took a corner at speed and Bryn almost lost her balance. Lights flickered by, bright images cast on the far wall of the van. Then its path ran straight.

Bryn's sense of danger eased, although her thoughts felt slow and dull. A weight lay on her heart, on her spirit. Her mind could not quite encompass what had happened. Leonin had been part of her world and her hopes for the future for so long, and he had been her constant companion since that night at her sister's.

He's gone. He's dead. I'll never hold him again...or kiss him...or hear his voice...

There would be a time for grief, she supposed, but not while their lives were still at risk. Leonin had sacrificed his own to save them, and there was nothing she could do to help him now. Mourning him must wait. Right now, people depended on her—her father and Felicity. And Black was still hunting them.

Silently Felicity twined her fingers in Bryn's.

"You're going to have to make some decisions real soon," said the Free Worlds man. "They're tracking this vehicle, certain."

The booster lay on her open palm. She stared at it, thinking that Leonin had expended his dying breath to give it to her. Captain Wie had said he'd wait. She might still be within the time window. Praying she was right, she thumbed the call button.

Done. It's done.

If only we hadn't run... If only Black hadn't found us...

He's gone.

He's gone.

Don't think that now!

"I need to go to—" and she gave the man the coordinates of the landing place.

When she started to explain about Wie's ship, he said, "I don't need to know any more than that. Don't want to. We'll change vehicles in just a bit or rather, you will."

That made sense in the slow, numb way everything else did right now.

"Now get yourselves ready to jump out," the man said. "We'll stop only long enough for me to pass on your destination."

With those words, he went forward and spoke a few words with Felicity, who was still murmuring encouragement to Ernst and then the driver. A short distance later, the van swerved, straightened, and screeched to a halt.

The door jerked open from the outside, and Bryn scrambled out. Her first impression was of being in a tunnel or underground structure. The only illumination was from a single red-tinted source like an emergency light. The air smelled musty.

The next moment, Felicity and her father joined her. He looked pale, nearly fainting. Bryn took his hand.

The van sped away and a second vehicle, a passenger sedan, pulled up. It was by no means new, the sort of transport passed from one generation of impoverished students to the next. She opened the nearest door and along with Felicity managed to get her father into the back seat.

"Where are we going?" Bryn asked as she climbed in beside the driver.

"Better not to talk."

The driver took them through a series of detours and back roads until Bryn's sense of direction was utterly confused. She hoped the same would be true for anyone following them. Each circuit brought them farther away from the center of the city until they were speeding down a lightly-traveled rural throughway. She thought it might run parallel to the tram she and Leonin had taken into the city, but she couldn't be sure.

Leonin... No, don't think of him now. There will be time to grieve later.

"Where are we going now?" Ernst asked, his voice querulous. "Where are you taking me?

"It's all right," she called over her shoulder.

"I want to go home."

"We're on the way home, Father, but it's far away. Can you be patient a while longer?"

He mumbled agreement, then Felicity said something low and soothing.

Bryn hated to hear her father sounding so miserable and peevish. She'd hoped that as soon as he was away from the laboratory, he'd improve. That wasn't the case. Her father was still under the influence of the theta-corticator, and his mood and level of understanding were unpredictable. He needed help, and Alpha with its labs and psychotechnology was no longer safe. Alpha, once the safest, most civilized planet in the entire Alliance! Was *any* place beyond Nagy's reach? Beyond where Black could hunt them down?

Not Terra. Not Vainwal or Renney or Campta.

But not all inhabited planets were part of the Alliance...the Class D Protected Worlds the Alliance had pulled back from in the tumultuous years when the first Nagy came to power...worlds that had gone their own way, developed their own techniques…

Telepathy.

Darkover.

She touched the pocket holding the tab containing the data on *Project Telepath*. One of Leonin's gifts had been his paranoia, insisting that she have a backup plan if the rescue didn't go as planned. The Darkover telepaths might not be able to restore her father's mind, but they were the best chance he had. She didn't know anything else about the planet. For all she knew, it might be barely habitable, the last place Nagy would think to look for them.

First thing, we need to get off Alpha.

The vehicle slowed, rolled off the roadway onto a dirt surface surrounded by trees, and finally drew to a halt. The driver flicked off the headlamps. Bryn waited, hardly able to breathe. Except for the faint creak of the cooling engine and the even fainter susurration of their breathing, the place was utterly silent.

"Where are we?" Felicity asked.

"The rendezvous place," Bryn said, opening the door and sliding out. She pivoted, studying the landscape. "I've been here before, but it was daytime."

Felicity helped Ernst from the vehicle. A moment later, it took off. Bryn felt a shiver of fear, but muted as if someone else were feeling it. They were in no immediate danger. Her skin wasn't prickling.

Her fingers tightened around the hard shell of the booster. With any luck, Black hadn't been able to trace it.

"What's that thing?" Ernst asked.

The booster panel was glowing, readily visible in the near-dark. "It's how we contact the captain of the ship that brought us here."

"You have a way to get off-planet," Felicity said. "Excellent!"

Matters could have been worse, Bryn supposed. She'd managed to find her father and free him. They'd gotten away—

—but Leonin *hadn't—no, don't remember him lying there, those last precious moments—*

"I'm relieved," Felicity was saying, "for neither you nor your father can safely remain here, especially not since StarOps has traced you. Alpha may have the most sophisticated technological resources in the Alliance, but its academic environment is porous. Nothing stays hidden for long here, and I do not doubt that the StarOps agent—Black is his name? how appropriate—has sources of intelligence that would make your detection and capture both inevitable and rapid. Since you have another option, it's prudent to take it. Almost any other planet would be preferable under the circumstances."

"I agree! The sooner we're off-world, the better," Bryn said. "For all we know, StarOps can trace my father through the implanted electrodes."

"My dear." Felicity fumbled for Bryn's hands, found them, and squeezed gently. "I do not score high on warmth and sympathy indices, but I am not indifferent to what just happened. I am well aware of the deep mutual affection between you and your lover. To lose him so suddenly, and by violence following a period of tremendous anxiety—"

Bryn shook off the proffered comfort. If she gave in to grief, even for a moment, she would surely drown in tears. "Thank you, but this is not the time or place."

"If you do not acknowledge your loss now, when will be the right time?"

"I don't know! When it's safe? When we're no longer fugitives?" *When my father has regained his wits? When Black is dead? When Nagy is removed?*

"Bryn, sweetheart." That was her father, who had overheard the conversation. "You're distressed."

Bryn reached for her father, trying to think of what to say to him. His hands felt cool and dry, the skin papery over bony knuckles.

"What's going on?" He sounded confused, veering back toward the peevishness of earlier.

Bryn forced cheerfulness into her voice. "We're waiting for a ship to take us away from here. Won't that be good?"

"If you say so. I don't understand how any of this is helping First Minister Nagy and the Alliance. No, that's not right...I have to get away..." He turned away just as Felicity slipped her hand through his elbow and restrained him.

"Thank you," Bryn said to Felicity. "I don't know how I would have managed him without you—or how I will, until I can get his brains unscrambled."

"I should think it obvious I am coming with you."

Felicity couldn't go back as if nothing had happened. She'd face charges for her part in the rescue.

"You don't understand," Bryn said. "I'm taking him to Darkover, to Cottman IV. It's a long shot, but it's outside of Alliance territory. If the natives are anything like they're described in Project Telepath, they may well be able to help my father."

"A Class D planet? My dear, that's brilliant. Nagy will never suspect."

"But you, *you* must stay here. Invent an excuse for your part in all this. Say I forced you, kidnapped you. I'm sure you can invent a credible excuse. You must not abandon your work here. Darkover's a primitive world."

"Alpha is no longer the haven for me that it once was, but that has been true for some time. When the theta-corticator experiments took a turn into territory so morally abhorrent that I could not in conscience be a part of it, I was reduced to teaching subjects I could recite backward in my sleep. I soon lost what little patience I had with the idiocies of bureaucracy. I know perfectly well the reputation I gained as being a bully toward staff and students alike. But the opportunity to free your father from the implanted corticator, to truly make a difference, to know that my work has meaning once again..." Felicity raised both hands in an eloquent gesture. "I grasp this chance with an eager heart, as the poet says. And if there is any way I can help defeat the monstrous regime that did this to the Senator, I will gladly do so."

Before either of them could say more, a wind descended from above. Bryn glanced up to see the stars blotted by a rounded shape. A circle of lights, yellow-hued against the darkness of the sky, marked the underside of the descending shuttle. The noise was so loud, she had to shout to be heard, ushering her father and Felicity out of the way. The craft settled onto the grassy spot, a door whooshed open, a ramp extended, and a man Bryn recognized from Captain Wie's crew appeared in the opening. Connison, she thought his name was. First mate.

She couldn't hear him above the sound, but his gestures were clear: *Hurry!*

Bryn clutched her father's hand and made for the ramp, grateful that he didn't resist. Felicity was right behind them.

"Is that it?" the crewman asked. "Where's Vargas?"

Leonin.

"He—he didn't make it."

"Damn. Captain will be pissed. They went way back." His breath hissed between his teeth. "You three all wanting passage?"

"Obviously," Felicity snapped as she strode up the ramp. "And we're being pursued by a singularly unpleasant squad of StarOps agents."

"Yes, ma'am." Connison nodded. "Best be on our way, then."

◆◆◆

A short, breathless time later, the three of them nestled into their seats and the shuttle took off. The cramped space was even noisier than Bryn remembered from their arrival. She couldn't understand anything the crewman spoke into his headset. To distract herself from the discomfort of the flight, she focused on what she could see around her, a technique she used with her young patients. She'd made the focusing exercise into a game: *Name a black thing, name a white thing, find something you don't know the name of, name a hard thing, name a soft thing, name a silly thing...*

Really, what did that matter? What mattered was how thick and sore her throat felt, as if to keep from sobbing. What mattered was the image of Leonin, lying in her arms, fighting for breath, his body so broken, so broken, the light in his eyes dimming.

Stop remembering! We're not safe yet.

Closing her eyes, Bryn felt the vibration of the shuttle all through her body. She imagined it rattling her bones...shaking loose her thoughts.

She thought of Project Telepath, with its summons for people with *natural* psi powers, who could speak with their thoughts, move objects with their minds, and do other things once thought impossible. People who knew how telepathy worked. People who could, if there were any luck in the universe, use those abilities to free her father's mind.

The shuttle docked with the ship, and Connison explained the situation to Captain Wie. Wie showed no visible emotion at the news of Leonin's death, and in his silence Bryn sensed as much grief as he would allow himself to show. Instead, he snapped out a series of orders to prepare the three of them for interstellar flight. Felicity and Ernst went first, strapped into the acceleration couches. They quickly succumbed to the drug-mediated sleep. Wie entered the cramped passenger cabin just as a crew woman finished attaching Bryn's equipment.

"StarOps frigate in orbit, not long now." *You know anything about that?*

"Black—I don't know if he has another name," Bryn murmured. The drugs were beginning to take hold and each syllable was progressively more difficult to pronounce. "Sorr—sorry. Must have—followed me here—"

"As may," Wie replied sardonically. "We gone before he notice. By the by, and since I would honor my friend, what's your destination? I won't take you back to Terra, nor Ephebe or Renney or any other hot spot. Time for small fish like me to lay still while the sharks hunt."

"Cottman IV—Darkover. Take us to Darkover."

Wie consulted a ship-wide link strapped to his wrist. "You in luck. Got the language modules. In flight, you hook up to them." He clapped her on the shoulder and faded into the darkening haze.

She closed her eyes and waited for the drugs to take her. Sounds muted. She felt herself floating, falling...

◆◆◆

...and jolting awake. Every nerve shrilled. Her heart beat so hard, it threatened to leap into her throat. As if across a vast distance, she heard an alarm—a klaxon, going *Ah-ooh! Ah-ooh!*

She tried to open her eyes. Her lids refused to comply. Red tinged the dark inside her skull. She could barely feel her body or the surface beneath her.

No nightmare, this. Something's happened.

Panic seized her—the need to free herself—to escape—

danger-danger-danger—

Shock waves rippled through the couch that held her prisoner. *And the ship itself,* she realized. The words echoed weirdly through her mind, Terran Standard overlapping another dialect, one that sounded like a cross between ancient Spanish and Celtic. *Casta*, her memory suggested. A Darkovan dialect. Her unconscious mind had been under the language learning program.

Something had awakened her and triggered her danger-sense. She was too far under the soporific drug to do anything.

The klaxon repeated, *Ah-ooh! Ah-ooh!*

She felt another shudder, the metal encasing her recoiled from a terrible blow—a series of blows.

The ship's under attack!

Pirates? Spaceforce?...Black's found us!

She struggled to sit up, but she was too disoriented to get her bearings. Her body wouldn't obey her and her mind refused to wake up.

Space itself seemed to break apart, whirling out in all directions, gravity lost—

No, *she* was spinning, or the ship around her was.

Help! Oh, help!

HELP ME!

...I am here...

The sensation of uncontrolled rotation receded. The world—what she could feel of it—steadied. Yet in that instant, she received the distinct impression that someone very far away had heard her plea.

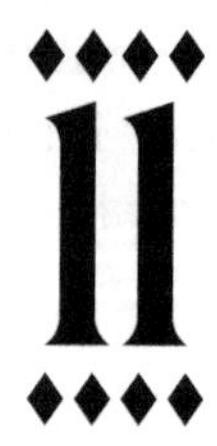

Someone was calling her name. And shaking her...no, the surface on which she lay was shaking. Her eyelids were stuck together, her skin felt as brittle as chalk, and she wanted to throw up. It must be a reaction to the sleep drugs and the hurried prep. She'd traveled between planets before but had never been this sick.

Nightmare...

For the moment, the best thing was to get moving. She was still strapped to the couch. The crew woman released the restraints, lifted her up, and shoved a bulb of liquid into her trembling hands. She sucked on it, trying not to give in to the waves of nausea. The medication did its work, however, and a short time later she was feeling much steadier.

Wie summoned her to the cramped, instrument-laden bridge. "Your friends still waking up. Wanted to talk to you first. Leo left you in charge. Decision yours."

"Yes, I suppose so."

"Now you listen good," he said, brows tightening in a scowl. "Just out of Alpha, rocket from Alliance ship, hiding behind moon—*bam!*"

Bryn remembered the ship recoiling like a stricken animal. Remembered, too, her own skyrocketing danger-sense.

Wie's expression was shuttered. The damage had been survivable. They'd made it.

"—halfway here," he went on, "something else on our tail. Maybe Rift sharks, raiders out of Wolf V, who knows? Lost the trace but that don't mean they not still there. Not going to wait around, see what shows up. Sending you down in shuttle. Near settlement. Can't risk more, not even for old friend. *Not waiting.* You kien?"

"I kien."

"Here now, where you asked. Planet down there—" with a jerk of his chin in what Bryn supposed was the horizon below, "—Class D world. Spaceport or two, used to be. Maybe still, maybe not. Feds—no Alliance then, not yet. Federation same as Empire before, same stupid laws—they pull out many years ago, no way of knowing if we can land, let alone refuel. No Spaceforce out here, backass of nowhere, no bigcorp traders. No tourist, sure. Maybe raiders looking for easy pickings. Few smugglers happy to hide no one's looking too close." The way he said it, he included himself in one of those categories, maybe both.

Bryn felt the corners of her mouth tighten in a tentative smile. Leave it to Rashid to have friends who frequented the dubious side of the line between what was strictly legal and what was creatively opportunistic. If Darkover was no longer under Star Alliance surveillance, so much the better. She'd take her chances with a few smugglers, especially if they were like Wie.

At the same time, Bryn gathered that Wie's honor went only so far, and the captain wasn't willing to hazard his ship against whatever had trailed them from Alpha. He meant to swing in and out, dropping her and her friends on this backwater planet. He certainly wasn't going to land, where the ship would be even more helpless to escape an incoming threat. She didn't blame him.

"You *stuck* here, you kien?" Wie said after a pause. "Call booster won't reach into space."

"I'll find a way to contact you again. I *will.* There must be radio equipment in the spaceport or the old Terran embassy. Some of it must surely be still operational."

"Old Terran spaceport, mebbe." Wie looked thoughtful. "Used to be smugglers' base in desert area, probably gone now but worth looking for." He waved off her further protests and left her.

There is a way off Darkover, she promised herself. *And when we are ready, I will find it!* Chance and resourcefulness had gotten her this far but without Leonin—

No, don't think of him.

◆◆◆

By the time Felicity and Ernst were awake and Bryn had brought them up to date on plans, it was time to board the shuttle. As Bryn had suspected, the ship carried two of the smaller craft. Perhaps out of a fleeting sense of guilt, Wie supplied them with thermal clothing, including headgear and gloves, in addition to food concentrates and water. He also gave Bryn a hand-held so that she could access the data in the tab.

I'll have a map, and with the language program I should be able to speak to the natives. I can do this.

The shuttle's interior was little more than a cockpit with four gravitational couches and a divider walling off the tiny storage area. It smelled of recycled air. Most of the illumination came from the banks of instruments. There were no personal decorations, not even initials scratched in a corner surface or a patch of adhesive where some past crew had pasted a picture of a loved one.

Connison, the first mate, settled them in the shuttle and took the pilot seat. The doors closed with a bang and the hiss of the seals cycling shut. Then they were free of the ship.

Accelerative forces pressed Bryn into her couch as the engines cut in. The sensation gave way to the floating feeling of microgravity. Nausea flared and receded. Her father muttered something about spaceflight never being quite this uncomfortable before. She didn't feel much better. Without a horizon to focus on, she was having trouble keeping her balance centers steady. There was nothing to do but wait out the discomfort. Glancing back, she saw that Felicity looked tense and pale.

What have I done, dragging two elderly people off to a planet on the rim of the galaxy, a place we know almost nothing about? It was far too late to consider the question. There had been no other option, and here they were.

Connison touched a sequence of panels and the opaque inner shields slid back, revealing a sweep of stars against the void. Bryn stared, momentarily speechless, at the massed brilliance, like a glowing, milky swathe shot through with tiny diamonds. Darkover was situated far out on the galactic arm, so she was now seeing the Milky Way edge-on. The perspective from the surface must be equally breathtaking.

The planet itself came into view. Haloed in the blue haze of an oxygen-nitrogen atmosphere, it arched out in a generous curve. At first, she could make out little beyond the swirling whiteness, but then, as the shuttle began its inward spiral, she caught glimpses through the gaps in the clouds: the slate blue of deep ocean, a bit of coastline, the dense blue-black of forest, a stretch of fawn-pale terrain that must be the desert area Wie had mentioned, and a distant stretch of polar ice.

"It's cold down there," Felicity said. "I'm sure the natives have developed appropriate compensatory technology."

Lightning flashed beneath thick gray clouds as the ship dropped lower. Then they hurtled through a clear patch, the clouds parting like curtains on a stage, and there lay the shimmering whiteness of snow—thousands of acres of it, bright enough to blind in full sun. Even from this altitude, Bryn could not mistake the range of glaciated mountains. Nothing on Terra compared to them, not even the great chains of the Himalayas or the Andes. Then the clouds closed over.

"Descending," Connison said. "Air turbulence might get a bit rough."

The clouds soon hid the terrain from view. Without warning the shuttle plummeted, dropping so sharply that Bryn's teeth snapped together. Then it regained a measure of stability.

"Good heavens!" Felicity exclaimed.

"You okay back there?" Bryn called over her shoulder.

"Yes, I believe so," her father answered. "That's quite enough excitement, young man."

"Sorry," the pilot muttered. "Unstable air mass."

Bryn peered through the view shield but saw only unending eddies of gray on white. Her mouth went dry, and her heart rate speeded up. Her danger-sense roused again, gathering urgency but not yet critical. "What's below us?"

"Hellers Mountains. Don't worry. We pass over to reach the landing spot."

Through Bryn's escalating danger-sense came mental images: permanent ice blanketing row after row of peaks; bone-numbing cold; the sweet, heady tang of air untouched by industrial pollution; trudging beneath a swollen red sun beside a horned pack animal that resembled a miniature reindeer—

"Half the damn planet's snowed under," the pilot continued. "Don't know why they didn't name it Winter. Uh oh—hold on."

The shuttle dropped again, so precipitously Bryn's stomach shoved into her diaphragm. Air currents pummeled the side of the craft. Its nose pointed downward. Bryn would have fallen out of her seat if she hadn't been strapped in. The clamor of engine and wind filled her ears. The world outside flipped over, and again, and again: they must be spinning along their long axis. She couldn't tell which way was up or down.

Now she was screaming as loud as she could draw air into her lungs.

Other cries echoed in the confined chamber. On the edge of her vision, she glimpsed the pilot wrestling with the controls.

Winds pounded the shuttle. Flurries of ice crystals blanketed the view, so Bryn seemed to be tumbling through a sea of whiteness. The light caught her up, buoyed her, drenched her senses. It filled her lungs as she inhaled, white and gray and shimmering pale blue that glowed as it burned. She could no longer hear screaming, her own or anyone else's.

Silence, silence as she drifted through that ocean of blue-tinged brilliance.

Her terror vanished.

Her sight turned oddly doubled: one instant, she floated in a pale azure mist. The next, she stood upon a plain of endless gray beneath a featureless, ashen sky, the ground solid beneath her feet. In the distance, a structure like an obelisk or tower loomed above the horizon.

A voice sounded in her mind, speaking words she almost, almost understood.

Who are you? What are you doing in the Overworld? Don't you know how dangerous it is for the untrained to wander here?

Before she could even absorb the question—*The Overworld? What was that?*—the blue-white light disappeared. With a jolt, she found herself back in her body. All around her, metal shrieked. Even though the straps anchored her to the couch, acceleration forces tossed her this way and that.

We're going to crash.

She heard a woman murmuring, a chant low and intense like an invocation—

Breda, *where are you?*

Breda? No, I'm Bryn!

Then: *I'm going to die.*

A gap opened in the blizzard. As the shuttle tumbled, she glimpsed a sloping expanse of snow. Then the crazed spinning of the craft took the field out of view. Something struck the shuttle from the outside—air currents, wild and powerful.

With a deafening, bone-rattling thump, the shuttle collided with something massively solid. It bounced skyward, briefly suspended. Bryn's stomach lurched into her throat. Then she was fighting for breath, struggling against the sick, cold grayness lapping at her vision—

Blackness.

12

Bryn rose slowly to consciousness, like a swimmer who has escaped drowning but is still caught in a current. Voices echoed in her hearing. Through her closed eyelids, she sensed a brightening in the air, a curtain drawn aside. Coming back to herself, she opened her eyes. She felt nauseated and disoriented, but she was alive. She lay at a slant, halfway under her acceleration couch. The interior lighting flickered. Fumes and the reek of charred synthetic material filled the compartment. Her eyes stung and she felt an overpowering urge to cough. A weight compressed her chest and her lungs ached for air.

Wriggling gained her a small measure of room. Once she could take a full breath, she managed to maneuver herself into a position where she could get a better look at her surroundings.

"Father? Felicity? Are you all right?"

Silence.

"Connison—?"

Around her, metal groaned. The shuttle shifted, settling beneath her.

Bryn redoubled her efforts to free herself. Her legs were still held tightly; there was only enough slack so that she could still feel them, but not enough for her to draw her knees up and use leverage to propel herself forward.

Panting with effort, she eased off. She was beginning to feel dizzy again. Sweat beaded her exposed skin, yet she felt chill. It was getting perceptibly colder. She remembered crashing into a massive snow bank. The dropping temperature suggested that the shuttle's internal heating had failed and the hull insulation was no longer intact.

"Father?" she yelled. "Felicity? Can either of you hear me?"

Her only answer was the continued creak and *ping!* from the cooling hull. She told herself that an absence of response didn't mean they were dead. More likely, both were unconscious, as she had been. Unconscious and needing her help. *Right now.*

What do I do? What can *I do?* wailed through her mind. She'd never faced a problem like this. She knew what to do when a traumatized child went into crisis or how to present herself to her father's colleagues in the Senate. This was different, this looming threat of physical harm—of *death, don't fool yourself.* Leonin would know—would *have known*—

But he wasn't here to steady her. To have her back. To guide her. And he never would be again.

Her vision blurred. A lump formed in her throat.

Stop it!

Grief was a luxury she dared not afford. Once she gave in to it, she might never emerge.

Time ticked by, marked by the beating of her heart and the sound of the cooling metal. There was no one else, no one but her.

All right, then. One step at a time.

"Come *on*!" she shouted as she shoved against the couch. Was it her imagination or did it slide a little to one side? She heard a groan from the second row of seats. Shifting position, she braced herself. This time, she pushed and *pushed* for all she was worth—until her arms straightened completely. The weight lifted from her legs.

She lay back, catching her breath, then flexed her knees, jammed her feet against the nearest surface, and pushed again. Her thigh muscles burned, threatening to cramp, but she kept on. Movement was slow, one awkward inch at a time. But move she did. Again. And again, until she tumbled free onto the floor, or rather the side of the compartment. The shuttle lay partly on its belly, partly on its side.

The groan came again. This time she recognized the voice. "Father? Are you all right?"

"I appear to be." He spoke with a slight hesitation as if pausing for breath. "I cannot say the same for our companion. She's unconscious, and I see blood on her temple."

"Can you get to her?"

"I believe so. If you will check on our pilot's condition, I will attend to the professor."

Bryn felt a rush of relief at how lucid her father sounded. How like his old self.

The angle of the shuttle made getting to her feet awkward, and her vision tended to spin as she worked her way to the pilot. Wreckage completely engulfed his seat. The shuttle had come to rest at an angle, and the nose had been crushed. Debris and the shattered remains of his couch covered most of his body. One arm was partly exposed, the uniform torn to reveal drying blood. His skin was cool and slack. She felt her way along the forearm to the wrist and searched for a pulse but could detect nothing. Perhaps it was very faint or slow, or she was probing in the wrong place.

If the pilot was still alive, she must do whatever she could to help him. His injuries might be beyond her lay medical skills and whatever supplies might be stowed on the shuttle. If he wasn't, she would waste valuable time. The temperature was falling, and two—or, dreadfully, one—no, it must be *two* people—Felicity *had* to be alive—depended on her.

She didn't know the pilot. He meant nothing to her. But she'd been powerless to help Leonin, and she would have given anything to save him. For all she knew, the pilot—Connison, he had a name—had a family, friends. People who loved him. He was a human being. Had been.

A sob clotted in her throat. She could tell herself it was beyond her physical ability to free him from the wreckage. She could repeat it for the rest of her life with the dreadful certainty that this decision, either way, would haunt her.

Have I brought us all here to die?

No pulse. She checked again. No pulse.

"I'm sorry," she whispered. "I'm so sorry." And clambered back to where her father had finished removing Felicity's harness.

Felicity wiped the blood from a gash in her scalp. "Dare I ask what happened?"

"We crashed," Bryn said.

"So I gather."

"The pilot's dead. The ship's life support and insulation have failed. It's undoubtedly warmer inside than out in the snow, but I don't know how long that will be true."

Bryn's head throbbed. She hoped it was from the altitude and not a skull injury. She tried to think what to do first to ensure their survival.

"Open the storage compartment and retrieve the supplies," she said. "Thermal clothing's top of the list, but we'll also need food. I'll see if the radio is functional."

The interior lighting flicked on and off as she made her way to the nose of the craft. The navigational instruments and radio were completely smashed. After some exploration, she located a flat box that looked as if it might contain an emergency beacon. But when she opened the clasps, she found only a collection of star charts, compasses, and similar devices.

Ernst and Felicity emerged from the back compartment, arms filled with clothing and backpacks. As they were changing into thermal gear, the lights dimmed and went out. A diffuse gray illumination, shaded with crimson, shone through the view screens. The interior of the shuttle felt suddenly colder.

"Ah!" said Ernst. "That should be enough to find the emergency circuits."

"Father, I had no idea you knew about such things."

"I've tinkered a bit with craft like this now and again over the years, as much to take my thoughts off the political crisis of the moment as from any real thought I'd have practical use of it. Dr. Sage, you have small hands. Would you assist me?"

Felicity agreed, sounding relieved to have something to do.

"I'm going to take a look around outside," Bryn said, gathering her feet under her. "I won't go far. Call if you need me." But neither paid attention; they were already prying off one of the panels below the instrument bank.

By a stroke of good fortune, the angle of the shuttle had not blocked the hatch. The door was slightly warped and resisted at first, but Bryn was able to get it open. She clambered through the opening, stumbled, and fell to her knees in the snow. The shuttle had plowed through a bank, its path marked by a wide channel, carved out by the heat of re-entry.

The sun was setting behind a row of immense, snowy peaks. She'd seen mountains on Terra and other worlds, but nothing like these. The sun appeared huge, as if swollen with age, and red. The shuttle's violet-tinged shadow followed the axis of the channel exactly, which meant its nose was pointing approximately east.

A wind came whipping down from the heights, so cold it burned on her exposed skin, although the thermal layers kept out the worst of it. It reminded her forcefully of the necessity of shelter. The three of them could not possibly travel at night, that much was sure. The one saving grace, if it could be considered so, was that she felt no sense of pressing danger. On that thought, she returned to the shuttle.

Ernst and Felicity crouched around the opened panel, through which Bryn spied a bank of lights. A moment later, overhead lights illuminated the compartment, not as bright as those when the shuttle was fully operational, but a relief nonetheless. Bryn felt a whisper of warmer air on her face. They'd have to plug the openings as best they could, of course, but now they should have enough warmth to make it through the night.

"A small amount of planning now and making the best preparations we can will increase our survival odds," Ernst was explaining to Felicity. "We have light and heat for a limited time. An endless water source lies just outside the door. None of us has fully recovered from the crash and a night's rest will do us good. Tomorrow we must inventory the supplies and fabricate what we do not have, sledges if we can manage them, as it takes less effort to drag smooth runners over snow than to carry the same load. Layers of clothing instead of thermals only. Snowshoes so that we can save energy by walking on top of the snow instead of wading through it and risking injury on an uncertain surface below."

Bryn sat down on the edge of an overturned couch, heartened by her father's clear reasoning and fluent speech. But, she wondered, where had he learned all this? He must have caught her bewildered expression, for he paused, his eyes glinting. "I used to go glacier trekking when I was a young man."

"I didn't know that. You are full of surprises."

"Those days were behind me when you and Sara were born. I had already embarked upon my political career and saw little chance of returning to the adventures of my greener days."

"I for one am grateful that *one* of us has expertise in cold climate survival," Felicity remarked. "But these are temporary measures at best. We cannot remain here."

"If we were on any Alliance planet, the best thing to do—the thing all the survival experts advise—is to stay where we are and wait for rescue," Ernst said.

"Even if this shuttle has an emergency beacon, who would receive it?" Felicity said.

Who indeed? Bryn hadn't considered that when she searched the equipment.

"It's highly unlikely the natives would have received a distress signal as this ship went down, or known how to locate us," Felicity continued.

"I agree," Ernst said. "If we have the energy tonight, it would be prudent to re-assess the communications equipment on the off-chance that some of it can be made functional."

If Black somehow managed to track us here, we need to get as far away from the shuttle as possible.

"The equipment was destroyed when the shuttle crashed," Bryn said. "That's just as well since we don't want to risk a signal that might be picked up by Spaceforce. More than that, we need to make contact with the native telepaths, and to do that, we need to know which way to travel."

Felicity drew her brows together, wincing. "Don't you have a hand-held with a data tab on this planet? Doesn't that include maps? Or is my memory faulty in that regard?"

Bryn found her satchel and dug out the hand-held. The outer case was cracked. When she inserted the data tab, the screen lit up sluggishly. Lines of fuzzy static broke up the images. It must have been damaged in the crash, like so much else. Worse, its power supply was nearly exhausted.

"Maybe I can still bring up the suite of maps of Darkover," Bryn said. To her relief, the screen yielded a patchy image of the major continent.

"Okay," Felicity said when Bryn turned the screen around so the other two could see it, "so where are we?"

The Hellers Mountains, the pilot had said. That was a start.

Bryn located the massive range on the maps and enlarged the area. She lost the image several times when the screen turned dark or the lines of static obscured details. Felicity dug around in her shoulder bag, extracted a notepad of real paper and a carbon stylus, and began sketching the map.

A handful of settlements dotted the Hellers Mountains. Nevarsin. Tramontana. Caer Donn. Further south, places called Armida and Serrais. And what appeared to be the capital city, Thendara. Thendara, Caer Donn, and Port Chicago were marked as having had Terran consulates. Ah, there was the desert Wie had mentioned, with Carthon and Shainsa indicated. Smuggler bases didn't strike her as the safest options, but they wouldn't be likely to collaborate with Spaceforce. The names were oddly familiar, but then, this was a Lost Colony World, so they would have had Terran origins. At that point, the hand-held went dark and refused to start again. She couldn't even get a battery measurement.

"So we're somewhere in the Hellers," Bryn said, trying not to feel discouraged, "but that covers a lot of territory. We need to know where we are starting from."

"Actually, we don't," her father said. "We can use the sun's position for general orientation and head south. The maps tell us that much. Our best tactic is to go downhill whenever possible and look for a stream or a river. People tend to settle on the banks for water, fishing, and easy transportation."

"That makes sense," Bryn said. "It's a good thing Felicity thought to sketch a map."

"My colleagues considered me a Luddite for carrying around pieces of paper instead of relying on electronics, but sometimes the simpler technologies are superior," Felicity said, looking pleased.

"We should leave as early as we can, to maximize the available daylight," Ernst said. "Let's prepare as much as we can now."

Felicity discovered a tent, as well as oversized, thigh-length jackets of water- and wind-resistant fabric. Meanwhile, Bryn pulled out couch insulation while her father devised frameworks for the sledge and snowshoes. She glanced at the pilot's couch and sighed.

"I wish we had a way to bury him, or at least send word to his family."

"They may never know what happened to him," Ernst said, "but then, since he operated on the fringe of the law, he may not have had anyone to come home to. These mountains are as fitting a burial place as any."

"Father." He met her gaze, his expression alert and yet gentle. "I'm glad you're back with us."

His fingers closed over hers. "For some time now, I have wished we spent more time together. There was always a reason to put it off, one crisis after another or a challenge that only I could meet. I would not have chosen these particular circumstances, although since I find myself marooned on a half-frozen planet on the edge of the galaxy, it is no small blessing to have you here with me. But, Bryn—"

With one hand, he indicated the electrodes implanted in his skull. "Bryn, there is something seriously wrong with me."

How much does he remember? How much should I tell him?

"My memories are fragmented," he said. "I remember preparing a speech calling for negotiations between the Alliance and the Vainwal independence leaders. I cannot quite recall the content. When I try, it slips away from me. I am sure I felt passionately about it. I must have been abducted. That's the only logical explanation of how I got to the place you found me—the laboratory at Alpha University, correct? But I have no *memory* of it."

He averted his face, shadows masking his expression. Bryn thought that for a man who had lived by the sharpness of his intellect and his keen moral sense, such an admission must be especially painful. She said, "It's a good sign that you can recall events from before you were taken. The electrodes are the external receptors for a version of the theta-corticator." She explained a little about the technology, adding, "We didn't try to remove them. Felicity thought we're beyond the range of the transmitters."

For a moment he was silent, pensive. Then: "Which leaves the logical conclusion that the damage is permanent."

"No! You mustn't think that!"

Felicity sat beside them. "What symptoms are you having? Headaches, visual disturbances? Flattened affect—or unusually intense emotions?"

"Memory gaps. Thoughts and feelings I know are not mine. I was telling Bryn that I remember the Vainwal situation and how I acted—I *became* a pawn of Arthur Nagy."

He sounded so distressed, Bryn took his hands in hers. "That's why we're here on Cottman IV, to seek specialized help to undo the effects of the theta-corticator."

He did not look very convinced.

Felicity said, "I am familiar with the device used on you as I helped to develop it, but the implanted electrodes were never part of the design. The effects you describe are a kind of mechanical brainwashing. Unlike the old technique of hypnosis, which could not compel a subject to behave in a way contrary to his or her values, the theta-corticator can create a second, false persona that then dictates speech and behavior, even internalized values quite contrary to those previously held."

"So you are saying this repugnant indoctrination is part of me now?" Ernst said, gesturing again to his head, "That it may take me over again?"

"I cannot guarantee that it will not," Felicity said. "Until I remove and inspect the device, I cannot be certain whether it passively transmits those attitudes from an external source or functions independently."

"Either way, I dare not risk their taking me over again. Under Nagy's control, I might say—might *do*—terrible things. I refuse to become a weapon in his hands! As long as there is a chance I might be mind-washed, I must never go home."

Bryn had never before heard her father sound so grim, so desolate. "No. *No.* You are right, you must never become Nagy's puppet again. But at the same time, you must not give up hope. Those devices are not the only means of controlling another person's thoughts. The reason we've come all this way to Cottman IV is that of all the planets in known space, here is where people have developed *natural* telepathy." She hesitated, unsure if she should mention her danger-sense, then decided to keep it private. "The natives of Darkover used those abilities to prevent the old Terran Empire from overrunning their world, then enforced their Protected Status. If there is any way of countering the *mechanical* mind control Nagy's developed, it is here on Darkover."

He placed one of his hands over hers. "My dear, determined daughter."

◆◆◆

The next morning, Bryn found herself buried under a heap of insulation from the crash couches and faintly nauseous. She'd been dreaming of that eerie gray plain, searching for someone or something. Or someone was searching for her, asking where she was. The fading moments of the dream echoed with *Hold on, we're coming.* The words had not been in Terran Standard but one of the Darkovan dialects imprinted on her mind. If she was dreaming in that language, that boded well for her ability to make herself understood by the natives. She hoped they wouldn't automatically reject her request for help because of past frictions with Terra.

She sat upright, shedding the layers of insulation. The air in the cabin was chilly, and the interior lights had failed overnight, indicating that the batteries were drained. The light from outside suggested early morning. The sooner they got going, the more daylight they would have.

After a quick breakfast of emergency food supplies, they loaded up the sledge with its improvised harness, donned their packs and makeshift snowshoes, and set off. The position of the sun gave them a general east-west orientation, although the compasses did not work. The planetology summary indicated that Cottman IV was a metal-poor world.

Bryn, as the strongest, pulled the sledge, finding that once she overcame the initial friction, it glided easily over the snow. Her father and Felicity walked single-file, stepping in each other's footsteps. The air was cold but smelled fresher than any Bryn could remember, and the pounding of her heart reminded her that it was also thin.

They planned to head south, keeping to lower ground and hoping to come across a waterway that would lead them to a landmark recognizable on the map or, better yet, a settlement. And what would she do if they found such a place? What would be the best way to enlist the natives' assistance? The anthropology files in the data tab suggested that the mountain communities placed a high value on hospitality. But these tribes also engaged in raiding for livestock, resulting in long-running feuds.

We come in peace. We mean you no harm. Please help us, she rehearsed silently in the two primary languages Wie's sleep-learning program had instilled in her mind. *My father and my teacher need medical care*—no, that was too complicated for an initial greeting.

Rocky outcroppings broke through the snow-covered ice. Sometimes they had to take extensive detours and then consult the maps to make their best estimate of the direction they were supposed to be following. Bryn's heart raced as she struggled to maneuver the sledge. Felicity hadn't complained but was clearly struggling. When they stopped to melt snow for water and eat lunch, she asked her father about what might be done for altitude sickness.

"The best treatment is descent, which we are already doing as quickly as we can. None of us are coughing or short of breath at rest, or confused, so we seem to have escaped the most serious symptoms. Staying warm and hydrated and continuing on our way at the best safe speed are the most we can do for now."

Toward the end of the afternoon, mauve-tinged shadows fell across thick, layered ice. The wind died down just as the sun passed beyond the line of peaks and light seeped out of the sky. The temperature dropped, and where the surface of the snow had melted at midday, it was now re-freezing. There was no point in trying to go farther that day.

They didn't have a large store of food and canned fuel, but it was concentrated and reasonably palatable, and Ernst was experienced in preparing it. There were even several packets of sweetened, highly enriched powder that, when mixed with melted snow and heated, produced a drink that warmed Bryn from the inside. Felicity had no appetite for solid food but was able to sip one of the hot drinks.

After they'd tucked away the packaging, the three settled down for the night. The tent was just barely big enough, being designed for only two people. They placed Felicity in the middle to keep her the warmest.

◆◆◆

The next morning, Bryn felt sore but otherwise well. Felicity was too nauseated to eat and turned pale when she tried to stand up. She didn't argue when Ernst and Bryn insisted that she ride on the sledge. This meant dividing the other supplies between the sledge and their packs.

The sky clouded over as the day wore on. A dull gray light washed over the landscape, and the temperature, which had begun to rise at midday, dipped. Bryn called for rest stops more frequently. Somewhat to her surprise, she'd stepped into the position of leader. Although her father had greater expertise in mountain travel, he deferred to her suggestions. From time to time, he would look distracted, his focus turning inward. She wished there was something she could say to ease his worries. The truth was that she *hoped* the people of Cottman IV could undo the distortions of the theta-corticator, but she didn't *know* they could or would.

As they continued their descent, wind rushed down from the heights. As Bryn watched the clouds thicken, her danger-sense prickled. Just as she was beginning to feel a twinge of desperation, they came around the shoulder of a steep slope. A vista stretched out below them, ending in the ragged, dark green edge of a forest. It was still some distance away, more than they could make before dusk, but Bryn fell to her knees, so profound was her sense of relief.

Felicity came to stand beside her. "Oh! We've made it!"

"To the tree line, anyway," came Ernst's voice behind them. He was breathing hard. "We'll still need to descend further to be safe from altitude sickness."

"But we'll stand a better chance against the elements among the trees," Bryn pointed out. The gathering clouds worried her.

"Trees that will make it more difficult to follow our planned route," he said. "Not to mention that the sledge will be harder to pull once we're off the snow."

As they went on, the sky darkened. The patches of snow thinned to rocky soil. The sledge kept catching, even with all three of them pushing and pulling. Bryn's shoulders ached with repeatedly having to jerk it free. Felicity insisted on walking, and their pace slowed. The tree line was visible now as a blurred line in the distance.

We can't go on like this. Bryn held up one hand to signal a halt. She looked around for a place that might serve as a campsite. They had a tent, after all, but it would be better to get out of the wind—

—the wind that even now brought thin, flurrying snow. Flakes touched her face, melting instantly. Soon they would stick. They no longer had the luxury of searching for a perfect campsite. At the moment, a simple windbreak would have to be enough. But where?

"Look!" Ernst unclipped the sledge harness and came to stand beside her. He pointed. Following his gesture, Bryn saw a gorge bounded by steep, bare rock that might afford protection from the wind. The snow was another matter, but there was no better choice. Felicity looked to be at the end of her endurance. They must take whatever shelter they could find.

By the time they reached the mouth of the gorge, all three were stumbling with weariness. Once they passed between the walls of rock, however, the wind died and the air felt warmer. Bryn wondered if there might be caves, which would give them even better shelter, but didn't see any.

They set up the tent. After a brief dinner, they all nestled into their sleeping bags. Bryn drifted off to the snores of her two companions.

And woke in utter darkness at the sound of a piercing wail. Like a siren it rose and fell, so unearthly, so downright *eerie* that it sent shivers through her marrow. Her danger-sense shrilled along her nerves. For a moment, she couldn't breathe.

"What is it?" Felicity whispered. Bryn thought if she tried to answer, it would come out as a terrified squeak.

"I don't know," came her father's voice. "Bryn, do we have a weapon of any sort?"

Bryn started to say no, of course not, why would any of them have such a thing? Then she remembered Leonin thrusting the neural tangler into her hands. She'd fired it—she'd been holding it when the van had pulled up outside the laboratory complex and the three of them had scrambled inside. Had she kept it—and if so, where? She reached for the clothing she'd worn beneath the thermals. Pawing through it, she touched something hard and about the right size. It was too dark to see, but once she'd taken it into her hands, she had no doubt she was holding the tangler.

She lowered herself back, holding the thing close. What was she thinking, to have kept it, this thing whose only use was to maim or kill, but if she hadn't—they would be defenseless against the screamer in the night—who knew if a Terran weapon would even *work* on whatever it was—

—and she was going to drive herself crazy, thinking like this—

—and if the screamer found them, she might not have a choice.

Meanwhile, it was too cold to sit up, waiting. She arranged her bedding so that at a moment's notice she could throw it off.

The yowling came again, no less blood-chilling than before but less loud, as if whatever made it was moving further off. Bryn listened, hardly daring to believe their luck, but did not hear it again. Her pulse slowed as adrenaline drained from her body. Her danger-sense receded. Her father yawned, and then Felicity did, and then Bryn. She pulled the sleeping bag around her shoulders, although she kept hold of the tangler.

Whatever it was is gone now, she told herself. *It must have missed us in the dark.*

She slipped into uneasy dreams in which a featureless gray shape stalked their trail. When she glanced back or peered out from a hiding place, she could not make out what it was, only that it was large and cold and deadly. The terrain over which she fled shifted. In the way of dreams, all color drained away, leaving her wandering through a forest of ancient, gray-boled trees or dashing across a flat gray plain under a sky the same color.

Where are you? came a ghostly voice.

Wheeling, she darted away.

The gray sky lowered over her. The faster she ran, the lower the clouds sank until she could almost reach up and touch them. The plain had vanished, replaced by walls like the gullet of a living thing. A ravenous thing.

The sky pressed down on her. The walls closed in. With every step, she fought to move, to breathe. She tried to cry out, but her voice came out as a strangled, barely human sob.

The sound jarred her awake. She tried to sit up, but her head pushed against a barrier. There were only a few inches of clearance between the top of her head and the tent. The fabric sagged, as if under an immense weight, and the air felt close and humid. Their combined exhalations must have condensed on the inside of the tent fabric.

Bryn touched the lowest point of the bulge. It was cold, as she expected, but it gave only a little, resisting her pressure. The realization struck her: while they'd slept, protected from the wind in the narrow gorge, snow had fallen.

They were buried. How deeply, she did not know. Without tools or outside help, they might not be able to dig themselves out.

Bryn forced herself to breathe slowly. It was harder than she expected. She imagined their pocket of air turning stale. What were the symptoms of anoxia? She couldn't remember—did that mean her brain was deprived of oxygen? A part of her, that terrified monkey at the back of her brain, yammered at her to get out *now*.

Panic will only use up the air faster. Think!

The moment she eased away from panic, she realized that her danger-sense, while humming away, wasn't urgent. Not yet, anyway. She still had time to assess the situation, time to plan.

She wasn't dead. Or badly injured. Or gasping for breath. She wasn't in the dark, so the snow must be shallow enough for light to penetrate.

She also wasn't alone. Her father knew about survival in cold weather. Felicity had a keen analytical mind. Together, they could surely reason out how to proceed.

As if in answer to her thoughts, the two older people began to stir. Ernst started thrashing, mumbling incoherently. Gently Bryn shook him. With an explosive, "What!" he came awake.

"Father, it's all right. I'm here."

"Where are we? What's going on?"

"We're on Darkover—Cottman IV, don't you remember?"

He poked the sagging roof of the tent. "What is this thing? It's cold!"

"It's snow that's fallen on our tent," Bryn said. "Better not to touch it until we know how deep the snow is."

"I'm not supposed to be here..." he mumbled, subsiding.

"Do I understand correctly that we have been buried under snow?" Felicity asked quietly. "I take it that is quite a dangerous situation."

"Yes, and I think so," Bryn replied, trying to keep her voice calm. "We have air for now, but for how long I can't tell. I also don't know if we can dig ourselves out—I remember something about people getting caught in an avalanche not being able to do that most of the time."

"That's outside my area of expertise," Felicity said.

"We'll need a probe to determine the thickness of the snow and also how compacted it is."

"Yes, that is a logical way to proceed. But with what?"

"Something thin enough to slip through the snow without compacting it, and as long as possible. How about one of the tent struts?"

"An excellent first thing to do," Ernst replied, emerging from his confusion, "and not too difficult. There should be a pocket at the end of one of the tent fabric channels."

Felicity, who was closest to the opening of the tent, kept the tension on the fabric while Bryn and Ernst extracted the strut. The tent sagged further but did not collapse. They marked the strut in half- and quarter-meters. Felicity maneuvered it out through the tent opening and upward. She wasn't as physically strong as the others, but she had by far the best leverage. After several attempts, she managed to position the strut and begin pushing it up. Moment by moment, bit by bit, the strut slid through the snow.

Half-meter...three-quarters... Bryn felt as if she were counting heartbeats instead of marks on the strut.

A meter...another quarter...

We're in too deep. We can't dig through that much snow. And nobody knew they were here. No rescue would come. No friendly hands would lift them out.

Felicity stopped pushing. "The resistance just gave way. I think I'm through."

Digging themselves out was much harder than Bryn expected. Not only was it strenuous work but it had to be done carefully to not cause the snow to collapse on top of them. They also had to extricate the tent and their belongings. The sledge proved to be too difficult, but they should not need it much longer. By the time they had gotten everything to the surface, all three of them were tired.

"We can go slowly, but we must keep on," Bryn said. "We have to get out of this snow."

"As much as I would like to rest, you are correct," Felicity said.

As they descended, the air seemed less thin, and no one complained of altitude sickness symptoms. Seen close up, the trees appeared to be conifers, and although the cones were oddly shaped, the smell was pleasant. Resting at a vista point, Bryn looked back the way they had come.

Overhead, a large bird, an eagle or a hawk, soared, its cry piercing and lonely. That night, as Bryn settled into sleep, she thought she heard the distant howling of wolves.

The next day, they came across a narrow, flattened ribbon of a trail that wound its way along the lowest part of the cleft between two rising peaks. It led in the direction they were going and provided easier and safer footing. Another couple of nights brought them even lower out of the mountains. Here snow clung only in the deepest shadows. Rain rather than sleet fell at night, and not every night at that. At midday, the sky turned bright and clear, and the air was warmer and laden with the smells of wet earth and green, growing things.

They camped on a wide, flat area just off the trail, bordered on one side by a tree hedge and the other by a rocky slope. The air was still and sweet-smelling and clear. Overhead arched a river of stars. Pinpricks of light glittered like gemstones, dwarfed by two of Darkover's four moons, one with a faint peacock hue. The sight took Bryn's breath away, hungry and weary though she was. She crawled into her sleeping bag as soon as she'd finished her meager rations and fell asleep almost instantly.

She awoke, heart pounding, to the gut-wrenching certainty that something was wrong. That some threat was almost upon them. Fire raced along her nerves.

She forced herself to lie still and listen. From the direction of the tree hedge, she heard the sound of rustling, as if some creature—or some *one*—was moving stealthily over the dry leaves. It stopped, then came again, this time doubled and slightly out of phase. *Two* of whatever it was?

A voice reached her ears, a rough-edged, masculine, *human* voice speaking so softly and in such hurried, urgent tones that she could not catch the meaning. The voice was answered by a second, even more faint and unintelligible.

Moving as silently as she could, Bryn slipped her feet into her boots and dug out the tangler. She parted the opening to the tent and peeked outside. The fire had burned down, but embers still gave off a faint glow. Clouds muted the light of the stars, but through a gap one moon shimmered like a pearl. As far as she could see, the site and its surroundings were undisturbed.

"We come in peace," she called in *cahuenga*, one of the dialects she'd sleep-learned in flight. "We mean you no harm."

Nothing answered her, not even the crackle of a dried leaf. She imagined the skulkers out there, perhaps gesturing to one another, curious mountain dwellers, perhaps, who'd been drawn to the fire.

Bryn tucked the tangler into her waistband and crawled out of the tent. Straightening, she held her hands up, palms facing out in the universal human signal of peaceful intentions. "It's safe to come out. We're friends."

One long moment melted into the next. The chill of the night seeped into the bare skin of her face and hands. She turned in a slow circle, pausing to face each direction as she peered into the darkness. Several times more she repeated the words of welcome.

"Bryn—" came her father's sleepy voice from inside the tent. "What's going on?"

She heard shouting in a dialect she couldn't follow. Then someone kicked the banked embers, sending up sparks and a rush of flames.

Rough hands grabbed her from behind. She was jerked off her feet, pinned against a thick, masculine body. Her assailant wrapped one arm around her neck. Fetid odors washed over her—the rank, salty reek of old sweat and wet fur. Gagging, she clawed at the arm at her throat. It might as well have been steel beneath the greasy leather. She gasped, struggling for breath. She had to act fast, before she passed out.

She shifted her attack, twisting as best she could, then made a fist and punched down and behind her as hard as she could. Her hand collided with soft flesh. With a grunt, her captor loosened his hold.

In that instant, Bryn threw all her weight against the arm that held her and jerked free. She spun around, backing up out of reach. The dull glow of the embers and the light of the moon fell on the features of her assailant. She couldn't make out more than a patch of pale skin above a beard, and a thick, fur-trimmed parka and pants. He crouched over, holding his groin. His breath came in agonized wheezes.

Whirling around, Bryn searched for the others. She didn't see Felicity, but Ernst was grappling with another man on the ground. The fight was so fast—just as when Leonin had wrestled with that man back on the riverbank or when he'd tackled Black.

She jerked the tangler free from her waistband. "Stop! Stop or I'll fire!"

Moonlight flashed on a length of metal—a knife as long as her forearm. The assailant hauled her father to his knees, blade at his throat. The man shouted something in his mountain dialect, but she couldn't understand him. His meaning was clear.

"He's an old man," she pleaded in *cahuenga*, hoping that at least he could understand her plea. "Don't hurt him!"

The man responded with more shouting, repeating the same phrases. Two others appeared in the periphery of her vision, closing in on her. One carried a sword, held low.

"Stay back!" she cried, swinging the tangler from one to the other.

The next round of shouting ended with a choked-off scream from her father. His captor had cut him with the knife edge.

"All right, all right!" Raising her hands, she lowered herself to one knee and placed the tangler on the ground.

The two men to either side grabbed her, hauling her roughly to her feet. One of them jerked her hands behind her back and tied them together with coarse rope that bit into her skin. A few minutes later, she was sitting beside her father and Felicity, both similarly bound, while the bandits pawed through the contents of the tent. The clothing and snowshoes interested them and were set aside. One squatted beside the fallen man and helped him to his feet. Another built up the fire, although by now, gray light swept across the eastern horizon. It was bright enough to make out the spatters of blood on her father's jacket.

The tangler lay half-covered in dirt where Bryn had set it down.

While the bandits finished going through the supplies, the sun had cleared the eastern heights. Bryn started shivering, and blue tinged Felicity's lips. Ernst sat, bowed over and expressionless. The tent had been turned into sacks for carrying the loot. Once the bundles were prepared, the bandits left them in a heap and went aside, leaning close and speaking in hushed tones. From time to time, they gestured toward the prisoners. The discussion then shifted as the leader stared at her pointedly and with an expression that unnerved her. Her danger-sense shot up. She had no doubt that Felicity and her father were of no use to the bandits. But she was.

She fought the sudden rush of bile up the back of her throat. *Think!*

It would take a few moments to clamber to her feet. The tangler was still on the ground.

No, don't look directly at it—

He was coming toward her now, lips drawn back in an unmistakable leer.

She lashed out with a kick just as he came within reach. Her foot collided with his knee. She felt something give beneath her foot with a sickening snap. He shouted at her as he bent over, hands over his knee, and she didn't need to know the language to understand the nastiness of his cursing. One of the others started laughing, and that only made him more furious.

Bryn scooted away, feet slipping on the dirt, thinking only to get as far away as she could before the bandit recovered. The toe of one boot caught on something—a bit of rock, maybe—and she kicked upward. Dust and pebbles billowed into the air and hung like a brownish curtain. As it fell away, she saw the bandit leader straighten up and take a limping step toward her. His face turned dusky, distorting into a grotesque mask. This time he didn't yell at her but came on in silence that turned her blood cold.

But only for a moment. Her temper was up now. She wouldn't—she *couldn't*—stop fighting. She kicked up more dust, shouting back at him. Swear words, insults, anything she could think of.

Her voice faltered when, a few moments later, one of the man's comrades joined him, coming at her from the side. The second man pushed her flat on the ground and held her while his friend loosened the ties of his pants. Tears of futility stung her eyes. She felt a rush of savage energy such as she had never experienced.

Bryn dug her teeth into one of the hands that pinned her. She almost gagged, the skin was so rank and layered with filth. The man bellowed and jerked away. She bucked and writhed, trying to bring her feet around to kick him. She jerked at the rope binding her wrists, but it held. Her assailant grabbed for her legs. He got a hold of one foot, just as she managed to smash the knee of her free leg into his face—his nose, from the crunching sound and the howls.

Snarling and spitting blood, he hurled himself flat across her torso. No matter how she lashed out, she could not break free. He was too heavy. Hands pawed at her hips—she felt a searing line of pain along one thigh—a knife, cutting her clothing away. She kept struggling, kicking, squalling in rage, but the weight across her ribs was just too much—she couldn't draw more than a shallow breath. Her adrenaline-fueled strength was fading.

"Ai-ai-ai-ai!" A chorus of high-pitched cries filled the night. And the sound of galloping hooves.

"*Comhi-Letzii!*" The man holding her down spat out the words like a curse. The next moment, his weight lifted from her. She rolled away as best she could with her hands tied.

The campsite roiled with mounted fighters, darting back and forth, uttering those strange, ululating cries. Dawn's ruddy light flashed on the blades of the riders. Metal sang as one of the bandits parried a blow. The next instant, he was down, fighting on his knees against the rider who attacked him with strokes so fast, the short sword blurred. The other riders wheeled their horses to cut off the remaining bandits, encircling them. The bandits fought back, but the riders had the advantage of height, the nimbleness of their mounts, and the coordination of their attack.

One moment, screams and war cries filled the campsite, and thudding hooves and the clash of steel. The next, a deathly silence fell.

The riders halted their horses and dismounted. Bryn counted four—no, five of them. One checked the fallen bodies. Another approached her, drawing a long knife from a belt sheath. Bryn scuttled away as best she could with her hands behind her. These riders were clearly enemies of the bandits, but they might be equally hostile to all strangers, and who knew what their attitude toward Terrans might be? Darkover was a much more dangerous place than she'd thought.

The rider loomed over Bryn for a moment before flipping her over to lie face-down. With a *snick!* the rope holding Bryn's hands fell away. She lay there, heart pounding. Her shoulders burned from having been wrenched during her struggles. She raised her head, awkwardly pushing herself to sit upright. The rider who'd freed her had stepped away, joining the others as they moved about the camp.

Father? Felicity?

She heard Felicity's voice from across the camp as the older woman conversed with the riders in halting *cahuenga*. Surely that was a good sign. But she couldn't hear her father. Half-sick, half-numb, and dreading the worst, she clambered to her feet. There he was—alive! But he gave no sign he was aware of her presence. His eyes were glassy, his expression slack, as if the bandit attack had fractured his fragile sanity.

No, no, no, no!

"Bryn!" Felicity called out. "My sweet stars! They're *women*."

Bryn huddled in front of the fire, which the women riders had built up again. She couldn't stop shaking. Her father sat beside her, staring at the flames. One of the riders had draped a sleeping bag around his shoulders.

Felicity wrapped one arm around Bryn, murmuring comfort. "It's all right, it's over. You'll be fine now."

Bryn wanted to throw up—to hit something—to run and keep running—to collapse into helpless tears—to scream. She didn't know what she wanted.

Snap out of it! She'd be no good to her father like this.

Her attention was caught by two of the women riders dragging the bodies of the bandits to the edge of the campsite, where they laid them in a line. She stood up.

"No," Felicity protested, "it's gruesome—don't look."

With dry eyes, Bryn stared at the mangled corpse of the man who'd assaulted her. With one foot she prodded his body and felt the clay-like inertness, the terrible stillness. She studied the blood, the swollen, discolored mouth, and other injuries, and felt not a shred of emotion.

Suddenly anger engulfed her, a fury she'd never known before. Her hands balled into fists. Her breath quickened, muscles tightening. Her boot slammed into the dead man's body.

"Take that, you bastard—and that!—and *that!*"

Again and again, she kicked him. She thought of pummeling him with her fists as well, but she didn't want to touch him. Didn't want to get that close to him. He didn't deserve to be treated with respect, even dead. He was a thing—a vile, disgusting *thing*—a thing to be trampled underfoot. Energy rushed through her, sweeping away the last vestiges of weakness. She no longer needed words—only her voice, wild and furious.

No one tried to stop her or urge her to be reasonable.

In a corner of her mind, she realized the therapeutic value of what she was doing. She'd used similar techniques with her child patients. At the moment, though, she didn't care. The only thing that meant anything was the utter destruction of the man who'd tried to rape her.

Name a black thing, name a white thing. Name it. Rape.

At last, she came to the end of her onslaught, left with the exhilaration of standing tall and free over this lump of a man who would never threaten her again. She was breathing hard and sweaty but no longer shaking.

One of the riders had mounted up and ridden off. Around the camp, the others were sorting through the contents of the tent and folding up the tent itself. One of them paused in her work to give Bryn a long, hard look.

Felicity came up to Bryn. "Better now?"

No. Yes. I don't know. Can I ever be better again?

"Better, yes."

"Come on, let's sit down." Felicity put her arm around Bryn. "I'm concerned about your father. He's barely responsive. I don't know if he's traumatized or if this is an effect of the theta-corticator and being out of range of the transmitter for so long."

Bryn lowered herself beside her father. She could do nothing about the dead bandits. But she could do something for *him*. She knew how to do this, how to comfort, to support. To heal.

"Father, I'm here. I'm with you." When she stroked the side of his face, he did not flinch or pull away. Instead, he turned to meet her gaze. His expression shifted to one of puzzled awareness.

"What is this place?" he asked. "How did we come to be here?"

"It's Darkover, Father. Cottman IV. I've brought you here from Alpha."

A vague look passed over his face. "Alpha...was in another lifetime, or someone else's. My memory is full of gaps, like alpine cheese."

"Do you know who I am?"

"Oh!" He touched her cheek. "You are my own sweet Bryn. And since I am in need of aid, I can think of no one I would trust more. Together, I am certain, we will solve the mystery of what has happened to me."

The leader of the women riders sat down in front of them. Seen up close and in better light, she was of middle years, with wind-roughened cheeks and strands of gray in her dark hair. There was no mistaking her air of command and quiet competence. And ruthlessness, Bryn thought, remembering the efficiency with which this woman and her comrades had dispatched the bandits.

The woman gestured to herself. "Martina n'ha Riva." Gesturing to each, she named her comrades: blonde Devra, the fighter who had freed Bryn; red-haired Arliss; Leeanne with her long black braid; and, with a wave in the direction the last one had gone, Bettina. Then she pointed to the Terrans, clearly demanding their own names and then repeating them. She called Bryn "Bruna" and Felicity "Felicia," but had no difficulty with "Ernst."

"Thank you for your help," Bryn said. "You arrived just in time."

"We were sent for you. Escort. Protect."

"Sent? Who sent you?"

"The—" a word Bryn didn't recognize; *sorceress*? "—of Nevarsin Tower."

Nevarsin, that's one of the settlements on the map! If it was big enough to be designated, they might well find proper shelter, food, and medical care there.

"Sorceress?" Bryn repeated.

"I think the word means *female aristocrat*, although it might have a specific, honorific connotation," Felicity said, with an expression that said she was in the process of analyzing cultural linguistics.

How was it possible that this *sorceress* had dispatched a troop of women fighters to arrive just in time to save them from the bandits? "Nobody knew we were here," Bryn said.

Then in a flash of memory, she stood once more on the featureless gray expanse and heard the voice in her mind—*I will find you.*

I called for help and she answered. This must be one of the telepaths Bryn had come to Darkover to find.

"She explains when you see her," Martina assured them. "We take you to her at Nevarsin Tower."

"So you're mercenaries?" Felicity said. "Guards? Security for hire? All women?"

Martina made a dismissive gesture, speaking rapidly so that Bryn caught only the general sense of her meaning. The band of women was part of a gender-segregated society, whose name translated roughly as *Free Women-Warriors*. Clearly, they were adept at mountain travel, not to mention combat. Martina insisted that the bandits had broken their laws, for which the penalty was death.

"Fascinating," Felicity murmured as she discreetly drew out her notebook from her shoulder bag and made notes.

Bettina, the woman who'd ridden off, returned with four animals that looked like a cross between ponies and reindeer. Two were saddled and the others carried wicker panniers on either side. At Martina's orders, the other women packed up the remains of the camp and distributed them between the animals. Bryn was mounted on one, her father on the other, and Felicity behind Devra, the smallest of the women, on one of the horses. The horned animals, which she gathered were called chervines for their goatlike qualities, had an unfamiliar but not unpleasant smell and a choppy gait, as she discovered when they set off down along the trail, riding single file. Leeanne went first, scouting out the trail.

They kept a brisk pace where the trail was smooth and even, slowing when it hugged the steep rock sides. Just before dusk, they arrived at a rough-hewn cabin with a pole corral for the livestock. Everyone dismounted, the women alighting as if in a dance, Bryn and her father awkward with stiffness. Felicity would have fallen off if Devra had not eased her to the ground. Bettina and Leeanne took charge of the animals and led them away to the corral.

Bryn leaned on the door frame of the single-roomed cabin, grateful to be standing instead of riding. "What is this place?" she asked Martina, who was bringing in an armful of rolled blankets that had been tied to the saddles.

"Trail shelter. Open to all. In winter, save lives. Truce holds here."

In winter? This isn't *winter*?

The women set about unpacking and making the trail cabin ready. Arliss carried in an armload of wood and laid a fire on the stone hearth. Martina and Devra wrestled the panniers inside. Bryn stayed out of the way as they deposited the load in what looked like a storage alcove, tucked away from both the hearth and the bunks.

"Can I help?" Bryn asked.

Devra continued on her way back outside, but Martina paused. "You know tending chervines? Rubbing down horses, checking—" she used a word Bryn didn't recognize but probably meant *feet* or *legs* or *hooves*.

Bryn shook her head.

"Cook over fire?"

Not likely. "I'm sorry, no."

Devra called from the threshold, "Could use another hand here."

Under Devra's watchful eye, Bryn lugged in more wood and buckets of snow. When she was done, she was so tired, she thought she'd fall down if she stopped moving.

The fire had begun to warm the inside of the cabin. Water simmered in a metal pot, while Arliss bent over another, which gave off a savory smell.

Arliss shyly asked Bryn something that the language program failed to translate. That could have been due to a natural drift in the language or a heavy accent, divergences from the original form the program had been based upon.

"Arliss is healer," Martina explained, once she understood the difficulty. "She asks if there is any pain or sickness in you."

Bryn pointed to her knees and then her bottom, at which Martina erupted in laughter. "Arliss has—how do you say? *medicine?* for trail sore."

After the evening meal, Arliss brought out a flask of sharp-smelling herbal liniment and a pot of ointment. Ernst turned away politely while Bryn tended to her saddle sores. She was surprised at the rush of soothing warmth.

Felicity and Ernst were already in their bunks and, by their deep breathing, asleep. Leeanne took the bed above Felicity, and the other women placed their bedrolls to one side of the middle of the floor, clearly intending to sleep there. Bryn was too wound up to sleep. She sat with Martina and Arliss over cups of a tisane that tasted of mint and chamomile. Now that their work was done for the day, they were as curious about her and her party as she was about them. They settled on alternating questions.

Bryn went first with, "The woman at Nevarsin Tower, who is she?" *Whose voice did I hear on the gray plane?*

Martina said, "She is a great *leronis*, the Lady of Nevarsin. When she send to Guildhouse, she say that the need was urgent."

"Your turn now," Bryn said. "What would you like to know about us?"

"Which Zandru's demons possess you to camp in bandit stronghold?" Arliss blurted out.

Zandru? A local god?

"We had no idea they were there," Bryn said. "Our shuttle crashed high in the mountains, and we followed what we thought was the most direct route to a settlement."

"They are *Terranan*, as the Lady said," Martina explained to her companion. "That is why she speak odd accent and does not know what simplest child is taught." Turning back to Bryn she added, "You fought well for one not trained."

Bryn flushed, remembering the struggle and how close she had come to losing—and the fury that had engulfed her. All her life, she had been taught to express herself in nonviolent ways. And yet, that anger had saved her life. She was a survivor, not a victim.

"Better than most women," Arliss added.

"Tell me about this fellowship of yours," Bryn said. "You live apart from men, right? Forgive me, but that sounds so strange."

"We are *Comhi-Letzii*," Martina said, almost chanting the phrases, "women who, from Ages of Chaos—"

Ages of Chaos? There was so much here she didn't know!

"—freed ourselves from the rules of men. We renounce both their chains and their protection, so we call ourselves Renunciates. Even today, most women of the Domains—"

Felicity would have loved to hear this, but Bryn thought it better to let the old woman sleep. There would be time enough to tell her.

"—and *all* women in the Dry Towns," Arliss broke in, her tone emphatic.

"—live under the control of men. Be it from father, husband, lord, or the entire Comyn Council, few of us are free unless we make ourselves so. Is this not the case in your world?"

A denial leaped to Bryn's tongue. All her life, she had seen herself as independent. She'd been headstrong as a child, she'd studied what she wished, and she was a professional in her own right. Then she remembered how Leonin had taken charge of their mad flight from Terra. Perhaps she had not always been as self-reliant as she liked to believe.

"People behave differently under different circumstances," she said. "We are all more assertive at some times than others."

"We are as the gods have made us," Martina said. "Some women are good fighters—I am not among them, although I can hold my own well enough on the practice yards. Others have a talent for training animals or baking bread or arranging comfortable travel or any of a hundred ways of earning a living honorably." She paused, giving Bryn a curious expression. "What work do *you* do, beyond tending your father?"

"I am a therapist specializing in pediatric trauma recovery." Seeing the expression of incomprehension on both their faces, she explained, "I help children who have been damaged in their minds by war or natural disasters. You do not have such a profession here? If I had been a child and *that—*" with a tip of her head back in the direction they'd come, "—had happened, who would have helped me?"

"Your family," Arliss replied, "or if they could not, they bring you to Tower. *Leronis* there, she heal mind."

There was that word again, *leronis. A telepath who acted as a therapist?* She had to stop thinking in terms of Terran science. This was Darkover, a world that had developed its psychic abilities.

"When you meet the Lady, you will understand better," Martina said in a kind tone. "Now time to rest."

Breakfast the next morning was meat-laced porridge left over from dinner. Bryn was stiff and sore, and also hungry, as were her father and Felicity, which she judged to be a good sign. Devra, the cook that morning, smiled when they all asked for seconds. Everyone pitched in to scrub the pottery dishes and leave the cabin tidy for the next travelers. Brianna mounted Bryn on a horse today, the others rotating between horse and chervine, except for Ernst, who was too heavy for a chervine.

The day began clear, and the Renunciates sang as they rode. The melodies sounded vaguely Celtic to Bryn. She caught a phrase here and there, something about a couple newly in love, walking on the banks of a lake of clouds. The minor key made the song sound sad, as if a tragedy had befallen them.

Early on the fourth day, they reached the summit of Nevarsin Pass and dismounted to let the animals breathe. Before them, the trail descended between glaciated slopes. Nestled against one of these, as if carved from the snow itself, Bryn spotted a cluster of gray stone structures, the first permanent habitation she had seen on Darkover. Although distance blurred the outlines, it appeared to be a walled city.

"Nevarsin," Martina said. "The City of Snows. It's one of the oldest settlements on Darkover. 'Tis said to have been founded by St. Valentine himself, he for whom the monastery is named."

Felicity came to stand before them. "This is a splendid prospect, indeed. I had no idea that Darkover possessed religious communities. I'm afraid our cultural orientation was woefully inadequate."

Martina raised one eyebrow, eloquent. "Indeed?"

"We meant to learn more of your world and its customs before we arrived," Bryn explained.

"You speak well enough," Martina said.

It took the better part of the day to arrive at the gates of the city. Two guardsmen asked their business but stood back for them to pass after Martina said they were bound for the guild house. By this time, Ernst was holding on to the pommel of the saddle as if for dear life, and he answered in monotones when Bryn spoke to him.

"We're almost there, Father. Hold on just a little while longer."

They made their way down a steep cobblestoned street lined by two-story buildings with overhanging, stone-shingled roofs that almost touched in the middle. Lanterns glimmered on corner buildings, and orange lights glowed through windows of thick, dimpled glass.

With a moan, Ernst toppled sideways. Bryn jumped to the ground and ran to him. Martina, who had been walking beside his horse, caught him before he reached the cobblestones. Together they eased him to the ground.

"You there—and you—lend a hand!" Martina called out to a handful of men in the street.

"Where shall we take him, *mestra*?"

"The monastery, for he suffers from cold and fatigue." Without hesitation, the men swiftly carried Ernst away, disappearing up a street at the nearest intersection.

"He will receive the care he needs all the sooner this way," Martina said to Bryn. "Do not trouble yourself. The *cristoforos* know what they are about when it comes to injuries from cold."

"I should go with him," Bryn protested. "We must not be separated!"

"That is not possible, for they do not permit women within the premises, except in the Stranger's Room."

"How do we know those people will take him there? Anything could happen to him. They could rob him—hold him hostage—"

"Such things may be commonplace among the *Terranan*, who lack any pretense to honor. Here in the Hellers, folk do not betray one another so casually. The bandits you encountered were the exception, much to their sorrow. Your father is now under the protection of the monastery of St.-Valentine-of-the-Snows."

Bryn, catching the flash in Martina's eyes, remembered the swift deadliness of the fight with the bandits. There remained the question of where she and Felicity were to go. "What now? Will you take my teacher and me to the Lady of Nevarsin Tower?"

"Not quite yet. My sisters have long maintained a guild house—" she pronounced it as if it were one word, *Guildhouse*, "—here as in other major cities. We will inform the Lady of your arrival. Until she issues an invitation... I believe I promised you hot baths and soft beds?"

Despite her anxiety for her father, Bryn's spine melted at the prospect.

"Come then, for they await us."

The Guildhouse turned out to be a rambling, two-story structure of stone and wood, set back from the street behind a gated wall. After ringing the bell outside the gate, they were greeted by a young woman dressed in a belted tunic over loose trousers.

"Martina! Devra! Leeanne! We were beginning to worry—come in, come in!"

"Enough of your chatter," Martina said, her tone making it clear she was not displeased. "We are too hungry and tired for long stories. This is Bruna n'ha—I am sorry, I never inquired your mother's name."

"Tamryn."

"Bruna n'ha Tamara. And *Mestra* Felicia, a great scholar."

The Guildhouse courtyard was bounded on one side by a stable, with the house on the far side. Their greeter took the reins of the chervines and the horses, who practically dragged her toward the stable. Entering the house, Bryn and Felicity passed through a foyer of sorts, then a room with a huge fireplace that gave off waves of warmth. A woman with white hair, short-cropped like the rest of them, gave a series of orders regarding hospitality, a hot meal, and rest. In the bustle that followed, Bryn caught the phrases *dinner ready* and *which room* and something about her hair or her clothing, she couldn't tell which. She and Felicity were seated and offered steaming, aromatic tea.

"Martina has related much of your story and of course, we have been expecting you since receiving the Lady's message," said the older woman. "More must wait for when you have rested."

The tea tasted of licorice and honey and other herbs, a surprisingly delicious combination. Warmth spread through Bryn. Her vision sharpened and so did her thoughts.

"Now, I am Venezia n'ha Lauria, and I am the Nevarsin Guildhouse Mother."

"Martina used that term before, *n'ha*, but didn't tell me what it meant." Felicity asked, "Is it an honorific or a denoter of unmarried status?"

"None of us are married," Venezia said. "*N'ha* means *daughter of*, followed by the mother's name."

"Some Terran women still change their surnames on marriage—my mother did—but that's rare among professionals. I'd always thought of myself as a Haslund, my father's daughter."

"It is our custom to leave behind the name of any man, be it father, husband, or lover, and to be known only as our *mother's* daughter. Would you surrender your name to your husband, as if your life had no separate identity from his?"

"On Alpha, it is not the custom for either to change their name upon marriage," Felicity said. "In any event, it would be more likely that, given my established professional reputation, my husband would change his name to mine."

The question had never come up between Bryn and Leonin. *Leonin.* A pang shot through her. It had been days since she'd thought of him.

"Now then," said Venezia, "I presume you would like to wash away the grime of the trail. We have a freestanding bath house, or if you'd prefer a more private setting, I can arrange for a bucket of hot water, soap, and towels in your room."

"The bath house will suffice," Felicity said.

"Will you join us for dinner afterward? I can have a meal sent up."

"A communal meal sounds appealing. I have so many questions yet to ask. I hope you will also excuse me if I am too fatigued."

"That is understandable. You are not accustomed to travel under hard conditions."

Devra and a couple of her friends, including the young woman door guard, took Bryn outside to the bath house. It smelled of the sulfurous water that was piped into a wooden tub big enough for three or four. One had brought a lantern, which she hung from a hook inside the door. After stripping, Renunciates got in the tub with a good deal of splashing and giggling. Bryn couldn't help noticing how lean and muscular they were, like athletes.

She eased into the water and settled on the ledge. Her skin stung in a dozen places, every cut and scrape making its presence known. Within a short time, however, the stinging eased and the aching fatigue melted from her muscles.

Bryn was not especially modest by Terran standards, and the women seemed to have no inhibitions about nudity, yet she noticed the two younger women sneaking shy glances at her.

Devra, noticing the interaction, sent a splash of water at her friends. "Where are your manners? *Mestra* Bruna is our guest."

The young women hung their heads. Bryn couldn't make out their expressions, but she imagined them blushing. "Really, it's all right—"

"They should know better." Devra's tone was severe.

"Your accent *is* very strange," the door guard said. The other poked her in the ribs with an elbow, which occasioned a new round of splashing and giggling.

When Devra began to scold them, Bryn interrupted her. "I am pleased that you're relaxed enough to behave as if I were not here. I mean, as if I were one of you."

"It is good to see a new face," said Leonie, the other young woman. "I am newly sworn and still in my housebound year. And after that, I mean to go to Thendara and join the Bridge Society there."

"Will you join us on the training yard tomorrow, Bruna?" another woman asked.

"*Hist*, Doranne! Must I remind you yet again that she is our guest?" Devra said.

"Doranne just wants to show off for you," said Leonie. "She's *very* good. She could single-handedly hold the Guildhouse gates against a mob of drunken Dry Towners."

"Please, there is no offense," Bryn said. "Tomorrow I must inquire after my father. He's at the monastery, and I must also be ready for when the Lady of Nevarsin Tower can see me. But I am honored by the invitation and hope I will have the chance to observe your fighting techniques. I've already witnessed them in action. Did you tell them, Devra, about how Martina and the others rescued us?"

Devra told the story in dramatic fashion, drawing out every moment with details of exactly which fighting technique each Renunciate had used.

A communal dinner awaited them back at the house. A table had been set in the kitchen with baskets of thick-sliced bread, and platters of braised root vegetables and soft white cheese. Within minutes, everyone was seated on the benches and passing the serving dishes. Felicity, seated between Venezia and Leonie, was clearly making mental notes.

After the meal, Devra took a lighted candle and conducted Bryn up a stairway at the rear of the house. Felicity, apparently, had a room to herself, but Bryn was to share one.

"Zenia's off to visit her son in Temora," Devra explained, "so her bed's free."

The chamber itself was small, crammed with beds, chests, a huge wooden armoire, a pair of chairs, and a dresser on which sat an assortment of brushes, candlesticks, and what looked like knitted mittens and bits of harness. Devra rummaged in one of the chests and brought out a nightgown of thick flannel with a tracery of embroidery at the neck and cuffs. "It's a bit large, but it's warm. Zenia wore it when she was pregnant."

As she pulled off her clothing and donned the nightgown, Bryn made a mental note to tell Felicity that being a Renunciate didn't imply renouncing men. The bed, a pad over leather straps on a wooden frame, rustled as she settled under the comforter.

♦♦♦♦

16

♦♦♦♦

Bryn woke to brilliant sunshine and shivering cold. The single window in the room, high and narrow, was covered with oiled cloth that obscured the view outside but glowed as if ignited. The other two beds were unoccupied, the covers neatly arranged. A basin and ewer sat on the dresser, and a pile of folded clothing on the nearest chest; beside the chest stood a pair of worn boots lined with sheepskin. Much to her relief, there was also a chamber pot. From the courtyard below came women's voices, whooping and shouting.

Face splashed, dressed, and considerably more comfortable, Bryn made her way downstairs. The kitchen was empty, although a loaf of bread was laid out on a cutting board, along with pots of honey, jam, and soft cheese. Martina came in, took a mug from the stack on the drain board, poured herself a cup from the pot of *jaco* on the hearth, and sat down at one of the stools beside the table. Bryn followed suit. The *jaco* was surprisingly mild, and the bread was still warm and laced with chopped nuts. Bryn was on her second slice when Doranne came in, grabbed a slice, and left.

"Now then," Martina said when they were both sipping the last of their *jaco*, "I will take you to the Tower."

How did one greet someone of great stature after a desperation-fueled telepathic communication? *The same way you greet anyone else*, she answered herself. *With courtesy.*

"What about Felicity? May I bring her, too? I'm sure she has many questions for the Lady."

Martina gave Bryn a hard look, as if she'd broken an unspoken law. "The Lady's concern is with you only."

"I am here on Darkover on my father's account," Bryn began, then realized how that must sound to this woman who had redefined herself on her terms alone. Martina had abandoned the privilege and security of her father's house, or whatever her particular circumstances. She'd chosen to be known only as the daughter of her mother.

The voice in the gray plane, the voice of the Nevarsin Lady who had heard her silent screaming, that voice had spoken to her alone. Her own importance, her own destiny, emerged as separate from her father's or anyone else's. But in the end, it was her father, not she herself, who had the power to bring Nagy to account.

◆◆◆

Bryn followed Martina through the town to a tall building that looked to be part fortress and part lookout, with stone walls and heavy wooden doors. Martina knocked and the door swung open. A man about Bryn's age stood there. The first thing she noticed about him was his shoulder-length fiery red hair. He wore the kind of belted tunic over leggings she'd seen on the other men of the city and was of medium height and build.

"Martina n'ha Riva. You have returned." His gaze shifted to Bryn, his almost colorless eyes brimming with light. The air between them seemed to shimmer with the sheer force of his presence, quickly muted. "I am Desiderio of Serrano Heights, matrix mechanic."

"Bryn Haslund. Pleased to meet you."

The man stepped back, indicating for them to enter. "Welcome to Nevarsin Tower, Bruna Haslund of Terra."

These people are never going to get my name right. Bryn followed Desiderio inside, then Martina. If that were the worst misunderstanding she ran into, she'd count herself fortunate.

Desiderio led them through a narrow hall covered with wooden panels that would likely have ended up in a museum on Terra with their exquisite carving. The hall opened into a room in which a pair of chairs and a loveseat, all liberally strewn with cushions, were drawn up around a fireplace. Other seating and a couple of low tables occupied the rest of the room. Softly glowing globes set in wall brackets illuminated the space. They didn't look like solar lights, and Bryn couldn't imagine what else might power them or why the Renunciates didn't have similar conveniences.

An adolescent red-haired girl sat on the carpeted floor, feet tucked under her skirts, beside another girl and a boy a little older. The three were eating pastries, and the smell of honey hung in the air. They looked up as

Bryn and the others entered, then the second girl and the boy returned to their food while the redhead watched Bryn solemnly. Bryn supposed the people here didn't see many strangers. The feeling of being followed stayed with her after they had left the room.

Beyond the parlor, a winding staircase led upward. Tucked beside the base of the stairs was a narrow archway, the door itself so delicately carved it looked like an entrance to fairyland. Desiderio tapped on the door. A voice from within, recognizably feminine, called for them to enter. He lifted the latch and stood back.

Bryn stepped into a small but beautifully proportioned chamber, with every detail, from the mantelpiece of shimmering pink-white stone to the chairs and desk and sideboard, exactly right for the diminutive woman who sat in the central chair. Once Bryn's gaze met the woman's, she could not look away.

The woman was old, even accounting for the differences between planets and the lack of anti-aging treatments. Despite the snowy braids coiled low on her neck, her eyes were clear and intense. At one time she must have been an astonishing beauty. She wore a long dress of dark green and a shawl of a slightly lighter hue. Her slender hands lay still on her lap. Yet there was such a presence about her, such an aura of *authority*, that Bryn had no doubt she was in the presence of a person of immense, hard-won power, the Lady of Nevarsin.

Such a person clearly required a different protocol from the straightforward camaraderie of the Renunciates. Even Martina had referred to her with reverence. Bryn wished she'd asked about the proper mode of address, but it was too late now. She'd have to do the best she could, drawing upon her experiences meeting her father's colleagues. She adopted a politely neutral expression and waited for the Lady to make the first overture.

That piercing gaze flickered to Martina. "Thank you for delivering her safely. Hjalmar will arrange for the payment of your fee."

Martina inclined her head and left the chamber. Ah, so a formal bow was not expected.

"Please sit down," the Lady said in archaic but understandable Terran Standard. Making note of the language facility, Bryn sat.

"Pardon my poor manners. When one has achieved my age and when one is accustomed to speaking mind-to-mind, one loses facility with the accustomed phrases. My name is Alanna Alar. I am a *leronis*, that is, one trained in the use of *laran*, psychic ability. I have lived and worked here at Nevarsin Tower since shortly after your people left Darkover."

"Bryn Haslund, child psychologist."

"So you are the *Terranan* woman whose mind reached me across the vastness of space and then in the Overworld. I suppose you have no idea how unusual that is, even for those who are highly trained. It was a good thing I found you, or things could have turned out very badly. Our archives contain many tales of those who venture into that unliving land, searching for loved ones, never to return."

"I'm not here on my own behalf, but that of my father, Senator Ernst Haslund. I learned about your world's Project Telepath and came here in the hope that Darkover's psychics might help him."

Alanna touched the neckline of her gown, revealing a heavy copper filigree locket nestled between the folds of the shawl. "We know that extreme conditions can cause people, even ordinary folk with only the most rudimentary *laran*, to achieve feats far beyond their normal capacity. And for those who truly do possess the Gift, such events can catalyze their awakening. Tell me, have you felt ill since our mental contact? Difficulty eating or sleeping? Strange dreams? Visual distortions?"

"Thank you for your concern," Bryn said. "I assure you, I'm fine. It's not my health that concerns me but my father's."

"Hmmm. Perhaps you have escaped threshold sickness, or perhaps your Gift awakened at the usual time but the symptoms were diagnosed as something else."

"Your language and customs are new to me, so I ask your pardon if I behave inappropriately. Please understand that I mean no disrespect. At the same time, I might not have made myself sufficiently clear. Let me try again. Out here on the galactic arm, you've been shielded from the rise of the tyrant, Arthur Nagy. He's used increasingly brutal military force to subdue anyone or any world that defies him. My father is a statesman of immense stature, the only one capable of holding Nagy to account and restoring justice to the worlds of the Star Alliance. Now my father's mind is compromised. I believe the telepaths of Darkover represent our best hope of freeing him. That and that alone is why we have come here."

"Forgive me," Alanna said with a graceful inclination of her head. "I meant no discourtesy. You have been through a terrible ordeal and are unfamiliar with our ways. Let us begin again."

She was trying to be friendly, even though they'd had a rough start.

There were bound to be initial misunderstandings when it had been so long since their peoples had had any dealings, and those not the most harmonious. And she was one of the telepaths Bryn had come here to meet, a powerful one by all indications.

Alanna inclined her head and the young red-haired woman from the parlor entered, carrying a tray with a teapot, two elegant cups and saucers, and a plate of cookies. She set the tray down on the nearest table and departed, all without a word.

"It's not tea, at least not Terran tea," Alanna said as she poured out the steaming, honey-gold liquid. "No place on Darkover is warm enough, as I understand the requirements of the tea plants." She handed a cup and saucer to Bryn.

Bryn sipped the tea, which was unfamiliar but pleasant and settling to her stomach. She hadn't realized until then that she'd been slightly nauseated, for how long she wasn't sure. Alanna, for her part, sipped the tea while she ate a half dozen cookies. Bryn watched with astonishment that someone so slender could pack away so many sweets. It must be the climate and altitude, which might also explain her persistent queasiness.

"Now then," Alanna said, brushing the crumbs from her fingers, "it is clear that we have different priorities. Mine is my responsibility to you, a newly discovered, untrained telepath. Yours is to your father, about whom you are deeply troubled. Is that a fair summary?"

"Yes. I'm sorry if I sounded ungracious after you hired that troop of Renunciates to rescue us. None of us would have survived without them."

"I am glad of it. Those of us Gifted with *laran* are not so numerous that we can pass over a single potential. Allow me to propose a bargain. I will attend to your father's condition if you will permit me to test you and supervise whatever treatment or training I deem necessary."

Bryn shook her head. "I can't agree to either treatment or training, since I don't know what they might entail. I don't see the need for either. I came to consult with you, not to present myself as either a patient or test subject. But I'll go along with the evaluation as long as it does not delay my father receiving help."

"Then we are in accord." Alanna did not offer her hand to shake, which to Bryn suggested a taboo against touching among telepaths. "I understand your elderly father is presently in the care of the monks at St. Valentine's."

"I'm sure he's receiving adequate physical care, but I honestly don't know how much good prayer and hot food can do for his mind."

"Prayers and hot food can do a great deal. The monks are unusually skilled at treatment of exposure to cold."

"Of course, his physical health is important, but as I told you, he suffers from a malady of the mind. An impairment of will. My teacher and I rescued my father from the laboratory where this was done to him, and Nagy's agents have pursued us ever since. We don't have the resources to remove it, but when I read about Project Telepath, I believed that your natural telepathy might provide the solution. That is why we've come to Darkover."

"Mind control generated in a laboratory?" *Tell me tell me tell me...*

A weird reverberation gave the words an auditory aura like a shimmer of sound. Bryn blinked in surprise. Had those two words been spoken aloud? She gathered herself. "He's been subjected to a device that can alter brain waves and mood, even break down normal resistance to suggestion and create unthinking obedience. It's mediated through technology similar to what we use for rapid learning of languages, only in my father's case the device is implanted in his skull."

Despite Bryn's expectation that her words would mean nothing to the native woman, Alanna did not look at all confused. Her face hardened, revealing nothing of the emotions beneath. "And this...*device* then controls his behavior?"

"It does! When it's active, he barely knows who he is, let alone what he believes—used to believe."

Alanna turned even paler, so that her lips were no darker than her porcelain cheeks. The calm in her voice when she spoke was terrible. "This device *controls another person's mind*?"

"Yes. I saw it not only with my father, who went from being Nagy's most eloquent critic to supporting him unconditionally, but also with an entire mob. In that case, there was no direct contact between the device and the people, and the behavior was fairly basic. They just dispersed—who knows what they were thinking, if they were at all?"

"I had no idea the *Terranan* were capable of such barbarity," Alanna murmured, half to herself. "We always knew that many among them lacked all sense of honor, that they stooped to the use of Compact-forbidden weapons—coward's weapons that destroy everything they touch. But this, *this machine mind-control*, it goes beyond all decency."

Bryn could feel the Lady's abhorrence and visceral disgust in her own body. "I should warn you that our presence may bring Darkover to the attention of the Star Alliance. Nagy's agent tracked us from Terra to Alpha, where we found my father imprisoned in a secret laboratory. The captain who brought us here could not be sure we weren't followed. I'm sorry if we've put you at risk."

"No more risk than we have already survived, but I thank you for your candor. 'Tis a thing highly valued in the Domains. In fact, *the word of a Hastur* used to denote an unbreakable oath. Now I must see for myself what has been done to your father." Alanna rose with surprising vigor. "We of the Towers have resources for repairing damaged minds that go far beyond those of ordinary healers. If he can be returned to his true self, I will see it done."

This was exactly what Bryn had hoped for, but she did not have the chance to express her relief. The door swung open and the red-haired girl stood there.

"Adriana will see you to the Stranger's Parlor, where you will wait until your father has been transported here and we have had a chance to examine him," Alanna said. "You will be informed of our findings."

◆◆◆

Sunlight streamed through the mullioned windows of the Stranger's Parlor, a small room on the ground floor. A divan and two chairs filled the space, with knitted throws in bright colors folded over their backs. An array of foods and a couple of pitchers, one containing *jaco*, were laid out on the sideboard.

Bryn settled herself in the chair nearest the fireplace with a plate of pastry and a mug of *jaco*. The food tasted even better than it smelled. She felt as if she were inhaling its energy, replenishing everything the long, cold journey had drained. A sense of inner quiet and safety filled her, the certainty that here in this Tower, behind these strong walls, no hostile force—not the bandits, not Spaceforce, not Black, not even Nagy himself—could reach her.

Sounds outside the door brought her alert. She flung the door open. There, in the vestibule, stood her father, supported by two strong-looking men in the same rough woolen clothing she'd seen in the streets. Behind them, in the courtyard beyond the steps, she glimpsed a curtained sedan chair.

For a heart-stopping moment, his gaze slid aside, unfocused. Unrecognizing.

"Father!"

"Oh, it's you," he said in that same tone she remembered from the lab at Alpha, when his mind was still in the thrall of the theta-corticator. Desiderio, the red-haired man who'd first greeted her, emerged from the depths of the Tower.

"What is this place?" Ernst scowled at the sedan carriers. "And who are these people? What do they want with me? Don't they know I have important work to do?"

"You've been ill, don't you remember?" Bryn slipped her hand through his elbow. "The monks were taking care of you."

"Care? If you can call it that. Herbal potions and chanting. Superstitious nonsense, all of it. There's nothing wrong with me that getting back to work won't cure."

Desiderio gestured toward the stairs and said in heavily accented Terran Standard, "*Dom* Ernesto, if you would—"

"I would not! Not while the Alliance is in danger! Consp-p-piracies and sp-p-pies everywhere—First Minister N-N-Nagy needs my sup-p-p-port."

"Which is why you must recover as soon as possible," Bryn cut in, alarmed at the stuttering. Her father had always been a smooth orator, without any trace of speech impediment. Did this indicate further deterioration? "This place is a sort of hospital with specialists to help you."

"Doesn't look like a hospital to me."

"We're on Darkover now, Father. Cottman IV. Don't you remember the mountains where we landed?" Bryn led him toward the stairs. To her surprise, he came willingly. "It's a Lost Colony, so of course, everything looks different. But these people are highly skilled and Dr. Sage is here, too. So all will be well."

"Dr. Sage? Dr. Felicity Sage, who was your mentor? I remember her from Alpha. And the mountains. I remember..." He halted. Through her grasp of his arm, Bryn felt him tremble. He covered his eyes with his free hand. "I don't know what's wrong with me or if it's even possible I *can* be helped. It's as if I've become two different people, at odds with myself. Have I had a mental breakdown?"

The despair in his voice tore at her heart. She wanted to assure him that yes, he could and would be restored to himself, but she could not promise such a thing. She glanced away from her father to see Alanna standing in the doorway to her parlor, eyes filled with inner light. Bryn felt as if the Darkovan woman sensed her despair and answered it with a pulse of hope.

I reached her once, mind to mind. She had enough faith in that contact to send a rescue. And if that much is true, what else might be possible?

Bryn waited while her father ascended the stairs, pulling himself along by the handrail, managing one step at a time with painful dignity. Desiderio went with him, positioned to catch him should he lose his balance. After they turned a corner and were lost to sight, she turned back to Alanna, still standing in the doorway to her parlor. "What happens now?"

"Your father will be escorted to a psychically isolated chamber. What happens next—that is, how the examination and healing will proceed—is up to Adriana, our Keeper. She'll work closely with our monitor, Sylvie, and others in the circle, as she sees fit. You met both of them in the common room when you first arrived."

"I did, but both of them seem so young, barely more than children. On Terra, they'd still be in school."

"We do things differently here," Alanna said with a flicker of a smile. "Come, let's sit together again."

Bryn followed the older woman back into her parlor and sank into the same chair as before.

"From everything I have heard, the worlds of the *Terranan* prolong childhood dependency," Alanna said. "Not having traveled off-world myself, I cannot say. But here on Darkover, young people assume adult responsibilities as soon as possible."

Bryn's patients fared better with tasks that enhanced self-worth. Meaningful work was helpful in a variety of psychological disorders. But what jobs could children perform in the technologically developed worlds of the Alliance?

"Children here contribute from an early age," Alanna continued. "Every pair of hands is needed for survival. Comyn youth traditionally train in martial arts—sword skill, of course, and unarmed fighting, horsemanship, and the like. Perhaps it's not so much the case now. I don't know, I've been away from Thendara for a long time. But I think—" with a tilt of her head that gave Bryn an inkling what a lively young woman she must have been, "—that not much has changed, men being what they are."

"You mean, creatures ruled by their hormones and therefore given to violence? Isn't that a product of socialization and cultural expectations?"

"You *Terranan* regard sword fighting as barbaric. But how is a sword that brings the one who wields it into equal risk as his opponent less civilized than a blaster, which can kill not one but many at a time, while the person using it remains safe from harm?"

The fight at the lab—blasters firing wildly, the neural tangler in her hands, Leonin falling…

Spaceforce ships over Campta and Ephebe and Renney…the dust of cities, the ruin of forests...

The nightmares of those children who survived.

"There must be better ways to resolve differences than either a sword or a blaster," Bryn said.

"Perhaps we shall live to see such a world. In the meantime, each of us, *Terranan* and Darkovan, Comyn and commoner and Dry Towner alike, must live as best we can. And that means ensuring that weapons are never seen as toys or used lightly." She paused as if reflecting on a memory of personal darkness. "That is as true, if not more so, regarding the powers of the mind."

So we've come back to training. Alanna had brought the conversation around so naturally, Bryn was curious to hear more. "You mean *laran*?"

"Indeed," Alanna said. "Which is why those of us with the Gift must learn to use it in a disciplined manner. The powers of the mind are not parlor tricks to amuse the gullible but weapons capable of terrible destruction. We of the Towers have an old saying: *An untrained telepath is a danger to herself and everyone around her.*"

Does she mean me—or herself? Bryn flushed under Alanna's gaze. *She means both of us. That's why she feels so strongly about the matter, because she sees herself in me.* The longer she was in Alanna's presence, the stronger and more disturbing were such thoughts.

"So you see, we take a tale such as yours seriously. You spoke of a way of controlling the thoughts and actions of others that requires no discipline to earn it—a mechanical *laran*—" Alanna broke off with an expression of repugnance. The next moment, the previous icy calm settled over her features. "I will consider what you have said. Meanwhile, let us allow Adriana and Sylvie to do their work. Once they report their findings, we will have a better notion of how to proceed."

"After all we've been through, I don't think we should be separated. Should anything happen—I must be nearby in case my father needs me. He might experience another episode of disorientation and not know where he is or what's going on. In the past, I've been able to talk him through those. And I can't abandon my teacher, Dr. Felicity Sage, even though no doubt she's happily studying the customs of the Renunciates. I understand that women are not permitted at the monastery. Does this Tower have guest quarters that would accommodate all three of us?"

"It does not. The work we do requires a place apart from ordinary minds."

Bryn felt as if the walls of the Tower were closing in on her. If she were here, her father at St. Valentine's, and Felicity at the Guildhouse, and something were to go wrong—

"I will secure suitable accommodations for your father and your teacher together, if that is what you wish," Alanna went on. "*You* are another matter. I have fulfilled my part of our bargain. Now it is time for you to honor yours. You agreed to permit me to test your *laran*."

"I did," Bryn admitted. "But I didn't agree to live here."

"If you were an ordinary, head-blind commoner, it would never be mentioned. Everyone would be more comfortable if you stayed somewhere else. But comfort is not the issue here."

"Are you reading my mind?"

"No, *chiya*, I assure you I would never do such a thing without your leave. We of the Towers take an oath to never enter the mind of another except to heal, never to harm, and then only with permission. I have... personal reasons to regard that oath as binding. But you and I have been in—I do not know the *Terranan* word. We call it *rapport*. We have been *in rapport* since you first reached out to my mind. I have the training to shut off the connection, but I did not do so, not when your life and those of your companions depended upon it. And now that I know more about why you are here and what has befallen your father, it would be irresponsible of me, a breach of honor, if I were to abandon you just at the time your Gift is awakening."

"I don't understand any of this. I'm not psychically gifted."

"Perhaps you *were* not, but now? How else do you explain what happened between us?"

"I just— I can't. I heard your voice in the gray plane as clearly as I do now. I've been able to sense danger, even when I saw no rational cause. But until a month ago, I didn't believe telepathy existed. What if those experiences were caused by stress and will never recur?"

"Let us err on the side of caution," Alanna said in an encouraging manner. "If you do have *laran*, I fear what might happen if it should manifest further when you are among those without the skill to help you."

"I appreciate your concern," Bryn said, hearing the stiffness in her own voice. "I'm sorry, but I don't know you and you don't know me, either. You don't know what I've been through. To me, the greater risk lies in being separated from my own people. However, I did agree to the testing. If you will kindly help us find lodgings together, I will make myself available."

Alanna remained silent for a long moment, her expression fading into the same unreadable mask as earlier. She looked visibly older than earlier, as if the effort of maintaining control had overtired her. "Very well, it shall be as you wish. But you must send word at the slightest difficulty. It's unusual for an adult to experience threshold sickness, but it's not a thing to be taken lightly."

After Bryn agreed to these terms, Alanna left her in the Strangers Parlor for what seemed like hours. Finally, Alanna returned to say that a nearby inn had prepared rooms for them.

"Adriana performed a preliminary analysis of the device implanted in his brain and temporarily blocked its action," Alanna added.

Bryn exhaled in a rush of relief. "That's excellent! When can I see him?"

"He's resting now but will be ready to be transported to the inn soon. We will arrange for a sedan chair. But our measure is only a respite, not a cure. We may not be able to accomplish more. We have never developed such devices, and while a working circle can move small masses, doing so within a living human brain may prove too delicate a matter to risk. Repairing damaged blood vessels, even in the brain, or removing tumors, these things we know how to do, but they involve restoring normal physiological function, not extracting a piece of metal. For that, you might need a larger, more skilled circle, and for that, you would have to go to one of the major Towers, Arilinn or Hali, even Comyn Tower in Thendara."

"But he's stable for now?" Bryn repeated.

"He is." With that, Alanna departed.

Ernst didn't appear distressed by the treatment he'd received. If anything, he looked more robust. His posture conveyed a renewed vigor, and his eyes were clear.

"I'm so glad to see you looking more like yourself," she said after a long hug.

"Don't trouble yourself about me, sweetheart," he said. "I feel more myself than I have in some time. They tried to explain it to me, but between the glitch in my brain—" he touched one of the implanted electrodes, "—and the local idioms, I failed to discern what they were talking about. Psychic powers or some such."

"*Laran*, it's called. I don't understand it, either."

The chair arrived and they proceeded along the narrow, cobbled streets. It had been late afternoon when the Terrans and their Renunciate escort arrived in Nevarsin. Tired and distracted, Bryn remembered little beyond the steepness of the streets and the overhanging roofs. Now her attention was drawn by the people: women swathed in shawls and voluminous skirts, men in sheepskin jackets, here and there a cloaked and hooded figure on a tall horse, a cart drawn by two oversized chervines, and an occasional, fleetingly glimpsed furred shape. As they passed through an open market square, she inhaled the smells of roasted meat, incense, and savory herbs.

The inn was a short way beyond the market, a brightly painted, two-story wooden structure. The sedan chair carriers set Ernst down and withdrew, bowing. Bryn and her father entered a large common room paneled in rough wood, with tables and a long bar set with pottery jugs. A robust, gray-haired woman emerged from a door at the far end of the bar, carrying a tray stacked with dishes. The brisk, no-nonsense manner with which she approached them reminded Bryn of the Renunciates.

"Ah! Be the strangers wanting rooms, yes?" She was missing several front teeth, and her heavy accent took Bryn a moment to understand.

"Yes. Alanna—the Lady of Nevarsin—sent us."

"Bags aloft already. Two rooms, meals, all set. Ah, and the *mestra* just arrive. Stair's there," with a jerk of her head. "Go on up."

Bryn and her father exchanged glances. She shrugged, indicating, *Maybe that's the way things are done here*, and he nodded, *We'll figure it out.*

They went up the stairs, which were dark and narrow by Terran standards. At the top was a short corridor with only two doors, one along the side and the other at the end, which was open, revealing Felicity, notebook in hand.

"My dears, I'm so glad you're here! This place is amazing, is it not? So reminiscent of pre-industrial Terra! Ernst, come and sit in this chair. They've given us adjoining rooms, did the innkeeper tell you? She's the most extraordinary character—I must interview her. My stars, I'm speaking too fast, aren't I?"

"Yes, you are," Bryn replied with a smile. Felicity's excitement was so *normal.*

The room itself was airy and pleasant, although narrow. The center was occupied by their piled possessions. There were two wooden-frame beds covered by faded comforters, a table with an ewer and basin, and a couple of chairs, one of which Ernst settled into. A door at the far end stood open, leading to a second room of about the same size but with only one bed. Clearly, these were places to sleep, not live.

Felicity insisted on examining Ernst, but without instruments she could not determine what had been done to him. "If anything," she muttered. "Of course, any perceived improvement could be part of a cycle of remission and exacerbation…"

The three set about dividing their baggage, placing Ernst's in the single room. By the time they'd finished, Ernst was fading. Bryn fetched a pitcher of water and a mug from the bar and left him dozing.

Felicity was too excited to remain indoors, so she and Bryn ventured forth. The rest of the afternoon was spent exploring the immediate neighborhood. Often they stopped to gaze awestruck at the soaring, snow-draped peaks of the Hellers.

"It's hard to believe we made it through those," Bryn said.

"And, from what I have been able to deduce, we are still quite high up compared to other areas." They stopped before an apothecary's shop and Felicity drew out the map she'd sketched from the data tab.

"It looks like we landed here," Felicity indicated an approximate area, "based on its proximity to Nevarsin Pass and the city itself. Not that this constitutes a city by Alliance standards, but it appears to be quite ancient, a millennium or more. Venezia at the Guildhouse referred to it as one of the oldest settlements on Darkover. Half the buildings appear to have been carved out of the mountain itself, and the other half constructed out of the rock removed in the process. Oh, and have you seen any of the nonhuman races? There appear to be several, of various degrees of sapience. *Kyrri, cralmacs*...I don't recall the others."

"Speaking of maps, it would be good to have one of the city. I was so worried about Father when we arrived, I didn't get a good sense of its layout. Do you think you could undertake it while Father and I return to the Tower for his treatments?"

"I'm perfectly capable of escorting him, and I would very much like to investigate the buildings and their inhabitants. Do you know that the tower is said to have been constructed using psychic powers? What a fascinating myth!"

"I don't think it *is* a myth." Bryn started walking in the general direction of their inn. "We know very little about what Darkovan *laran* can do. I met the most extraordinary woman, the one Martina called *The Lady of Nevarsin*. Her name's Alanna Alar, and she's old enough to remember the departure of the Federation."

"Extraordinary, indeed. I must interview her, too."

"I'm not sure how she would take such a request. She's rather...I suppose you'd say, *dignified* or *reclusive*, for that."

"I presume you have an explanation for why *you* are granted an interview but *I* would not be."

Bryn stepped aside as a string of heavily laden chervines and their handler, a pre-adolescent boy, passed by. "She's convinced I have *laran*, the Darkovan psychic talent, and that my health is at risk because of it."

"And is she correct?"

"I'm not sure. I don't know. I feel well, given everything we've been through." She was about to list the reasons why Alanna was right about her having *laran*, but Felicity might start offering rational explanations for the voice in her mind, her danger-sense, and everything else. It was simpler to say, "At any rate, I agreed to allow her to test me, so the next time Father goes back, I'll go with him."

"I'll have plenty to study," Felicity said. "I do wish I had a tri-vid recorder, though."

"These people have been cut off from Terran culture for a long time," Bryn said. "The Renunciates, the monks, the Tower telepaths, they all have different customs. I wish we hadn't lost access to the data tab. So far we've been fortunate in not creating serious misunderstandings, but we can't count on our luck holding. The more we learn about these people and their expectations, the better our chance of success."

"Indeed. It is likely that we fared well with the Renunciates because of their straightforward communication style. They offer women a non-traditional community, which says much about women's roles and status.

From what you've said about Lady Nevarsin, she falls into neither of those categories."

At the inn, they found Ernst in the common room, looking much better as he ate a stew of root vegetables braised with shreds of meat. The innkeeper emerged from the kitchen with two more bowls, accompanied by a basket of crusty bread.

"Thank you," Bryn said, looking around for eating utensils. She spied a pair of women in the ubiquitous shawls and full skirts at a nearby table, using spoons of horn or antler. Ernst held out his, carved of similar materials. Without a word, the innkeeper left them and came back with two more, scratched but still serviceable.

"Customers generally bring their own," Ernst remarked. "Two meals a day come with our rooms. The innkeeper wouldn't hear of taking payment, not that we have local currency. I'm not sure whether the Tower paid for us or it's a courtesy to them. From everything I can see, the *leroni*—the Tower sorcerers, and most notably the Lady—are held in almost superstitious awe. Pass the bread while it's still hot."

Bryn had seen the reverence with which Alanna Alar was held. If the Tower had been built using *laran*, that was even more cause to respect its power.

◆◆◆

The next morning, Ernst appeared in good spirits to get out and explore. Bryn was anxious about him overtaxing his strength or somehow negating the benefits of the Tower healing. Felicity wanted to return to the apothecary shop, which interested neither Bryn nor her father, so they set out by themselves.

As the hours passed, a sense of disquiet grew in her mind, vague and unformed. She glanced around as they went on, although she saw nothing even remotely threatening. The weather was fine, and the people seemed to be friendly.

Just as they were about to head back to the inn, a dark, fleeting shape flitted through the edge of her vision and disappeared around a corner. Her pulse sped up. *Black? But how could he be here?* She whirled around and darted in the direction she'd seen it. This led to a blind alley between two buildings, more an alcove than the end of a street. It was empty of everything except a wooden planter containing a straggle of gray-leaved succulents.

Ernst caught up with her. "What is it, sweetheart?"

"I thought I saw—never mind. I was mistaken. Are you too tired to walk back?"

"I'm a little tired, yes, but those meat skewers at the crossroads we just passed smelled appetizing. I believe I could eat a portion."

"But we don't—" Perhaps the vendor would be willing to accept something in trade. She wasn't sure what, but she had taken her satchel as they left, out of old habit, and surely there must be some bit of Terran origin that would suit. "Yes, let's do that."

When they arrived at the cart of the meat skewers, the vendor would not hear of payment. The woman, young and red-cheeked, smiled broadly as she handed over the food. "Oh no, *mestra, mestre.* 'Tis an honor. When folks hear as you give us favor, they'll all want the same."

It seemed ungracious to refuse. The meat was not beef but a bit like venison, marinated and then quickly cooked so the interior of each chunk was juicy. Ernst ate all of his and one of Bryn's, which she decided was a good sign. Every time they stopped to admire a leather belt, a woven shawl, or a pottery bowl, or to smell the savory spices or honey-nut aroma of pastry, the merchants urged their goods upon the Terrans, saying how much honor it would bring them. It was all Bryn could do to usher her father back to the inn, although they got turned around and lost their way twice. He was flagging, and her belly was unsettled. She put it down to unfamiliar food.

The next day, Ernst slept in. Bryn felt faintly nauseous and remembered that Alanna had asked about that particular symptom. Otherwise, she would have thought it was due to the stress of mountain travel and too much animal protein. She ate lightly, mostly bread and fruit, thinking to ease the load on her stomach. But the day after that, her father was noticeably confused again and her symptoms were no better. *Just give it time,* she told herself. When a messenger from the Tower arrived, inviting him to a second session, she accompanied him.

As before, Ernst was escorted up the stairs. Alanna was not available, so Bryn waited in the Stranger's Parlor. An adolescent boy brought in a pot of herbal infusion. Bryn sipped it, relaxing in the warmth and calming effects of the herbs. If only Leonin were here to share it...

Leonin.

His face rose up in her mind, the way the lines around his eyes crinkled when he smiled, the warmth of his voice, the tenderness when he touched her.

Suppressed grief.

Ever since that day in Terra Central, Bryn had been running from one crisis to another without a chance to process her emotions. She'd seen the same thing in her young patients. Many had barely escaped with their lives. Some were the only survivors of entire families or villages. They'd shut down emotionally, sometimes to the point of being unable to speak. It took time, but under skilled professional care the frozen state melted, the dam broke, and the children began to feel again.

"*Mestra* Bruna—" Alanna stood there, one hand still on the latch of the door. "I apologize for interrupting your meditation. Shall we begin our testing?"

Bryn felt unsettled from the spasm of grief, but her memories of Leonin were too tender, too private, to speak aloud. *Better to get the testing over with. Maybe my lack of focus will result in failure.*

Alanna took a seat opposite Bryn and held out one hand. Her fingers hovered over the bare skin of Bryn's wrist. The other hand cupped a ball of blue light. "If I may—?"

Bryn's instinctive reaction was to flinch away, to retreat, but she sensed that Alanna would not touch her without her consent. What had Alanna said earlier?

An oath to never enter the mind of another except to heal, never to harm, and then only with permission.

Throat dry, Bryn managed a nod. The touch was butterfly-light, the fingertips, cool. For a long moment, nothing happened, just that evanescent pressure and her body rocking with the force of her pulse. Almost imperceptibly, her vision went hazy. Not white like mist but pale, pale blue. The mist thickened, brightening moment by moment until the room faded.

She was floating in a sea of blue light.

The strangest thing was how readily her mind accepted what was happening as good and natural. Her sense of time faded into relief at how *safe* she felt. Nothing could reach her in this endless light. Nothing could harm her.

The light gradually fell away, or perhaps she emerged from it, rising like a dolphin from the depths.

Alanna held out a goblet. "Drink this."

Bryn took a sip, and then another. The liquid was cool and slightly lemony.

"I'm sorry to be a bother," Bryn said, clambering to her feet, "but could I trouble you for something to—ooh!" She broke off as the room tilted sideways. She fell back into her chair.

Sylvie arrived with a platter heaped with pastries glistening with honey and studded with dried fruit. Ordinarily, Bryn would have turned her nose up at such sticky sweets, but now the aroma made her mouth water. She took one and nibbled a corner. As soon as the concentrated sweetness hit her tongue, she gobbled the whole thing in just a couple of bites. Another followed, and two more after that. Finally, her gorge rose at the smell.

"Ugh. I've never eaten so much sugar at one sitting in my life." She stared at her fingers, coated with crumb-sprinkled honey. "Not even when I was a child."

Alanna chuckled. "That's the case with many of us. Honey is costly to produce, and sugar is a *Terranan* delicacy. We can grow beets, although our local varieties are not high in sugar. But *laran* work is energy-intensive, and we must replenish those resources."

"I believe you are jumping to conclusions. What I experienced was an episode of delayed grief. The blue light is likely a metaphor for recovery."

"You have no cultural context for understanding *laran*, that is all. You were brought up in ignorance of your Gift. Did I not make myself clear earlier?"

"You mean about our mental contact?"

"That, and a not inconsiderable degree of precognition."

My danger-sense?

Tell me.

Haltingly, Bryn described her danger-sense from her earliest awareness, a mere prickle, to insistent near-panic. Alanna was such a good listener that Bryn went on to describe the sinister, fleetingly glimpsed figure. Alanna nodded as if it all made sense. Maybe on this world, it did.

"You have most likely been experiencing threshold sickness, which often accompanies the awakening of *laran*," Alanna said. "Among us, this happens most often with the stirring of sexual energy during puberty. It can be severe and debilitating, sometimes fatal. Over time we have learned how to treat the worst symptoms, so we no longer lose our young people. *Kirian* helps," with a nod to the goblet that Bryn had set on the table. "It's distilled from the flowers of the *kireseth*."

"I'm sorry, I don't know what that means."

"*Kireseth* is a flowering plant that grows throughout the region. Its pollen is psychoactive and quite dangerous, but it can be distilled into useful compounds. Unseasonable warmth produces widespread flowering, resulting in a Ghost Wind, with mass hallucinations, loss of inhibitions, and orgiastic behavior. That can still be a danger to travelers, as it was to our earliest ancestors. Some speculate that the origin of the Comyn—the aristocratic caste, with the highest frequency and strength of *laran*—lies in the mating of those human settlers with telepathic *chieri* during those Ghost Winds. That makes more sense to me than the story of how we are all descended from Hastur son of Aldones, Lord of Light, and his human bride."

Bryn felt as if her head were spinning. "Okay, enough about *laran* and your nobles. What is *chieri*?"

"They're one of Darkover's intelligent nonhuman races, very old and once space-faring. They're extremely rare now, although every generation or two, someone encounters one."

"I think I saw one of those alien—excuse me, nonhuman—races. It was furred, but no one took much notice of it."

"A *kyrri*, most like."

Perhaps that's the shadowy form I saw and not my anxiety about Black acting as a shadow on my mind.

"As for you," Alanna went on, "it is clear that you do have *laran*. I agreed to test you only, but as a result of what I saw, I urge you to reconsider. If you leave here now, I fear your *laran* will be a danger to you. You are welcome to remain while you learn to master your Gift."

"To study with you?"

"Study a little. And rest, knowing you are safe. This Tower is a sanctuary. I came here many years ago, seeking refuge mostly from myself. As a child, I was never taught self-discipline. So when my Gifts awoke, well—it was only by the most extraordinary luck that I did not bring more sorrow to those who loved me than I did. Here I learned to trust myself by *becoming* trustworthy."

In Alanna's words, Bryn heard the voice of a young woman, still a child, at odds with herself and horrified by what she had done and might yet do. If Alanna had still been that child and had been entrusted to her therapeutic care, she would have known how to respond. The mature woman facing her was another matter. "Why are you telling me this?"

"Perhaps so that you can be sure I speak from the heart and not an arbitrary set of rules. We mean you only good, Bruna of Terra. Will you trust us? Will you trust *me*?"

For a long moment, Alanna held Bryn's gaze. The light in the eyes of the *leronis* reminded Bryn of the sea of blue radiance. It felt as if she'd been running and hiding and running some more for a long time. But her father wasn't well yet, and there were practical matters to consider.

"I will try—but on two conditions."

One fine brow arched upward. "And they are?"

"As I said before, I am responsible for two other people. I brought them here to Darkover and I cannot just abandon them to their own devices. I need to consult with my father and my teacher before agreeing."

"While I respect your duty to your kin, you must not allow a false sense of obligation to interfere with what is necessary to preserve your health. They are *Terranan* and cannot understand the risks of untrained *laran*."

"I will make up my own mind, but I insist on speaking with them first."

"Very well. And the second?"

"That you call me by my proper name, not Bruna but Bryn."

"Bryn is a *Terranan* name and as long as you hold to your allegiance there, that must be your name. But should the time come when you see your heart belonging to Darkover, you will become Bruna in truth."

To this, Bryn had no answer.

◆◆◆

When Bryn escorted her father back to the inn, Felicity was still out, exploring and investigating. It wasn't until later, when night had fallen—no, draped itself like a diamond-studded velvet blanket over the city—that all three of them sat together over bowls of bean soup and toast. They ate in the common room, with the gentle murmur of other conversations in the background. Felicity had a host of observations about how Darkovans of various socioeconomic classes greeted one another, although these did not include either the Tower people or the monks.

Bryn related what had happened earlier in the day, ticking off the evidence for her having *laran*. Her father nodded from time to time.

"My dear, you must look after your well-being," he said. "If I had not experienced the unorthodox techniques of these people for myself, I might hesitate to recommend it to you, but as it is…"

"What a marvelous opportunity to study the Tower procedures from the inside," Felicity began.

"I'm sure it is, but that's not why I've been invited. If the first test is any indication, I wouldn't be able to explain it to you, anyway. Despite the translator programs, there's still so much we don't have a vocabulary for."

"I'm sure there will be ample opportunity to interview them once you are done with your testing and Ernst has received the maximum benefit from their psychic healing," Felicity said. "Meanwhile, you must not worry about us. The innkeeper here takes excellent care of us, and I do not anticipate a single moment of boredom, I assure you!"

That sounded so exactly like Felicity at her most scientifically curious, Bryn could not resist a smile. "I'm glad to hear it. There are things we need to do here, yes, but what then? Just because there are inexhaustible sources of interest—I'm not saying this very well. Nevarsin—and Darkover itself—is just a waystation, a place to restore Father's mind and sort out whatever's going on with me. It's not a permanent home. Do you follow me? The end of our journey is not here. It's back on Terra, with Father in full possession of his faculties."

Ernst looked troubled. "What if that is impossible? What if this—" with a gesture at himself, "—is the best I can hope for?"

"We will deal with that *if* it happens," Bryn said. "Meanwhile, Nagy is extending his autocratic rule over more planets, and that snake Black is out there. We must never forget our enemies, as they will not forget us."

"Well spoken!" Ernst exclaimed. "If the worst should come, I nominate you to take my place."

"I am no politician, as you know, Father." Bryn laid her hand upon his arm. "So I have both of your agreements to study at the Tower, if only temporarily?"

"You need not ask, after making such a compelling argument," said Felicity.

◆◆◆

"You're to room with me," Sylvie told Bryn upon her return to the Tower. "I'm so pleased! We have more than enough space for each of us to have our own chamber, but since you are new to us, Adriana thought it best that you not be alone. There's an entire closet of extra clothing and bedding."

Bryn had no idea what to say to any of this. She didn't mind sharing a room, not after the variety of sleeping accommodations during her flight here. The younger woman's effusiveness was so good-hearted, they might become friends.

Sylvie led the way up the narrow, spiraling stairs. Luminescent globes cast a chill, gray light. At the top, she threw open a door, stepped inside, and twirled around, holding out her hands in welcome. "My abode!"

Bryn's first impression was a riot of warm, vibrant colors. Woven hangings covered the paneled walls, and a carpet in shades of garnet and lapis cushioned her feet. Furnishings included an armoire, a sideboard or credenza on which sat a basin and ewer, and two beds laden with pillows and comforters quilted in equally bright shades, with chests at the foot of each. While there was plenty of floor space, there was an equal lack of privacy.

"Which—?" she murmured.

"Blessed Cassilda! What am I thinking?" Sylvie gestured to the right-hand bed, carefully avoiding touching Bryn. "Here, this one is yours. You must be exhausted—and famished! *Domna* Alanna said you'd had a bout of threshold sickness yesterday. How dreadful, and at your age! Are you dizzy? Nauseated? Here, lie down and I'll monitor you."

"I'd like to *just* lie down, thank you."

"Oh!" Sylvie flushed, then turned pale. "I've been terribly rude. Your pardon, *mestra*. It's just that—the people from your world may not be familiar with threshold sickness, but here on Darkover we take it very seriously." Her hands balled into fists at her sides. "I am the circle monitor and therefore am responsible for your well-being, quite apart from us sharing a room. I'm sorry if I offended you with my enthusiasm at meeting my first *Terranan*. I will try to be more restrained in the future. I will leave you in solitude if that is what you wish, but only on the condition that if you experience any further symptoms, no matter how fleeting, you will report them to me."

Bryn stared at her, unable to think what to say.

"Do I have your word?" Sylvie said in a tone that meant she expected a solemn promise.

If that's what it takes to get a little peace and quiet... "You have it."

After Sylvie left, Bryn lay down on the bed that was to be hers. It was surprisingly comfortable, a thick comforter of down or some other feathers, over a mattress that had just the right combination of softness and firmness.

Instead of getting relaxed, however, her muscles felt more tense. She couldn't lie still although the bed was perfectly comfortable. Finally, she threw back the comforter and sat up, thinking that moving about the room might help. Before she could swing her feet onto the floor, trembling seized her entire body. A frigid wind blasted her skin and a metallic taste filled her mouth. Sweat broke out on her face and hands.

Help, I should call for help. Her jaw muscles clamped shut. She gasped for air through her clenched teeth, but could not draw a full breath.

Alanna! Sylvie—?

A jolt of electricity shot from her feet to the top of her head. She tried to lift her arms and legs but could not move them, could not even feel them. Abruptly, a thousand butterflies flew out of her chest, each one taking away a bit of her mind. The pieces hung in the air, slowly drifting apart. They glittered as if they were bits of metal foil or tiny gemstone shards. Of all her senses, only vision remained, moment by moment growing dimmer.

Chill brought her back to herself. Sight returned. She was lying on the floor in a tangle with no memory of how she'd gotten there. She was trembling again, only this time with the cold. Her head ached; touching the back of her skull, she felt a tender lump. Groaning, she managed to roll over onto her side. Her stomach rebelled. She retched dryly and groaned again.

The door flew open and Sylvie dashed into the room, closely followed by the young man from the parlor on the day of her arrival.

"No, don't move," Sylvie said, pushing Bryn down when she tried to rise. "Ramon-Luis, the comforter, if you please. And two pillows."

Together the two Tower workers swaddled Bryn in the comforter after placing a pillow under her head and another supporting her knees. Bryn couldn't tell if her eyes were open or not, for everything she saw was in constant motion, elongating one moment and shrinking in the next. Colors took on an eerie, surrealistic glow and voices echoed sickeningly. She wished they would go away and leave her in peace, leave her to drift...

"Bruna! Bruna, stay with us!" Flashes of blue light accompanied the words, as bright as the voice was urgent.

The rim of a cup pressed against her lower lip. "Drink."

"Go 'way!" Bryn snarled, flailing out with her hands. Someone grabbed them and held her fast.

"It's *kirian,*" said the same irritatingly persistent voice. "You've had it before. It will do you good."

"Nnnnn—" Bryn threw her whole body from side to side, as best as she was able against the restraining hands. *Don't want!*

You idiot girl! Can you not tell when someone is trying to save your life? This masculine voice was different from the one before, echoing with painful loudness inside her skull. It insisted, over and over, in words that battered her until surely her brain must be bruised and bleeding, until she opened her lips. She felt the hard curve of the cup. Lemon-tinged liquid rushed into her mouth and she swallowed.

Again! The voice would not let up until she had gulped and gulped. With each swallow, a little more of the fight went out of her. Warmth spread out from her belly along channels like nerves but not quite. She had the sensation that her usual physical body had dissolved and left in its place a network of glowing threads joined by nodes like miniature suns. Here and there, the suns were red and sullen like dying stars, and the threads connecting them pulsed in shades of purple and brown.

Out there, somewhere in space, Nagy was hunting her...

DangerDANGERDanger!

"Seizure," someone said, the voice distorted as if from the end of a long tunnel.

"Not over the worst," someone else said.

Sleep, said the voice that had commanded her to drink.

She slept.

◆◆◆

Bryn jolted awake to find herself propped up on pillows and buried under mounds of comforters. The light was all wrong. Her body didn't belong to her. She recognized the person holding out a spoonful of something steaming and nauseating-smelling: Adriana, looking too somber for her youth. She might have been all of twenty.

Bryn made a pushing-away motion with her hands. "Take it away. I don't want it."

"You must eat. It will help your symptoms."

Oh! Threshold sickness? Dimly she remembered Alanna saying that could be fatal. "I've been ill?"

With a grim expression, Adriana set the bowl and spoon aside. "You are *still* ill. I am trying to help you. We all are. I know that you have not been brought up with any understanding of *laran* or respect for the expertise that we of the Towers have."

As Adriana spoke, her words began to echo. The effect intensified Bryn's nausea, so she felt increasingly disoriented. She wished the young woman would go away and leave her alone. Closing her eyes, she turned her head away. The movement sent her whirling through space, falling into a sea of surging, rusty tides.

◆◆◆

"But a *Terranan*—" came a man's husky voice. *Desiderio*?

"We have no choice," a woman said, "if she is to live." *Adriana*?

◆◆◆

Light. Blue and piercing. A million glittering shards of light.

◆◆◆

"Take this," the echoing voice commanded.

The light dropped into her palm and kept going downDOWNdown, dragging her along with it. Together they fell, she and the light, into the endless void. The light wrapped itself around her as if it were a lock and she were the key.

Bryn could not remember being so hungry. Her entire body craved food. Other than that, she felt surprisingly well as she slid out of bed, wrapped the topmost comforter around her shoulders, and padded over to the nightstand. The light slanting through the narrow window offered few clues as to the time of day, but she thought it must be late morning or early afternoon, not sunset. A pouch of silky material hung around her neck on a braided thong. She decided it would be wiser to not antagonize her hosts by removing it.

Underclothing included a chemise of a fabric she didn't recognize but that slid over her skin like silk. Over this went a full skirt and long-sleeved woolen dress, belted at the waist. In the chest she found socks, clearly hand-knit, and suede ankle boots, also a shawl knitted in an intricate cable pattern.

She followed the smells of baking bread and *jaco*, and after a number of wrong turns discovered the kitchen. No one else seemed to be around, so she helped herself to thick slices from the loaf on the cutting board, found a pot of jam, poured herself a mug of *jaco*, and settled on one of the stools beside the table. Finally, when she'd finished a third slice of bread and all the jam, she become aware that she was not alone.

Adriana stood in the doorway. "Shall we begin?"

Bryn followed the younger woman up the stairs, past the level of her shared bedroom. Adriana opened a door at the next landing. As soon as Bryn stepped inside, a profound sense of stillness enveloped her.

"This chamber is telepathically isolated," Adriana said. "In this way, we can perform delicate *laran* work without the risk of either disturbing others or being distracted, ourselves." She led Bryn to the central round table, where they sat facing each other. "We will now begin our lessons in the use of your starstone."

"Excuse me, my what?"

Adriana touched her own locket. "They're also called matrix stones, psychoactive gems used by individuals Gifted with *laran*. They don't create *laran*, but they do enhance—focus—it. You were given one. Before going further, I must ascertain whether you are keyed into it properly."

Bryn fumbled with the drawstring of the silken pouch. A crystal tumbled into the palm of her hand, translucent blue except for the very center, where a twist of brightness was suspended between the facets. The point of contact with her skin flared, so intense and unexpected that she almost dropped it. Without conscious thought, she curled her fingers around it. The burst of energy faded, or perhaps melded with her skin...flowing along her nerves...infusing her blood, her bones, the very fiber of her being...

Exactly so, said a silent voice with the stamp of Adriana's personality.

Bryn glanced up, astonished. "I heard you—was that telepathy?"

"Indeed," Adriana replied with a smile. Bryn noticed then that she held a similar gem, a nugget of blue-white fire. "No, don't look at my stone. It's keyed to my mind, not yours. And another thing, before we go any further: You must never let anyone handle your stone, except your Keeper. The touch of anyone else, no matter how much you love and trust them, will deliver a powerful shock. It might even stop your heart or burn out parts of your brain. Do you understand?"

"I do, but what's a keeper?"

"Not a what. A who. I am yours for as long as you remain under my care here at Nevarsin Tower. If you go to Thendara, I cannot say. It is better to err on the side of caution in such matters and safeguard your starstone."

"All right." Bryn sat straighter, cupping her starstone in both hands. "You haven't answered my question. You say you are a Keeper, *my* Keeper, but I don't know what that means."

"Most *laran* work requires the coordinated strength of a number of *leroni*, and so is performed in circles. The Keeper occupies the centripolar position— I'm sorry, I see I've lost you again. The Keeper links the minds of the others and weaves them together into a functional whole. It's very demanding work, and only a few of us can do it."

"But you're so—so young."

"I have trained to be a Keeper since my Gift awakened when I was ten. Once—before the time of Cleindori Aillard, the Golden Bell of Arilinn—a

Keeper was rigorously isolated from human touch, especially sexual contact." At Bryn's horrified expression, she hurried on, "Oh, we don't insist upon lifelong virginity any longer! Who could live like that? Yet the prohibition wasn't entirely without sense. The same channels carry both *laran* and sexual energy, which is why both tend to become active at puberty. Since your Gift did not, at least not in its full expression, things may be a bit confusing to you for a time."

At least, there was no longer a question in Bryn's mind about her having *laran. I can sense impending danger. And I have telepathy, both the ability to send and to receive.* Once those statements would have struck her as bizarre, delusional really, but now she felt nothing but relief.

When Bryn lifted her gaze, Adriana was smiling and nodding. "That's better. Now, shall we begin?"

For the next several hours, Adriana guided Bryn through round after round of exercises. *Take the starstone out. Place it on the table. Look at it. Look at it with your eyes closed. Put it back in the pouch. Look at the pouch. Look at it with your eyes closed.* Around and around they went until Bryn couldn't keep track. She began to see the stone—that twist of light she now knew like the inside of her skull—with her eyes open or shut.

When Adriana said, "Enough for today," Bryn was so tired her muscles trembled. Tired and hungry, every fiber craving fuel.

Laran *work burns up energy.* Adriana set a platter of nut-covered honey pastries between them. As the concentrated energy lifted her blood sugar, Bryn felt a rush of heat. Her vision sharpened, as did her thoughts. "What happens next?"

"Rest, and exercise, and chores. We fare better without the chatter of mundane minds in our working and living spaces, and we don't employ *kyrri* as servants, so we divide up the housekeeping among ourselves. Do you cook, by any chance?"

"Not on equipment you're likely to have here."

"I thought not. Beren will find something you can do. And then you'll have lessons. And more lessons—" Adriana giggled, for a moment looking like the very young woman she was. "—until you will *long* for those chores!"

◆◆◆

A few days later, Bryn received an invitation from Alanna for mid-afternoon tea in her parlor.

"How are you getting on?" the Lady asked, once they were settled with cups of straw-colored herbal tisane and a plateful of spiral buns.

"Honestly, I don't know. Adriana has me staring at my starstone and doing impossible things with my mind. Scrubbing pots in the kitchen is actually a relief." Bryn met the older woman's gaze evenly. "But you knew that already." *You know everything that goes on in this place.*

Indeed, I do. But it opened the conversation, yes?

"Bruna, one of the first things you must learn about living with telepaths is that it is pointless to attempt to disguise how you feel, at least until you develop proper barriers. While I am interested in your progress, I could as well ask Adriana for her assessment. You have been through a terrible ordeal, not just your flight from Terra and your journey through the mountains, but your near-fatal episode of threshold sickness." Alanna set down her cup.

I am in part responsible for you. Every person in this Tower is under my care.

"I'm grateful for your help. It was indeed terrifying."

"Gratitude is not required. Honesty is."

"All right, then. I do find you intimidating and my situation confusing. There's so much here I don't understand, and our objectives are different, perhaps incompatible."

"You feel yourself dependent upon my goodwill for your father's treatment."

Bryn took a deep breath. "Let me ask you frankly, do you intend to hold me here, even after he is well? Will you help us find a way back to Terra?"

"To the first question, not if you wish to leave and it is safe for you to do so. You must trust my judgment on this, and that of your Keeper. Remember that if you are not of sound mind, there is nothing you can do for your father." Alanna's eyes darkened. "As for where all this may lead, only the gods know. There is an old saying here on Darkover, that nothing is certain but death and next winter's snows. Forces are now in motion. I cannot tell where they may lead, and that troubles me. For today, however, you are safe among us."

Bryn considered this for a moment. "I had hoped to arrive on Darkover with at least a rudimentary understanding of your ways, but the teaching module was damaged. What must I know to behave properly, not just toward you and the other Tower workers but in the larger world?"

"Adriana tells me you are mastering your *laran*, and that is enough for now. I understand that you share a room with Sylvie. I commend her as a loquacious and sensitive teacher. She may, as the saying goes, talk the antennae off a scorpion-ant, but her judgment is sound."

"I have often found that talking too much is a great deal better than not talking enough," Bryn remarked.

A smile played across Alanna's face, one that struck Bryn as sad. "I am remembering my foster mother, *Domna* Marguerida Alton. She, too, was a Terran, but she made this planet her home. She believed that most problems could be resolved if people would simply talk it over with one another. Such faith in the power of persuasion! Well, she had that faith in plenty, although I did not properly appreciate it at the time. But being who she was, she understood and forgave. So when you tell me you are afraid of giving offense, please believe that I have done that to someone who loved me dearly. I cannot judge you for an honest mistake."

"I hope you will never have cause," Bryn said, her voice thick.

"But enough of this! Next, we will be weeping like a pair of old crows. Go now to your rest, and let healing do its work."

◆◆◆

"Does everyone on Darkover have *laran*?" Bryn asked one afternoon as they sat together on Sylvie's bed, legs crossed and mugs of steaming spiced cider cradled in their hands. "I mean, I gathered the Renunciates don't, nor the merchants in the square. But what are the rules of who does and doesn't have it? And other than Tower etiquette, what are the social conventions when dealing with those that do?"

"You know what the Comyn are?"

"Aristocrats, I gather."

"Yes, that. They rule the Seven Domains, and *laran* runs strongest in those families. It is said that back in the Ages of Chaos, their breeding programs selected for ever more powerful *laran*, often with disastrous results. Now the strongest telepaths still come from the old families, like *Domna* Alanna. With so many *nedestro* lines over the centuries, common folk like Illona Rider are just as likely to possess *laran* Gifts."

"I've heard that term, *nedestro*, but I don't know what it means."

"Born outside formal marriage, I think is the best way to put it. Among the Comyn, that would be *de catenas*."

"Historically, we'd say *illegitimate*, the original meaning of bastard. I take it there's no shame attached to it."

"Aldones, no! 'Tis a source of pride to have such parentage. Often the children are legitimated and can inherit. It's a way of keeping both *laran* and power within the family line. My mother was a *nedestra*, but the Leynier family claimed her and I bear their name. And Desi's an Alton by the same process and has a place on the Comyn Council. Or would have, if he bothered to attend. He says his work here is more important than a bunch of political speeches."

Bryn had the dizzying feeling that every time Sylvie answered a question, two more arose to take its place.

"To begin with," Sylvie said, "there are seven Domains. Hastur, Elhalyn, Alton, Aillard, Ardais, Ridenow, and Aldaran, although for a long time no one had any contact with Aldaran, dating back to the Ages of Chaos..."

Sylvie's explanation of the Comyn Council was more confusing than enlightening, since it apparently did not correspond to a Senate or other ruling body. A Regent held executive power, but not really. The Elhalyn were kings who refused to rule. Council members included the heads of the Domains but also others. Darkovan politics, Bryn concluded, were positively Byzantine in complexity.

At some point, she'd have to negotiate with these people to find a way off the planet once her father was restored to himself. That, or contact the smugglers' base in the desert. She wasn't sure which alternative was more daunting.

◆◆◆

At the end of the second tenday, Adriana announced that it was time for Bryn to undertake real work. Not as a full member of the circle—that required years of discipline—but as Sylvie's apprentice. Bryn would be acting as junior monitor for the working circle, stretching her new abilities to assess the physical and mental well-being of the *leroni*.

The circle had been assembling a new matrix screen to carry psychic messages from one Tower to another. Darkovans had developed a parallel but effective technology, devices that enabled near-instantaneous communication across mountainous regions too rugged for air flight. Her job would be to watch the members of the circle for distress. Once she would have thought the notion of perceiving another person's bodily state *with her mind* was a laughable hoax. Now she knew better.

As the circle took their places around the table, Desiderio nodded to her in his usual reserved manner. A skilled matrix mechanic, he was responsible for the precise attuning of the individual stones to function as an integrated unit. Bryn perched on a bench as she had been instructed, spine straight, hands resting on her lap and loosely cupping her starstone. Although she concentrated on her breathing and the now-familiar twist of light in its heart, she experienced nothing. Silently she urged herself to have patience and keep an open mind. After some time, her left leg was going numb but her leg was fine.

Oh, she thought. She *had* felt it. But it wasn't *her* leg. It was Desiderio's.

As her awareness shifted from imagination to conviction, she felt the prickle of returning nerve flow, the warmth of circulation...and the evanescent touch of Sylvie's mind, a whisper of silk as the monitor eased the problem. Sometime later, Bryn noticed another twinge and then a dryness in the throat. Each time Sylvie deftly intervened, and each time Bryn perceived the problem a little earlier.

The circle broke up, its work completed. The individual members roused. One stretched, spinal joints popping audibly. Another rolled his shoulders. Adriane yawned, a hand covering her mouth.

"That was amazing," Bryn said to Sylvie. "What I caught of it, that is—goodness knows how much else I missed."

"You did well for your first time. Sometimes novices can't sense anything."

"I had a good teacher."

Sylvie turned away, but not before Bryn caught the flush of pleasure on her cheeks.

◆◆◆

After Bryn had practiced monitoring several times more, Adriana summoned her for a private conference. The small workroom was chilly, but Adriana had brought a couple of shawls, as thick as blankets. Bryn took one, wrapped herself in it, and settled on a bench beside the battered old work table. Adriana made a circuit of the room, causing the *laran*-charged glow globes to emit their characteristic pale blue light.

"The Lady requested that I evaluate your training to see if there is aught else that might benefit you beyond the basics of monitoring."

I know so very little.

On the contrary, you have learned an astonishing amount since you came to us, Adriana said silently. *Your skills as a monitor are already progressing, and Sylvie tells me you improve daily. Your telekinesis may not be strong, but your telepathy most certainly will be.*

She gave Bryn a sidelong look of amusement. *Or have you failed to notice that we are no longer speaking aloud?*

Actually, I had. I suppose I've grown accustomed to it.

"Of your other talents, your danger-sense is perhaps the most problematic," Adriana said aloud. "I believe it is akin to the Aldaran Gift of precognition but poorly shaped and apt to be distorted by possibility streams. That is, many who have this Gift do not sense *the* future, but one or more *possible*, often contradictory, futures. It's not an easy thing to live with, and in the past, was considered an affliction apt to drive a person mad."

"I've never seen actual visions," Bryn said. "It's been more like a sensation of prickling or heat just below my skin. Not very specific, I admit."

"No, I expect not. But your ability to detect falsehood might be useful. It's not very strong or reliable, but I believe it will allow you to use an ancient technique of *truth spell*, which I propose to teach you before you leave."

"A spell, as in magic?"

"It's not magic," Adriana said, "it's simply a way of using *laran* to create a radiance that bathes the features of the speaker and persists only as long as they utter no falsehoods. Once it was considered vital to diplomacy, particularly between adversaries, and any *leronis* trained in its casting was valued."

"I don't see how it could work, but then I've seen a couple of dozen impossible things since coming here, so who am I to object?"

"I will cast it upon you first." Adriana took out her starstone, which flashed when it touched her bare palm. In a low, soft voice, she chanted, "In the light of the fire of this jewel, let the truth lighten the space where we stand." She pronounced the words with a peculiar accent that, more than the stilted phrases themselves, told Bryn that the text was very old.

With each phrase, her starstone pulsed brighter and brighter, until it seemed to Bryn that it filled the entire chamber. The effect continued after Adriana's words died away. Closing her eyes, Bryn felt a mist-like sensation on her face. It did not fade when she opened her eyes again, nor had the light diminished.

What now? How does it work?

Wait.

"What is your name?"

"Bryn—Bryn Haslund." Nothing happened. The light continued as before.

"Who are your parents?"

"Elise and Ernst Haslund." Again, no change.

"Why are you here?"

Here as on Darkover? Here as in Nevarsin Tower? Or here as in what is my purpose in life? Bryn decided to try an experiment. "I'm an agricultural agent on a mission to introduce fig orchards to Nevarsin."

The light winked out. "That's how it works," Adriana said. "You use the phrases to build the field, layer by layer."

For the next hour or so, Adriana took Bryn through the steps of casting the spell. Bryn failed her first few tries, until she focused on the individual skills involved. The core telepathic structure, linking her mind, the light from her starstone, and the perception of veracity in the speaker's thoughts, made intuitive sense to her. It was no more irrational than an antique polygraph. She loved the way the blue light suffused Adriana's face as she created the field.

"The Lady thought it might be useful," Adriana said as they headed for the door. "We have learned to rely on her judgment. In her youth, she possessed the Aldaran Gift of precognition, although she does not often speak of it."

◆◆◆

As Bryn recovered from her threshold sickness, her thoughts turned more toward her father. With Alanna's permission, she arranged for him to visit her at the Tower. Ernst and Felicity arrived at the Stranger's Parlor, where she joined them. Her father's face appeared less drawn than the last time she'd seen him, and he had a bit of color in his cheeks. Felicity looked weather-browned and well.

"It's wonderful to see you, Father. And you, too, Felicity!" Bryn embraced them in turn. After living among telepaths, who avoided casual physical contact, it felt good to be hugged.

Ernst eased himself into one of the chairs. "You look well."

"I feel well, thank you. And you, Felicity, you've clearly been out in the open air."

"It's the wind. I've been walking everywhere and trying to encourage Ernst to get more exercise. This city is so old it's practically an historical midden, and for all the resemblances with ancient Terra, it's surprisingly sophisticated. The evolution of Terran folklore, the adaptation to a cold, unforgiving climate, the relations between human and alien species, and even the socioeconomic groups, all could easily furnish an entire college of scholars with more than ample fields of study. Unfortunately, the industrial technology is so rudimentary, I haven't discerned anything like a proper laboratory, not even at a pre-spaceflight level."

While Felicity was talking, Ernst reached up to rub his temples, where the discs of metal gleamed.

"Are the electrodes uncomfortable?" Bryn asked.

His features tightened. Bryn reached out to his mind, only to sense a jangle of fractured mirrors instead of natural human patterns. She slammed her mental barriers tight. The brief contact left her feeling as if someone had sandpapered her brains and then rubbed in salt.

If it's this bad for me, what must he be suffering?

"Don't worry about me, sweetheart," he said with a pained smile. "Most of the time, thanks to the healers here at the Tower, I'm fine."

"*Most* isn't *all*," Felicity said.

Bryn gazed at her father. "What does she mean?"

"This mechanism appears to be activated by my thoughts. During ordinary conversation, I'm unaware of any activity. I feel like myself, normal. I can relate many aspects of my previous life. But if I try to—if I even *think* critically about Arthur Nagy—no, why would I do such a thing? It would be the height of disloyalty—everything I believe—no, I can't—you see what I mean—don't listen to me—" White ringed his eyes, his eyes like those of a trapped animal. Sweat broke out over his forehead and his face turned dusky.

"I remember the certainty of what was right, the necessity of speaking the truth—how the words flowed through me." His chest heaved. The muscles in his neck stood out like cables, and a vein pulsed in one temple. "I remember how it seemed I spoke not for myself only, but for those who had no voice. I advocated for their dreams for peace, for their children and their children's children, for understanding and tolerance—"

He turned to Bryn with an expression that clawed at her heart. "I know all these things were true, but when I try to remember exactly what I thought and did and said, I hear *other* words in my mind. The voice tells me I was duped into treason, that now if I speak at all I must tell the real truth—Arthur Nagy is a great man, the savior of the Alliance. Yet those words fill my mouth with poison. I cannot utter them, but neither can I deny them. What happened, Bryn? *Were* we all deluded? Was it all a lie?"

Bryn said, "Stop, please!" at the same moment as Felicity snapped, "Enough!"

Ernst pressed his lips together and closed his eyes, then opened them a moment later. He still looked troubled, although no longer wild with panic. "There, that's over now. I suppose we'll have to make the best of it and never discuss politics again."

"We must not give up now, not when we've come so far and endured so much," Bryn said.

"What other choice do we have?" he asked. "The Tower healers have done all they can for me. Most of the time I feel tolerably well."

"Except when you try to think critically about Nagy and the Alliance," Bryn pointed out.

"Except then," he agreed, and Felicity nodded.

"Well, that's no good," Bryn said, trying to keep her tone light. "We didn't come all the way out here just to exchange one form of thought censorship for another. I'll talk to *Domna* Alanna about what else can be done."

"Come inside," Alanna said, gesturing to her parlor. She and Desiderio were standing outside the door, talking, when Bryn approached. "It is time you learned the whole story. Desi, please bring us a simple meal and a pot of sweetened *jaco*. I would not want Bruna to faint from hunger before I have had my say."

Desiderio bowed, one uplifted eyebrow hinting of humor, and left them. Bryn followed Alanna back down the corridor to the parlor, where the two settled on the pair of chairs before the fire.

Alanna said, her tone gentle, "You have seen your father."

"Yes, after his last session."

"As you know, I discouraged earlier contact. It was important that you concentrate on mastering your *laran* without outside distractions. You are now past the most dangerous time."

"I understand. But now that I've seen him, I'm concerned. While he appears to have improved in some ways, he's still under the influence of the mechanical device. The healers here have worked with him for several sessions. Can they do anything more for him?"

"I wish I could offer you hope that continuing as we have been would result in further progress, but I cannot do that in all honesty. Ah, here is Desi with our *jaco*."

Desiderio entered with a tray. He set it down on the little table in front of the fireplace and pulled up a third chair for himself, then poured and distributed mugs of the steaming brew.

Why is Alanna including him in our discussion? Bryn liked him well enough and he had gone out of his way to encourage her. Her time at Nevarsin Tower had given her a healthy respect for his abilities as a matrix mechanic, equally skillful although of a different specialization as the Keeper.

Alanna, clearly catching Bryn's thought, said aloud, "I have asked Desiderio to be present here because if you agree to my plan, he will be part of it. He is aware that we have reached the limitations of what we can do for your father. We are a small circle, only one, focusing primarily on the needs of the local population. Other Towers are more powerful and experienced."

"I did not want to accept that this was as good as my father would ever be," Bryn said. "If that were true, we might remain here, hoping to stay hidden. You say there is still hope?"

"That I cannot promise, only that we have not yet exhausted the possibilities. I propose to send you and your companions to Thendara. Desiderio will accompany you."

According to the data tab, Thendara was the major city of the Domains and the site of the old Federation headquarters. When the Terrans departed, they likely left behind laboratory facilities and communications equipment. That sounded promising. "And Desiderio? Do you have business in Thendara as well?"

"Thendara is much larger and more complex than Nevarsin," he said. "It is no simple matter to deal with the Comyn Council, who may have much to say about your mission and your very presence on Darkover. At the Lady's request, I will endeavor to instruct you and ease the way."

"Desi is being modest," Alanna said. "His family, the Altons, are ancient and prestigious, and he has the right to participate in council meetings. He has powerful kinship and personal connections, as well as knowledge of courtly customs. You could not ask for a better mentor."

"I had no idea," Bryn said. She had respected him for his skill as a matrix mechanic and never thought of his position beyond the Tower walls. "Thank you in advance."

He inclined his head in acknowledgment.

"That brings us to the second reason to send you and your party to Thendara," Alanna said. "Through our telepathic relays, I have spoken with the Regent and the Council, and the Keeper of Comyn Tower, as well. They agree that, even without your father's need for further treatment, your very presence here threatens Darkover, and that threat must be addressed at the highest level."

The skin along Bryn's spine turned cold. *Black? Has he traced us here already?* "Please go on."

"To explain why we are all so concerned, I must recount a little of the long and often tempestuous relationship between my world and yours."

"I know that Darkover—Cottman IV, as we call it—is a Lost Colony, settled by humans long ago and then rediscovered. And that Darkover managed to negotiate its autonomy with the Federation, based on the value of its unique telepathic abilities."

"Indeed, although some would say it would have been better had we remained lost. We were, as you put it, *rediscovered* in the time of King Stephen Hastur. The *Terranan* set up their bases here because of our location on the galactic arm, or so they said. Then came traders and industrialists as well as diplomats, men looking to strip our poor world of its few resources, to turn our people into the same mindless workers as on every other planet. At one point, these companies even attempted to destroy Darkover's ecology to bring us to the bargaining table as beggars."

I wouldn't put it past the Nagy regime to try the same thing.

"As a result of the incursions of the World Wreckers, Regis Hastur himself created the Telepath Project," Desiderio said.

"I've heard of him, always with tremendous respect," Bryn said. "And I know of the project, for that was why we came to Darkover rather than another distant world."

"Just as the Terrans brought their machines and Compact-banned weapons," Alanna continued smoothly, "they also introduced their ideas of progress. Not all of these changes were bad, as the Bridge Society healers have demonstrated. But the *Terranan's* technological superiority blinded them to the truth that we are not ignorant savages. The powers of the mind can be just as devastating as anything from their laboratories. The Sharra matrix, woken in arrogance and raging uncontrolled, destroyed the spaceport at Caer Donn, did you know that?"

Bryn shook her head.

"After that, your authorities developed a more suitable respect for why we forbid distance weaponry, but they never truly comprehended that Darkover is not helpless. Most of them continued to treat us as a colony world to be dominated. As you can well imagine, when the *Terranan* withdrew from Darkover, many rejoiced. I was still very young and very preoccupied with my own concerns, but I remember those years vividly. Time passed, as it always does. We might have been abandoned but we were not forgotten. It wasn't long before your people returned—smugglers and those who hunted them. Mercenaries, you understand.

"Now," Alanna concluded, "we have come to the attention not only of raggle-taggle bounty hunters or scavengers but of the Alliance's power-enforcers."

"How do you know this?" Bryn asked, her heart suddenly hammering in her throat.

"We lack the instruments to detect the approach of spacecraft," Alanna admitted. "But instruments are not the only way of detecting dangers ahead, as you well know."

My danger-sense. Earlier, Alanna had mentioned a talent for precognition. What was it called?

The Aldaran Gift, Alanna answered mentally. *Which I have had since my* laran *arose.* Aloud she said, "It took me many years to master it. The Aldaran Gift does not show *the* future, but only *a possible* future. I have deliberately avoided using it until now."

"And now you have?"

"I needed to know the risks of your father's presence here."

Bryn sensed the old woman's self-discipline, the way she allowed no hint of her emotions to show.

"I saw a shape, moving through space. It was heading toward us, keeping to the shadows in the manner of a cloud leopard stalking its prey. A dark ship…a deadly ship. A ship with fire in its belly. Fire to rain down on Darkover—" Alanna's voice broke, but only a little. "I cannot know if this is what *will* happen, but everything you have told me convinces me that the threat must be taken seriously."

"This is my fault," Bryn said. "If I hadn't found those entries about Project Telepath, if I hadn't conceived the idea that natural telepaths could prevail against corticator technology—at least enough to restore my father's mind—the Spaceforce agent, Black, would not be on our trail. He tracked us from Terra to Alpha, where I found my father. He's tenacious. He won't give up. For all I know, his ship is even now approaching Darkover, and it will be armed." She blinked away the sudden blurriness. "What must I do? What *can* I do to make this right?"

"That I do not know," Alanna replied with a hint of a smile that struck Bryn as sad. "Yet oftentimes we are given the opportunity to make amends in unexpected ways. You are precious to us, for we value every person with *laran,* and yours is considerable. As to what may be done, that is for the Regent and the Council to say. They desire to interview you and your father, and for that, you must go to Thendara."

"But not you?"

"Oh my dear, I gave my word that I would not return until I—unless I—and the years rolled by and then I found my life and my work were truly here. Now the time when such a journey was possible has passed, as such things do. There are those I would be glad to see again, but I am content to never do so."

Bryn understood. Not every sorrow, or every disappointment or regret, could be completely resolved. The ability to be at ease with unsettled issues was a gift indeed.

I wish I had the chance to hear her story and know her better.

"If you have no other commitments, Bruna," Desiderio said, once Alanna had left them, "we can begin with an overview of the Domains."

"Sylvie's already given me the basics, but going over them can't hurt. However, I think my father and my teacher ought to be part of that conversation. After all, they have as much need for the information as I."

"That is certainly true, although I must point out that neither your father nor your friend is likely to negotiate on his behalf. *You* are."

"My father can make his own case."

Your father does not possess laran.

Stung, Bryn opened her mouth to reply that it should make no difference. Then she realized that it *did*. On Darkover, *laran* meant everything.

"Very well, so long as they are prepared for what we must deal with." The weight of responsibility pressed on her. She'd never sought any of this—not being spied on, not being gassed, not running for her very life.

Desiderio was staring at her with an unreadable expression. Bryn wished she knew how he felt—sympathy? outrage? incredulity? Without thinking, she reached out with her mind. A presence washed over her—and a rapid progression of emotions—suspicion, astonishment, disbelief, confusion—all tinged with welcome.

You are not alone. You will never be truly alone here.

Her gaze met his, his eyes wide and face newly, utterly open. *I could love him*, she thought.

Why had she not noticed how handsome he was, so deliberate in his strength? Because she had seen him before only through her physical eyes?

And then, from him: *No, that's an illusion born of the rapport. You're not accustomed to the intimacy. It's natural to mistake it for something more.*

"Working so closely, it's natural to experience attraction," he said aloud with the disconcerting directness she'd experienced from Adriana and others of the circle. "It's not unusual to become lovers for a season, minds in tune and bodies with healthy needs. We understand it is only the pleasure of the moment. We enter into it with no promises other than honesty when it's over. But you, with your grieving heart, for you it would be something more. A lifeline in a storm, a balm that is the seeming of comfort only. When it ends, as it must, you will be hurt, angry—looking for someone to blame. Anything but at peace with yourself, which is all I or anyone here wishes for you."

He brushed his fingertips over her wrist, the evanescent touch she had observed among other telepaths, and that brief contact brought a tenderness that took her breath away. At that moment, she was not alone, adrift, bereft, perplexed.

You understand, now, what binds us together.

It was love of a sort, the meeting of minds if not hearts, and it was also immense power. *This is why the* Terranan *must never be allowed to exploit us,* she answered.

"You understand now why we cannot—*dare* not—simply go on with our lives, allowing you to do the same," he said aloud. "Not if there is the remote chance your enemies have followed you here."

"Darkover cannot stand against the Alliance, not under Nagy's rule." Bryn lifted her chin. "Teach me whatever I need to convince this Comyn Council to help my father."

The next few days passed by in a whirl of preparation for the journey. Alanna contracted with the Renunciate Guildhouse for trail guides, led by Martina and assisted by Bettina and Leonie, who was to join the Bridge Society in Thendara. Felicity was particularly interested in learning more about the Darkovan women who had adapted Terran medical technology.

"I don't hold out much hope for laboratory facilities, but still, a visit will be interesting," Felicity remarked to Bryn and Ernst after one of their tutoring sessions with Desiderio. "But there are the abandoned Terran bases, assuming the equipment is still functional."

"And assuming the Comyn Council, which I gather controls such things, gives us access," Bryn said.

"There's that," Ernst said. "At this point, I don't care which technology we use, so long as something works. I can't shake the feeling that our time here is running out."

"I have not observed any signs of significant neurological deterioration," Felicity said, "although without proper instruments I cannot be sure."

The Federation had departed in haste, so they might not have taken everything. The headquarters must surely have included a great deal more than just medical work spaces and laboratories. Communications equipment, for example...they might have a way to contact someone who could transport them to Terra. That assumed their arrival here had gone undetected by Black, Ernst could be returned to his normal self, and that the interstellar radio was still functional.

Black... It was all too easy to imagine his ship coming into orbit around Darkover, intent on hauling them all back to Terra and Nagy.

No time to lose.

◆◆◆

Bryn had almost nothing to pack beyond a small amount of clothing and personal care items. Her remaining nights were taken up in drilling everything she'd learned at the Tower and learning diplomatic and courtly skills.

On the morning of departure, she woke to Sylvie bending over her, holding a single candle. Shadows shrouded the room, without a hint of daylight through the window.

"It's time. I tried to let you sleep as long as possible, but if you don't get up now there won't be enough time for breakfast, and I don't know about you, but *I* wouldn't want to be all day on the trail without something hot in my belly first." Sylvie said all this without pausing for breath. It was so like her that Bryn couldn't help laughing.

"I'm going to miss your chatter." Bryn flung herself out of bed.

Sylvie opened her chest and drew out a long cloak with a hood lined with fur. "Something to remember me by. Not to mention keeping you much warmer than that *Terranan* jacket."

"Oh! I couldn't accept this." Bryn couldn't guess how much the cloak must be worth, but that was in Alliance terms, where expertly handcrafted goods were at a premium. Not to mention real fur.

"All right, then. Don't take it. See if I care if you freeze!"

Bryn stared at her, for a moment speechless, before she realized Sylvie was teasing. In her former life, she'd had only a few close women friends, most of them from her student days, and her relationships with her colleagues and her father's associates had been civil but never more—and with that thought, she burst into tears.

◆◆◆

Bryn emerged through the front door of the Tower, Sylvie's cloak over her old jacket. Snow had fallen the night before, leaving the air shiveringly clear. Adriana and a handful of other Tower workers were waiting for her, Desiderio among them. He looked up at Bryn's appearance and lifted his cup in salute. A moment later, Alanna came down, wreathed in furs, to bid them farewell.

In a short time, Bryn and Desiderio were mounted, she on the same horse she'd ridden before, he on a tall, elegant black. They made their way to the city's lower gates, where Ernst and Felicity met them, along with their Renunciate guides. Bettina spotted Bryn and grinned at her, hands busy with the lead lines of the laden pack animals.

The road from Nevarsin was wide enough for two or three to ride abreast. Bryn reined her horse behind Leonie, who was chatting in an animated fashion with Felicity.

"Oh yes, I have wanted to train as a healer since I was a child," Leonie was saying. "In my village, we had a midwife and we thought her more than enough for our needs until one winter two of the men were badly hurt when a frost-killed tree fell on them and they both died. Then we had lung-fever for weeks, and it seemed to me that the herbs helped only those who would have lived anyway. The midwife did not survive, which made our situation even worse. Then during my housebound year, I heard about the Bridge Society, which trains healers in the best of our traditions *and Terranan* science. That's been my dream ever since."

"It is a laudable one," Felicity said, and began probing Leonie's preparation for studying medical sciences. She was in full academic curiosity mode, and Leonie was clearly flattered to have such an interested listener.

Desiderio drew even with Bryn. She noticed the sword strapped to his saddle and wondered if he expected to fight alongside the Renunciates, should there be more bandits.

"I don't know much about horses," she said in an effort to divert her thoughts, "but I believe that one is particularly fine."

"She is an Alton black, a gift from my kinsman, Arnad Alton-Hastur."

"Alton *and* Hastur? So which Domain does he belong to?"

"Our naming conventions must be confusing to outworlders, although your father doesn't seem to have trouble with them."

Bryn laughed. "He's had a lifetime of diplomatic training. My expertise is of a very different sort."

"Mending the spirits of wounded children. Yes, *Domna* Alanna told me. It is honorable work."

"I always thought so, although I don't know when I might practice again."

"There will always be a need for insight and compassion."

"And knowledge of how broken minds can be mended," she said, pensive. "Enough of that. Tell me about the Alton-Hasturs."

"This particular branch goes back to the time of Regis Hastur," he said.

"Before he fathered heirs of his own, he adopted Mikhail Lanart-Hastur, his sister's son, and Mikhail then married Marguerida Alton."

"*The* Marguerida Alton?"

"There's just one. Their firstborn and heir was Domenic Alton-Hastur, and his son, Varzil, is now regent."

The Comyn seemed to practice inbreeding, but that was true for other aristocracies, the better to hold power or, in this case, to concentrate *laran* Gifts. "Then who is king if he's regent?"

"There isn't one, and that's the point. Historically, the Elhalyns held the throne, but they haven't shown any interest in ruling for a long time. The real power lies with the Hasturs."

Clearly, the Hasturs are the power-behind-the-throne. "And your kinsman, Arnad, he's Varzil Hastur's what? brother? son?"

"Cousin. His mother is the daughter of Mikhail and Marguerida. He's honorable and fair-minded, not one of those you'll have to watch out for."

"Yes, you've warned me already."

"I meant it. Varzil is not Regis Hastur, but he is wily enough in his own right. You must take particular care with what you say to Vittorio, the Ardais heir. There will be meanings within meanings in every encounter. Not all the Council members will look kindly on you. They will see anyone assisting your father as facilitating re-contact."

"Then we must convince them that Darkover may already have come to the attention of the Alliance and their best hope of autonomy lies not in secrecy but in bringing down Nagy's regime."

"*I* am not the one you must persuade."

◆◆◆

The sun warmed the air, and last night's snow melted. Everyone's spirits were high. The Renunciates sang as they went along, call-and-response tunes followed by a funny song about an old monk and all the ridiculous things he carried in his pockets. Desiderio's clear baritone voice joined in on ballads that sounded like very old versions of Terran folk music.

"I enjoyed that so much!" Bryn said to Desiderio when they paused beside a rushing brook to water the animals and eat a light meal. "I hadn't realized how much I've missed music. You have a fine voice."

Desiderio, munching on a mixture of nuts and dried apple slices, made a dismissive gesture. "By Darkovan standards, only fair. I'm a much better dancer than a singer, but so is everyone. Have you heard the old saying that whenever two Darkovans get together, they hold a dance?"

"I'm not surprised." She took a swig of water from the teardrop-shaped skin. "I didn't see any dancing during my time at Nevarsin, perhaps because I so rarely left the Tower. Will there be much at Thendara?"

"Since it will be Comyn Council season, families will converge from the various Domains. There will be balls and impromptu dances at least every day, not including dancing in the streets and marketplaces. You *can* dance, I hope."

"By Terran standards, I'm adequate. I use art and movement therapies in a professional context with my patients. Children who are emotionally paralyzed by what they have experienced can sometimes draw or act out their feelings when they can't speak of them. But I don't suppose Darkovan dances are anything like that."

"No, I think not." He sobered. "Do not be deceived, however. Dances are serious business here."

"Match-making, you mean?"

"That, of course, and contending for power. Brokering treaties between Domains. Inciting duels or resolving rivalries."

"I hope I won't be involved in those!" Bryn said with a laugh.

"Not directly, but you must be wary. Allowances will be made for your being an off-worlder, although that will add to your allure."

She stared at him, open-mouthed, as she realized he was being perfectly serious. "You mean one of these Comyn lords might try to seduce me? On the *dance floor*?"

"Do you think so little of yourself that such a prospect is impossible?"

Bryn looked away, pretending to be interested in unwrapping a cheese bun. She could not imagine welcoming such an overture but now, in this fleeting moment, she felt a pulse of warmth from Desiderio. Respect. Tenderness...and a flicker of her own response. An instant of acute awareness of his physical presence. The warmth radiating from his face, as much imagined in her skin as felt. The curve of his lips, caught in a half-smile as he waited for her answer.

No, she could not deal with a new relationship. *Even* if her goal in Thendara were not so critical, *even* if she were not still mourning Leonin, the shadow of the assault by the bandits was still too fresh.

"We are not all such savages," he went on quietly, and his tone told her that he had followed her thoughts. "I know that you do not need protection, but if you will allow it, I will endeavor to make sure you are never placed in such a vulnerable position."

"Thank you, but I can take care of myself!" Through their rapport, she sensed that he took no offense from her sharp words. Nevertheless, she regretted her tone. "I spoke ungraciously just now. I appreciate the warning. I will be prepared."

His expression shifted, opaque. "Even for those who have grown up immersed in Comyn politics, the unexpected can take us unawares. Be on your guard, but trust your instincts."

"Point taken. Speaking of preparation, what can I expect in Thendara? Will we all stay at an inn?"

"No, indeed. We have spent so much time talking about Domains politics that I have been remiss in issuing a formal invitation to you and your party to be my guests at Comyn Castle. There's a guest suite with accommodations for you all in the Alton quarters. An old family friend will act as housekeeper to ensure your comfort."

"That's very kind…thank you."

What more they might have said to one another went unsaid as Martina called for the party to move on.

Past midday, clouds scudded across the sky, blurring the great red sun. The trail dwindled to a thread that wound through increasingly steep and rocky terrain. Pockets of snow dotted the bare stone faces like bits of frosting. The wind picked up, carrying an icy edge.

They halted for the night while light still lingered in the west. The Renunciates and Desiderio set about taking care of the animals and unpacking their gear. They made camp, the two men in one tent and the women in pairs in others.

Leonie brought the Terrans mugs of herbal tisane. "This will strengthen you for the days to come."

Felicity tasted her drink and made a face. Bryn sipped hers and found it as bitter as she'd feared.

"Drink, drink!" Leonie said. "These plants have long been known to prevent or lessen the severity of mountain sickness, what you call altitude sickness. The Pass of Scaravel lies before us."

Desiderio brought Bryn and the others trenchers of trail stew. As she accepted hers, she felt the gentle touch of *laran*. A presence, a pulse of friendly reassurance swept through her. She could not see his expression, for he had turned away, but she did not need to. It felt as if their hands had clasped invisibly, clasped and held.

We're in rapport, she thought.

We have never ceased to be.

She listened to the dying echoes of his thought in her mind and knew she had nothing to fear from him. Rapport was not love, at least not romantic love. In a way, this undemanding resonance of mind was far stronger. She might grapple with her grief for Leonin, her fears for her father, her fury at Arthur Nagy and that snake, Black, but she would never again be alone.

◆◆◆

Gradually the party ascended the slopes leading to Scaravel Pass. Beyond it, Martina assured Bryn, the going would be easier. The pass itself was over seven thousand meters high, and the approach led along sheer cliffs through slanting sleet. Often they had to dismount and lead their animals.

One night, Bryn snuggled into the cocoon of her blankets. She'd gotten used to sleeping on the hard ground, and the altitude had left her tired enough so she had no difficulty falling asleep. She stirred as her tent mate, Doranne, slipped inside. Just as she was dozing off again, she heard a familiar, eerie wailing. She jerked fully awake, her muscles tense. Her heartbeat sounded unnaturally loud and fast.

"It's a banshee, isn't it?" Bryn whispered.

Doranne reached for her long knife. "Aye, but still far off."

The cry came again, rising and falling. Bryn could not tell if it came from farther than before, or if the mountainous terrain made it seem so. She grabbed her boots.

"Where do you think you're going?"

"You said it was far off." Bryn shoved her arms into the sleeves of her jacket. "But it's terrifying, that cry. I'm going to check on my father and my teacher." She hurried out of the tent, Doranne on her heels.

The arc of stars and two glimmering moons cast enough light to make out the contours of the camp, the still-glowing embers of the banked fire, and the shapes of people moving about. At the picket lines, the animals shifted about, restless. Bettina and Leonie were stamping out the embers.

Martina had once remarked that the giant carnivorous banshees were blind to light but hunted by detecting heat.

Desiderio stood outside the men's tent, holding the door flap open and speaking in low tones. "No, *mestre*, you must remain within. Should the banshee approach, we will do our best to defend you."

"Desiderio, would you please ask Felicity to join us so we're all together?" Bryn ducked inside and knelt beside her father. His face was an ashen oval in the shadows. "Father, let's stay inside. We should let those with weapons—Desiderio and the Renunciates—do their job."

"Knives against whatever that thing is?"

"Banshee, it's called. Remember we heard one before, on our way to Nevarsin? And yes, this is their world, and they know how such a danger is to be met. If they want us to stay out of the way, that's what we should do."

Again came the chilling wail, rising and falling. It sounded louder and nearer. Goosebumps flared over Bryn's arms. With an effort, she prevented herself from covering her ears. That would only alarm her father. No, she must appear calm and confident, even if terror shot along her nerves with each ululation.

Fumbling in the near-darkness, she took her father's hand. He was trembling. "The banshee hunts by immobilizing its prey. The sound is meant to frighten us. Your body is only doing what it's supposed to. It's a natural reaction."

Before she could say more, Felicity pushed her way into the tent. "Brrr! What a night! They don't want any of us wandering around, getting in the way, and I shouldn't wonder. I'm unable to judge how far away that noise is. It's better to be together, don't you think? Ah! I wish that thing would shut up!"

The next time they heard the banshee wailing, it sounded farther off, and the time after that, even fainter. After a half hour or so, strain as she might, Bryn heard no more cries.

Martina ducked her head into the tent. "The banshee's moved off, but I've doubled the guard to be on the safe side. You can go back to bed."

Bryn returned to her tent, numb and overwrought. Doranne had not yet come back, since she was on first watch. Drawing her blanket around her shoulders, she waited. Minutes passed, one growing from the last, yet sleep would not come. She felt for the silken pouch nestled between her breasts. Her fingertips outlined the hard crystalline contours of the insulated starstone. *Her* starstone. She remembered handling it for the first time, the moment when it made contact with her bare palm, the way its blue radiance had flared like a living thing, reflection and complement to her mind.

She slipped her starstone out. Light pulsed through her. It filled her, soothed her. Drowsy, she drifted on the patterns of brilliance that were as familiar as the hardness of her bones, the inside of her closed eyelids.

Safe, it was safe to sleep now...

Gradually she became aware of her surroundings. The light shifted from blue to watery gray. All the warmth seeped out of it, like the sullen overcast of rain not ready to break. The grayness before her was not uniform but darker in some areas, lighter in others, the patterns suggesting a person or a far-off structure, a Tower perhaps.

She was in the Overworld.

Something long and sleek passed overhead, a shadow on the gray firmament. A hunter, searching...searching...

There was no place to run, nowhere to hide.

This is the Overworld. There is nothing to fear, except from my own mind.

Alanna's warnings rose in Bryn's mind, but also that here it was possible to meet the dead she had once loved. She turned her attention back to the distant figure.

Leonin?

As if summoned by her silent plea, the shape became clearer. Hope beyond hope, she had been given this last chance to see him, to speak with him, to hold him in her arms. She tried to move in his direction but the ground was insubstantial and she could not gain traction. In desperation, she reached out with her mind. To her astonishment, she made a connection. It was fragmented, a reflection seen in the shards of a broken mirror, but enough for her to discern his response. She could not make out words, not even her name, only a silent cry. At the same time, she became aware of a bone-deep chill creeping across her skin.

Alanna's warning echoed in her mind: *Those who venture into that unliving land, searching for loved ones, become lost...never to return.*

She dared not linger—but just a moment longer—if she could only make out what he was trying to tell her—this was no place for the living—she might become trapped here forever—one final glimpse of him—

Blue light flared. The distant figure grew no closer, but she heard, faint but clear:

Don't waste my death!

Bryn turned and fled. Grayness clung to her like a miasma. Fog-like tendrils surrounded her like a cage. Try as she might, she could not free herself.

Let go, whispered through her mind, bearing the distinctive touch of Desiderio's *laran. Reach for the light…the blue light.*

Blue light…starstone…it brought me here, it can take me home.

In her mind, she pictured the twisting brilliance in the heart of her matrix gem. It took form, moment by radiant moment turning her flesh into living glass.

And then she was in her tent once more, her chest heaving. Her fingers cramped from gripping her starstone. The faceted edges bit into her skin. In the frigid air, her breath came as vaporous plumes. For all that, she was back in her body.

Glad to hear it.

His mental voice awoke a thrum of gladness in her. Or relief, she could not tell.

You're still with me, she said.

Always. Did I not tell you it would be so?

Were you with me in the Overworld? I knew better than to go there. Alanna warned me.

It was understandable, given how recent and unhealed is your loss.

After a pause: *You did not need my help, you know. You were not…committed to the place. You sought not death, only answers.*

Thank you for pulling me out.

I might have given you a wee bit of a reminder, but 'twas your own strength that saved you.

My own strength… At the moment it seemed he believed in her more than she believed in herself.

◆◆◆

Past the Kadarin River, the landscape became progressively more welcoming. Mountain terrain gave way to gentle foothills and pastures, trails to well-marked roads. Even the weather conspired to lift their spirits, for although it rained occasionally at night, the days were bright and sun-filled. Finally, they came down out of the hills and looked down on Thendara. In the distance, the city was both familiar and exotic with its rambling stone buildings, plazas and alleys, and gardens and walled compounds.

"Look there!" Felicity exclaimed. "Those buildings aren't native stone. See how the light's reflected! That's plasteel and glass. It must be the Terran base. And beyond it, there on the very edge of the city, the spaceport!"

"Aye, that it is," Martina said. "You have good eyes."

"I can't discern any deterioration at this distance, though. Can you, Bryn?"

Bryn shook her head. In Darkover's climate, it was unlikely that Federation buildings would be in pristine condition.

"What's that?" she asked, pointing to the massive complex dominating the older part of the city.

"Comyn Castle, our destination," Desiderio said, reining in his horse beside hers. "It's said to be millennia old and every generation has added to it, or so it seems. The place is an amalgam of architectural styles and a warren of passageways, many of which don't go anywhere. If anyone's considered remodeling for the sake of consistency, their skeletons are probably moldering in one of the dungeons."

"Dungeons? You can't be serious."

"I am assured they do exist, although despite my most determined searches, I never found any. My kinsman, Arnad Alton-Hastur—I told you about him, remember?—he once claimed he'd discovered bandit treasure in the bowels of the castle, but we were only eight at the time and he never produced any proof."

"Did you spend your childhood in the castle, then?"

"No, I was fostered at Armida, which is where Arnad and I became friends. A great place for wild boys, Armida—" he gestured expansively, "—a big house in the country, herds of horses, beautiful pastures. We all crammed together in the Alton quarters during Council season."

From what Bryn had seen, Darkovans were more comfortable at close quarters than many Alliance cultures. Desiderio made it sound fun, the way festivals on Terra brought families together, often under the same roof. As he nudged his horse down the slope and she kept pace, she reminded herself they were not here for entertainment.

When they reached the outskirts of the city, the great red sun had dipped behind the horizon, bringing a brief, shimmering twilight. They halted at a checkpoint where pedestrians, some of them pushing hand-carts or leading laden pack animals, mixed with riders on horses or chervines and an occasional wagon.

Shadows lengthened, clotting into darkness, as they proceeded into the city. Lanterns provided illumination along the broad avenue, and warm orange lights glowed behind windows of dimpled glass. On they went, drawing ever nearer to Comyn Castle. From the slopes of the hills, it had looked huge, but now she saw it was like a walled city unto itself. As they approached the gates, guards bowed and stood aside.

A man in a long, belted robe emerged. Metal keys swung from his jewel-set belt. "*Dom* Desiderio, welcome. And your companions as well. We've been expecting you."

"It's good to see you, too." After dismounting, Desiderio clasped arms with the man. He turned to Bryn, who was helping first her father and then Felicity from the saddle. "This fine man, aptly named Fidelio, is the *coridom*, the steward you would say, for all of Comyn Castle. We've been friends for many years. These are my companions, *Mestre* Ernst Haslund, *Mestra* Bruna Haslund, and *Mestra* Felicia Sage."

Fidelio bowed to each of them in turn. He clapped his hands and a handful of men and women emerged from within the gates to carry away the baggage as it was unloaded.

"Here we part ways," Martina said. "We have fulfilled our contract."

Bryn clasped arms with the Renunciate leader. "I cannot thank you enough for all you have done for us. Not only for rescuing us on the mountain but also for your friendship. If there is ever an opportunity to repay your generosity, consider it done. I wish you success in your future endeavors, and you, especially, Leonie—" turning to the younger Renunciate, "—I hope your studies at the Bridge Society are as rewarding as you so richly deserve."

"*Su serva*," Leonie replied with a dip of her head.

"Thank you all," Felicity echoed. "We would not have survived without you, although I expect you are well aware of that. Your insights into the role of women in Darkovan culture have been fascinating."

"Good fortune to you, my friends," Martina replied. The Renunciates mounted up again, disappearing back into the city along with their unloaded baggage animals.

From beside the gate, Fidelio made a sweeping gesture of invitation. They followed him inside, across a paved yard, and into the castle itself. They passed more servants, identifiable by liveries in different colors. One of them, a girl of seven or eight, trotted along behind them. Fidelio kept a measured, easy pace, wordlessly accommodating the gait of the older people.

As they went along, Bryn noticed the carved wooden paneling, the tapestries, and the ornaments. Some were bright, obviously new, but others, faded with age, were no less beautiful. The level of craftsmanship was very high. At times both Felicity and Ernst exclaimed at a detail or made a comparison with the finest of Terran art.

This is a living culture, one that values both beauty and utility, Bryn thought. *It's not primitive, no matter how closely it resembles that of Terra's distant past.*

"What's down there?" she asked Desiderio, indicating an archway.

In response, he sent a telepathic image of a map: the central hall through which they'd entered; a flagstone square lined with benches and fragrant yellow flowers; an enormous chamber with partitioned seating areas, saturated with multi-hued light; barracks and training areas; kitchens; a zig-zag maze of passages leading to a Tower—

Comyn Tower?

Yes. And here we are at the living quarters of the Comyn, both those in residence and attending Council season.

Fidelio conducted them through wide double doors, polished golden wood below a carved crest with the motto, *Fortuna Montani*, then down a branching corridor and finally to a smaller door, which he swung open and stood back for them to enter.

"I trust these chambers will be satisfactory and that you will be at your ease here, as guests of Alton," Fidelio said. "If you want anything, do not hesitate to ask. Maralise here," with a nod to the girl who had followed them, "will take messages."

They entered a generously proportioned room furnished as a sort of parlor with chairs, a pair of divans, and side tables. The far end of the room, through opened partitions, revealed a table set for a meal. In the fireplace, glowing embers gave off a gentle heat. Ernst lowered himself onto one of the well-padded divans and closed his eyes.

A woman emerged from the dining area. She looked to be in middle age, robust and energetic, and wore a long-sleeved tunic over full skirts, the whole draped by a tartan pinned at one shoulder.

"Welcome home, *Dom* Desiderio," she said in perfect Terran Standard. "And these must be the *Terranan* guests."

Desiderio introduced the Darkovan woman. "May I present *Mestra* Ishana Reed, who is showing off her language facility. Her father was Jeremiah Reed, a soldier who stayed behind when the Federation departed."

"'Tis only common hospitality to greet guests in a tongue they ken," Ishana replied with a tone of affectionate familiarity. "And 'tis the tongue of my childhood, so it's I who should be giving thanks for the chance to speak it again."

"Have it your way, Shana," Desiderio replied. "Clearly, I've brought these travelers all the way from Nevarsin and the stars just to indulge your nostalgia."

Ishana turned her attention back to the Terrans. "Welcome to Thendara and Comyn Castle! This suite of rooms is to be yours for as long as you are guests of the Altons, and I am in charge of ensuring your comfort." Her gaze flickered from Bryn to Felicity and then alighted on Ernst on the divan. "Forgive my presumption, *mestre*, but you look fair done in. Are you too fatigued to come to the dining room, or would you prefer to have a tray sent to your room?"

Ernst made an effort to sit up straighter. "Of course I—who am I kidding? All I want right now is to lie down."

"And so you shall, with a bowl of soup and hot spiced wine right to hand." She led him through the dining area to one of several doors on the far side.

"I believe I will emulate him, or would if I knew which way to go."

Felicity turned to Maralise and switched to *casta*. "Child, do you know where I'm to be ensconced? To sleep?"

"Yes, *mestra*. Please follow me." The girl led Felicity through a second inner door.

"And now," Desiderio said to Bryn, "I must pay my respects to the head of my family. I'll be staying in my old chamber just down the main corridor, left branch. Should you need me for any reason, send Maralise."

Left to herself, Bryn wandered over to the fireplace. The room felt peaceful, with the flames giving off warmth and soothing crackling sounds. If she strained to hear, she could just make out voices from behind the closed inner doors.

One of the doors opened and Ishana emerged. "*Mestra*, you look as done in as your father and the other lady. Shall I show you to your sleeping chamber?"

"I'd rather have something to eat." Bryn glanced down at her travel-stained clothing. *And a bath.*

"I've a proper meal ready. Or I can send for something lighter, as you wish."

"Whatever you have prepared will be fine."

"This way, then."

Beyond the parlor lay a combination dining area and office. On a marble-topped sideboard sat an array of covered chafing dishes. Up close, the smell of the food almost brought Bryn to her knees. Ishana steered her to the nearest chair and placed a filled plate and goblet in front of her.

Bryn picked up the two-tined fork and took a bite of the slivered meat in sauce. It was so tender she barely needed to chew it. With the second bite, she felt renewed energy flowing to her muscles. She forced herself to slow down and take a morsel of bread and a sip from the goblet. Thank whatever gods they worshiped here, it wasn't wine but a room-temperature beverage that tasted of honey and mint.

"This is very good—no, it's delicious. Please forgive my manners. Are you going to eat, too?"

Ishana responded with a warm smile. "I shall convey your compliments to the cooking staff. I dined earlier, but please do not hold back on my account. If it would make you feel more comfortable, I'll have a little of the tisane and a bit of bread."

They sat for a time in silence as Bryn ate and Ishana sipped and nibbled. Finally, Bryn laid down her fork. "Thank you! I feel almost human again."

"Shall I show you to your sleeping chamber, then? Or would you like to bathe first?"

"A bath would be heavenly."

Ishana led the way to a tiled room with a tub, a remarkably Terran-like toilet and sink, and wicker shelves holding thick, folded towels. She clapped her hands and the girl, Maralise, presented herself. Within a surprisingly short time, Maralise had trotted off and returned with two yoked buckets of steaming water that looked to Bryn to be far too heavy for her. Nevarsin Tower was built in an area with natural hot springs, so the issue of indoor hot water had not arisen.

"Should she be doing that?" Bryn blurted out. "I mean, she's still a child."

"Would you prefer a *cold* bath? This is honorable work, far more pleasant than what the girl would be given at home." Ishana poured the water into the tub. "She comes from a poor farming village, and otherwise would have no prospect beyond an early marriage and a lifetime of grueling labor. In exchange for a few hours a day running errands about the castle, she receives an education, room and board, and likely an eventual post as a teacher if that is her area of interest."

"That makes sense. It's strange, compared to how I was brought up, to see work as the result of a prolonged period of formal education."

Ishana ran in cold water and tested it for temperature. "I understand your concerns perfectly well. As a girl, I remember my father—who was of your people, you know, a soldier left behind when the starships withdrew—of him telling me of the other places he'd seen. It seemed to me fantastical that there were whole worlds among the stars, lands where snow never fell, or endless deserts of black sand. He made it sound rather romantic." Her expression turned serious. "After the wars he had seen, the death and maiming from weapons *we* would never use, I expect he was entitled to embellish a little."

"Your father did not make up those worlds. I have seen some of them myself, and more besides. I spent summers on Thetis, which is more ocean than solid land."

"What a wonder!"

"Right now, the wonder is this bath!"

"Then I will leave you to it. There is a robe beside the towels. If you bring me your clothes, I will see to it they are cleaned and repaired, or if that is not possible, others are provided for you."

The moment Ishana closed the door behind her, Bryn stripped off her clothes and eased into the bath. The tub was a tight fit, but that was just as well since a child had carried in the heated water. And it was indeed a pleasure, warm enough to melt sore muscles and yet not unpleasantly hot. She let her head rest against the lip of the tub and closed her eyes, thinking that her father and Felicity were going to love this…

A tap on the door roused her. Bleary-eyed, she tried to focus.

Ishana poked her head in. "You poor thing, you are nigh as exhausted as the others. I feared you had fallen asleep. 'Twould not do to drown in a tub!"

Bryn sat upright, sending the water sloshing. "I'll be out in a minute."

She dried herself on a towel, wrapped the robe around her, and gathered up her clothes as requested. Ishana guided her to one of the doors beyond the dining and office.

Bryn was dazedly aware of a softly lit room, a scent like lavender and marjoram, with two beds and assorted furnishings, of Ishana helping her off with the robe, a moment when the air was entirely too chill on her bare skin, then the softness of a long, full nightgown, and finally sliding between sheets. The mattress shifted slightly as Ishana tucked the covers around her, a move so reminiscent of Bryn's childhood, so reassuring, that Bryn fell asleep almost at once.

◆◆◆

Bryn rummaged in her pack, found the comb that had been a parting gift from Adriana, blinked back tears, and yanked it through her tangled curls.

I need a haircut. At this rate, I'll have to use a butterfly clasp to keep it in order.

Garments of the sort she'd worn in the Tower were folded neatly over the chest at the foot of the bed: a long chemise of silky *linex*, over which went a long dress and a knee-length sleeveless vest that laced to fit. Layers made sense in this climate, and the style was flattering.

In the dining area, she helped herself to *jaco* and meat pies from the sideboard. She was joined around the dining table by her father and

Felicity, both of whom were dressed in Darkovan fashion. By their still-damp hair and flushed cheeks, they had availed themselves of morning baths. Maralise took up her station beside the sideboard, looking pleased with herself.

A tap on the outer door signaled the arrival of Desiderio. "Good morning. I hope you've all rested."

"Please, sit," Bryn said, indicating a vacant chair. "Would you like something to eat? Or *jaco*?"

"Thank you, no. I've already broken my fast. I come with news. The Regent wishes to see you this morning. I ran into the cadet carrying his message and decided to deliver it myself, since I will be escorting you."

"That soon?" Ernst said.

Bryn cast an anxious glance at her father. He looked drained by the journey and repeated struggles with the corticator, not at all prepared to make a crucial first impression.

"Father, you won't have to face this interview alone," Bryn said. "I'll be with you—and Felicity. If you agree, I can speak for you. Act on your behalf."

"There's no set protocol beyond the usual etiquette of greetings," Desiderio explained. "In fact, there's no precedent at all for why you're on Darkover. The audience might be a brief formality or it might be more complicated. I'm afraid I can't offer you more guidance than that. You'll have to use your judgment as the interview unfolds."

Bryn couldn't help a shiver of anxiety. This sort of thing was more her father's area of expertise, not hers, but he was in no shape to plead his own case.

"All right, then," she said, shoving away the plate with a half-eaten meat bun. "Do we wear anything special?"

"You are perfectly fine, and more than fine. You look enough like Darkovans to not rouse immediate hostility as *Terranan*, but you clearly aren't courtiers. You are slightly exotic and non-threatening. Anything you get right will be to your credit."

"I should hope that is the case," Felicity said dryly, "after all the tutoring you've given us."

Desiderio refused to take offense. "I would not expect too much. The Regent is likely to be polite, even cordial, but he may not be able to promise anything, even if he desired to do so. Comyn season is just beginning and the Council has not met yet, nor have the Keepers assembled."

Bryn could tell from her father's expression that he easily followed Desiderio's remarks. She hoped it would not be long before he received the help he needed.

With that, they all rose from the table. Maralise was already clearing the dishes as the door closed behind them. Desiderio took them down a broad corridor, up a flight of stairs and through an archway, and then across a wide foyer, with so many twists and turns that Bryn lost her sense of direction. Along the way, they passed more servants, all in livery, several young men in military-looking uniforms, and men and women in gorgeously rich attire. The foyer itself was dotted with people, mostly men, standing around talking. Most of them wore swords.

Felicity was clearly taking mental notes, and Ernst's gaze moved about the room, occasionally pausing but never for long. *He's looking for patterns,* Bryn thought, *patterns of movement, of association, the subtle signs universal to humans everywhere, signs that reveal dominance or deference. He knows how to do this—it's what he's done his entire career, judging the lines of influence and power.*

"*Terranan...*" someone muttered, and not in a friendly way. Felicity flinched. Bryn kept her gaze forward, doing her best to ignore the comment, and Ernst appeared not to have heard, concentrating on walking straight ahead. When Desiderio moved to the front of the party, making himself easily seen, the comments shifted, respectful now.

"*Comyn...*" someone uttered, and "*Vai dom,*" and then there were no more murmurs.

They neared an ornate pair of doors on the far side of the lobby. Guards armed with swords and grim expressions stood to either side.

"A fair day to you, Raymon," Desiderio said. "Is he ready for us?"

"Aye, *Dom* Desiderio. I expect he'll welcome the distraction. Go on in."

Inside lay a reception area, not a throne room although there was a large, imposing chair at the far end, a space in front of it, and benches arranged on either side of a central aisle. Courtiers parted as Bryn's party approached. She got a good look at the man on the throne, pale-skinned as so many Darkovans were, his red hair streaked with white, wearing an elaborate jacket and fitted pants of dark blue, ornamented with silver embroidery.

Desiderio halted before the chair and bowed. "*Vai dom,* I ask leave to present *Mestre* Ernst Haslund, his daughter, *Mestra* Bruna, both of Terra, and Doctor Felicia Sage of Alpha. *Dom* Varzil Alton-Hastur, Warden of Hastur, Regent of Elhalyn and of the Comyn."

"Enter and welcome, come in peace," *Dom* Varzil said with a smile that struck Bryn as carefully modulated. His voice was smooth and pleasantly resonant. "Speaking on behalf of the Comyn, I extend our hospitality to you all in the sincere hope that, whatever the past differences between our worlds, you will find yourselves as friends among us."

Past differences… Bryn sensed the slight stiffening in her father's muscles, although he had not moved, nor had his expression altered. She wished she knew what he was thinking. Without a conscious decision, she softened her *laran* barriers. And immediately barricaded her mind again. In that split second, she was inundated by a rush of broken phrases from her father's mind.

"Worlds breaking apart… Nagy's strong hand at the helm… Defiance swiftly punished… Treasonous rebels…"

NO! Must—not—give in— Not—my—thoughts—

"Together The Future. Together The Stars. One Alliance, One Hope." NAGY!

Breathe…just breathe…

"Once we were in danger of becoming merely another Terran colony," *Dom* Varzil went on, "but now we greet each other as equals."

Visual fragments flashed across Bryn's mind—*ships like star sharks, circling a planet around a swollen red sun…laying down line after line of bombs…*

Terrible things Nagy would not think twice about ordering. Things the corticator would force her father to support.

He was fighting it. She felt his struggle in the jagged mental currents. She saw it in every rigid line of muscle and tendon, the clenching of his jaw. He was terrified of how easily and unexpectedly the corticator gained control of his mind. Thendara was not safe, not when the instrument of treachery lay within him.

His fears, not mine. His.

She shuddered, the room suddenly chill.

How does he bear it?

Dom Varzil continued, stringing together flowery phrases filled with allusions to Darkovan legends about the blessings of hospitality and the truce that reigned there.

He's implying that anyone who breaks that truce on either side will suffer lasting punishment. She supposed that made sense, given the brutal Darkovan climate. But his words struck her as more veiled threat than reassurance.

Finally, *Dom* Varzil paused, his expression expectant.

"Thank you for your welcome," Bryn said, taking a half-step forward to make it clear that she spoke for their entire party. She was a little surprised to find her voice steady, her tone confident. "And to the people of Darkover, who have extended such generous hospitality to strangers."

"I am glad to hear you have been well treated. Lady Alanna sent word of your coming, and also your purpose here. These we will discuss in private, as is appropriate. You've arrived at the onset of Council season, so much of my time is not my own. For this hour, however, consider yourselves our honored guests. If you are at liberty, we will dine tomorrow night in the Hastur quarters. One of the cadets will escort you."

"*Vai dom*, that won't be necessary," Desiderio said. "I will accompany them."

"Very well. I look forward to seeing you all at the appointed time."

Desiderio replied with a few impeccably polite phrases, as it was clear they had been dismissed. Apparently, no greater formality in taking leave of the Regent was expected. Bryn didn't notice the tightness in her breathing until they were back in the corridor. Ernst had gone very pale. She slipped her arm beneath his elbow and felt the faint tremor of his muscles.

"My father needs rest," she said to Desiderio.

"It's not that," Ernst said. "Or not *just* that. I had—"

"I know what happened," Bryn said. "You don't need to explain, especially here." With a tilt of her head, she indicated the courtiers, a blur of color and motion.

"He's had another episode?" Felicity said, only half a question.

"Indeed." Ernst wheezed out the word. "It has passed now."

"We've got to get my father back to our rooms," Bryn said.

With Felicity leading, they made their way back toward the Alton wing. The noise of the public areas fell away, the quiet a balm to Bryn's nerves. Ernst had recovered his composure by the time they arrived back at their suite of rooms. He lowered himself into the divan in the sitting room. Ishana was directing a couple of servants in cleaning the dining area. She took one look at the Terrans and shooed the servants out.

Felicity began questioning Ernst about his symptoms. Any nausea? Headache? Visual distortions? Persistent, unwanted thoughts?

"Stop fussing," he said, waving her away. "I don't need a neurological examination." Ishana brought out a cup of steaming, straw-colored tisane. He accepted the cup and took a sip. "Thank you."

"It's a calming blend," Ishana said, "with a bit of mint and honey for taste."

"It's very good, just what I need."

"What you *need*," Felicity said, "is to get that infernal corticator removed from your skull."

"What I *need* is rest—and quiet!"

"Stop, both of you," Bryn said. "This isn't helping."

"You're right," Felicity said after a moment.

Ernst hauled himself to his feet and, shaking off Felicity's attempt at support, went off to his room. Ishana remained, watching him with a worried expression, then returned to her work in the dining area.

Bryn waited a few more moments, then tapped on her father's door.

"What is it?"

"It's me. May I come in?" At his mumbled response, she lifted the latch and entered.

The room beyond was in much the same style as the one she shared with Felicity: two narrow beds, a dresser with pitcher and basin, an armoire, and a couple of comfortable-looking chairs. A carpet patterned in dark colors covered the floor.

She lowered herself to the bed beside him and took his hand between her own. Beneath his cool, dry skin, his joints felt swollen.

"How are you, Father? Really?"

He folded the pillow to prop up his head. "I can't deny that this latest episode has taken a deal out of me."

"Something during the interview must have triggered it."

"Don't be disingenuous. We both know what it was."

"I'm so sorry."

"My dear." His fingers tightened around hers. "This is in no way your fault. The Regent was correct, you know. Given the difficult history between Terra and Darkover, we cannot expect to find a smooth path forward."

"You're right, it's early days yet. It's just difficult to be told we must wait, given how hard it's been to get here."

"Wait? I can't imagine you sitting still."

"Waiting is exactly what I'll do if you need me here."

A sigh. "Given past experience, the best thing I can do is sleep as much as I can and give my brain the quiet it needs to recover as best it can. I felt better after the sessions in Nevarsin."

"We mustn't give up. Alanna believed the *leroni* here could do much more."

Ernst seemed to have aged a decade since fleeing Alpha. For as long as she could remember, he had worked tirelessly for the causes that mattered to him. It was all there in the sagging flesh, the hollows around his eyes, the lines bracketing his mouth. She wished—oh! how she wished—she could ease his anguish. In a moment of insight, she realized that she had chosen her profession not solely because it wasn't overtly political and therefore different from his. Even as a child, she'd known how much he'd poured out from himself. His words, his long hours of work, the thousand tiny daily sacrifices. He had never meant to neglect her. She had never doubted his love for her. Her young life had been marked by those moments of absence, of silence. No wonder she had sought out work that trained her to bridge those losses, as if by reaching her patients, she could also reach him.

Her monitoring skills— But no. She wasn't even remotely qualified to blunt the corticator's influence, which had required the combined talents of the Nevarsin circle. Besides, it was dangerous if not unethical to work on family members.

"You need not watch over me while I nap," Ernst murmured. "You have other matters to attend to. Go, go!"

With a kiss on his forehead, Bryn went.

"Do you believe *Mestre* Ernst is in immediate danger?" Desiderio asked once she had closed the door behind her.

"No more so than he's been all along, and besides, there's nothing we can do at this moment." Bryn fell back in one of the chairs beside the fireplace, thinking, *Nothing* I *can do*. Rousing herself, she said, "You said the Keepers' Council had not yet met, but can I contact them individually? Surely, with the recommendation of Alanna Alar, they can at least begin their evaluation of my father's condition."

"The most influential living *leronis* is Illona Rider, the old Comyn Tower Keeper," Desiderio said. "She is quite elderly and has retired to the Tower, but her word carries great weight."

"Then I should speak with her as soon as possible."

"I doubt you would be admitted, even with Lady Alanna's introduction. I don't know if *Domna* Illona is open to receiving visitors at all."

We'll see about that. Manners were one thing; the health of her father was another. Quickly, she quelled the thought, but he didn't seem to have picked up on it.

"Is there no one else?" she said. "I don't want to wait for the Council to make up their minds. The reason we came to Darkover in the first place was the advanced state of their telepathic abilities. My father needs help now."

"I don't know which Keepers have arrived, but I shall make inquiries. This may take some time, so be patient. Council season proceeds at its own pace."

"Well, I for one am not going to sit around." Felicity began to pace, gesturing with her hands. "Further sessions with telepathic techniques may not be any more successful. If we wait to find out, we'll be in an even more disadvantageous position than we are now. Bryn, you know I hold your father in the highest esteem and I have not the slightest doubt about your clinical acumen within your field, but in this matter I must trust my own judgment, which is that the theta-corticator device must be surgically removed, not merely blunted."

"You mean to cut the device from *Mestre* Ernst's brain?" Desiderio asked, clearly appalled.

Felicity shot him a pointed look that said his opinion was unsupported by scientific rationale and hence, unworthy of consideration. In her student days, Bryn had seen such looks reduce a research assistant to tears. Desiderio just stared back at Felicity, unintimidated.

Bryn's determination hardened. Felicity wasn't going to wait around while the Regent or the Council or whoever else made up their minds? Well, neither was she. She would seek out Illona Rider or another Keeper now gathering for the Council season and enlist their help. At least, they could judge the likelihood of fully disabling the corticator.

"First, we must locate appropriate resources." Felicity paused in her pacing. "Will you come with me, Bryn? I could use a second opinion."

"I don't know how much use I'd be," Bryn said. What was she thinking, to leave her father alone in such a state? No, it was too risky. She'd have to wait for another chance. She felt as if half the air had gone out of the room. "I don't think it's wise—I dare not leave my father. You go on without me."

"I'll let you know what I discover." Felicity gathered her shoulder bag and notebook, then left.

Desiderio sat down on the edge of the chair facing Bryn. "I do not like to see you forced into such a choice. Your teacher has asked for your opinion, and surely that is not a small thing. I would offer to sit with your father, but I have obligations today. Is there no one else you would trust to look after him?"

"It should be me," Bryn said. "Another episode might leave him confused, and he'll need someone he knows and trusts. You need not remain since you have other commitments." She heard the stiffness in her own voice and caught the hint of recoil in his expression. She hadn't meant to hurt him by her rebuff, but it could not be helped.

She wasn't sure what she felt as he bowed and took his leave. Regret? Sadness? *In the end, what does it matter?* she asked herself. And yet it did matter.

"Excuse me." Ishana stood on the threshold between the dining and sitting areas, a pottery pitcher in hand. "Forgive the intrusion, but I would be happy to stay with your father. I'm not kin, but he knows me. And I've experience as a nurse."

Bryn considered the way Ishana had calmed her father with a cup of tisane, and the older woman's calm demeanor and quick action. "I would appreciate your remaining here, if my father agrees. I have an errand of my own."

"Will you be requiring an escort? A guide?"

Bryn hesitated. It would definitely be easier to find Comyn Tower with someone who knew the way. Desiderio had tutored her on the power structure of the Comyn, not whether she would attract attention by wandering these corridors alone. "Yes, thank you, a guide. Maralise, if she has no other duties."

"I'll summon her."

Bryn knocked on her father's door. He was awake. When she explained the situation, he agreed with her reasoning. He said he liked Ishana and felt comfortable with her.

"After today, it's clear I can't go on the way things are," he pointed. "I'd rather risk surgery, instead of enduring another such attack."

Bryn laid her hand on her father's shoulder, feeling the bones that protruded too sharply. "I will find a solution."

Back in the sitting area, Maralise was waiting beside Ishana, her face glowing as if she'd just been invited to a party. "On your way, then," Ishana said, and went back to the dining area, where she could hear Ernst if he called.

"Oh, *mestra*! Where would you like to go?" Maralise bounced on her toes as they left the suite. "The Escalia flower markets? Threadneedle Street with its fine cloth? A stroll through the Old Town?"

"Comyn Tower. And I would rather my visit not attract too much attention. I'm presenting greetings from the Tower where I studied in Nevarsin, although I haven't received an official invitation yet. It might prove embarrassing if they're not ready to receive me."

With an air of solemnity, the girl led Bryn back toward the main part of the castle. Here and there they passed a knot of people, nobles or higher functionaries by the elaborateness of their dress and by the way they ignored the young servant and Bryn in her ordinary Darkovan clothes. They crossed a courtyard, a flagstone square lined with benches and trees. A trio of ladies twittered like songbirds as they hurried in the opposite direction. Re-entering the castle complex on the far side after the brightness of the day was like plunging into a cavern. Bryn stumbled to a halt while her eyes adapted. Maralise slipped her fingers into Bryn's and gently pulled her forward.

The way twisted like a maze, so Bryn would have gotten lost if she'd tried to find her way without a guide. It was a misnomer to call this place a castle; it was a midden of castles, layer upon architectural layer. The final passage led to a door lit by a globe set in a wall bracket. The blue-tinged light reminded Bryn of a starstone, and she remembered Silvia mentioning that *laran* could be used to power such a device.

Maralise hung back as Bryn approached the door.

"Come on," Bryn said. "You needn't wait outside."

"Oh, no! 'Tis for *leroni* only, and I'm none of that!" Maralise exclaimed with such alarm that Bryn refrained from urging her further.

At the lift of the latch, the door swung open. A young woman stood just inside the door. She was about Bryn's age, pale and very stern-looking, her flame-bright hair tied back so severely, it looked painted on her skull. Like the matrix workers at Nevarsin, she wore a robe of soft gray. Her expression was calm as she lifted one eyebrow in unmistakable inquiry.

"I'm Bryn Haslund. I studied at Nevarsin Tower and I'm here to convey greetings from Lady Alanna Alar. May I speak with one of the Keepers?"

"Please come in." The young *leronis* moved back for Bryn to enter. Beyond the entrance hall, a small arched doorway opened to one side, and stairs led upward into darkness.

Once inside, Bryn felt a subtle buffering of the ongoing low-level telepathy of the outside. She followed the young woman up a spiraling staircase and onto a gallery overlooking the entrance hall. The young woman said nothing, only paused outside the door at the end of the hallway and sent a mental signal, *She's here*. Then she opened the door and stood back.

Light streamed through the high, mullioned windows, filling the room with warmth. A half-dozen chairs, either upholstered or strewn with enough embroidered pillows to afford equal comfort, formed a rough circle. End tables held pitchers and goblets and plates of the pastries that accompanied any *laran* working. Two women and two men, clad alike in crimson robes, sat there.

Bryn Haslund of Terra, be welcome among us. The telepathic message came from the nearer of the two women. *I am Fiona Dellerey of Comyn Tower, and I bid you welcome to Comyn Tower.* "Alanna Alar has sent word of your coming and of the dangers she believes follow in your wake."

"We have the highest respect for *Domna* Alanna," said one of the men—*Robert Syrtis, from Neskaya*—"but we prefer to draw our own conclusions."

"I believe Lady Alanna's concerns are justified," Bryn said.

Then came a presence, like light refracted from a diamond. Bryn turned to see an elderly woman standing quietly just inside the door. In a rustle of clothing, the others stood.

"Please be at your ease, all of you." The voice, reedy with age, was still strong. "I'm Illona Rider, once Keeper of this Tower, now occasional counselor and repository of history." Aided by a stout walking stick, she made her way to an empty chair.

"I—we—came here in the hope that *laran* healing could free my father's mind from the mechanical thought-control device implanted in his skull by agents of the Star Alliance despot, Arthur Nagy. Lady Alanna felt that the existence of such a device and the risks posed by Nagy's ambitions are of concern to Darkover, as well. It would be to your benefit that my father regains mastery of his own mind, as he is the single greatest obstacle to Nagy's reign."

A moment passed in silence, and then another, during which Bryn struggled against the thought that she had committed a grievous offense. Her fear urged her to make appeasing gestures, to back down, to pretend she had not said what she had. *No, not in this place of truth. I will put my faith in the fact that we cannot lie to one another when speaking mind-to-mind.*

Truly, you are one of us, a Darkovan by spirit if not by birth, someone said.

A smile lit the face of the old Keeper. "Let us hear what has so convinced our Alanna of the importance of your presence on Darkover. Laurinda, bring up a chair."

And now for your story. Illona's mental voice, resonant with power, filled the chamber. *Not aloud. Let your memories guide us.*

Bryn cast her mind back to that fateful day when the sky had seemed on fire, the beginning of all her running and searching. She lingered over finding her father on Alpha, the horror of how the corticator technology had been perverted, the testing of mind control on a crowd, and the treacherous words spewing from her father's mouth. Although she kept Leonin's death as a private grief, a gentle pulse of sympathy enveloped her. Black, always she returned to Black, following implacably after her, perhaps even now discovering where she and her father had disappeared, if Alanna's vision were accurate. The Keepers' circle sensed every moment, their presence like featherdown. How much time elapsed, she could not tell, only that when she came back to herself, her palms were slick with sweat.

One of the men held out a goblet whose contents smelled faintly of lemon.

Kirian.

Bryn took the goblet and sipped. Starstones flared, evoking a glimmer from Bryn's own. Through it, she sensed the silent conversation, the judging and weighing, the sharing of other memories—mostly from Illona—and the tales. *Ages of Chaos* and *Sharra* she recognized, but not other fragments.

Movement rippled through the circle. "We cannot judge the likelihood of the Star Alliance searching for you here," Fiona said, "but if they do, given what you have shown us and what we know about the direction they were taking when they left Darkover, that risk is serious, indeed. We cannot stand against their weapons, not without using those we have forsworn for many generations, and perhaps not even then."

"The only way that is possible is if my father controls his own mind again. Alanna believed that your resources here exceed those of the healers at Nevarsin. Will you at least look at him?"

"I think we must," Laurida said. "But not today. And of course, if we were to attempt dealing with this mechanical device, we would require the entire Keepers' Council, and we are not fully assembled yet. Tomorrow evening would suit us for a preliminary examination, though."

"Unfortunately, we have a dinner engagement with the Regent," Bryn said.

"Perhaps the following afternoon? One of us will come to you." Laurinda named the hour.

Bryn and Maralise arrived back at their quarters to find the door ajar and the rooms in an uproar. Raised voices reached them, men shouting and Felicity shouting back, even more loudly.

Bryn burst into the sitting area, Maralise on her heels. At a glance, she took in Felicity, fists on her hips, facing four uniformed men. Each of them towered over her slight frame. Grim-faced, they kept their hands on the hilts of their swords. Ernst stood at the threshold to the dining area, with Ishana a pace behind.

Felicity spoke very quickly, barely pausing for breath as she switched back and forth between *casta* and Terran Standard. "I am a full Professor and Distinguished Research Fellow at the University of Alpha, and I have not come all the way to this forgotten Class D planet, only to have some pea-brained soldiers stand in my way."

"Please calm yourselves, everyone," Ernst said as he approached the guards. "There is no reason for a confrontation. Doctor Sage is not a criminal but an honored scholar and guest of the Regent. Surely there has been a misunderstanding."

"Your pardon, *mestre*, but the meaning is clear enough," the captain said. Now addressing Felicity directly, he continued, "In plain terms, *mestra*, you are guilty of criminal trespass."

"Balderdash!" Felicity snapped. She glowered at the captain in a way that would have reduced her teaching assistants to tears. "It is luminously apparent that your Regent is not in possession of the pertinent facts."

"I don't know what *balderdash* is—some version of off-worlder *reish*, most like. You failed to heed our warnings, and you're very lucky I chose not to throw you into the deepest dungeon beneath the castle, there to await the Regent's disposal of you."

"*Disposal*?" Felicity's voice rose in volume but dropped dangerously in pitch.

"Will someone please tell me what's going on?" Bryn said, her voice ringing through the pause.

The captain did not take his eyes off Felicity. "Doctor Sage attempted to enter the Terran Base without authorization. She was informed that the Regent has forbidden unauthorized access. I escorted her back here with a warning, rather than placing her under formal arrest. I have been attempting to explain to her the gravity of her situation and the necessity of refraining from a further incident."

Felicity folded her arms across her chest. Her lips tightened into a downward-curving line.

"Your consideration is appreciated," Bryn said to the captain. She gestured toward the door, angling into the personal space of the nearest guard. The guard responded by edging toward the exit.

"Who will be responsible for her behavior?" The captain asked.

"We will *discuss* the matter," Bryn said in a tone meant the conversation was at an end. With a brief bow, a mere nod of the head, the captain left the room, followed by the other guards.

"Well!" Felicity unslung her shoulder bag and threw it down on the floor beside one of the chairs before the fireplace. She slumped into the chair and closed her eyes, a signal that she wished to be left alone for the moment.

Bryn went to her father. "Are you all right?"

"Yes, yes, sweetheart. I'm fine, just a bit startled by the ruckus. Now we'd best find out more about the present situation."

Ishana let out an audible breath. "I'll make tea."

Ernst walked over to Felicity's chair. Bryn lowered herself into the opposite seat, studying her mentor's expression. She couldn't read much on Felicity's face, but indignation and frustration shimmered in the psychic space between them.

Felicity's chest rose and fell rapidly, slowing now as her color returned to normal. She opened her eyes, glancing from one to the other. "You needn't fuss. I'm not about to repeat my lapse in judgment."

"Yes, but what happened?" Bryn asked.

"Obviously, when I arrived at the Terran Base I was refused entry. The place is practically a military fortress with fences and locks and sword-wielding goons everywhere!"

Bryn reflected that Felicity was not only accustomed to coming and going from the university laboratories as she pleased, but she also had the typical Alphan attitude toward armed guards. "That must have been disappointing, to say the least."

Felicity sighed, a release of tension. "To say the least." She sat up straighter. "Well, I must endeavor to think of today's obstacle as an unexpected result, not a door slammed in my face. Which it amounted to, although not literally. I never reached the doors."

"Darkover is not Alpha or even Terra," Ernst said. "We must adapt ourselves."

"As I am now reminded. Stars, I've overcome worse obstacles."

"Hopefully, this too will prove to be a delay, not an end," Ernst said.

Felicity's expression shifted. "There's something else. Setting aside my dislike at not being able to inspect the facilities, it strikes me that someone went to inordinate lengths to secure those premises. I'd expect a modicum of security, if only to safeguard the equipment that couldn't be removed. Any weapons that might have been left behind, that sort of thing. These precautions seemed excessive. There were too many guards, too much—dare I say it?—paranoia."

Alanna's vision of the ship like a shark of the skies... Had the base detected Black's ship on approach?

"Too many men walking about with swords," Felicity said.

"Swords, so primitive," Ernst said.

"Yet they are permitted under the Compact," Bryn said. "Swords and knives are limited in their reach. The aggressor runs the same risk as the target. It's a matter of honor. To Darkovans, the alternative is not disarmament but a return to times past, when *laran* generated instruments capable of widespread destruction. In comparison, a few swords and knives seem innocuous. After all, they require skill for effective use, not pulling a trigger."

An image rose in her mind, the weight of the tangler in her hands on Alpha. The weapon had felt cold in her grasp, inert but malevolent. And heavy, as heavy as grief. This thing *killed* people, she'd thought. Now she felt sick.

"My dear?" Ernst bent toward her, concern plain on his features.

"I'm sorry, I was remembering— It doesn't matter now."

A knock on the door announced Desiderio's arrival. He entered in a flurry of chilly air, his cheeks reddened as if he'd hurried in from the outside. "I came as soon as I heard. A *Terranan* woman tried to break into the old base." To Felicity: "I assume that was you."

"I did not *try to break into* anywhere," Felicity said, clearly annoyed at having to explain what happened yet again. "I approached the perimeter fence and was summarily escorted off the property."

"You attempted to enter the Terran Base without the Regent's permission?"

"We have already been welcomed by the Regent," Felicity replied, as if that were a sufficient invitation. "It's incomprehensible to me that an innocent investigation should be misconstrued as if it were an act of espionage."

"With all respect, Darkover is not your academy."

Ernst made a *calm-down* gesture. "Alienating our hosts will only result in further delays. We are strangers here, after all, and still learning Darkovan ways."

Ishana emerged from the dining area with a tray bearing a steaming pitcher, enough mugs to offer one to Desiderio, and a pot of honey. She poured out tea for everyone and handed it around. Ernst took a seat, although Desiderio remained standing. Ishana retreated to the food preparation area.

"I knew what Felicity proposed to do," Bryn said, once everyone seemed calmer. "I saw nothing wrong with it. In fact, it made sense to me to gather information about a surgical solution to my father's condition as a backup if the Keepers' Council couldn't help him. I am as much at fault as she is. More so, perhaps, since while she was attempting and failing to enter the Terran Base, I was meeting with members of the Keepers' Council."

"You were?" Desiderio stared at her, as did Felicity and Ernst.

"Please stop acting as if what we did was scandalous. Neither Felicity nor I acted irresponsibly. We harmed no one. We wouldn't have even annoyed anyone if those guards hadn't tried to arrest her. All we were trying to do was ask for help. I was not aware we needed permission to do so."

"I know you both meant well," Desiderio said, "but unfortunately the Regent may see *Mestra* Felicity's actions in another light. As for meeting with the Keepers, they do not answer to either the Regent or the Comyn Council, although they would probably not act against the direct wishes of the Comyn, at least not under ordinary circumstances. Well, it is done now, and not all the smiths in Zandru's forge can put that chick back into its egg. May I ask how your visit was received?"

"They were happy to meet me, one *leronis* to another," Bryn said, smiling a little at the memory. "Lady Alanna's introduction opened the door, so to speak, and they understood our need for help. The Keeper of Comyn Tower has invited my father for an evaluation the day after tomorrow."

"Excellent!" Ernst said.

"I'm happy that *one* of us was successful," Felicity said, "although that does not diminish the urgency of my own investigation. The most likely location of medical facilities is still the Terran Base. Even though the laboratories and operating rooms may have been closed up for years, the equipment remains. It should have been constructed of durable materials. Stored properly, many of the drugs and disinfectants would still be usable, or if not, I could employ computer-assisted manufacture."

"Your pardon, *mestra*." Ishana emerged from the dining area, a fresh pot in her hand. "Do I understand that your objective this morning was the medical wing of the Terran Base?"

"The very same. Please do not give me yet another argument about my failure to ask leave of the Regent. I will not be scolded."

"Even if you had gained access, it would have made no difference in the end." Ishana set the pot down on the table beside the hearth. "I did not understand earlier, or I would have saved you the aggravation. You *cannot* enter that part of the base."

Felicity made a dismissive gesture, but before she could say anything, Bryn asked, "How is it impossible? Besides being fenced off and guarded?"

"The scientific areas were sealed off, and I believe the medical ones as well. Much of the equipment has been—I do not know the correct term—paralyzed?—and the chemicals made unusable. Even if you could hack your way through the doors, it would do you no good."

The three Terrans reacted to this statement with stunned silence.

"Why...why would anyone do that?" Bryn murmured, recovering the quickest. "Why destroy precious resources?"

"You will remember that at the time of the Trailmen's Fever, the Federation had already left Darkover, but some of its people remained. My father, Jeremiah Reed, was among them. He had served in the *Terranan* military, and his work involved the deliberate creation of plagues and deadly agents akin to those we ourselves developed during the Ages of Chaos."

Bryn's stomach roiled. Felicity was silent, her face pale, and Ernst sat, immobile.

"He related to me how he used the Federation's scientific equipment and computing devices to create a treatment, although in the end, it required *laran* to perfect the serum. When it was over, a small group of leaders decided that such resources must not be allowed to fall into the wrong hands. There had already been one insurgency, led by the Ridenow. It was deemed too much of a risk to simply lock those areas. My father said it was a difficult decision, but he had seen the terrible effects of *Terranan* weapons on other planets. This was the only way he could protect Darkover from becoming a similar battlefield."

If Jeremiah Reed had been part of his generation's military, he might well have felt a special guilt. And an equally potent desire to make sure it never happened again.

"Thus was the Compact born during the time of Varzil the Good," Desiderio said, "although those weapons were created using *laran*, not *Terranan* science."

"I cannot fault the decision," Ernst said. "And I speak in the full knowledge that I myself may suffer if the Keepers cannot remove or disable this device in my skull. Weighing so many lives against only one—even if it is mine—the choice is clear."

"I'm very sorry to be the bearer of ill news," Ishana said. "I hope that you will find another way."

"Well, I for one do not believe it!" Felicity said, having recovered her composure. "I *refuse* to believe it until I have examined the premises and equipment for myself."

"That is unlikely, as the Regent has not given you permission," Desiderio said.

"If the Regent can forbid access, he can also authorize it," Ernst pointed out.

"Why would he, when those areas of the base are already inaccessible?" Desiderio said.

Bryn took another sip of tea. If Varzil Hastur were looking for an excuse to refuse his cooperation, Felicity's actions might well have provided him with one. She didn't know him well enough to have a sense of how he'd respond. Yet, she reminded herself, if anyone could smooth over a misstep like this one, it was her father.

"It seems I shall be required to apologize for what I have done *and* ask permission for what I intend to do in the future," Felicity said. "However, the base laboratories are not the only resources. There's a university, I'm told. Leonie, the young Renunciate who came with us to Thendara to study at the Bridge Society academy, said they train midwives in surgical techniques."

Desiderio cleared his throat. "*Mestra* Felicity, I commend your desire to be open and aboveboard with *Dom* Varzil. That will go a long way toward mollifying any offense he may have taken at today's incident. At the same time, I caution you to not give him reason to refuse. Give the matter time to settle, at least until tomorrow's dinner."

"What do you propose, then? Staying here and creating surgical equipment out of rolled-up napkins?" Without waiting for an answer, she gathered up her shoulder bag and retreated into the dining area, where she proceeded to set out her notebook and stare at its pages.

◆◆◆

The following evening, Ishana presented all three Terrans with clothing suitable for a dinner with the Regent. For Bryn and Felicity, there were ankle-length gowns with bands of embroidery along the cuffs and necklines, the fit adjusted by lacings up the back, topped by long sleeveless vests slit up the sides; for her father, a loose robe belted over shirt and trousers. Desiderio presented himself at the appropriate hour, his appearance elegant but restrained. As he bowed ceremoniously to them all, his gaze lingered on Bryn a trifle longer. She could not read his thoughts, yet her mind was aware of his.

Outside the windows, full night had fallen, but glowing globes filled the hallways with blue-tinted light. A servant in blue and silver livery admitted them to the Hastur quarters. A blaze churned out heat from the immense fireplace along one wall of the dining area. The table, chairs, and sideboard were massive, the wood dark with age. Even the jewel-toned carpet beneath their feet was threadbare in places.

Varzil Alton-Hastur had been standing with a small group of people on the far side of the fireplace. He came forward as they entered. "Welcome, my friends! And Desiderio, it's good to see you again."

Desiderio bowed. "*Vai dom*."

"Let us not stand upon ceremony. We'll have more than enough of that once the season gets properly underway." Varzil indicated the other guests, who now approached. "My dear," he said to the woman, "allow me to present our *Terranan* guests, Ernst Haslund, his daughter, Bruna, and Felicia

Sage. *Mestre* Haslund is a statesman, *Mestra* Sage, a scientist, and—" to Bryn, "—I'm sorry, I don't quite understand your profession, *damisela*."

"To tell the truth, I'm not sure anymore."

"My wife, *Domna* Liriel MacAnndra-Hastur," Varzil said, to more bows all around. "And here is my oldest son and heir, Felix, and our cousin, Arnad Alton-Hastur, and Vittorio Ardais."

Everyone said hello, the Darkovans responding with *Z'par servu*, the local version of *At your service*. Ernst, refreshed by a day's rest and thoroughly in his element, answered with ease and charm. Felicity was not nearly as affable, but she had always hated faculty meetings. Bryn murmured responses when appropriate, while observing their hosts and other guests.

Alton...Hastur...Ardais. Three of the Domains were represented here.

"I am especially pleased to make your acquaintance, *Mestra* Bruna," Arnad said. He was a personable young man about Desiderio's age, with dark chestnut hair, calm gray eyes, and a faintly military bearing. "My cousin has spoken of you with warmth."

"And he has told me much about you and your boyhood adventures at Armida."

"None of it true, I assure you!"

Their conversation was interrupted when *Domna* Liriel offered goblets of wine to everyone. When Varzil proposed a toast to friendship, Bryn took only a sip and noticed that her father did likewise. It wasn't a particularly elegant vintage by Terran standards, especially since it had been heated and heavily spiced. Felicity lifted hers but did not partake. Desiderio met Bryn's gaze over the rim of his own cup and she saw his approval—felt it, for they were once again in light rapport. His glance flickered to his friend, Arnad, and then to Vittorio Ardais.

Tread carefully, he meant.

I intend to.

A bevy of servants carried in covered trays, everyone took their seats as directed by *Domna* Liriel, and the meal began. Bryn's danger-sense prickled, although she could not discern its source. There was no reason to believe these people meant direct harm. The conversation began with general comments about the food—richer than Bryn was accustomed to—the weather, and preparations for a gala ball.

"You must forgive me for staring," Felix Alton-Hastur said to her, since they were seated side by side. "I've never met anyone who was born on another planet. Off-worlders, we call you."

"What, did you think they had horns and hooves or were as blue as Zandru's demons?" Vittorio Ardais tossed back the contents of his goblet and held it out for a servant to refill. He clearly meant it as a joke, but there was an edge to his voice. Felix flushed, the color obvious on his pale complexion.

"Let us not oppress our guests with the superstitions of our ancestors," Varzil said. "Folklore and legend are all very well, but we are modern, educated people. It wasn't that long ago that our world was part of a star-spanning empire." To Bryn's ears, he did not think this an evil. She made a mental note of it, and watched her father's expression shift slightly, indicating he was doing the same.

"And for that, we must take pride?" Vittorio scowled. "Your pardon, *vai dom*, *vai domna*, and honored guests, but the Federation went its own way a generation ago. If we mattered that much, if we were truly essential to the progress of civilization, surely we would have been re-contacted by now." He gestured with his goblet, as if the wine had loosened his tongue, but Bryn noticed his eyes had not reddened, nor did he slur his words.

An act, to put us off our guard?

"And yet," Arnad cut in, "here they are."

"In no way do we represent an official delegation," Ernst said. "The tides of fortune have cast us upon your hospitality, at least until we discover how we may repay you."

"Surely the discharge of an honorable duty is recompense enough," *Domna* Liriel said with the practiced charm of a hostess.

"So Darkover and the Terrans have not been in contact since the withdrawal?" Bryn said, taking advantage of the brief pause. "I had heard there were more recent, unofficial visits."

"Not through proper channels, that much is true." Varzil's expression darkened. "Darkover was not entirely forgotten. Our position on the galactic arm offers the same advantages to smugglers and outlaws as it once did to legitimate traders." He paused to take a sip from his goblet.

The table grew quiet as Bryn's danger-sense flared. "I'm sorry," she said, "have I said something amiss? Please accept my apologies. I spoke out of ignorance of your customs."

"Child, your intentions were innocent," Liriel said with a kindly smile. "No one here thinks the worse of you. But contact with your people remains a...delicate subject."

"One perhaps best reserved for the proper time and place, which is not at the dinner table." Varzil gestured for the servants to remove the dishes. "Come now, shall we have some music? Desi, you'll sing for us."

"If you wish it," Desiderio replied.

An assortment of musical instruments had been laid out in an adjacent room, including a lap harp. Liriel accompanied Desiderio for a couple of ballads in what must have been very old *casta*, and then duets with Arnad and Felix. Bryn was impressed with the quality of the singing, clearly well-practiced. Of course, with Darkover's long winter nights and an absence of vids or even books, people would have to create their own entertainment.

"And you, *damisela*?" Varzil asked during a break. "Do you sing or play? I would very much enjoy hearing *Terranan* music."

"I'm afraid I don't. It's not common on Terra, except for professionals."

Arnad started to laugh, then sputtered in an effort to smother it. "Your pardon, please! It's just that in *casta, professional singer* is a polite way of saying—help me out, Desi—"

"A courtesan? But there are also legitimate forms of vocal music."

"Oh," Felix said with a dismissive wave of one hand, "*Terranan* opera was one of *Domna* Marguerida's enthusiasms, you know, and continues in favor with certain elements within the Comyn and wealthier merchants. I never could find anything of interest in it, myself."

Liriel said, "I believe Lady Alton composed several operas on Darkovan themes, thus creating a musical art form that bridges the two worlds."

"Do you care for opera?" Varzil asked Felicity.

"Me? I hadn't thought about it, one way or another, but I believe I do. It harkens back to a time when people relied on their own talent and training for entertainment."

"So you might say that opera arose during that era, when Terra was not very different from Darkover," Ernst added.

"Each world is best left to its own development," Vittorio added in a lower tone.

"I know little of the ancient history of Terra," Arnad said, raising his voice, "and therefore defer to our learned guests. I believe the Thendara Opera Company is putting on a new production for the season. It's based on the legendary *Lady Bruna's Ride*, I believe. Since it is in your honor," with a courtly nod to Bryn, "we must plan an outing together."

Legendary? Bryn thought. *That explains why everyone insists on calling me* Bruna.

Liriel clapped her hands like a delighted child, although neither her husband nor her son looked particularly eager at the prospect. Vittorio scowled at the prospect of attending the opera, which did not surprise Bryn in the least. Felix muttered words about the demands of the Council.

"Well, well, we mustn't deny our guests the amusements of the season," Varzil said. "There will be time for serious matters, as well as the usual round of balls and parties."

Yet more social events while there is no progress toward helping my father! Bryn forced a polite smile. She was not here to be entertained with musical evenings or flirtation.

"Speaking of amusements, we would like to visit some of Thendara's points of interest," she said, addressing Varzil. "I understand that access to the Terran Base is restricted, but would there be a similar problem in visiting the university? Doctor Sage, as a noted scholar from Alpha University, has a particular interest in Darkover's educational institutions. And the Bridge Society academy, as well?"

"Of course, you are all free to explore the city as you wish," Varzil replied. "I will arrange for an escort to ensure your safety." He seemed pleased at the prospect of their visiting the university.

"*Dom* Varzil," Desiderio said, "I would be honored to accompany our *Terranan* friends."

"And I," said Arnad. "I look forward to another stimulating discussion of off-worlder customs." He nodded to Bryn and her companions. "Tomorrow, if you are not otherwise engaged?"

"There is nothing I would like better," Felicity said.

"Excellent, most excellent," Varzil said, although Vittorio Ardais exuded an aura of subtle disapproval.

"Thank you," Felicity said. Anyone who did not know her well would have thought her subdued, but Bryn knew better.

Glancing at her father, Bryn noticed that he was slumping a little and his face looked ashen. What was the proper way of excusing themselves?

"Well, my dears," Liriel said, setting aside the lap harp and rising, as if she had read Bryn's mind. "It's late and I'm afraid we have kept you overlong."

After several rounds of bowing and appreciation of hospitality and *think-nothing-of-it*, Arnad took his leave. Bryn, Ernst, and Felicity headed back to their suite, Desiderio with them.

Ishana was waiting for them with an offer of honey-sweetened chamomile tisane. Bryn wondered silently if the woman's response to any event was to make tea, but the timing was perfect. The warmth soothed her stomach after the tension of the dinner.

"If you don't need me for anything else," Ishana said, "I'll bid you goodnight."

"Yes, thank you."

After Ishana and Desiderio had left, the Terrans gathered around the fireplace.

"So what did you think of this evening?" Bryn said. "What was really going on?"

"Clearly, there are fractures within the Comyn," Ernst said. "Factions, and factions within factions, I don't doubt. I believe our host is essentially neutral, at least when it comes to our presence."

"You think *Dom* Varzil is neutral?" Felicity said. From her disapproving expression, she still regarded him as an obstacle.

"He made sure to include those expressing two opposing views, which suggests he does not subscribe to either of them. Vittorio went to lengths to appear inebriated, but he was clearly in command of himself. His antagonism to contact with the Alliance was unmistakable."

"Yes, I thought so, too," Felicity said.

"As did I," Bryn commented. "I noticed that Varzil specifically did not agree with Vittorio. Arnad and Desiderio were the only overtly friendly people there, if you discount *Domna* Liriel, with her gracious hostessing."

"At any rate," Ernst said, "if Vittorio represents the anti-Terran faction, clearly Arnad as the representative of Alton speaks for those who would welcome renewed relations."

"So we can assume Ardais wants continued isolation, but Alton would favor engagement, and Hastur is neutral," Bryn said, ticking off the Domains on her fingers. "That leaves four more—evenly divided, do you think, Father?"

He favored her with a smile. "Had the division been unequal, Varzil would not have set up his dinner as he did. Now that we are forewarned, we can look forward to seeing how these divisions develop."

"And how much they interfere with our mission," Felicity said.

"Perhaps we will learn more on our tour of the university tomorrow," Bryn said, smothering a yawn.

The next morning, Desiderio and Arnad presented themselves to the suite just as Bryn and the others were finishing breakfast.

"Where would you like to go first?" Desiderio asked.

"The university," Felicity said firmly. "It is the most likely to have the equipment I'm looking for or the Darkovan equivalent, anyway."

Together they ventured out into the city. It had rained overnight, leaving the streets glistening and the air fresh if chilly. Quite a number of people filled the streets, obviously in a holiday mood with bright ribbons and entertainers on the plazas they passed. Arnad and Felicity carried on a lively conversation.

"Tell me about the university," Felicity said, turning away from the market. "Did you attend there?"

"I cannot compare them," Arnad said. "And I am no scholar. We Comyn generally have tutors at home or study at Nevarsin, that is, St.-Valentine-of-the-Snows, and as for farmers and hunters and horse-traders, what need have they of book learning that helps them not at all but ruins their eyesight?"

"We do not educate our young people in quite the same way," Felicity began.

"He does have a point, though," Bryn said.

Arnad went on, "I learned statecraft mostly from my grandfather, *Dom* Domenic Alton-Hastur, who was the son of *Domna* Marguerida Alton. She established the university we will visit."

Their destination turned out to be a nobleman's city house. Like much of the Darkovan architecture, the construction was primarily stone, with panels of translucent blue framing the more recent wooden doors. One of the doors opened and a handful of young people trotted out, talking animatedly. A few carried satchels over their shoulders. They looked and sounded so like university students that Bryn thought bemusedly that they must represent a universal constant.

"Shall we go in?" Felicity said, gesturing toward the half-opened door.

"I'll wait out here," Arnad said. "Desi, please go if you wish."

Bryn, Felicity, and Desiderio entered a foyer lined with racks for cloaks and benches for outdoor boots, and a board on which flyers were tacked, everything a bit shabby with wear. Beyond the entrance area, a staircase spiraled upward, and corridors led to either side. From above came music, a harp of some sort accompanying a soaring soprano.

A middle-aged woman in loose trousers and tunic, her hair cropped short in Renunciate style, came down the stairs and approached them. She introduced herself as Julianna n'ha Caitlin, the dean of students. Desiderio bowed and the others said their names.

"I also teach at the Bridge Society," Julianna said. "I am Guild sister to your friend, Martina n'ha Riva, who has told me much about our *Terranan* visitors, although I did not think to encounter you so soon. May I have the honor to display our university to you?"

They followed Julianna into a spacious room, perhaps originally meant for formal dining or dancing but was now arranged for small group discussions. At one end of the room, an older man sat with three younger students, one of whom was reciting aloud. At the other, a girl barely in her teens read from a book while another wrote in a notebook.

"Here are where lessons take place," Julianna said.

"Not in classrooms?" Felicity said.

"Yes, that, upon occasion. Of course. But it's Council season, so many of our students are on holiday with their families. And we prefer this mode of instruction, where each student may progress at their own pace, as in a traditional apprenticeship."

Bryn said nothing. This place, with its small groups and absence of formality, reminded her more of Nevarsin Tower than an academic institution. These students had the benefit of a mentor, rather than being lectured to in large auditoriums. She found herself unexpectedly homesick for the Tower.

"What about laboratories for natural sciences?" Felicity asked.

Julianna's expression shifted, rueful. "Such areas of study are beyond the scope of this university. We specialize in history, philosophy, and music, according to the wishes of our founder. We have found the best approach is a flexible one that incorporates small discussion groups, mentoring, and library study."

No natural science. That means no medicine and no surgical facilities. Bryn was surprised at her own disappointment. After all, Felicity had desired to remove the corticator device surgically. Her father surely must have understood the importance of what Julianna had just said, but his expression continued to reflect interest, not concern.

"Might we see your library, then?" Felicity said.

"Certainly. Come this way." Julianna led them back to the spiral staircase.

At the second floor, Julianna opened the door to a narrow room, bounded on one side by shelves, with a reading desk at one end and a small table with a basket of white cloth gloves occupying most of the center.

"Excuse me—this is it?" Felicity asked. "For the entire university?"

In answer, Julianna donned a pair of gloves and took down a book from the shelves. It was bound in leather, the pages not paper but animal skin, vellum by its whiteness, and the text was calligraphed by hand.

And illuminated, Bryn thought, bending over for a closer look. *It's a work of art.* Aloud she said, "This collection must be very valuable."

"Indeed, the contents of this room are worth more than the building itself," Julianna said, carefully replacing the book before stripping off her gloves.

"I believe my family donated a number of volumes," Desiderio said. "It's good to see they are being put to use in educating the next generation."

"Tell me more about the academy," Felicity said. "I'd like to visit it next."

"It began as a joint venture between the medical staff at the *Terranan* headquarters, back when they still maintained a presence here, and Renunciate healers who wanted to combine the best of both traditions. At first, they trained midwives, women who tended primarily to other women, but since the departure of the Federation, they are the best clinicians we have and are trained in treating a wider range of ailments."

"That sounds encouraging," Felicity said.

"Leonie, one of the Renunciates we traveled with, is to study there," Bryn said.

"And she is most welcome," said Julianna.

◆◆◆

Like the university, the Bridge Society academy had been set up in a remodeled residence, but unlike the university, the place was primarily wood, resembling ancient Terran half-timbered style. As they approached, a pair of women, one of them a Renunciate by her clothing and close-cropped hair, the other a traditional Darkovan, burst out the front door and raced up the street, bulging leather satchels on their backs. Bryn pulled Felicity out of the way to avoid a collision.

"Well!" Felicity said, brushing off her arms. "*Someone's* in a hurry."

"Babes often are," Julianna remarked. "You've now encountered two of our midwives. Come in, come in. All except you," she added to the men. "This is a school run by women for women, so unless you're a patient near death, you may not be admitted."

Desiderio acknowledged her pronouncement with an inclination of his head.

"I see my presence here adds nothing," Ernst said. "Rather than waiting here, I'd like to see more of the older parts of the city."

"I would be happy to show you," Arnad said. After he and Ernst left the others, Desiderio retreated a short distance from the Bridge Society building so that he would not cause questions from the women coming and going.

The door led to a foyer with pegs for cloaks and a bench for muddy boots. The first room off the hallway was used for classes, fairly small ones at that, judging by the seating, but airy and well-supplied with windows. Chalk diagrams of human anatomy adorned the slate board on the far wall. As at the university, there were no books in evidence except for a large, leather-bound volume on the podium. The next rooms followed the same general plan, but in the one beyond them, a lesson in suturing wounds was in progress using a living model, a middle-aged man with weathered cheeks and blood soaking half his upper body. A half-dozen women students, masked but not in surgical gear, watched as an elderly woman demonstrated how to make the stitches. She looked up, snapped, "Get out!" and went back to her lesson.

Julianna closed the door behind them. "She's just a bit possessive."

"Please tell me that wasn't a surgical suite," Felicity said.

"As close to one as we have, yes. Generally, male patients aren't brought here but are treated at home. I believe this man is kin to one of the senior students. Occasionally a teacher will combine treatment with a demonstration, as we saw."

"Where do you take them, then, if a more extensive surgery is required, one that necessitates anesthesia, for example? Or quarantine for infectious disease?"

Julianna raked her fingers through her short, graying hair. "You're asking if we have the same level of medical technology that once existed at the Federation Headquarters. The answer is no. We don't have the machines or the metal with which to fabricate them. Likewise, we're limited in what medicines and other chemicals we can produce. Ordinary cleanliness and anti-infectives derived from Darkovan plant species suffice for most purposes. If a patient is so ill or badly injured as to be beyond these remedies, we send him to the nearest Tower—Comyn Tower, here in the city, or Hali Tower, a short distance away."

"I take it that there is no equivalent of a modern surgical facility," Felicity said, tight-lipped.

"I understand that you're disappointed," Julianna said with unexpected kindliness. "Come to my office. I'll have one of the students bring us *jaco* and we can talk. Perhaps we may find another solution to your search."

A short time later, the three of them were seated in what must have formerly been a small parlor. Shelves held books, animal skulls, and shells. A student, a freckled teenage girl, brought in a tray with the ubiquitous *jaco* and a plate of nut-bread.

Felicity accepted a steaming cup. "Forgive me, Julianna. I don't deal well with frustration. I was hoping the academy might provide the resources necessary to perform a surgery."

"Is it possible to modify the existing surgical classroom?" Julianna asked.

"The room I saw? No, absolutely not. All that dust, plus contamination from the organic materials. I don't see even a remote possibility of making it acceptably sterile. But there are still the facilities at the Terran base. I understand they're restricted, but if I can gain access, I might be able to salvage what I need."

"I wish I could accommodate you." Julianna nodded, considering. "When the Federation departed, they shut down everything except for a few areas, like the radio listening post, and that requires permission from either the Regent or the full Comyn Council. It's been so many years since the question came up, I'm not sure."

"That seems to be the case," Felicity said.

"Would you consider giving a guest lecture to our students?" Julianna asked. "It would have to be fairly basic, I'm afraid, but they have never had the opportunity to hear such a distinguished scientist. You would be an inspiration to them."

From the flash of interest in Felicity's eyes, Bryn thought her mentor would not only be delighted to lecture but to establish an entire curriculum and research laboratory. After a small hesitation, however, Felicity shook her head. "Perhaps later, if time allows. I cannot allow myself to be distracted from our primary purpose here."

"Of course," Julianna said. "Consider the invitation open whenever you can come."

Toward the end of the afternoon, Desiderio went to attend to family business in preparation for the Council season. Ishana served a light meal to Ernst and Felicity, then left them. Bryn wasn't hungry, though. She sat staring into the fire, telling herself over and over again that finding proper surgical facilities had always been a long shot and there was no reason to be disappointed. Felicity's solution was not their only option. The Keepers had yet to examine her father.

"*Mestra*, do you wish for anything?" Maralise said.

"No, thank you."

At the sound of tapping, light but firm, on the door, Maralise hurried to answer it. A young woman entered, with fire-red hair and that uncanny self-possession characteristic of those who had spent years of study mastering their *laran*. She paused before Bryn and inclined her head in greeting.

"I am Verana, monitor at Comyn Tower."

"I am Bryn Haslund."

The young woman's aloofness softened a little. "Yes, I saw you when you visited the Tower. May I come in?"

"Yes, of course. I'm sorry, I was expecting one of the Keepers. I learned a little monitoring when I was at Nevarsin Tower, and have nothing but respect for that skill," Bryn said. "Forgive me if I was rude."

Verana held out one hand, fingers down. *May I?* When Bryn nodded, she brushed her fingertips against the back of Bryn's wrist, a telepath's butterfly-light touch. Bryn felt a subtle lightening as the two merged in rapport. Verana's mind reminded her of a garden, sunlit and fragrant.

"Who is it?" Ernst called from the dining area.

"It's a *leronis*—a monitor—from the Tower," Bryn answered. Ernst and Felicity approached.

"Keeper Laurinda Hastur of Arilinn Tower asked that I evaluate a patient here," Verana explained. At Bryn's gesture, she stepped into the sitting room. "*Mestre* Ernst Haslund?"

"I am the very same. This is our friend and colleague, Doctor Felicity Sage."

Verana acknowledged the introductions with an inclination of her head. "Might we have a quiet, undisturbed place to work?"

"Would my room suffice?" Ernst said.

Verana indicated that it would.

"Maralise, please stand here at the door so that we are not disturbed." Bryn then turned to Verana. "May I observe? I understand that it is not good practice to treat our relatives, for it is impossible not to lose judgment with those very close to us."

"If you give your word—" with a slight emphasis that *word* meant *solemn oath*, "—that you will not interfere. I would not require that if you were Tower-trained from youth. You are *Terranan*. Otherwise, the bond of kinship or affection can enhance healing rapport."

"I did not realize."

"No, of course not. Why should you?"

"What about Felicity?" Ernst said. "Might she observe?"

"What's involved?" Felicity said, joining them in the parlor area.

"Your pardon, *mestra*, but it seems you do not possess *laran*," Verana answered without any hint of judgment. "Of course, I cannot be sure without testing you, but at your age, it is unlikely to be latent. You would not be able to sense anything."

"Visually, there will be nothing much," Bryn added. "The monitor sits still, focusing on her starstone."

"Nevertheless, I haven't had the opportunity to observe such a procedure before," Felicity said. "I do not want to pass up what may be my only chance. So yes, if it is permissible, I would like to be present. May I take notes?"

Bryn gathered from Verana's hastily masked expression that such a thing would be a distraction, turning a clinical examination into a spectator event.

"Well," Bryn said, "perhaps not. My father might be more comfortable if the lighting was dim."

Felicity having no further objection, they proceeded to Ernst's room. Maralise carried in a stool and an extra chair so that everyone had a place to sit. Verana pulled up the stool, and Bryn and Felicity placed their chairs along the far wall. Ernst lay back on his bed. Verana took out her starstone, its blue light tinted very slightly with green, like an ocean under calm skies, and held it in her upturned hands. Bryn took out her own, concentrated on it, and then closed her eyes.

The familiar currents of luminous energy bathed her. She saw her father as a tangle of glowing strands. In places they intersected, creating beads of brilliance. Here and there, a node pulsed dully, dark as rust. Temptation rose in her, to smooth those congested areas as she had been taught at Nevarsin. How easy it would be! But she had agreed to stay on the sidelines, so she held herself still.

Verana scanned Ernst's psychic form, her focus like a searchlight that penetrated and illuminated. Bryn sensed the warmth wherever the younger woman's attention lingered. In all her time at Nevarsin, she had never seen such a delicate touch. One of the congested nodes softened, and the sullen red seeped away. His breathing deepened. Oxygen flowed through his tissues. His muscles relaxed. His thoughts drifted toward light sleep.

Bryn followed Verana's scan of his spine and sheltered cord…his brainstem… The neurons were like holiday lights, each active synapse a minute, sparkling point. The implanted corticator did not gleam like metal, nor was it ruddy like the congested energy nodes. She saw it—she *felt* it—as a void, a tumor composed of nothingness. It dominated the surrounding cortex…the centers of thought…of personality…of will…

On the bed, Ernst moaned, thrashing weakly. Felicity uttered a soft cry, quickly smothered.

Now the device appeared in Bryn's inner sight as a gray-on-gray-on-black sphere that sent out many fine filaments. She couldn't tell whether they were physical connections or patterns of energy. The sphere itself felt impenetrable and alien.

Verana tried breaching the sphere one way and then another. Each probe slid away as if magnetically repelled. How long Verana continued her efforts, Bryn could not tell, but at last the *leronis* withdrew. She came back to herself. Verana's face was flushed and glistening with sweat. Her chest rose and fell with exertion.

Her father stirred, then sat up. "Is it over?"

"How do you feel?" said Bryn. Her muscles felt like jelly and her balance was uncertain. She dropped down on the bed beside him and took his hand.

He managed a smile. "Weak. Shaky. Like I've just had a fever and it's broken." He looked at Verana. "It didn't work, did it? I can feel the block in my mind. Whenever I try to remember the position I held in the Alliance—the wrongs committed—the abuse of power by Arthur— No, I can't even speak his name without a flood of thoughts of how good and noble he is. I know that at one point in the past I challenged him, but—" He looked imploringly at the *leronis*. "Please tell me there is a way to rid me of this mental enslavement."

"It wasn't my intention in this session to disable the device, only to determine if such a thing were possible," Verana said. Her voice trembled in the first few words, then steadied. "I detected what the Nevarsin *leroni* accomplished. It was more of a buffering zone, an envelope, if you will. But it's breaking down under the sustained influence of the—the device, which has its own protective measures. I couldn't get through them to see how it works. Without that knowledge, I don't think it's possible to turn the device off." She took a heaving breath. "I'm sorry."

Bryn's heart beat too loudly in her ears. *This can't be the end. There must be something more we can try!* "I—that's a great deal to take in."

"You are sure nothing can be done using your mental powers?" Ernst's expression was carefully neutral, but Bryn recognized the iron control behind it. The only hint of Felicity's reaction was her tightly pressed lips.

"You may of course consult with the Keepers," Verana answered, "but in my opinion, without being able to perceive and analyze the mechanism, *laran* is useless in this case. I do not come to that conclusion lightly, you must understand. We of the Towers have perfected our Gifts and their usages since before the Ages of Chaos. But this *Terranan* device is not natural. Its technology is foreign to us. We have no framework with which to comprehend it."

"Nonetheless," Ernst said, "you have my gratitude for attempting to do so."

"And mine," Bryn added. "I hope you will not take it amiss if I ask for a second opinion."

"Of course not. While we are all fallible, I know my skill as a monitor. You will not receive a different answer." Verana excused herself to return to the Tower.

Ernst turned to Bryn. "Do not look so downhearted, sweetheart. We may be able to make lives for ourselves here. Certainly, we have begun to form friendships and alliances."

"Ever the optimist," Bryn said, sighing. "I wish I could borrow some of yours."

"As do I, for that would in no way diminish my own supply of hope but rather, by sharing, increase it."

Bryn accepted his kiss on her cheek. She and Felicity left him. Once in the sitting room, Felicity let out a sigh of exasperation. "I can't say I'm surprised—"

"Please," Bryn cut her off. "The whole thing is upsetting enough as it is. I don't need to hear about the limitations of Darkovan *laran* or whose approach was correct. Unless the Keepers have a different opinion or we can find a way to get into the old base *and* the equipment there is salvageable, we're out of options."

"There are always options," Felicity said, "although I confess I have yet to discover our next step. If we were on Alpha, I would know where to look."

"I'm sorry to have dragged you into this," Bryn said with a sudden rush of feeling. "You left your position, your research—your entire academic life. I can't imagine that teaching at the university here would in any way make up for that."

And what if the Alliance finds us here?

Felicity's expression softened. "I believe that if our roles were reversed, you would tell me to take time to process my very natural disappointment and then return to the problem. And if I were me and you, you, I would tell you that obstacles are common in research. One might even say they are obligatory. We never give up at the first failure. We repeat our experiments, we re-examine our research design, we recalculate statistics. In other words, we question our assumptions."

"I do not know which assumptions to question."

"But you will, once you have had a break. As for myself, I maintain that our best hope is still a surgical solution. I do not believe we have exhausted every possibility. Just because we have not thought of it yet does not mean the answer is nonexistent."

With a murmur of thanks, Bryn returned to her chamber. Once she closed the door behind her, she collapsed on the edge of her bed. She felt hollow, as if her strength had been drained.

What if she couldn't find a way? What if her father remained under the corticator's control? Could they still make lives for themselves here, assuming Darkover remained unnoticed by the Star Alliance? If Nagy's hound, Black, tracked them here and her father's will was not his own—

No, that was a fate too terrible to contemplate. She was discouraged, that was all, fueling her fears. None of these things might come to pass, although she recognized that Black had been often in her thoughts. Her danger-sense stirred at the memory of him, but perhaps that was all, just a memory. As for the future, she wasn't out of options yet.

Bryn emerged from her room to find Desiderio chatting with Felicity. "I came by to see how you fared," he said. Clearly, Felicity had filled him in on the results of Verana's monitoring.

"Better now," Bryn said. "I was disappointed at first, but as Felicity advised me, it's too soon to give up and there's too much at stake. We have something else to try."

"There may come a time when all paths have been explored to their end, and then you will make a new plan," he said. "But as the old saying goes, we will fly that hawk when its pinions are grown."

Felicity lifted one eyebrow, but Bryn smiled. *Such a Darkovan phrase.*

"I want to be absolutely certain the corticator device can't be disabled by *laran*," Bryn said. "I hope the assembled Keepers will have the skill to accomplish this."

"Such a task would require a circle," Desiderio said. "All of us are taught monitoring, as you were, but not all of us have the aptitude to do it at a high level of skill. The Keeper's talent lies in her ability to weave together the mental power of her circle. She might not be more than adequate in monitoring. I am a skilled matrix mechanic, and offer myself as part of such a circle."

"Thank you. Anything that furthers our chances of success is welcome."

"Meanwhile, you look as if you could use fresh air. How about a stroll in one of the courtyard gardens?"

At his words, Bryn felt as if a fragrance of sunshine and something like lemon and roses passed across her mind. Felicity had been right, she could not think clearly with her mind tied up in disappointed expectations. "Yes, I'd like that."

◆◆◆

Bryn's request for the Keepers to examine her father was swiftly granted. From the way Fiona of Comyn Tower responded, she understood the concern that all doubts be laid to rest. *You are one of us*, the Keeper seemed to be saying, *and we would not have you uneasy in your thoughts.*

Desiderio accompanied Bryn and Ernst to Comyn Tower. As they entered, the stones of the walls hummed a welcome in her mind. She didn't understand how such a feeling of being at home could arise from a single, brief visit. Her time at Nevarsin Tower, and the readiness with which the *leroni* here accepted her, meant that she was already part of the larger community of those Gifted with *laran*. She remembered Desiderio saying, "Once, long ago, Towers were ruled by kings for whom they produced *laran* weapons. With the adoption of the Compact, the Towers became self-governing, a force unto themselves. They admit whom they will, choose their work, and generally remain neutral in Comyn politics."

Fiona accepted Desiderio's offer gladly, for she had been his first teacher when his Gift awoke. The circle gathered a circle in the primary working chamber, with a healer also in attendance. Besides Desiderio and Verana, acting as monitors, there were three others, all members of Comyn Tower.

Bryn was permitted to watch but was strictly enjoined against any participation that might distract the Keeper or taint her findings. Fiona worked quickly, gathering together the circle with a powerful yet silken mental touch. Truly, Bryn thought, this was one of the most skillful *leroni* in Thendara, in all of Darkover most likely. Fiona followed the same general method as Verana had, channeling the combined psychic energy of the circle. She began with a scan of Ernst's energy body and spiraled in to focus on the corticator device. *Laran* energy flowed freely from Desiderio and the other circle members into the Keeper's hands. As before, however, the device proved opaque to psychic probing. One after another, the circle's efforts to penetrate it failed. Bryn's heart sank with each attempt.

The examination came to an end with a graceful lightening of *laran* presence. So precise was Fiona's control that Bryn felt not even the slightest jarring. She already knew the result, however.

"I am sorry," Fiona said, meeting Bryn's gaze with a somber expression. "I cannot determine how this thing exerts control over your father's thoughts and speech. It is simply too different from anything I have experienced. I do not think even the great circles of the Ages of Chaos, which could manipulate cell-germ material, teleport people halfway across the Domains, and charge batteries to power flying machines, could do it. All these things are native to Darkover and our psychic sciences, even if we have lost the specific methodology to re-create them. The device in your father's skull is not."

◆◆◆

When they arrived back at their suite, they found Felicity at the dining table with a book that looked to be a primer of Darkovan grammar, an assortment of colored pencils, and her notebook. A pitcher and several tall pottery mugs had been laid out.

"Any success?" Felicity inquired.

"I'm afraid not," Bryn said. "For all the marvelous things *laran* can do, it appears that disabling a piece of Terran neurotechnology isn't one of them. Why should it? I feel like a fool for even trying."

"We are no worse off than we were before," Ernst said. "All the attempt has cost us is a bit of fatigue on my part. I don't know why these sessions should be so tiring when all I do is lie there, but there you have it. If you'll excuse me, I believe it's time for me to rest." With that, he headed for his room.

Felicity followed him with her gaze, her mouth tightening. "I do not like how he looks. There is no logical reason why lying still for an hour is so debilitating."

Bryn knew from her own experience that *laran* work often left her hungry, but she had relied on the explanation she'd been given, that expending psychic energy also used physical energy. What if the corticator were programmed to react negatively to a probe, like *laran*? The idea horrified her.

She flinched when Desiderio touched her shoulder. "Do not lose heart," he said. "Your very natural fears for your father have led you to the worst explanation. When we heal people in the Tower, whether of physical or mental ailments, they often require rest and quiet."

"I thought that was only for the healers," Bryn said, feeling contrite. She should have remembered.

"You are distressed, Bruna *carya*, so of course your mind paints dangers where there may be none."

Bryn's cheeks felt warm and dry. "I'm sorry that I misunderstood, Felicity. In the end, I suppose it doesn't matter. We're at a dead end. Everything we went through to get my father to Darkover has accomplished nothing."

"My dear, don't say that." Felicity got up and put her arm around Bryn's shoulders. "We have achieved a great deal. You escaped Terra and rescued your father. He is no longer in Nagy's grasp. We are, for the moment at least, at liberty."

"To spend the rest of our lives in hiding?"

"To spend the rest of our lives in *planning*," Felicity said.

Desiderio laughed at that. Bryn summoned a smile, recalling her former determination. She gave herself the same advice she offered to her young patients whose lives had seemed unrelentingly grim and hopeless. *Things can always change. There is always hope.*

Ernst had not been settled for more than a half-hour and Desiderio had taken his leave, and Bryn was staring into the fire, letting the pattern of the flames soothe her, when a knock sounded on the outer door. Maralise ushered in two visitors. Bryn remembered Vittorio Ardais from the dinner with Varzil, especially his pretense of drunkenness and his rudeness. The other, Lewis-Ramon Ridenow, was older, sporting fair hair and a beard.

Bryn assumed an air of hospitality and invited the two to sit. They settled in the sitting room, where she perched on a chair. Felicity remained where she was, bent over her notebook, a clear signal she was not interested in conversation.

"Please pardon the intrusion," Lewis-Ramon said. "We Comyn are such a limited society, each new arrival becomes the subject of intense curiosity. The rest of us were envious when Vittorio had the first privilege of dining with you. Half of Thendaran society is looking forward to getting better acquainted with you, and the other half has no inkling of how enchanting you are."

"Since I cannot have the silence I require to work, I will pay a call on Julianna n'ha Caitlin," Felicity said, rising.

Don't abandon me to these two scorpions! Bryn pleaded silently. Lewis-Ramon turned to her with a startled look.

"It would not be seemly, even in this modern age, for a respectable unmarried woman to be left unchaperoned in the presence of two men not her kin," Vittorio said.

"Or her promised husband," Lewis-Ramon added.

My what? He was *flirting* with her. Odious man! Yet—what was he really after?

"Please stay, Felicity." Bryn added in Terran Standard, "For the sake of their *delicate sensibilities*."

Felicity took the chair opposite Bryn and said, also in Terran Standard, "Then let's dispense with preliminaries, the like of which I have not had to endure since my last faculty meeting." She switched to *casta*. "This is no mere exchange of pleasantries. You want something from us or want to communicate something to us. Which is it?"

The two Darkovans exchanged glances. They had undoubtedly encountered women who were forthright, women like Martina and her Renunciate sisters, and the *leroni* of the Towers. Felicity was in a league of her own.

"Yes," Bryn said in her sweetest tones, "exactly what do you want?"

"I told you they wouldn't be fooled by gallantry," Vittorio told Lewis-Ramon.

"Not yours, anyway. I crave your pardon, ladies. Our ways must be strange to you. We've heard your story from *Dom* Varzil, and it is so filled with wonders—"

Bryn held up her hands. "If you're going to engage in more flattery, we're done."

"Thank you, my dear," Felicity said dryly.

"We're curious, yes, but we're also concerned," Lewis-Ramon concluded.

"Your presence poses something of a dilemma for the Comyn, the ruling families of the Domains," Vittorio added.

"*Dom* Varzil made that clear," Bryn said. "We do not intend to embroil Darkover in our affairs or place your planet at risk."

"Nevertheless, here you are," Vittorio said, "and for good or ill, we have no choice but to deal with you."

"We understand that some of you wish to avoid future interactions with the Star Alliance," Felicity said, "but others are more open to engagement. I assume you both represent the former position."

"We do," Vittorio agreed. "Our world may be remote, but it was colonized once and then rediscovered. Because you chose us as your hiding place, we may be forced to deal with off-worlder powers, whether we wish it or not. Will you be content to live quietly among us? Or will you attempt to summon help from your people?"

"You mean by using the old radio equipment in the Terran base," Bryn said. A statement, not a question. His silence confirmed that equipment did indeed exist. And that there was a good chance it was still operational. If so, it could provide a way off Darkover if by some means Ernst was restored to himself. Bryn tucked the information away for the future.

Vittorio leaned forward, his gaze intent. "Will you give us your word that you will not contact your people but will respect the isolation that we, the Comyn of Darkover, have chosen? Do you promise to not endanger our world by recklessly bringing us to the attention of the *Terranan* forces?"

"We will do no such thing," Felicity said, "and it is outrageous for you—or whatever factions you represent—to demand it. You appear to think we are as foolish as we are ignorant. We may not be versed in the internal politics of your ruling aristocracy, but we very well understand *our own* priorities, beginning with the neuropsychological health of Senator Haslund. Only a simpleton would consent to such a limitation of options. No one can predict how events will unfold! Your present intention is clearly to make us feel unwelcome, which hardly furthers your stated objective of preventing us from initiating contact with Star Alliance forces. In plain language, do you want us here or not?" Felicity raised her chin in a way that Bryn had always supposed was daring the unfortunate student who was the victim of one of her orations to challenge her. Very few of them ever did, or ever attempted it twice.

For a long moment, no one said anything. Bryn couldn't tell if the Darkovans were trying to figure out what Felicity meant.

Lewis-Ramon stirred in his seat. "We truly meant no offense, and we beg you to accept our overtures in the spirit in which they were offered. Perhaps it would be better to begin again in a more congenial setting."

"I doubt whether a change in location would be sufficient to alter the odiousness of your demands," Felicity remarked.

Vittorio got to his feet. He was a moderately tall man, and he loomed over the two women. Bryn bristled, although Felicity remained perfectly composed. In a wild moment, Bryn was tempted to cast a *laran* truthspell over him, over both of them, revealing their falsehoods—or, better yet, a spell that *forced* them to tell the truth.

"Consider this not a *proposal*," Vittorio said, "that is, a suggestion that can be taken up or not with equal consequence, but as a *caution*. Offered in the spirit of friendship, if you will. Some might deem disregarding it to be unwise."

"That's enough!" Bryn broke in before Felicity could provoke him further. She strode to the outer door, laying her hand on the latch. "We've heard what you have to say. Thank you for the courtesy of your call."

The Darkovans responded with ritual phrases of leave-taking. Vittorio bowed to her, not nearly as deeply as he had upon entering. He kept his eyes fixed on hers. She resisted the impulse to knee him in the face, appealing as the prospect was. It wasn't like her to entertain visions of retaliatory violence, even when so well deserved. Vittorio represented a faction that didn't trust Terrans, and assaulting him would only prove how right he was.

Lewis-Ramon lingered after his companion had exited. "I hope to improve the opinion you must have formed of us—of me. First impressions are often unfortunate in the sense of being incomplete. Your concern for your father does you credit. I hope that in future conversations we will come to understand one another better and discover how much we have in common. Our goals need not be mutually exclusive."

"I, too, regret that we appear to be at odds," Bryn said, not that she had an overwhelming desire to be on amicable terms with this particular Darkovan lord, but the Comyn were as much a part of Darkover as her Renunciate friends and the Tower folk at Nevarsin.

Bryn closed the door behind him. Eventually, she and her father and Felicity would have to deal with either returning to the Alliance worlds or hiding here on Darkover. No matter what planet they ended up on, though, her father needed help *now*. The circle at Nevarsin had provided a temporary, partial measure, and now the corticator might be regaining control.

◆◆◆

When Bryn went to check on her father, there was no immediate answer when she tapped on the door. She waited a few minutes, then knocked again, more loudly. Alarmed by the resulting silence, she tried the latch. It lifted easily. The space beyond was dark except for the light from behind her, yet that was enough to make out her father's form on the bed. The air felt terribly still.

"Father?"

Fear clawed at her, a sudden terror that she would find him stiff. Cold. She bent over and reached out her hand. But the flesh beneath the clothing was resilient, warm beneath her touch. Her ears caught the hush of his breathing.

"Father?" When she shook him, calling his name, he did not rouse. She tried again, louder this time. She was afraid to shake him too hard for fear of injuring him. "Father, wake up!" she shouted. "Ernst! Ernst Haslund!"

Still, he did not wake or give any sign of awareness.

"What's happened?" Felicity stood in the doorway. "I heard you shouting."

Bryn swallowed, trying to steady her voice. "He won't wake up."

Felicity began examining him. Bryn understood what she was doing—checking pulse, respirations, spinal suppleness, reflexes, and reaction to the pain of a skin pinch. Felicity straightened up from peering closely at the corticator electrodes and shook her head. "His condition is not good. The irregularity of his respiration is an especially worrisome sign. I can't determine exactly what happened, not without proper instruments—it could be a seizure as a result of the psychic probing or a gradual deterioration that passed a critical point. If I could, I would operate as soon as possible, but I doubt I'll be allowed back on the base. I am not accustomed to being physically repulsed. I fear I was not exactly diplomatic in my language."

"I heard a sample of that," Bryn said. "What if I went to the Regent and pleaded to be allowed into the base laboratories? I am not you, and it's worth asking, isn't it? There might be something left that you can use. Maybe improvise an operating room at the Bridge Society academy? I know it isn't ideal, but I don't see any other choice. Should I gain permission, though, I'll need to know what to look for."

"You are not only resourceful, my dear, you are scientifically literate, capable of identifying surgical equipment, and you are familiar with the general specifications common to all corticator devices. I'll make a list and trust your judgment."

Seeing the Regent turned out to be more complicated than Bryn anticipated. When she arrived at the Hastur suite, she found the place bustling with activity. She'd been so preoccupied, it had slipped her mind that every day more Comyn arrived in Thendara for the season. A small crowd waited outside the entrance to the residential wing, nobles in gorgeous holiday garb, servants in Hastur blue and silver as well as other colors, and armed guards. She pressed herself against a wall, looking for an opening in the press of bodies. It was going to be difficult to push her way through. Through a chance gap, she spied Fidelio, the *coridom*, with a couple of younger men in similar robes. Standing on her tiptoes, she waved to him.

"*Mestra* Bruna, whatever brings you here?" He bent over so that his voice would carry over the lively chatter without shouting. "Did you have an appointment?"

"I was hoping to see the Regent about an urgent matter."

"I see you have not been in Thendara long enough to appreciate that *no* matters are urgent during Council season," he said. "All things happen in due course, whether in the Crystal Chamber or the ballroom floor. But now I crave your pardon. I did not mean to make light of whatever brings you here."

"You know we came to Darkover, seeking help for my father's condition? It's regarding that."

Gimlet-bright eyes regarded her. "Remain here, and I will see what I can do." He strode through the crowd toward the doors of the suite.

Bryn couldn't see much over the heads and shoulders of the gathering, but she caught phrases here and there, mostly about people and events she didn't know. When some of the courtiers and servants moved off, others took their place. At last, she saw Fidelio coming toward her.

"Come with me, *mestra*." Moving at a stately but consistent pace, he led her past the formal doors, then down a smaller corridor, and after several turns to a more modest entrance. He tapped, and the door swung open. A young man in blue and silver bowed to them.

"I will leave you here," Fidelio said. "Should you require an escort back to your chambers or anything else, do not hesitate to send a message."

"Please come this way." The young officer led the way to a sitting room appointed in modest, comfortable furnishings. A few minutes later, Varzil Hastur entered through a door on the far side. He looked harried, although his manner in greeting her was impeccably courteous.

"I'm sorry," Bryn said. "I hadn't realized you'd be so busy."

"Naught that passes during Council season cannot be delayed a few minutes. Will you sit? Shall I call for *jaco*? Spiced wine?"

"Thank you, no. I hope this can be resolved simply. I would like to inspect the medical facilities at the old Terran base. I understand they have been sealed off to prevent misuse, but my father's condition is precarious. Keeper Fiona tells me that she and her circle cannot help him."

"And you say this is urgent? Is he in imminent danger?"

"I cannot tell," she admitted. "But if something were to happen—if his condition were to deteriorate further… Tell me, Dom Varzil, if he were *your* father, far from home and in need, what would *you* do?"

After a moment he said, "Your loyalty as a daughter does you—and *Mestre* Ernst—much credit. You are right, I would go to any lengths, even braving the Regent of the Domains, to protect him. I will grant you permission in writing on the condition that you confine your search to the medical and science areas and not interfere with those at work elsewhere."

"Thank you!" While he called for an aide and wrote out a note, she added, "Forgive me if this is inappropriate, but I must ask. I assume it is out of the question for me to bring my teacher, Felicity Sage."

The look he gave her answered the question definitively.

"That is what I thought. I just wanted to be sure."

"You will, of course, have an escort," Varzil said, pen poised over the note.

"Do I really need one? I'm sure I can find the base on my own—"

Varzil went to the inner door and called, "Desi! In here!" A moment later, Desiderio appeared.

"*Mestra* Bruna has my permission to examine the medical wing of the *Terranan* base, insofar as it is accessible," Varzil said. "Would you be so kind as to accompany her?" *And keep her out of trouble?*

"With pleasure." Desiderio gave Bryn an abbreviated bow. *You will not have to do this alone.*

"Excellent, then." Varzil added a few words and handed the note to Desiderio.

After thanking Varzil again, Bryn followed Desiderio back through the private entrance, skirting the more heavily trafficked areas.

"I heard what happened with Lewis-Ramon and Vittorio," Desiderio said, once they were out of easy eavesdropping distance. "What they did was unpardonable!"

"They acted as they thought best. Compared to that StarOps agent, Black, they were models of courtesy. The visit was annoying at worst and illuminating at best."

"That's a charitable way of looking at it."

"I can't afford to take offense at every unfortunate encounter, especially at the cost of distracting me from what's important. And if—" she swallowed, her voice uncertain, "—if the worst happens and my father cannot be cured, and we remain here—then we must make a life for ourselves on Darkover, and that means getting along with people like Lewis-Ramon and Vittorio."

He said nothing, although she sensed his reaction that he would not be unhappy if she stayed on Darkover. To her surprise, she felt a shadow of sadness at the thought of leaving Darkover, with its soaring snow-draped peaks, the breath-taking sweep of stars across the night sky, the warmth of its people, the intimacy of being among telepaths…and him.

The choice was not hers, if indeed it was a choice. They might be marooned here no matter what happened. But out there, the Alliance was tightening its grip on its member planets…more children in desperate plight…and the new mind-control machines at Nagy's command…

I know, Desiderio said mentally. *But let us enjoy just this one summer day together.*

They passed the gates and made their way along a wide avenue toward the Terran base. Around them, the city filled with holiday gaiety, the bright colors of festive garb, flower garlands trailing ribbons, snatches of song and laughter. A band of fiddlers and flute players struck a merry tune, and a handful of dancers whirled around each other. She wished she could linger to savor it.

Finally, the tall, rectangular structures of the Terran Base came into view. They were unlike Darkovan buildings, steel and glass instead of weathered stone. Yet Bryn noted how the seasons and years had dulled the gloss and softened the architectural starkness. Terran engineering might have erected these towers, but Darkover would eventually make them her own. The thought, whimsical as it was, made her smile.

A heavily reinforced perimeter fence barred their way. At either side stood a pair of guards, hands on the hilts of their sheathed swords. Their expressions turned wary, suspicious. Then one of them, recognizing Desiderio, saluted.

"Hello, Donal," Desiderio said. "Bryn, this is my kinsman, Donal Vallonde."

"You're the *Terranan* newly come from Nevarsin! At your service, *mestra*. I believe you already met my less disreputable cousin, Arnad."

"Arnad Alton, who showed us around the city?"

"The very same."

"And I am Uriel Reed," said the other young man. "Rel to my friends. You know my aunt, Ishana."

"Good heavens," Bryn said. "Is everyone in Thendara related?"

"Not quite," Donal said, "although it seems so, come Festival Season." To Desiderio, "What brings you here on this fine day, kinsman?"

Desiderio held out Varzil's note. "I'm escorting *Mestra* Bruna, who has permission to enter the base on business of her own."

Donal took the note, his lips moving as he scanned the brief lines, then handed it back. "The medical wing, it says."

"Just so."

"Then keep to it, kinsman. The communications center—best you not venture there today. And you, lady. Rel, you remain here."

Accompanied by Donal, they crossed toward the headquarters building. The paving underfoot was weather-worn and cracked. Here and there green shoots poked through the gaps. The entrance came into view, doors of glass and metal. Bryn had visited, even worked in, buildings much like this one. Terrans carried their familiar designs everywhere.

Another guard stood just inside the doors. He, Donal, and Desiderio were all acquainted. *Kinsmen to some degree,* Bryn thought. Again the note was inspected, and the three entered.

The foyer interior bore an unpleasant chemical tang, momentarily dissipated in the swirl of outside air.

"You get used to it in time," Donal said. "The stink, I mean."

"I must say that Darkover *smells* better than most worlds I've visited," she said, recovering herself. "Not all, though. Some, like Thetis, are—were—relatively pristine."

"Were?" He gave her a sharp glance. "Rel's great-uncle Jeram fought for the Federation. He didn't talk much about what he saw and did, only that it was terrible. If your world, this Thetis, was one of the casualties, then I am very sorry."

She had not looked for sympathy or even kindness on a planet so determined to keep itself apart from the rest of human settlement.

The next moment, overhead lights flooded the space with warm yellow light. *Terran* light, Bryn thought, blinking in the brightness. Her eyes stung as she realized how long it had been since she stood under a sun with that light.

As they crossed the foyer, Bryn pointed down a corridor where light streamed from an open door. "What's down here?"

"That's our radio communications center, what's still functioning. We think of it as a listening post."

Bryn forced herself to speak slowly, calmly. "Can you also send messages?"

"I suppose, if there were a need. The isolationists insist we maintain it. For advance warning, you understand, in case the Federation decides to reclaim Darkover. But *Dom* Varzil has authorized your access only to the medical areas, and with what's been going on—never mind."

Bryn realized she'd made a misstep. "You are quite right, of course. I promised the Regent to restrict my visit."

Donal nodded. "It's this way. The elevators—is that the right term?—we call them rising shafts—anyway, we can no longer use them."

"I can climb stairs perfectly well."

They went to the very end of the corridor, then along a dog-leg, through another lobby, this one poorly lit through dusty windows, and then to a stairwell. The men climbed at an easy pace, one Bryn had no difficulty matching. The door at the top led to an open area that must have been for reception, given the size and placement of the desks. At the far end, wide corridors led to the right and left. Despite the size of the area, the air was close and stale. Overhead lights flickered and steadied at a low level. Dust filmed the surfaces, the computer units, the old-style flimsies, and small office instruments scattered on the desks. No one had been this way for a long time.

She'd been warned. Jeremiah Reed and the Darkovan leaders had been determined that these facilities were never to be used. But this was the last chance, the last remote chance. She couldn't give up without finding out, if she could, what lay beyond the closed doors and under the dust.

"Which way—" Her throat felt thick. She cleared it. "Which way to the surgical facilities?"

Donal said, "I don't know, I've never been in here before."

"There should be a map, a sign, or something. It's worth checking, rather than searching randomly. You look, and I'll see if I can find any digital records."

While the two men examined the walls, Bryn went to the nearest computer. The interface was generations out of date and covered with greasy dust. The keypad was inert, and the panels resisted her pressure before finally snapping free from their locked position, all with no result. She found the power button but it, too, wasn't functioning.

"Here!" Donal called. "I don't read Terran Standard, but this looks like a directional arrow." He pointed to a plaque secured to the wall. Sure enough, one arrow indicated *Medical and Surgical* and the other, *Basic Science Research Laboratories.*

"This is it," Bryn said.

The three headed down the hallway indicated by the former. About half the overhead lights flashed on as they approached, so at least some of the motion sensors were working. The hallway ended in another junction, and they took the branch indicating *Surgical.* Doors lined this passageway. They tried them, one by one. The first wasn't locked, although it required effort to twist the knob. It was clearly a janitorial closet, filled with cleaning equipment. Shelves lined two walls, holding bottles that were either empty or held small amounts of dark liquid or powders. A few had burst open, leaving a pungent, vile-colored residue on the floor.

The next two doors were labeled *Lounge* and *Conference Room*. She didn't bother with these. Beyond them, a doubled door wide enough for a gurney had been covered by an X of colored tape with the faded words, *Entry Prohibited.* Above it, a sign read, *Surgical Suites A-E.*

"We've found it!" Bryn reached for the tape, which came away in her hands, its coating turning to dust. Through the hair-thin gap between the double doors, she spied a bar like a magnetic latch that would keep the doors from swinging once someone had passed through. She pushed on the doors, but might have been trying to move a brick wall.

"Locked!" she said. "Look around, there must be a manual override."

"I'm sorry, *mestra*," Donal said. "I don't know what that looks like."

Bryn looked around, hoping to find a box or panel labeled *For Emergency Entry*, but found nothing. She shoved the doors in frustration.

"Bruna," Desiderio said. "That will not help."

"There must be a locking mechanism," Donal said, "but being *Terranan*, it could look like anything."

"Not *anything*, kinsman." Desiderio pointed at a small blue-white gem perched on the bar between the inner edges of the doors. Bryn could have easily missed it, had the angle of the light been different. It glinted, tiny and bright.

A starstone?

"A matrix lock," he responded aloud. "Doubtless placed here by the *leroni* who assisted in sealing this area."

Bryn had heard of such devices but didn't have any experience with them. "Can you unlock it?"

"I can try. It usually requires the combined application of *laran* and a specific psychokinetic pattern."

"Which is why you will have to try it," Donal said with a rueful half-grin. "I'd be hopeless." To Bryn he added, "I was tested for *laran* like everyone else at the suitable age, but mine isn't strong enough to be worth training. All I'm good for, apparently, is standing guard in out-of-the-way places at the whim of the Regent."

Desiderio slipped out his starstone from a spidersilk-lined locket on a chain around his neck. The psychoactive gem flared as it touched his skin. He closed his fingers around it. With his eyes half-shut, he silently mouthed a few phrases. Bryn tried to follow what he was doing, using their rapport. Most of it was too technical for her, but she sensed his use of *laran* in scanning the stone, opening his mind to the residue of the correct formula. He was looking for a combination of a psychic pattern and a gesture. For a time, attempt after attempt, both eluded him. Then a part of a pattern emerged…and then, as if overlaying it, a second fragment. The pattern fell into place.

What does it do? Bryn wondered.

You hold it in your mind like an invisible key, Desiderio answered silently. *The gesture turns the key in the lock.*

Bryn thought for a moment. *What's the gesture?*

That's the question. He raised one hand and curled his fingers in a twisting motion. Nothing happened, although the pattern wavered, blurring.

Not that, then, said Desiderio. He tried another hand gesture, with the same result, and then another. Each time it took longer for the pattern to come back into mental focus. He, too, was worried about the effect of repeated failures.

Let me try, Bryn said, thinking that perhaps another person's *laran* would amount to starting over. Holding the pattern in her mind, she studied the matrix lock.

A memory leaped to mind, of play-acting stories with her young patients. With the most profoundly damaged, she would encourage them to become magicians, unlocking the doors inside their minds. *Imagine there is a treasure inside*, she'd say, *the most wonderful thing in the world, the thing you long for the most. Don't tell me what it is, just hold it in your heart and whisper, "Open!"* More often than not, that whisper would be accompanied by a dramatic hand movement.

What she wanted more than anything else was for her father to be well and whole again. *"Open!"* she whispered silently, and raised her hands…

The lock clicked open. *Yes!*

You did it! Desiderio slung one arm around her shoulders and pulled her close, an unusual gesture given the years he had spent in a Tower where casual touch was discouraged.

Doors lined the corridor on both sides, glass or half-glass, and doubled but not locked. Bryn peeked inside each door as they came to it. The lights in the first two had failed, leaving the spaces beyond in near darkness. The lights in the third, which had a wider entrance, came on as they entered.

The center of the room was dominated by a heap of metal and plas, in parts smooth as if melted under tremendous heat, in others jagged-edged. It looked as if everything portable had been piled onto immovable equipment and then raked with a blaster on full setting. Blackened furrows scored the walls, fusing storage compartments and their contents with the surrounding materials. A faint reek of overheated metal and burned synthetics hung in the air.

"No, no, no, no…."

Underfoot something crunched, small and splintery. Glass or fire-hardened plas, or even metal turned heat-brittle, she couldn't tell. She ran her fingers over the shards protruding from the amalgamation, but nothing moved, nothing came free.

"It can't—this can't—"

In her mind, she heard Ishana's voice, saying, *"It was deemed too much of a risk to simply lock those areas. My father said it was a difficult decision, but he had seen the terrible effects of Terranan weapons on other planets. This was the only way he could protect Darkover from becoming a similar battlefield.*" At the time, she hadn't understood, truly understood, the extent of that *protection*.

Bryn searched for anything that might have been missed—a scalpel, a cauterizer, something still usable or reparable—anything!

Nothing, there was nothing…

They didn't just lock it up, they destroyed *it.*

They destroyed it all.

Behind her, the two men murmured to one another in *casta*. She caught their meaning, "So the stories are true…" "...had no idea…" "...reason it was hidden…" and then, "...Compact-banned weapons." If she was appalled by the waste, the colossal *waste*, they were equally sickened by the reminder of the weapons that were responsible.

They were so afraid of this tech, they destroyed it, echoed through her mind. What would the Darkovans think of the weapons capable of laying waste to entire planets, and the will to use them?

It's just one room. There are others—there might still be something… She could not think of a reason why the other rooms would be any different, but she had to be sure.

Silently Bryn left the ruins of the operating room and headed for the next one over.

"Bryn, wait!" Desiderio called after her, but she ignored him.

The equipment and supplies of each one had been rendered useless in the same fashion.

She fell to her knees in the last room beside the tangle of fused metal and plas. So many of the overhead lights were inoperable that the place felt like a cave. Tiny shards bit into her skin. She welcomed the pain.

I've failed, she thought. There was nothing left to try, no other hope.

No, came Desiderio's distinctive telepathic voice. She felt his nearness as he came to stand inside the door. *This was decided long ago, for reasons that seemed good at that time. They could not have foreseen your needs, and you cannot change the past.*

She turned toward him, her vision blurring. "I don't know what to do now."

"You have taken a blow. It is natural to feel discouraged. Take time, gather your thoughts, and consult with others. You will find a way—"

A ripple through the psychic plane brought him up short.

A jumble of emotions swept through Bryn—shock, excitement… dismay. She couldn't make out more than that.

"It's coming from the communications center," Desiderio said. "Something's happened."

Alanna dreamed of a ship like a shark…

Bryn bolted for the door. Donal moved to cut her off, but she swerved around him. He reached out to grab her. She jerked free.

"No!" Donal cried. "*Mestra*, you're not allowed—"

She rounded on Donal, chest heaving with the rush of adrenalin. "If there's even the slightest chance they're here—the Alliance!—if they've tracked us down—I have to find out!"

"Kinsman." Desiderio's voice was low and intense. "She has a right to know if her enemies are in our skies. I will take responsibility for her."

Donal's eyes widened as he caught the formal phrase. He stepped back, hands falling to his sides.

Bryn raced back the way they had come, Desiderio only a pace behind her. Donal followed as they slammed through the doubled doors, heading back toward the stairwell. Bryn clattered down the stairs as fast as she dared. She was shaking and stumbling by the time she reached the bottom of the stairs.

Words racketed through her mind: *How many ships—? How far distant?*

One radio burst—then another—cannot ascertain—two separate vessels—

Certain—from the Star Alliance—?

She braced herself against the wall, gasping and trying to collect herself.

Desiderio touched the back of her hand, catalyzing their rapport. *You must shield yourself.*

She nodded. *Laran* barriers might be second nature to him, but she had not had years of training.

Near-silence blanketed her mind. Her thoughts were once again her own, not the people in the communications center.

"Better?" he asked.

She nodded.

"What is it?" Breathing hard, Donal reached them. "I caught something—but I couldn't tell what was happening."

"The listening post picked up signals from incoming ships," Desiderio said. "Might be the people from the Star Alliance, the ones Bryn and her father were fleeing."

"We'd better find out." Donal pushed through the door and into the foyer. "This way," he said, pointing to where another pair of guards bracketed a door halfway down a corridor. The guards came alert as the three approached. They bowed to Desiderio before exchanging a few words with Donal.

"Please," Bryn said, struggling to keep her tone reasonable. "I need to know what's going on."

"With respect, *mestra*, this is Comyn Council business, not your concern."

"With *respect*, it is indeed my concern! If you've detected a signal from StarOps, they're after my father."

"*Dom* Desiderio, we cannot let you and this woman enter," the other guard said.

"They're under my supervision," Donal said.

"The Regent's orders—"

"Is that Desiderio Alton? And *Mestra* Bruna?" The voice from inside rang with authority. *Felix Hastur.* "Let them come."

The three entered a large chamber, made cavernous by the absence of windows. A pair of *laran*-charged globes gave off a cold blue light, added to that from the overhead fixtures. Once this room must have been a hive of activity, Bryn thought, and instruments studded with winking lights. A team of technicians would have tended them. Now most of those banks were shrouded, dark.

Three men and a woman clustered around the single functioning console. Their Darkovan clothing seemed out of place beside the sterile gray walls. A young man was wearing an antiquated earphone, his hands hovering over a central panel marked by colored lights. Bryn had not seen equipment that old, although she had read about it.

"Desi. Donal. And you, *Mestra* Bruna." Felix inclined his head to each of them. "I should have known you would make your way here, being unable to resist stirring up a scorpion-ant nest."

Felix's gaze bore into Bryn. She held her ground, her expression carefully neutral. "Well," he said after a moment, "since you're here and you are correct, this does concern you *Terranan*, you might as well learn the truth. It will all be made public in a short time, anyway. I am to report to my father and then to the Comyn Council this very day."

He gestured toward the bank of equipment. "About a tenday ago, we detected a signal far out in the Cottman system. It was so faint and erratic, we couldn't be sure it was not just random noise from our equipment. As you may note, *Mestra* Bruna, these instruments are old and not in optimum condition. With every decade since the Federation withdrawal, we have had fewer capable of its maintenance, not to mention replacement parts. Although there have always been young people enthusiastic about communicating with other worlds, we lack the knowledge to train them properly. With each generation, our skills decline."

Sooner or later, Bryn thought, *Darkover will either re-establish contact with the Alliance or its successor, or it will eventually lose the ability to do so through disuse and attrition.* She did not know which future to wish for, only that in *this* time and *these* circumstances, this signal meant danger for everyone here.

"We have continued listening," Felix said. "At times, we could not detect the signal, and at others it appeared to be coming from more than one source."

"Although that could have been because the ship was moving very fast," the young man at the console said.

"Or it could have been nothing," the woman said.

"That turned out to not be the case."

Bryn and Desiderio exchanged glances. With a Terran ship headed toward Darkover and communications equipment at least marginally functional, no wonder Felicity had been barred from the base. Lewis-Ramon and Vittorio could not be alone in their fear that their *Terranan* guests would try to contact the Alliance.

They had it all wrong, Bryn thought. *That's the last thing we would do, so long as the corticator is active.*

"There they are again." The woman indicated the identification symbols, bright against a black background, and the curved lines that slowly moved across the screen.

A voice issued from the speaker panel, speaking in Terran Standard interrupted by bursts of static noise. "Alliance..." a series of numbers... "on approach Cottman IV...*StarOps captain*..."

Static.

"Hailing...hailing...

"Arrest warrant... fugitive... ordered to surrender... unlawfully resist..."

More static, then a pause.

"Hailing…hailing…captain…arrest warrant for Star Alliance suspect…criminal charges…"

Static blared.

"...Senator Ernst Haslund…ordered to surrender…

"Hailing Cottman IV…hailing…

"StarOps Captain Black…by authority of Star Alliance First Minister Arthur Nagy…you are hereby ordered…"

Bryn was already numb with despair after seeing the wreckage of the surgical areas of the base. Now her worst nightmare was coming true.

StarOps captain. *Black. With a warrant to arrest her father. Arrest him. Surrender. Black, here.*

I've got to get him away, out of the city, into hiding!

Was that even possible?

Desiderio touched her arm. She drew a breath, thinking to calm herself.

"How far away are they?" Desiderio asked.

"We thought from the first fragmented signals perhaps a month or two. But now—" Felix spread his hands. "—based on the speed of approach, two or three days to orbit."

The StarOps ship would arrive, and there would be no place to hide, and her father would be taken into custody no matter what. A ship and crew armed with Compact-forbidden weapons. Who could stop them from taking whatever they wanted? *Whomever* they wanted?

If the Darkovans resisted, they would stand no chance against the Alliance.

"Of course," Felix went on, his voice sounding to Bryn as if he were at the end of a long tunnel, "we could be in error—"

Renney. Campta. Ephebe. Vainwal, for all she knew. And now Darkover?

"*Mestra* Bruna?" That was Donal, looking at her with grave concern.

She roused herself. "I'm sorry. It's just bad news for me. For us. Very bad news."

"This StarOps captain is the one you told me about?" Desiderio said.

"The very same. Felix, what happens now? Will you just hand my father over?"

Felix looked visibly shocked. "There is more at stake here than one stranger, even if he is your kin. My father and the entire Comyn Council must examine the situation. We have had no contact with the *Terranan* for many years now, except for the incident with the smugglers in the Dry Towns."

"And the firefight in our skies," Donal said. "I grew up on tales of how only the intervention of a great *laran* circle prevented ruin from raining down upon us. The *Terranan* have always regarded us as resources to be harnessed for their own greed." He glanced at Bryn, flushing. "Present company excluded. No offense intended, *mestra*."

Bryn didn't have the energy to be insulted. "I hope that my father and I, and Doctor Sage, will be included in any formal discussions. For the moment, though…pardon me. This has been a terrible shock. I must go to my father."

"I will go with you," Desiderio said. *You should not be alone at a time like this.*

Bryn felt a pulse of relief at his steady presence and his strength. They turned toward the door.

"*Mestra* Bruna." Felix closed the door behind him. With her *laran* barriers in shreds, Bryn sensed his distress. "Forgive Donal's rash words. He grew up on stories about the confrontation here in this very spaceport. Bounty hunters—a privateer armed with enough firepower to level the city—tracked a rebel ship here. They would not respect our Protected World status, or so the story goes."

"He has reason to fear," Bryn said. "Please believe me, we never intended to place Darkover in danger. I'm sorry if we have repaid your generosity so poorly."

"You lend us grace, *Mestra* Bruna. Your honor is beyond question. I wish matters had fallen out differently, so that we might become friends."

Bryn thought of the beauty of this world, the vitality of its people, and the gifts of its *laran*, and how she had thought Darkover might become a home. Blinking back sudden wetness in her eyes, she said, "Your pardon again, I must go to my father and break this news to him."

"And I, to mine."

Bryn and Desiderio left the Terran base building and headed back across the cracked tarmac, through the guarded fence, and back into the city. She was silent, searching for the words to tell her father and Felicity that they had run out of time as well as options. The Comyn Council would have no choice but to turn him over. Whatever happened would be her fault because she failed to find a way to free him. He would be helpless against Nagy…he would use all his brilliance and eloquence in the service of that vile man! Worlds would fall and burn, and maybe Rashid and the Free Worlds Movement would eventually win…after Nagy died…or be crushed…and how many more children would stumble through their nightmare lives, the ones that lived?

Desiderio said nothing, although she felt his light, sustaining presence.

After a time, the festive air of the streets penetrated even her somber mood. She filled her lungs with the sweet Darkovan air, perfumed with flowers from the garlands bedecking stalls, balconies, and the braids of laughing girls.

"How I will miss this world," she murmured.

"And how Darkover will miss you."

She took a moment to let that sink in, but only a moment.

"If I could take my father away, back into the Hellers," she said, "to Nevarsin perhaps, where the Alliance will never find us, I would. But we do not live in a universe where escape is possible. They would find us, and many innocent people would suffer. And anyway, it must be my father's decision, and he would not have an entire world at risk because of him."

"No, he is not that sort of person."

They walked on for another time, until the gates of Comyn Castle came into view. "I wish we'd had more time," Bryn said. "I can't help thinking that if only we'd been able to salvage surgical equipment or—I don't know—upgrade the facilities at the Bridge Society academy—or train the Tower circle in corticator technology—"

Train the Tower circle in corticator technology…

She turned to him, wide-eyed. "Could it be that simple?"

"Could what?"

"Listen! Both Verana and Fiona said they couldn't disable the corticator because it was Terran technology and they weren't familiar with it. But *Felicity is.* And so, to a lesser extent, am I. What if—tell me if this idea is as crazy as it sounds—what if the Keeper could link with Felicity—or I could join the two of them, like a translator? Yes, that might work!"

He smiled. "I knew that you would find a way forward. You are by far the most *determined* woman I have ever met, and I have known Alanna Alar since I first came to Nevarsin, and Martina n'ha Riva almost as long."

"There is bad news and very bad news," Bryn said, once she and Desiderio sat down with her father and Felicity in their suite. "But there is also good—I hope, excellent—news."

"You were not able to examine the surgical facilities at the Federation base," Felicity said.

"No, they let me in, but the equipment's demolished. Everything portable was heaped on fixed stations and blaster-fused. Storage cabinets and their contents likewise destroyed."

"Oh no! Nothing salvageable?"

"I couldn't even pry a scalpel out of the melted-down mess," Bryn said.

"The inexcusable, the *criminal* waste!"

"The people who did it were determined that no one would ever be able to use that equipment again. I don't believe they made the decision lightly, but regardless of their reasons, there is nothing we can do about it now. That's the bad news."

"There's worse?" Ernst said.

Bryn steadied herself. She didn't want emotional reactions to divert the discussion from what they must do next. "While Desiderio and I were at the base, we were allowed into the communications center. They had been monitoring signals far out in the Cottman system. While we were there, they received a clear signal. An Alliance ship is on the way. It identified itself as a StarOps vessel, with Captain Black onboard."

Although neither Ernst nor Felicity spoke, their shock and dismay swept through Bryn. She slammed her *laran* barriers tight and went on. "The message says they have a warrant for Father's arrest. The ship is only a few days out. That's the very bad news."

She paused to give her father and Felicity time to take in the news, point by point. Ernst sagged, and Bryn was acutely aware of the frailty of his chest, how bony his shoulders had become. Felicity looked grim, her face pale except for two spots of hectic color.

Ernst recovered first. "I was beginning to fear that we had exhausted all avenues of remedy. It has not been all in vain. I have regained enough of myself to realize the temporary nature of the Nevarsin treatments. Without this respite, I would not be able to appreciate what I have lost. Am about to lose..." He drew in a breath. "Now, my dear ones, there is a difficult decision ahead. I cannot—I *dare not*—allow myself to fall into the clutches of Arthur Nagy."

"No, don't think that!" Bryn said, seeing where his argument was going. "I won't hear of it! You're jumping ahead— You haven't heard my *good news*! I've had an idea, one I think will succeed." In a rush, she explained that the Comyn Tower circle was limited by their lack of knowledge of the principles behind the theta-corticator. "But I am not—and Felicity is not!"

"I don't possess any psychic talent," Felicity reminded her. "I cannot join a circle. Are you saying they can *read my mind* and thereby obtain the specifications?"

"But *I* have *laran*, and I have worked in a circle," Bryn said. "I already know the basics of corticator functioning. If those aren't sufficient to disable the theta version, then you can fill me in and I can transmit the information to the circle."

"My stars," Felicity said. "I would never have thought of that."

"You're saying...there is a way..." Ernst said, hesitant to allow himself to hope.

"I think so!" Bryn responded with unfeigned enthusiasm. "I am certain we stand an excellent chance! So no more talk of doom, Father."

"I treasure your optimism, sweetheart, but even if this scheme of yours succeeds, the StarOps ship will still arrive, and we cannot expect our friends to resist them. One person's life is not worth that of an entire city, even if that life is mine." He gestured to the implanted electrodes, revealed by their slow-blinking lights. "When Nagy realizes these are no longer active and I am not under his control, he will silence me."

Bryn heard her father's thought as clearly as if he'd spoken them aloud: *He will execute me in the most public and brutally deterrent way.*

"Is there a way to mimic the device being active?" Desiderio said. "I confess I know not how it might be done, but every hunter knows that prey animals will pretend injury to draw the chase away from their young."

"I have been pondering this very question," Felicity said, with a glint in her eyes that betokened her fascination with difficult or obscure problems. "When I was pursuing a surgical alternative, I considered disabling the device's ability to influence synaptic patterns while leaving the physical housing intact. A placebo device, as it were. It should be a straightforward procedure to re-route the light circuits so that they remain active, although disconnected. A superficial examination ought to be unable to detect the differences."

"Can you do that without cutting into his head?" Desiderio asked.

Felicity rubbed the side of her nose, a nervous gesture. "I don't know if that can be done. In an operating theater, certainly. But there are several obstacles here. First, we must sever the connections—device to brain and inert device to lights—using purely psychic energy. Second, Bryn or I must transmit the specifications to the *laran* circle accurately enough, and in terms they understand."

"I can vouch for both the accuracy and power of the work a circle does," Desiderio said. "We can no longer modify genetic material, as our ancestors did during the Ages of Chaos, but we can manipulate individual nerve and muscle fibers, and bring up tiny bits of metallic ore from deep below the surface. As for power—consider that this entire Tower was built using *laran*."

Felicity was silent for a moment, and Bryn suspected that her mentor was not accustomed to being impressed.

Bryn turned to her father. "Even if all this succeeds, you would have to act as if you were still under its influence. Can you do that?"

"My dear, I am a politician. I have had a lifetime of presenting myself according to a preconceived script. I can parrot a few pro-Nagy slogans and assume a suitably glassy-eyed appearance. I am more likely to deceive StarOps than I am to fool Arthur Nagy, whom I've debated for many years. At least that will be on Terra. The universe is a strange and wonderful place in which our enemies willingly give us a ride home."

A brief discussion followed, in which it was decided that Desiderio would petition the Keepers for a second attempt. As he rose to go, Ernst said, "A word, if you please. In private."

The two men withdrew to Ernst's room. Bryn joined Felicity at the dining table, where the older woman was setting out her notebook and several sheets of thick, soft Darkovan paper. "What was that about?" Felicity asked without looking up.

"I don't know." Bryn could no longer sense Desiderio's thoughts. They were usually in light rapport when in each other's company, but now his mind was a blank. What were they talking about? *Leave it alone*, she told herself. People needed privacy, whether physical or mental. *They'll tell you if they want you to know.*

A quarter of an hour later, the two men emerged, Ernst's expression giving away nothing. His manner distracted, Desiderio took his leave.

The three Terrans settled around the table, pooling their knowledge of corticator technology and the specific modifications of the theta model. Ernst didn't have much to add, although he was curious how the devices worked. Bryn discovered that she knew both more and less than she'd thought. Felicity explained and then drilled her in the structural differences between the therapeutic and theta models. By the time Desiderio returned, they'd covered the dining table with charts and drawings, and Ishana had had to make a third trip in search of more writing materials.

Desiderio's news was good. "They're willing to try again, although I got the distinct impression some of them consider this an extraordinarily—um, creative—approach. They specifically included Doctor Sage, in case there are questions only she can answer. As time is pressing, the circle will convene this very night."

Desiderio appeared at the appointed hour and accompanied Bryn and Ernst across the castle to the Tower. Verana met them at the entrance. As she passed through the outer door, Bryn felt a mental hush, as if she were coming home at twilight. In a moment of wistfulness, she thought that if her father were not in danger, if the freedom of Alliance worlds did not depend on defeating Arthur Nagy, she would be content to live and work within these walls and with these people, who could read her thoughts as if she spoke them aloud.

They entered the Tower's primary working chamber, where the circle had previously worked with Ernst. As before, a healer was in attendance and Verana acted as monitor. Besides Desiderio and two other technicians, there were six Keepers, all wearing traditional red.

"The circle in Nevarsin aimed to calm the brain storms, not remove their source," Laurinda of Arilinn said.

"The very notion of introducing a metallic device into a brain is abhorrent to us," Robert of Neskaya added.

"We will leave this metal thing in place, as you asked," Fiona said. "We will do our best to modify its operation so that it appears to be functioning as before, yet it will have no power. In time, we hope *Mestre* Ernst's normal brain function will recover."

"I am in your debt for your sincere effort, regardless of the outcome," Ernst said.

"Last time, I asked that you remain apart from our circle, lest you interfere out of your emotional attachment for your father," Fiona said to Bryn. "Now you will join us as our guide. We can ascertain easily enough what is healthy tissue, but not how a thing of metal can alter its function." She turned to Felicity. "And you, *mestra*, please sit quietly—your place is there, on that bench—and do not interrupt. Should we require a consultation, we will advise you."

Fiona turned to Bryn. "As part of the circle, your mind will be attuned to ours, and your *Terranan* knowledge with it."

"Yes, that is my understanding and my hope."

"In that case," Fiona said, "let's get started."

The members of the circle began arranging chairs in a circle around a padded bench on which Ernst was to lie. Verana brought out a thick blanket and tucked it around him for extra warmth. Felicity sat on the bench along the far wall.

Bryn took her place, as directed, between Fiona and Laurinda and took out her starstone, focusing on it as she had been taught. Around the circle, the others were doing the same. The light from the gems pulsed, brighter and brighter until it merged. She closed her watering eyes and found that the blue-white effulgence also filled her skull. Gradually the intensity of the light gave way to an awareness of the other minds in the circle, but especially Fiona's. After a moment of reflexive resistance, Bryn opened herself to the contact. She felt herself lifted, buoyed, and then immersed in the flow of unified *laran*. The power of this circle dwarfed everything she'd experienced at Nevarsin.

Bryn sensed the shift as Fiona focused the circle on her father, perceiving both his physical and his energetic bodies. Overlaid on the lightly glowing threads that represented the electrical currents along his nerves ran a separate, parallel system of energon channels. From his neck down, the channels pulsed rhythmically, alive with life energy. His head was another matter. She wanted to soothe the angry, swollen red nodes and ease the congested channels. And that sphere of ash-dead blackness—

Don't monitor him, came Fiona's mental voice. *Just wait. We will need all your attention soon.*

Joined to the circle, Bryn's focus shrank, and shrank even more. Neurons loomed on every side, vibrating with the light of metabolic processes. She tasted the transmitters that bridged the gaps of synapses; here and there, a shimmering almost-light marked a wave of depolarization as a nerve fired. For what seemed a very long time, she lost herself in wonder.

Look...there.

Ahead lay a massive, foreign shape, a lacuna of nothingness. The void spewed forth wave after wave of electrical energy over the area in which it was embedded. A psychically inert zone surrounded it, the work of the Nevarsin healers, but the barrier was porous, fragmented. Slowly failing. Electrical pulses extended toward the centers of judgment and decision-making. The corticator was gradually imposing its own order on more and more of the surrounding organic tissue, and its influence was expanding.

We cannot perceive the interior of the machine, Fiona's mental voice said. *We can only attempt to mitigate the damage. Show us what you know.*

Softly, so as not to disturb the circle's rapport, Fiona invited Bryn to convey her technical knowledge, as if she were unfurling a tapestry. Bryn summoned a visual image of the corticator's architecture, beginning with the housing and then moving inward to reveal the interior components. Felicity had mapped out for her the hybridization of the old psychic probe and Q-alpha corticator technologies. The elements already familiar to Bryn became more clearly defined as the shell turned translucent and then diaphanous, merely a misty outline. Other areas remained murky.

Fiona focused on the connections between the modules. There...and *there*...where the physical links appeared weakest, she channeled the combined *laran* power of the circle, wielding it like a scalpel.

Within the corticator, a delicate coupling fell away, and then another. The artificial electrical rhythms faltered.

Yes! Bryn could not restrain a flash of triumph.

Quiet! came a brusque command—from Robert, she thought. *Do not disrupt our concentration.*

The next moment, however, the corticator settled into a new rhythm, just as regular as before.

The device seemed to know it was under attack and was re-routing its internal connections to maintain its programmed function. Or perhaps it had been designed to adapt to damage and create alternate pathways.

Undeterred, Fiona continued her work, but with each severing, the corticator's discharges resumed. This time, they spread even deeper into Ernst's brain tissues. The new patterns were slightly altered in frequency but higher in magnitude. Relentless.

The detached connections emitted harsh, coruscating flashes of electrical power.

An anguished cry. Stuttering breathing. Ernst's arms and legs jerked fitfully, were still, then moved again. On either side of his skull, electrode lights flashed wildly. Across the room, Felicity murmured words Bryn could not make out.

The unity of the circle wavered.

Hold fast! came Fiona's telepathic command. *Still yourselves. Wait.*

Bryn imagined the circle grasping hands, invisible radiance surging from one to the other and into Fiona's deft control. Verana was steadying the individual *leroni*, easing the irregular heartbeats and shortened breaths. Desiderio was like an anchor, his *laran* a steady beacon.

The circle seemed to take a collective breath. Gradually, the frenetic rhythms of the corticator slowed, although they did not re-assume their previous pattern.

I need a map of the obscured portion, Fiona said. *I fear that if we make another attempt, this machine will turn upon us all, your father primarily.*

Bryn's heart sank. She had already transmitted the most detailed visual images she had. They'd come so far, and now it seemed success was within reach—only to be snatched away. Yet this was the limit of her knowledge.

But not, perhaps, of Felicity's.

I must consult with my mentor, she said. *Will that disrupt the circle?*

Ordinarily, yes, Fiona said. *But we have more than one Keeper to maintain our psychic bonds.*

And I will hold your place until you return, Desiderio added.

Bryn dropped out of the circle and rose to unsteady feet. Moving as quietly as she could, she made her way to where Felicity sat. In the radiance of the starstones, the older woman's face looked drawn, seamed with worry.

"What's happened?" Felicity asked.

Bryn explained in a few sentences, and Felicity followed up with questions for clarification. After a moment of thought, Felicity said, "I believe the inaccessible area is the psychic probe-pulse generator complex, and possibly the neurostimulation and resynchronization components. Those aren't present in the therapeutic devices, so it's no wonder you're unfamiliar with them. From your description, I suspect there's been a further modification of the neurostimulation and modularity aspects since the time of my own research."

How am I going to convey all that? "Can you tell me how it's put together? How it works?"

Felicity's eyes gleamed in the subdued light, and Bryn recognized the fierce joy of an educator faced with a challenge. As Bryn listened, she tried to picture her teacher's words spinning a series of mental images. It could have been sheer imagination, of course, but it was all she had to go on.

"Think of it as a defibrillator for thoughts," Felicity concluded. "The sensors pick up synaptic patterns, then analyze and process them, triggering imposed neural discharges and creating the desired new pattern. Attempting to interfere with that feedback is then interpreted as unfavorable, anomalous cognition. That's a gross oversimplification, of course."

"I hope it's enough to make sense of the hybrid device, but it's all we've got."

Bryn returned to her place and focused on her starstone again. As he'd promised, Desiderio had created a Bryn-shaped energy halo that settled over her like a second skin.

As before, Bryn sent her visualization to Fiona. This time, the Keeper did not try to sever the corticator's linkages. Instead, she used the psychic power of the circle to modify them, to nudge the patterns of electrical discharge slightly out of true. The new frequencies no longer imposed patterns on the organic synapses. Had Bryn not known, she might well have mistaken the substitutes for the real thing, and yet there was no mistaking how their influence dropped to nothing. Verana and Desiderio set to work repairing the damaged brain areas, coaxing suppressed portions into balance and soothing hyper-reactivity in others.

So this is how you liberate the mind of a man? Restore his voice, his deeds, his very self to the rule of his own conscience? Who said that, Fiona or Desiderio or Laurinda of Arilinn? Or her father himself?

Bryn came back to awareness. The circle had broken, and around her the *leroni* were putting away their starstones. Allart Ridenow of Corandolis yawned and stretched. "Where's the food?"

Ernst had fallen asleep, but already his cheeks seemed less sunken. Under Bryn's fingertips, his pulse was steady and strong, his flesh resilient. Lights glinted through his hair, slowly winking on and off.

It worked it worked it worked! bubbled through her mind.

"I must confess, I did not believe it could be accomplished with such a perfect appearance of normality." Felicity moved to Bryn's side. "It is said that the greatest compliment a teacher can receive is being surpassed by her student. Well done, my dear. Well done."

A young Tower novice entered, carrying a platter heaped with over-sweetened baked goods. Everyone, even Felicity, helped themselves.

Ernst raised his head, sat up with surprising vigor, got to his feet, and stretched. "*That's* better."

Bryn rushed to him. *Is it really you?*

"My sweet girl." He held out his arms. "If it will reassure you, I can confidently assert that the Nagy party is the most vile, self-serving force of divisiveness ever to be loosed upon the fellowship of settled planets. Universal independence and cessation of all interstellar commerce are infinitely preferable to his tyranny. There! Are you satisfied that I am now free to speak my mind? Yes?"

"Yes!" Bryn felt the sting of tears at the return of the vital, eloquent father she knew. "Oh, yes!"

"Indeed," Felicity said, "you have proven that you are now restored to yourself."

"My thanks to you, Doctor Sage, for all your efforts on my behalf. And to you, Desiderio, for your tireless interfacing with the Comyn. And you, my daughter, who never stopped trying. And to all of you!"

Ernst offered Felicity a formal handshake, colleague to colleague, and then a Terran version of a bow to Desiderio, who responded in kind, and to the entire circle.

"Now let us waste no time in bringing an end to this despotic regime and restoring a just and equitable system," Ernst said. "Let's continue the discussion in a more private setting."

The hour was late but everyone was too excited to sleep. Ernst in particular was bursting with energy. He waved away Ishana's offer of *jaco* and paced up and down in the sitting room of their suite. Bryn, who was more tired than she cared to admit, sank into a chair beside Felicity and Desiderio.

"The timing is perfect," Ernst said, more to himself than the others. "We will solve several problems at once. StarOps will give us a ride home, believing they have succeeded in taking me into custody."

Pace, pace…

"Father, please sit down."

"But we must not let slip that this is exactly what we want. The Regent or the Comyn Council—" he paused, turning to face his listeners, "—must not be seen to accede to their demands too readily. It's to the interests of some we have met, certainly, but there must be at least a token resistance."

Pace, pace… "Not enough to trigger a demonstration of Terran weaponry, of course. Bargaining, but not too much. Perhaps minor concessions and assurances. What does the Council want that they might ask in return for handing me over?"

"The isolationists would like nothing better than to be left alone, impossible as that is," Desiderio reminded him. "Our location on the galactic arm makes us a prime location for smugglers, as we have seen in recent history."

"The Alliance won't agree," Bryn said. "Besides being First Minister, Arthur Nagy is also the leader of the Expansionist Party. It's their goal to extend and maintain control over as many worlds as possible."

Ernst paused. "Darkover will not be forgotten, that is true, but it *can* negotiate a measure of protection."

"What do you mean?" Desiderio sat straighter in his chair.

"Just this: a planet with no status has no one to advocate for it. It partakes in no treaties limiting the actions of the greater whole. But that can be remedied. Yes, an excellent bargaining point, one that will make perfect sense to StarOps and to Nagy himself."

Bryn felt a surge in her danger-sense, which had never been entirely quiescent since their first meeting with the Regent. "Vainwal was a full member and yet look at what happened when it declared independence."

"Darkover is not Vainwal," Ernst reminded her. "Look at it this way, my friends. It is far easier to place restrictions from the beginning than to extricate from a relationship as firmly established as that between Terra and its member worlds. No, Darkover will be in a far better position by insisting on neutrality and limited status from the outset. Remember, too, that this is for only a narrow window of time, just long enough to convince Nagy that he has won by promising Darkover protection in exchange for a prisoner. Assuming all goes well and I am successful in challenging him, I will be in a position to ensure that any terms between this world and the Alliance are fair and mutually beneficial."

"That's assuming all goes as we hope," Bryn said. "Black might not believe you're still under corticator control, or Nagy might suspect. And Nagy has the power to make anyone who threatens him disappear."

"We have gotten this far against many odds," Ernst reminded her gently. "Now is not the time to lose heart."

"You're right." She managed a smile. "I must be overtired, that's all."

"We could all do with a night's rest." Smothering a yawn, Felicity rose and headed for her chamber. She had been unusually quiet, as if churning matters over in her mind.

Ernst turned back to Bryn and Desiderio. "You young people should get some sleep, as well. I'll stay up for a bit. Many of the thoughts suppressed by the corticator are bubbling around in my brain. I'll calm down once I've released the pressure, as it were, and have had a chance to work on my plan."

"Do you need anything?" Ishana asked from the dining area.

"Nothing, thank you. It's very late for you, as well."

"I have a stake in what happens, too," Ishana said, a trifle stiffly. "Darkover is my home, and my father risked a great deal to protect this world."

Ernst took her hands in his characteristically warm manner. "I will do everything I can to preserve not only this marvelous planet, Darkover, but also all the Alliance worlds. And I will always be mindful of the debt I owe to everyone here, you included, for the freedom I now enjoy within my own mind."

"Very well, then. I'll see you at breakfast."

"If you would be so kind, deliver a message from me to the Regent, requesting a meeting with the Comyn Council."

With an inclination of her head, Ishana left them.

"I, too, bid you good night," Desiderio said, rising.

Through their rapport, Bryn sensed something from him—not distress, nothing that strong, but akin to unease. She went with him to the door. He held it open for her, anticipating her desire for a few words in private.

You fear what might happen, he said mentally. *As do I.*

"I can think of so many things that might go wrong," she said, "but my danger-sense isn't clear which."

"If you have a measure of the Aldaran Gift, which causes you to see a number of possible futures, I urge you not to dwell on them. In our long history of *laran* talents, none has led more often to madness."

I'll try.

He shifted his weight, signaling a change in subject. "The Comyn Council will hear your father's case in the Crystal Chamber, and I must warn you about the telepathic dampers. They prevent those with *laran* from influencing those who are weaker or entirely lacking. It's…unpleasant. The stronger the *laran,* the more difficult it is to ignore. I've heard it likened to suddenly losing sight or hearing."

"That I can well believe," she answered. "Thank you for letting me know what to expect. I hope the council believes my father will do what he can to protect Darkover."

"I don't believe any of them doubt his good intentions."

"Only his ability to carry them out?"

He sighed. "Until the Lady of Nevarsin heard your telepathic call and your ship crashed in the Hellers, we were ignored by outworlders, and therein lay our safety. Now it is not smugglers and privateers we must ward off but the Star Alliance itself, with all its military resources. As for me…I have done as the Lady asked in providing aid and advice, but I also cannot help but think that in doing so, I have put almost all I hold dear at greater risk."

Almost all.

"Desi—" She started to reach out, hesitated, then withdrew her hand.

"None of us can truly foresee what will happen next. Didn't you just counsel me against putting too much credence in my fears? Everything you have done so far has brought us to the point where we stand a chance, a real chance, of bringing Nagy down."

"With the blessing of Aldones, your words may prove true."

With that, they bade one another goodnight.

◆◆◆

The next morning an invitation arrived from the Comyn Council. Escorted by an honor guard consisting of four very serious-looking cadets, the Terrans made their way to the entrance to the Crystal Chamber, where the Comyn Council had met since its founding. A pair of guards and a handful of liveried pages waited outside.

"Wait here," one of the guards said, then cracked open one of the doors and slipped inside. A few minutes passed in awkward, silent waiting, and then Desiderio came out.

"They've called the roll of the Domains and are now ready for you. Bryn, you may take your place with the Keepers as their guest in recognition of your work in their circle. *Mestra* Felicia, *Mestre* Ernst, you will come with me. Seats have been provided for you, but not within the enclosure of any Domain. You understand this is to protect your neutrality. You must not be seen as allies of any particular House."

"Suitably diplomatic," Ernst said.

The chamber was divided into sections with a central open area. Railings separated each area and the benches were about half-filled with men and a sprinkling of women in formal wear, most of them staring at the newcomers. Prisms set in the ceiling refracted the light from above, creating a sea of rainbows. On the walls hung colorful banners representing the different Domains. It was beautiful and ceremonial and strangely lifeless. Bryn felt as if layers of gauze had just been dropped over her head. She could hear and see well enough, yet every sensation seemed muffled. She could not sense the living energies of the assembly, not even Desiderio. Their rapport had been completely severed.

Telepathic dampers. Desiderio had warned her the effect was unpleasant. He had not exaggerated.

Desiderio conducted her to a small railed-off area to join the red-robed Keepers and then took his place in the Alton enclosure. Fiona, sitting in the front row, smiled and gestured for Bryn to take the empty place beside her. Ernst and Felicity seated themselves a short distance from the massive age-darkened throne occupied by Varzil Hastur.

"On behalf of this council, I welcome you," the Hastur lord said. "It has been many years since we have had dealings with your people. Much has transpired on our world, and yours, since your Federation departed. We have no illusions that the Star Alliance is in any degree more benevolent."

Murmurs rustled through the assembly.

"Federation brought us technology—"

"Compact-banned *reish*!"

"Not helpless—destroyed Caer Donn base—"

"Hush, let's listen!"

"The Domains now face the question of our times," Varzil said, raising his voice, "whether to preserve the isolation that has allowed us to flourish, safely protected from outside wars fought with weapons of fearful destruction, weapons we forbade a millennium ago, or whether to re-engage with the planet that was the home of our distant ancestors.

"It is not our purpose here to elaborate on the long and often contentious history of our relationship with Terra. Suffice it to say that Darkover both benefited and suffered as a result. *Mestre* Ernst Haslund, we have asked you here to supply us with information about how your presence may affect the choices before us."

Varzil paused for dramatic effect, and in that interval Ernst rose to his feet. Bryn recognized his posture, his air of serene competence. Even before he uttered a single word, he drew the attention of the assembly.

"*Dom* Varzil, I thank you for the opportunity to address this council. I have immense gratitude for the kindness of the many Darkovans to whom I and my companions owe our very lives. We are in your debt." He spoke slowly in clear, accented *casta*, his voice carrying through the chamber. Bryn felt the shifting mood in the council. Even *Dom* Varzil's expression softened.

"How is such a debt to be repaid?" Ernst lifted his arms as he pivoted slowly to address the entire chamber. "Firstly, by validating your rational concerns about the Star Alliance under its present leadership and what it is capable of. You are *right* to suspect. You are *right* to protect. I have seen with my own eyes the fate of worlds that defied the Nagy regime. Campta and the moon base around Wolf: destroyed, uninhabitable."

The temperature in the chamber dropped. Bryn's heart beat faster.

Around the room, she read changing expressions, and only here and there, among the Ridenow and Ardais, did she see anything like suspicion, and that was guarded.

"Ephebe, Renney, and Thetis: under martial law. Vainwal with its daring bid for independence: who can say?"

"It cannot be!" someone cried.

"They have no honor!" The Comyn might have heard rumors in the years before the Federation withdrew, when the Expansionist Party came to power. But Vainwal was news to them.

"As for Darkover—" Ernst drew a breath, and Bryn heard a hushed, collective intake of breath. His next words rang out. "Darkover *must not* suffer the same fate!"

People pressed against the railings that divided the Domains sections. Listening.

"With so much at stake," Ernst said, "we must consider our actions with care. The reasons for Terran interest in your world have not changed—your natural resources, your potential as a market for finished goods, and most of all, your geographic location in the galactic arm. The Alliance may be distracted by other matters for a time, but sooner or later, my friends, they *will* remember Darkover and its advantages. The choice then becomes whether to control the inevitable recontact, ensuring it happens under *your* terms and on *your* timing, or to leave the initiative entirely with the Alliance."

When he paused to let his words sink in, Bryn thought how skillfully he had shifted the parameters of the debate.

"The question, my friends, is no longer *if* Terran forces will return, but *when.* If the swords worn by many of you are an indication, you think in terms of military strategy, and you know all too well that being on the defensive, reacting instead of acting, places you at an inherent disadvantage."

"Aye, that's true," came from the Ardais enclosure.

"And so we come to this moment and this choice. In a matter of days, the Alliance StarOps ships will make orbit. You have heard their demands for my surrender. For the sake of Darkover, and for the sake of Terra and the other Alliance worlds—" A pause. "—you must turn me over to them."

"Is he mad?"

"I thought he would plead for our protection."

"Hsst! I want to hear his reasons."

"I love Terra as much as you love Darkover," Ernst said. "We are united in our devotion to our homeworlds. I have served Terra for most of my life, first as a local official, then as an elected representative, and finally as Senator and spokesman for that institution. Always I have sought to find common ground between opposing factions. Peaceful, mutually beneficial solutions. Protection of the vulnerable and justice for those who have been wronged. And always—*always*—I have striven to serve not for my vanity, but out of duty and with honor."

Varzil nodded, as did many around the chamber. Honor, Bryn thought, was a thing Darkovans understood very well.

"I mentioned the fate of Vainwal and its bid for independence from the Alliance. I believed, and still do, that each planet has the right to self-governance and autonomy. That includes the choice to make alliances and dissolve them, as the people of each world deem best." As he spoke, Ernst allowed his voice to rise in intensity. "This is as true for Darkover as it is for any other world. *No one* has the right to dictate to you how you should conduct your affairs. Persuade, yes. Negotiate when others are concerned, certainly. But never to impose with a dictator's iron fist."

Applause and expressions of agreement swept the chamber. These men and women knew what it was to care deeply, fervently, about their world.

"*This* was the very principle with which I led the effort to negotiate equitable terms with Vainwal. *This* is how we can forge relationships based on mutual respect, goodwill, and trust." Ernst lowered his voice, and throughout the Crystal Chamber, the audience leaned forward to hear his next words. "*This* is the future I envisioned for the Star Alliance. And *this* is why I must return. For Terra, my world."

And for Darkover. He did not say the words aloud. They were implied and understood.

"For the sake of both our worlds, you must turn me over to the Alliance."

"*Mestre* Ernst Haslund," Varzil said. "Are you sure this is what you wish? You have made a persuasive case for the Star Alliance being ruthless. You will be one man against an empire."

"You are correct," Ernst replied. "I am one man. I ask that you not put your entire world at risk by defying StarOps for *one man*. They are the brutal fist of the Alliance, this is true. Therefore, use me to your advantage. Bargain for concessions to gain protection for Darkover. Force them to deal with you as equals."

Murmurs filled the chamber. Bryn could not make out what people were saying, only the emotional tones of surprise, then agreement, and finally admiration. Many were nodding, including those in the Ardais and Ridenow sections who had previously been suspicious.

"You present us with an interesting proposition," Varzil said, as the chamber quieted again. "I suspect, though, that you have specific demands in mind."

Ernst made a conciliatory gesture. "That is for you to decide. I would not presume to speak for Darkover. However, if I might make a modest suggestion based on the political institutions of the Alliance, it would be to insist upon a Darkovan representative—an ambassador, if you will—with guaranteed diplomatic immunity."

Varzil's eyes narrowed slightly. "Very well, we shall consider the matter. Are there any further questions for *Mestre* Ernst Haslund?"

A lady stirred in the Aillard enclosure, so heavily veiled that Bryn could not make out her features. "Do you have anyone in particular in mind?"

"Madam, I do not," Ernst said. "That is for you—this ruling council—to decide."

Vittorio Ardais stood up. "How do we know you won't cooperate with the Alliance, using your knowledge of Darkover against us?"

Arnad Alton sprang to his feet. "He speaks as an honorable man. Why should we doubt his word?"

"He is *Terranan*!" Vittorio shot back. "We cannot trust them."

"We were all *Terranan* once," came a booming voice from the Aldaran section. Outcries and general uproar followed.

"Silence!" bellowed an older man in a formal Guards uniform, insignias of rank glittering on a sash across his chest.

"*Mestre* Ernst?" Varzil stared at him through narrowed, calculating eyes. "How will you answer?"

All heads turned toward Ernst.

"It is a just question," Ernst said. "Even if I gave you the most solemn oath among your people and mine, it might be broken through no fault of mine—or yours. I might never reach Terra alive. Unforeseen circumstances might force me into a *compromise* that is less than what we agreed upon. Nagy might silence me and do as he pleases, or twist my words to brand me a traitor. I cannot promise what will happen. But I can promise you this—" looking now directly at Vittorio, "—that I will do my utmost to achieve a fair and honorable solution. If this is your goal as well, then hand me over, but do so with as much advantage as you can gain."

Vittorio sat down, followed more slowly by Arnad. There were no further challenges.

"On behalf of the Comyn Council, thank you for your frank words," Varzil said. "The council will now consider them. Guards, please escort our guests from the chamber."

As Bryn got up, Laurinda, who was sitting beside her, murmured, "Your father is a man of great courage. You did well in advocating for him. Do not underestimate what else you might accomplish."

Bryn nodded, then followed her father and Felicity from the Crystal Chamber.

◆◆◆

Rather than make the long trek back to their suite in the Alton section, the three Terrans were conducted to a small chamber, one used by castle guards when the council was on brief recess. The room was furnished with straight-back chairs, a table, and a few other oddments.

Ernst took one of the chairs. Felicity, looking thoughtful, sat in another. Bryn wandered around the room, examining the pegs inside the door, a rack that looked as if it was meant for weapons, and a few notices tacked beside the door. As soon as they'd left the Crystal Chamber, the numbing effects of the telepathic dampers had lifted, but her danger-sense increased. She didn't think the threat came from the council meeting. Once onboard the StarOps ship, though, or back on Terra… What then?

No matter how compelling the case Ernst made, Nagy would deny the charges. He'd say everything he'd done had been for the greater good, for public safety and order. He'd claim that Vainwal's declaration of independence, not to mention protests on half a dozen other planets and Terra itself, were engineered by criminal elements, renegade subversives, and traitors determined to undermine the Alliance. Those who knew the truth might come forward, but only if they had some hope of success. Otherwise, Nagy's vengeance would descend on them and their families. He'd spew out one lie after another, and he'd stoop at nothing to hold on to his power.

If only there were a way to force *Nagy to admit what he's done*, Bryn thought.

Alanna had once mentioned that any member of the Comyn Council had the right to demand testimony under truthspell. Bryn had been taught to cast it, back at Nevarsin. But Arthur Nagy would never submit to such a thing. He'd call it a subversive hoax, that the *leronis* who cast it had deliberately made the blue aura disappear, or that it didn't mean anything, anyway. Moreover, truthspell only *revealed* a lie. It could not *compel* the truth.

Bryn paused in her pacing, considering. *I'd need something that lowers inhibition and enhances the desire to comply with the questioner.*

Was such a thing possible?

The latch opened and Desiderio entered. "The Council has endorsed your proposal. They're sending a message to the Alliance ships."

28

Ernst and Felicity returned to their suite, but Bryn found her way to one of the castle courtyards and settled on a bench beneath a flowering arbor. The midday sun felt warm, the day mild. Her thoughts kept returning to how to compel Arthur Nagy's confession. She could cast truthspell on him, assuming she could get within range, but for it to be effective, the audience—and Nagy himself—must understand the meaning of the blue light. Even if they did, that wouldn't be enough. Nagy had plenty of self-control when it was in his best interest. He'd see the trap and simply refuse to say anything he did not know to be the truth.

By the shadows across the courtyard, noon was well past. At dusk the great red sun would dip below the western skyline and darkness would descend in a great rush, giving way to the sweep of stars that never failed to take her breath away. Now she was to leave it forever, leave the forlorn hope of joining a Tower community…leave Desiderio.

As if summoned by her thought, he crossed the courtyard to her. She felt his mind like velvet on hers.

What troubles you, preciosa? He sat beside her.

Bryn related her fears of Nagy's treachery and her determination to create a truth-compulsion spell. Rapport shimmered between them, a gossamer tapestry. As she spoke, she felt Desiderio's revulsion at the notion of leashing a mind to another's will, and realized how deeply it ran throughout Comyn culture.

"I've crossed a line, haven't I?" Bryn said. "The prohibition against entering the mind of another?"

"We cannot rely on forced rapport to execute your plan. I am Alton and have a measure of that Gift. It was bred into us in ages past—the Ages of Chaos. Much from that era has been lost, but even in modern times, some of us still have it. From childhood, I have been taught to never abuse that Gift, no matter how urgent or worthy the cause. The last time—let us just say that the consequences to both the victims and the perpetrators were grave."

Bryn lacked the deep resonance with Darkovan history, the horror of using *laran* as a weapon. Now that the idea of a truth-compulsion spell had entered her mind, she would not, *could not* give it up.

"Help me, then," she said. "Help me to find a way that doesn't violate your ethics or require forced rapport or telepathic coercion."

For a long moment, he was silent. "You said that while under the influence of the corticator device your father made statements he did not agree with, to violate his own principles?"

"Yes, that's true," Bryn said.

He looked away, his expression shuttered. "That is a chilling prospect. Your *Terranan* tyrant has created a machine without a conscience. For the sake of both our worlds, I will help you if I can." He shifted into teaching mode, as she'd seen at Nevarsin. "Let us consider how truthspell is usually set."

Bryn took out her starstone and recited the verse Adriana had taught her, back in Nevarsin:

In the light of the fire of this jewel,

let the truth lighten the space where we stand.

Blue light ignited, spreading a gentle radiance from her starstone. It filled her mind and reflected on Desiderio's face.

"It's a mirror effect," she said. "The mind of the person casting the spell is linked to the subject. The bond manifests as a blue aura. If the subject tells a deliberate falsehood, the bond breaks and the light vanishes."

"And why is that?"

"Expectations," Bryn answered without thinking. "The subject knows they're lying and *expects* the light to go out. That breaks the link."

"What about Nagy? Would truthspell work even though he doesn't believe in it? Is belief necessary?"

"I would assume so. It wouldn't mean anything to him, though, or to a Terran observer."

"So truthspell works regardless of the belief of the subject. Why does the light vanish?"

"The leronis casting it detects minute changes in the subject's physiology—heart rate, perspiration, electrodermal response, pupillary dilation, that sort of thing."

"An excellent surmise," Desiderio said. "But that isn't what causes the light to fail. Try again."

"I don't know—magic?" Bryn jumped up, facing him. "Stop playing games! You have something in mind, so just tell me."

"I am not trying to torment you, Bruna. But *you* will be the one facing Nagy if all goes well, so the insight must come from *you*."

Bryn lowered herself back on the bench. She imagined an auditorium, Nagy and her father on a stage with broadcast equipment, herself to the side.

Nagy begins to speak...I take out my starstone and focus on it...blue light surrounds Nagy...he speaks a lie...the light winks out.

She tried another, slightly different scenario.

Truthspell...blue light washing Nagy's features...he remains silent...I ask a question...silence...I demand an answer... concentration splits and the spell fails. The light vanishes.

She shook her head. "I can certainly manage to cast truthspell on Nagy, but as soon as I try to trap him in a lie, I don't think I can maintain both."

Desiderio nodded encouragingly. "Yes, I think so, too."

"So we need two people for a truth-compulsion spell. One for the blue light that reveals a lie, the other to pressure Nagy to answer directly for his actions."

"But not to *compel* him to speak using *laran*."

"Then what? Nagy will never incriminate himself voluntarily. We'll get only one chance."

Desiderio looked thoughtful. "Instead of compulsion, maybe we should look at persuasion. Even better, *permission*."

Persuasion? That would get around the ethical issues about using *laran* to impose another's will on a subject. Thinking aloud, she said, "Honesty is integral for most of us, as evidenced by the shame we feel when we lie and the relief when it is behind us. Sociopaths don't experience remorse when they lie, but I don't think Nagy is one. He's ruthless, but then, he had Sandra Nagy as a mother. He's likely a product of environment and nurture plus personal ambition, rather than extreme antisocial personality traits and absence of empathy. So if I found a way to reach the part of Nagy that *wants* to come clean, it wouldn't be prohibited mind control but more like mind *release*."

"That's it!" Desiderio said. "There is precedent for this, a legend from the time of the Hundred Kingdoms about a king who was confronted with his crimes through *laran*. The story goes that through a telepathic bond, he experienced the suffering and humiliation he had inflicted on others, and thereafter he amended his ways. If this king, who was reputed to be without mercy, had a conscience that could be reached, I believe that Arthur Nagy does, too."

"Only I'm back to the same problem of being only one person."

"Such a spell will indeed require two people, you to create the light and me to draw out the inner honesty of the man."

"You're willing to come to Terra with me?"

"*Dom* Varzil has already inquired whether I would be willing to accompany you and your father as the Darkovan representative. I wanted to speak with you before I said yes."

Until this moment, it had not occurred to Bryn that she might have an ally in dealing with Nagy. She imagined that her father would face down Nagy alone, and it would be up to her and only her to make sure Nagy couldn't lie his way out.

Images assaulted her—Desiderio in the cavernous streets of Terra Central—Desiderio in a world of head-blind—Desiderio in Black's cells—oh gods, the crowd on Renney—Nagy's mind-control machinery turned on Desiderio—

"Bruna." His fingers brushed the back of her wrist, a telepath's butterfly-light touch. *We cannot tell what will happen, and dwelling on possible futures leads to madness. We can only act with courage and honor, and we can do it together.*

Do it together... That was very much what she would have said to her young patients, or what her father might have said to her. Panic eased. The barrage of fear-driven images receded.

"We ought to practice," she said, once she could speak again.

"I agree, beginning with creating the spell's field without the blue light. It isn't strictly necessary that it be externally visible, you know, and it might be easier. You will know when it reacts to a falsehood."

That made sense. But before Bryn could say anything more, Arnad ran up to them. "Sorry to disturb you, kinsman—word has just come from the listening post—the Regent sent me to find you both—the *Terranan* ship is now in orbit and will set down shortly."

"I don't understand why you're going down to the spaceport," Ernst said. He was sitting at the dining table of their suite, notes and speech drafts spread over the dining table.

Bryn pulled on an unadorned woolen cloak with a deep hood that cast her features into shadow. "See? I look like just another Darkovan."

"Let the Regent's representative negotiate, as planned," he urged. "There's no need for you to go. What if you're recognized?"

"I'll be careful to not draw attention to myself," she promised. "I want to take their measure." *And to see if I can cast truthspell without their noticing.*

"Go on, then," Ernst said with a weary smile.

She pushed back the hood. "Father, did you get any sleep last night?"

"It's not important. Right now, time is more precious than sleep. I will catch up on the journey home." Meaning that they would all be under sleep gas.

We are each preparing as we think best.

Bryn rode out to the old Terran spaceport with the rest of the Darkovan embassy. Felix, representing his father, was resplendent in court finery under a cloak lined with marl fur. Desiderio, equally magnificent, rode a pace behind Felix, as did Bessamy Leynier, present to witness the arrival on behalf of the Keepers' Council. Guards bracketed them.

In the thin morning drizzle, the Alliance shuttle waited on the battered landing field. The tarmac still bore overlapping circular scars, relics of the ships that had once regularly landed here. Partly-dismantled scaffolding and loading platforms littered the field. The shuttle wasn't sleek and dark, a perfect predator, a shark of the skies from Alanna's vision. Space debris scored the length of its sides. In them, she felt the cold of space, the screaming need for haste. The menace in every line. Her danger-sense stirred, reminding her that nothing in this universe was truly safe, and then subsided to a low mutter.

The Darkovans dismounted at the edge of the tarmac and walked the rest of the way.

A ramp extended from the shuttle with an audible screech of metal on metal. Three men in StarOps uniforms descended, weapons displayed. One moved to the fore, the others flanking him in defensive positions.

"On behalf of the Terran Star Alliance, and in accord with the agreement with the Regent of Darkover," the StarOps officer said in Terran Standard, "we are here to take custody of the indicted traitor, Ernst Haslund, and to take his daughter, Bryn Haslund, and Doctor Felicity Sage, under our protection."

"Be welcome, and depart in peace," Felix replied with impeccable formality in that same language. Every Darkovan present understood the insult in his bow, that of a superior condescending to notice a social inferior. The StarOps men did not react.

It's a test, Bryn thought. *And they didn't even realize it.* That boded well for her experiment.

"I am Felix Regis-Rafael Alton-Hastur, and I speak for my father, *Dom* Varzil Alton-Hastur, Warden of Hastur, Regent of Elhalyn and the Comyn. Will you accept our hospitality under truce and accompany us to Comyn Castle?"

"We will remain onboard until the prisoners are surrendered," the StarOps man said.

Felix's expression did not change, coldly cordial. "I have guaranteed your safety under truce and on *the word of a Hastur.* Surely you and your crew are in need of rest and provisions. A few hours planetside can only benefit you."

The StarOps man hesitated just long enough for Bryn to see that he was tempted. He might not understand the full weight of the word of a Hastur, but he clearly had orders to not antagonize the local aristocracy.

While the two men exchanged polite expressions of invitation and regretful refusal, Bryn rested her fingertips on the pouch containing her starstone. A twist, and the stone fell into the palm of her hand, warming against her skin. She focused on one of the subordinate Terrans, not their leader. Carefully she enveloped his mind in the spiderweb-delicate *laran* field.

In the light of the fire of this jewel...

There was no outward change in the man's face, no visible blue light, but Bryn sensed the field like a silken web. As a test, she tightened the strands slightly. The agent frowned and shifted his weight. His boss, the lead StarOps officer, was responding to something Felix had said. Bryn heard the harmonics of tension in his voice. She imagined the blue light dimming as she allowed the spell to fall away.

"I appreciate your offer," the StarOps officer said, "but I must respectfully decline. My orders are to take charge of the Haslunds immediately."

"As immediately as can be arranged," Felix answered smoothly. "Surely that cannot mean depriving our guests of the necessities of a long journey, as well as time to make their farewells. Moreover, your Captain Black agreed to the inclusion of a Darkovan representative, who will be granted full diplomatic privileges. By virtue of his position, this representative is entitled to whatever accommodation he requires. He will not only be representing Darkover but the honor of your First Minister."

"Very well. An hour, then?"

"Two days at minimum."

"Tomorrow at dawn. But the Haslunds must remain under guard until then."

"You have my word on it that they will not escape."

"Two of my men will ensure that."

Felix paused just long enough to convey his reluctance, then nodded. "By law and custom, we do not permit Compact-banned weapons within the city. Your men may retain their knives, but they must leave behind their blasters and other illegal arms."

"That's not protocol—"

"Come now, officer. Surely two trained, fit soldiers such as yours can deal with one old man and two women."

"Tomorrow, then. Be sure they are ready to depart."

Without even a sketch of a bow, the StarOps contingent returned to the shuttle, followed by all but the two assigned to guard the Terrans. The landing ramp lifted behind them.

"Not very trusting, are they?" muttered one of Felix's guards in *casta.*

"I hope so," his partner replied.

Felix turned his gaze to Desiderio and then Bryn, his meaning clear: *I have bought you all the time I could, and this* Terranan *fool thinks he has gotten the better of us.*

Desiderio responded with a bow, slightly lower than was strictly according to form.

The party headed back to their horses and then to Comyn Castle. They rode slowly to accommodate the two StarOps men, who refused the offer of mounts. Once out of sight of the StarOps shuttle, Bryn felt as if a weight had been lifted from her chest. There was no turning back now, no uncertainty. The initial greeting was over, an agreement sealed. She glanced at Desiderio at her side and felt a pulse of warmth from him. He was so calm, so confident, and yet he had never been off Darkover before.

At the castle, Felix detained the two StarOps men to let Bryn slip away. Her father was waiting for her in their suite.

"It went better than we expected," she said. "Felix bargained well, and StarOps thinks they have the upper hand so they could afford to make a few concessions. We have until dawn tomorrow. Meanwhile, a pair of StarOps agents will be posted outside our door to make sure we don't escape. Exactly where they think we might go, with the Regent having given his word to turn us over, I have no idea."

"Typical Alliance paranoia."

Just then, Bryn felt the approach of two unshielded minds. Minds that were subtly different from those of the Darkovans around her. "They're here, by the way."

"Shall we invite them in for *jaco*?"

"Pffft!" Bryn glanced around the sitting and dining areas. "I should tell Felicity to be ready, as well. Where is she?"

"I did not see her when I returned last night. Since her door was closed, I assumed she had gone to sleep early."

Bryn went to Felicity's room and tapped on the door. There was no answer, either to knocking or calling. Finally, Bryn tried the latch. Beyond, Felicity's bedroom was dark and empty. A long white rectangle caught the oblique light. Bryn picked it up: a folded piece of paper addressed to her and her father.

Dear Ernst and Bryn,

After much reflection, I have decided not to return to territory held by the Star Alliance, either Terra or Alpha. As I said to Bryn when we left Alpha, my former life is over. I cannot in good conscience continue to develop technology that can be perverted for tyrannical usages. I refuse any part of it. In any event, I do not labor under the delusion that my academic reputation will survive the present events. Instead, I am remaining on Darkover and have accepted the invitation of Julianna n'ha Caitlin, Dean of Thendara University, to create a program of basic scientific education and training in research practices suitable for the technological level of this world. The Bridge Society was created to use the best of Terran and native methods, but without further Terran input, it has stagnated. I believe that with my knowledge and mentorship, much may be achieved. I look forward to this new challenge.

Should either of you return to Darkover, I would enjoy meeting with you.

Yours in all sincerity,

Felicity Sage

She showed the letter to her father. "I am not surprised," he said. "She went to visit Professor Julianna on several occasions. I'm relieved, for she is well out of what comes next."

I'll miss her, Bryn thought, remembering their reunion on Alpha and the comforting familiarity of the university there. The manicured gardens, the sense of safety that turned out to be an illusion. No, Felicity was right. Their way led forward, not back to the past.

◆◆◆

StarOps agents marched Bryn and Ernst, and Desiderio, as the Darkovan representative, out through the front gates of Comyn Castle. A castle honor guard led the way and brought up the rear. No one tried to make conversation. The early morning was mild, with mauve Idriel still glimmering above rooflines. Merry-makers thronged the markets that had sprung up on street corners, dancers and flower-sellers, carts selling skewers of roasted meat and spiced, baked apples.

As she walked the streets beside her father, surrounded on either side by a black-clad agent, Bryn focused on preparing a convincing facade.

Just remember, she told herself, *I'm a devoted daughter, so traumatized by my experience on a marginal world and so beset with anxiety for my father that I'll believe anyone who can help them.*

When Bryn set her foot on the shuttle's ramp, her danger-sense spiked. There was nothing she could do about it, and it made sense. She was on her way back on Terra, surrounded by StarOps, about to be delivered into Nagy's custody after who knew what kind of mind-meddling in transit. The prickling eased off without becoming specific.

Upon boarding, Desiderio was escorted into a forward section, leaving Bryn and Ernst with their guards in the same compartment. Both of them were restrained by wrists and ankles to their seats. A StarOps agent slipped oxygen breathers over their faces, then took the remaining seat. He held a tangler at the ready, his eyes watchful. As the shuttle launched, Darkover's gravity pressed against Bryn, as if the planet were reluctant to let her go.

The shuttle completed its docking maneuvers and Ernst allowed himself to be taken away, leaving Bryn in her restraints.

Meek...dutiful...awed by StarOps authority...

When at last an agent came to get her, she was hustled unceremoniously into a cryo-prep chamber. A woman with a medic insignia on her StarOps uniform issued a string of orders: "Drink this, hold out your arm, close your eyes, take a breath." She placed Bryn in a stackable tube bed of the sort used for transport of colonists, designed to accommodate the maximum number of occupants in the smallest possible space. At least she did not close the tube while Bryn was fully awake.

Drowsiness overtook Bryn. Her skin felt clammy where it had not already turned numb. A sweet taste filled her mouth, characteristic of the cold-sleep drugs she'd been injected with. She searched for Desiderio's presence in her mind but felt only a blurred dullness that was more ache than absence. He, too, must be succumbing to the drugs. She closed her eyes.

A voice came to her, the words unintelligible, the timbre unmistakable. She would recognize it anywhere, even drugged halfway to insensibility. Her eyes remained closed, resistant to her will. Her lips felt thick, unresponsive.

"Not quite under," the medic said.

"Will she remember?" *Black, that was Black.*

She could not make out the medic's answer.

"Not that it matters. Well, you've led us a merry chase, Ms. Haslund, but it's over now. I hope you've learned you can't win this fight. The force of history is on our side. There will soon be no one to stand against us, now that the Senator is back in the fold."

Hands fumbled at her head, tiny jerking movements this way and that. For several minutes, her thoughts were so sluggish, she could not imagine what Black was doing.

"You understand that we can't take any chances with things going wrong. You may be the biddable daughter who now regrets her earlier, unfortunate alliances and now stands with her noble father. Or you may think you're fooling us—"

As Black talked, she felt the wet slickness of electrode gel as the pads made contact with her skull.

Panic seized her. Despite her rising somnolence, she forced herself to think. *No, there's no drilling. Nothing* inside *me.* Then, as if Felicity were delivering a lecture on the corticator series: *The alpha models are designed to teach languages over interstellar voyages. The primary mode of action programs grammar and vocabulary directly into the synaptic architecture of the brain—*

"Sleep now," said the agent Black, "and learn your lessons well."

The voice within her mind grew louder. Devoid of the warmth of every telepathic communication she'd experienced, it repeated patiently, relentlessly:

Arthur Nagy is your leader. You owe him your utmost loyalty. Arthur Nagy is the savior of the Alliance. The welfare of humankind depends on Arthur Nagy...

Although Bryn couldn't reach her starstone, she imagined its light, clear and blue and penetrating. In her mind, she shaped it into a shield. *Not my thoughts!* she hurled against the invading voice. *Not the truth!*

...You will support Arthur Nagy to your dying breath. You will not resist him in thought, word, or deed. Arthur Nagy is your leader. You owe him your utmost loyalty...

No...

The light within her mind dimmed. Darkness swallowed her up, but the voice went on. As her consciousness faded, she clung to the memory of radiance the color of the sky, of the waters on Thetis, of the spell of truth.

Emerging from cryo was significantly less comfortable than Bryn remembered from her previous flights. The prep had been accelerated, the dosages of the drugs maximized for rapid induction. Fortunately, no such extreme measures greeted her at the end of her journey. She awoke on a cushioned, monitored bed, swaddled in foam that helped restore circulation and muscle tone. Warm and slightly orange-scented, it gave easily as she stretched her arms and legs, so she wasn't restrained.

In a spasm of panic she recalled the circumstances of being put under. The mental resonance was faint but discernible.

Arthur Nagy is your leader. You owe him your utmost loyalty.

Her gut clenched. Where was her starstone? Fumbling, she found it still within its pouch around her neck. Blue light pulsed through her mind as her fingertips brushed its faceted surfaces.

As a test, she silently mouthed the words, "Arthur Nagy is a despicable tyrant."

Nothing happened. No smothering internal silencer. No bolt of pain. Not even a shimmer of resistance. The sleep-learning device might have left a residual influence, but for the moment, her thoughts were her own.

A moment later, likely summoned by a sensor in the bed, a medic entered. "Awake, are we? How do we feel? Any nausea? Vertigo? Ready for something to eat? I see you've found your amulet. You had a seizure when we attempted to remove it for safekeeping. It was determined best to leave it with you."

Bryn murmured appropriate answers to the medic's questions, underwent a gentle examination and was given clothing, a flowing tunic and pants with an elegant hooded scarf of synthetic fabric. The brassiere felt stiff and confining after the softer Darkovan undergarments.

Outside, a man in a dark blue suit greeted her. Plainclothes StarOps, she reckoned, from the coldness in his eyes. "My name is Everard Jenkins, and I'll be your escort and liaison."

They crossed a sky bridge into what was clearly an elite hotel. Jenkins showed her to a suite, a bedroom with an attached spacious bathroom, and a living space with brocade-covered chairs. One wall was covered by a screen that displayed scenes from nature, but there were no exterior windows. She could not help comparing this suite to her quarters in Comyn Castle or at Nevarsin Tower, or even the Guildhouse. Those had been organic, bearing the mark of generations of previous inhabitants, whereas this was artificial...*manufactured.*

"My orders are to see that you are comfortable and that any reasonable requests are granted," Jenkins said. "The First Minister has gone to a great deal of trouble to rescue you."

"I'm sure," Bryn murmured. *Where is my father? Where is Desiderio?* Clearly, they were being kept separate so they would have no chance to speak. She cleared her throat and assumed a professional air. "When may I notify my clients of my return?"

"It won't be long," Jenkins said. "Meanwhile, may I order something to eat or drink for you? I understand you've been marooned on a Class D world, so you must have become accustomed to the bare minimum for survival."

"No, thank you. I would not wish to impose on the First Minister's generosity."

"Now that you and the Senator have been restored to us, you will see how much progress has been made in your absence. We've done away with poverty and homelessness here on Terra, and other worlds will soon follow."

Lies, lies, lies.

Bryn wondered what had happened to the river encampments and the ruins where Rashid's group had hidden out. Perhaps nothing. Perhaps they were simply ignored.

"You're skeptical, I see," Jenkins said. "Frankly, I don't blame you. I wouldn't credit all the advancements if I hadn't witnessed them first-hand. After today's ceremony welcoming the Senator, you'll have the chance to view them for yourself."

Bryn let him talk while her thoughts raced ahead. She needed physical contact with her starstone, and for that, she had to remove it from its wrappings. When Jenkins paused, clearly expecting a response, she excused herself and went to the bathroom. She lifted the tunic and slipped the starstone under the brassiere. It warmed instantly against her skin. After rearranging her clothing, she stared at her reflection in the mirror for a moment. The stone did not show at all. The skin around her eyes looked bruised, but other than that, she appeared to be the same calm professional who had glanced up at the sky and thought it was on fire. All the changes were on the inside.

A short time later, they were joined by a very fit-looking man wearing a StarOps uniform and armed with several visible weapons. He fell in behind them as Jenkins led the way towards a bank of elevator doors.

"We'll go straight down to the sub-level," Jenkins said, "and then via security vehicle to the studio for the Senator's official welcome." He gave Bryn another of his polished smiles as he inserted a key into the call panel. "Don't worry, the Senator has been given excellent care. You'll have ample opportunity to speak with him afterward, and of course you'll be presented to the First Minister himself."

After descending to an underground garage, Bryn and her coterie entered a sleek, heavily armored vehicle. The windows in the back compartment were darkened so that she couldn't see out. The vehicle made almost no noise as it glided along, and finally halted with a barely perceptible jerk. The officer in the front got out, there was some inaudible conversation, and then Bryn was allowed to exit. The vehicle had drawn up behind a sprawling, multi-storied building. A glance showed Bryn the heavily fortified gate through which they'd come. Above, the sky was unbroken overcast.

Jenkins steered Bryn into the building and through a checkpoint with multiple detection units. They emerged through a side door onto the speaking area of an auditorium, ringed by holographic news cameras. Representatives of each world in the Star Alliance sat at tables arranged in a half-circle around the stage. Space for the general audience flanked the sections on either side and the rear. Bryn knew this place. She'd attended sessions here with her father but had always sat in the audience.

A dozen people sat in double rows against the back wall of the stage. Bryn recognized some as her father's colleagues, leaders in the Senate and megacorporations. As Jenkins guided her to a place just behind the podium, several of them nodded in a friendly way to her. One said, "It's good to have you back safely among us."

Desiderio? She couldn't see him.

Her danger-sense surged. Something was terribly wrong.

She was already sweating under the lights as a side door opened and two heavily armed StarOps agents emerged. Arthur Nagy followed, walking beside another, and flanked by yet more. Her breath caught in her throat as she recognized the man striding so proudly at Nagy's side, a commander's wings glinting on his chest.

Black.

Black glanced at her before taking his place. Of course, he would be here. He'd evidently just been promoted to a senior office in StarOps as a reward for bringing in the renegade, Ernst Haslund. Waves of gloating and self-satisfaction rolled off him. As much as she wanted to, she couldn't—she didn't dare block him out; she must remain open to casting truthspell on Nagy.

Memories crowded around her, blinding in their intensity. *The taste of knockout gas...racing through the subterrane...her father's blank expression in the Alpha lab...Leonin, dying in her arms...*

Danger-sense shrieked along her nerves.

Trauma, that was it. Flashbacks. Panic. Shutting down. Fury. All normal reactions. *Normal.*

All too often, her young patients were too lost in their pain and confusion to describe what had happened to them. She had been trained to reach them, using awareness of the present moment. Not *then*, but *now*. She spoke to herself as she would to a child in her care.

Name a black thing, name a white thing...

Her pulse steadied. Her vision cleared.

A white thing, a black thing...

She could think again. Her fears no longer controlled her. Let Black think he'd won, let him think whatever he damned well pleased, *he* was not her target.

As best she could without drawing undue attention to herself, she searched the audience for her father or Desiderio. She found her father, off to the side of the speaking area, bracketed by StarOps. The harsh overhead lights washed the color from his face, but his eyes gleamed. His mind was still unfettered. So far, the plan was working perfectly. Why then, Bryn wondered, did she feel no lessening in the sense of impending catastrophe?

It will be all right. It must be.

Desiderio? She sent out a telepathic call. Surely Nagy would want the

Darkovan representative to witness this spectacle. Then she would have her ally, her partner.

But there was no mental answer. Desiderio was not there. Not in the audience nor the member worlds sections nor the stage itself.

He's not here, he's not here—there's some mistake—he's not here—

It's up to me now.

A hush fell over the assembly as Nagy stepped up to the podium. Then, beginning with the dignitaries and people on the stage, applause rippled through the hall. Nagy raised his hands in acknowledgment, the gesture magnanimous. In the overhead glare, his eyes glittered like those of a predatory bird. Every hair, even on his eyebrows, was in place.

"Citizens of the Star Alliance," Nagy said, "today we mark the dawning of a new era in our fellowship of worlds. We have emerged triumphant from a period of tumult. We have faced the forces of division, forces that challenged the very foundations of our alliance. We have heard the slogans of those who would see us return to the ages of darkness, with every world isolated and self-absorbed, at risk of interstellar conflict. Instead of surrendering to fear, we stood together, resolute and united. We have said NO to lawlessness and factionalization. We have said NO to violent protests in our great cities. We have said—"

Here he paused for the audience to echo, "*NO!*"

"—to all those who lurk in the shadows, conspiring against our leaders. We have said YES to our glorious future!"

After another round of applause, Nagy began an oration about Senator Ernst Haslund, his achievements, and his vision for the future, "—the terrible loss to us all when he went missing." How dedicated, loyal agents had searched for him. The perfidy of those who had kidnapped him. Fears for his safety, for his sanity. And then, after one empty lead upon another, success.

"And here he is, my friends, our returning hero. I give you the premier Senator of the Star Alliance, a champion now restored us—Ernst Haslund."

Bryn's father strode to the stage, pausing to touch her on the arm.

Through the hair on his temples, the electrodes winked their slow, deceitful rhythm.

Nagy completed his introduction, another round of applause burst out and faded, and now her father began his speech. Bryn heard the familiar rhythms, the smoothness, the timbre of his voice. He opened with a gracious acknowledgment of Nagy's introduction, gathering the audience to him with the skill she knew so well.

Taking deep breaths, Bryn tried to calm herself. To act effectively, alone, she needed to be able to think clearly. She pressed one hand over her chest, feeling the hard edges of her starstone against her skin.

"...heartening to be welcomed home so warmly," her father said. "Over the past period of time, I have thought frequently and with tremendous longing of this green planet, my home. Our home. Apparently, you have thought of me as well, for which I offer my gratitude. As difficult as it is to be a stranger in a new place, an exile no matter how unwilling, it is more tragic still to be forgotten."

As Ernst spoke, his voice and manner encompassed not just the immediate audience but everyone throughout the Alliance who was watching remotely through the holographic news camera.

"Once, as my esteemed colleague here will tell you, isolation was the universal condition of humankind. Confined to one world, we could only gaze at the stars and wonder. The more creative of us imagined far-flung worlds where we might someday walk. The strange races we might someday encounter. That *someday* arrived, and now our kind inhabits not one, not two, not ten, but dozens of worlds. Imagine the ages that followed our leap into space, the times of discovery and then of colonization. New ecologies, new starry constellations at night, new songs to sing to children at night. But never did our ancestors forget their origin. Always they carried not only the heritage but the dreams of their home, their world."

Nagy looked immensely pleased with himself. Through her starstone-enhanced *laran,* Bryn sensed him: attentive and eager, yes, but also wary. Not quite convinced.

"Of course, differences arose, but we stayed together. The Empire became a Federation, and the Federation evolved into the Star Alliance we know today."

Scattered clapping answered him. A few of the Senators and other dignitaries who were seated near the front in places of honor got to their feet, but others held back.

"Now we face a whole new array of challenges. Rumors of dissent arise in every corner. The Free Worlds movement grows in strength. Shortly before I departed from Terra, Vainwal declared its independence from the Star Alliance—not a faction here or there, but an entire planet! Think of it, my friends. An *entire planet* repudiates the principles of the Alliance. Wants nothing more to do with us."

Desiderio? Can you hear me? When there was no answer, Bryn focused again on the drama unfolding before her.

Ernst threw up his hands. "What can they be thinking to reject the benefits of association with other worlds? Commerce, scientific exchanges, mutual protection, cultural enrichment? All gone, and for what? For mere regional pride?"

He paused again, while the muttering quieted down. "I'll tell you what they were thinking, my friends. The problem with using our space forces to suppress dissent is not just the immediate harm—the death toll, the destruction of cities and entire ecologies—or even the moral cost to those who give the orders. That I leave to your consciences to decide. The problem is that once the apparatus for such ventures is established, it perpetuates itself. All an ambitious person has to do is reach out his hand to wield it. And if that person happens to be the heir of Sandra Nagy, who would question his right to lead?"

The audience shifted, uncertain. Bryn focused instead on Arthur Nagy. He clearly suspected her father was up to something, although he might not know exactly what. Black took a step to Nagy's side, hands resting on a holstered blaster.

Nagy was still smiling, his posture easy, but he had come alert, nerves taut. He was apprehensive, but he was willing to ride it out for the moment.

Let the confrontation play out, Bryn told herself. *You'll know the right moment to act.*

"A leader who has inherited power," Ernst proclaimed, "or one who has been placed in power through collusion or trickery, is a leader peculiarly vulnerable to the seductive nature of force. Our ancestors understood this, which is why they created this institution, the Senate, to be a moderating influence and a check upon the powers of the First Minister. In ordinary times, this would be the case. But extraordinary times tempt even the best of men, the most altruistic of leaders, to use every tool at his disposal for what he believes is the greater good."

Nagy's psychic energy darkened, although his physical appearance did not alter. He was definitely unhappy with the direction of Ernst's speech. Ernst had not yet committed himself to an attack; there was still time to change the thrust of his argument. Meanwhile, the audience quieted down again, their attention focused.

Ernst went on. "First, of course, he must cause the public to lose faith in anyone who dared to stand up to him—his critics in the Senate, resistance groups, local planetary governments who want to make their own decisions—even those sectors of the press who report on differing viewpoints or news that contradicts him. Resistance groups get labeled as insurrectionists and criminals. How easy, then, to smash his opposition—whether that means bombing other worlds in retaliation for their temerity to demand self-governance, traumatizing generations of children, devastating natural resources—" with each phrase, his voice gained in loudness and expressiveness, "—or exploiting our scientific technology to control the minds of those who would stand against him."

Angry cries broke out across the chamber, most of them towards the back and sides where those of lesser political standing had been seated. Those members of the press who were physically present jumped to attention and attempted to converge upon the stage. Uniformed security guards held them back.

She had to wait until Nagy spoke. At the rate the confrontation was unfolding, that could be any moment.

Desiderio? she tried again. *Where are you?*

I'm here... came from the very limit of her telepathic range. *I'm not sure...locked away...* His mental voice cut off.

"As incredible as these charges sound, they are true! I am the living proof. When I would have spoken for Vainwal's legitimate aspirations, the First Minister had me kidnapped and these devices implanted in my brain." Ernst pointed to the blinking lights on his temples. "*This* is what Arthur Nagy ordered done to me!"

At Black's gesture, a StarOps agent rushed toward the stage. Bryn cut him off, placing herself between him and her father.

"Stay back!" Bryn screamed in the agent's face. The starstone pulsed, hot and urgent, in time with her heart. Her veins felt as if they were on fire.

The agent hesitated.

"Let him speak!" she yelled, as much to the assembly as to the StarOps guard. "Let him speak!"

To her surprise, the cry was taken up, at first here and there, then with growing force. "Let him speak! Let him speak!"

Ernst kept on, his voice soaring over the muted uproar. "You heard the speech I gave that day, one of unequivocal support of his policies. I tell you now that every word I was forced to utter was a lie. If he did this to me, what is to stop him from doing it to you?"

"The Senator is not well," Nagy interrupted. "He has only recently returned from a primitive Closed World. His traumatic experiences have unhinged his mind. He doesn't know what he's saying. As a great statesman who had devoted his life to the Star Alliance, he deserves our thanks and our compassion but not our unquestioning trust."

"Is what he says true?" called one of the Senators near the front, a gray-haired woman.

"Senator Haslund's speech on Vainwal independence?" a reporter said. "Did you use mind control on him, as he claims?"

"Of course, that isn't true!" Nagy snapped.

Bryn's danger-sense pounded through her body. She'd run out of time. Whatever she was going to do, it must be now. She'd have to set the truth-compulsion spell by herself. She pressed her hand over her sternum, where her starstone rested against her skin, and felt the answering flare of power.

In the light of the fire of this jewel...

With her mental vision, Bryn saw the flickering blue radiance envelop Nagy like a veil. The next moment, it winked out. She cast it again, with the same result.

"Pay no heed to the Senator's ravings," Nagy's manner shifted to one of concern for his colleague. "If a man changes his mind after careful consideration of the facts, that is hardly mind control. But now, alas, I fear he has gone too deep into his delusions. Everything he says is a product of his illness. He poses a danger now not only to himself but to the entire Star Alliance."

The spell would not hold. It *could* not hold because Nagy was now spinning out lie after lie, shredding the blue aura.

Step by step. Begin again.

She had never cast the compulsion part of the spell. That had been Desiderio's responsibility, and it required her to maintain her own part. How could she do both? It was impossible, and yet she had to find a way.

In the light of the fire of this jewel...

Nagy's energetic body glowed, his energon channels like a webwork of molten wires. Shaping the blue light into a gossamer veil, she lifted it high above his head and allowed it to settle over him. Unaware, he continued to speak, to deny everything Ernst had said. A ripple passed through the audience. His words were mesmerizing, and they were accustomed to obedience.

How could she persuade Nagy to tell the truth? How to pierce the layers of delusion?

Then it came to her, half-memory, half-instinct.

Find a black thing, find a white thing,

Find a hot thing, find a cold thing.

Her young patients regained control over their lives by simply asserting that things were as they were.

Let black be black, let white be white,

Let hot be hot, let cold be cold.

The second part of the spell was not so much a compulsion as an affirmation.

Let black be black, let white be white...

Let water be water, let fire be fire...

Let all things be as they are...

Let truth be truth...

Persuasion, she reminded herself. *Permission.*

Let the peace of speaking only the truth guide you.

Nagy continued talking, although he sounded less confident than before. Bryn was aware of her father, still struggling as he was dragged from the stage. Her concentration wavered. Nagy's tone shifted, coaxing and persuasive, and utterly smooth. As she reasserted the affirmations, Desiderio's strength flowed into her own.

Let truth be truth...let the peace of speaking only the truth...

Nagy stood utterly still. She could not see his face, but she *felt* the shift in his mind. The surrender, and then the relief.

At the same time, her danger-sense kept hammering through her skull. Red washed her vision. She shoved it aside, holding onto the blue light.

Let truth be truth...

Then Nagy said, "I gave the orders to transport Senator Haslund to the biomedical laboratories on Alpha and there to have implanted an experimental theta-corticator device—"

The shouting from the assembled listeners almost rocked Bryn from her feet. Their voices rose like a wave, suffocating her. *Hold on*, she told herself. A few more phrases and they would have him.

No, came another voice in her mind, one that echoed oddly. Each reverberation formed her thoughts more deeply.

Arthur Nagy is your leader. You owe him your utmost loyalty.

Black's voice it was, and Black's words! Although at that moment she hated him with every fiber of her being, her brain responded as it had been conditioned.

Arthur Nagy is your leader.

Bryn's danger-sense shocked through her, stealing the breath from her lungs. Her knees buckled, and she slammed into the dais floor. Her father was shouting her name, but he was nothing to her. Only Arthur Nagy mattered.

Only Arthur Nagy was to be obeyed.

She moaned, her arms and legs thrashing weakly.

You will support Arthur Nagy to your dying breath. You owe him your loyalty. You will not resist him in thought, word, or deed.

Bryn... came another voice, one that sent shivers of longing through her. This voice did not compel, nor did it plead. It summoned.

Bryn, remember who you are.

Who I am?

"—for his own safety and well-being—" Nagy pointed to Ernst, standing between two StarOps guards. "He is clearly deranged, his once-brilliant mind unhinged. We must prevent him from harming our beloved Alliance."

No, that could not be right. The reason she was here—she could not remember why.

Bruna, whispered the other voice in her mind, the one that did not compel. The one her heart chose to listen to. *It's the mind control device, like the one they used on your father. This is not what you truly believe. You're here to reveal Arthur Nagy as a tyrant, not to do his bidding. You must find a way to fight the programming.*

Although each mental syllable seared her, she managed to form the thought: *Help me...to fight it. Take it...from me.*

Horror answered her. *I cannot!*

You can, she pleaded. *You have the Alton Gift. I give consent—*

But already the moment of clarity waned, leaving her feeling even more alone.

Arthur Nagy is your leader.

Let truth be truth. The words rose unbidden to her mind.

Another voice answered, *Let Bruna—let* Bryn *be* Bryn.

Arthur Nagy is my leader...and leaders do not oppress those who trust in them. They inspire, they sacrifice themselves, they turn away from pride.

Arthur Nagy is my leader, and leaders speak the truth.

A weight lifted from her mind, from her heart. Her vision regained focus. On the platform above her, Nagy paused. His body quivered, visible only to those who, like her, were close enough. He glanced over his shoulder at her. White ringed his eyes. His face was suffused with blood and glossy with sweat. His mouth opened and closed, but no sound came forth.

Leaders tell the truth. But Nagy wasn't saying anything.

Hold on! Desiderio called. *I'll get there as soon as I can.*

"Sir?" Bryn heard Black's voice, low and urgent. Her vision swam with the effort of maintaining the truthspell. "Are you all right?"

Nagy gave a little shake of his head, the only free action he was capable of at the moment. It broke his concentration just enough for Bryn to push further through his resistance.

Leader! Lead! Tell the truth!

"I—I—it is all true. I don't want to—I want to—admit it, but every word Ernst Haslund just said is true."

Silence blanketed the hall.

"So what?" Nagy snarled. "The Star Alliance is *mine*, mine by birthright! I'm not ashamed of what I have done to keep it! I knew what my mother did, how she squashed the opposition. She never tried to keep it a secret from me, and why should she? The old Federation was weak and corrupt, festering in its own degeneration. She saved it—she saved you all! The cost, a few worlds that were worthless anyway?" His chest heaved. "*I* am what holds this alliance together. *I* am the one standing between you and chaos! You should get down on your knees and thank me every hour, every day!"

Without missing a beat, he whirled to face Ernst. "As for *you*! *I* am the leader, not you, not any of these mewling cry-babies. So yes, I had you abducted. My scientists implanted a device into your brain. Since you wouldn't see reason any other way, I had no choice—"

"There's no need to say more," Ernst said. "We've heard enough."

Nagy whirled to face Ernst, then the audience, and finally Bryn. His eyes narrowed and his mouth tightened into a short, straight line, as if he had now pinned her as responsible for his confession.

Just a little while longer.

"I—I— I deny it all!" He turned back to the assembly. "Something's wrong. I never said those things. I never did those things."

"You cannot erase the truth." Ernst's voice rang out. "You cannot take back what you have done…but you can begin to set things right. In the name of the Senate and the member planets of the Star Alliance, I hereby relieve you of duty."

Wild-eyed, Nagy glanced at the guards standing nearby. "Do something! Arrest this man!"

"Come away." Ernst took Nagy by the arm. "These men will escort you to a safe place where you can rest. We will arrange for your care."

"You can't do this to me! I'm Arthur Nagy, First Minister of the Star Alliance! I will not be dismissed by a mere—mere—traitor—rebel—"

Truthspell still enveloped Nagy, a shimmering blue halo that only Bryn could sense. He truly believed what he was saying. The paranoia had always been there, but having once blurted out the truth, he was now unable to censor himself.

"Can't you see what he's doing?" Nagy screamed, pointing to Ernst. "He's been after me for years—he wants to—" He gestured at the assembly. "You're all in league with him! Conspirators, all of you!"

Throughout the chamber, members of the audience got to their feet. Many of them shouted angrily. They were too numerous for Bryn to make out individual words, but their meaning was plain. Their emotions rolled over her, a wave of outrage that pummeled her mind as well as her ears. She could not maintain her psychic contact with Nagy. Her knees were shaking and her concentration shredded.

"*Enough!*" Black drew his blaster and aimed it at Ernst. "This ends now!"

Bryn hurled herself in front of her father. A bolt of searing energy shot out from Black's weapon just as Bryn and Ernst tumbled to the floor. Pain exploded along her ribs. She landed on top, limbs flailing. The breath went out of her as if she'd been kicked in the solar plexus.

Through her blearing vision she saw Black take aim again—

—and Desiderio burst through a side door, coming up behind Black. A knife flashed in his hand. He tackled Black just as the StarOps captain turned his head.

Black's next bolt went wild.

A man shrieked, and then suddenly fell silent.

With an effort, Bryn managed to roll off her father. She landed on her side, facing him, unable to move. All she could do was pant, high and light in her chest.

His eyes were open, but unseeing.

Gray lapped at Bryn's vision. She fought to stay conscious, but her muscles seized up with every breath.

Someone leaned over her. Spoke her name.

Darkness took her.

A world spun of grayness. Gray beneath her feet. Gray above her head, arcing from horizon to flat horizon. When she looked down at her body, it was almost translucent.

And chill, as if this world—and she herself—had never known the warmth of a sun or the touch of a human hand.

Hands… She raised hers, fingers growing more solid as she focused her attention on them.

I'm in the Overworld. How did I come here?

Memory returned. Terra. The Senate hall. Nagy. Her father's speech. Black, blaster in hand—

Father!

This was the Overworld, she repeated, where thought shaped reality. Thought, and longing. Here she could summon the dead, especially those she had once loved. Carefully she built an image of her father in her mind, not just his physical appearance as she remembered him but his warmth, his keen intellect, his courage…

When she had searched for Leonin in the Overworld, he had appeared as a distant figure on the horizon. Now she could not detect any change, only a gentle swirling of gray-on-gray fog.

Father! she called again.

Again, nothing. Could that be because she was dead? The last thing she remembered was being shot by Black, collapsing on top of her father's inert body, and losing consciousness.

As the scene took focus in her mind, she felt a shift in the Overworld. Instead of a flat horizon, walls appeared on three sides. On the fourth, a curved space with ghostly outlines of an audience. Below her feet, a smooth surface. Above, brightness. In front of her, the figure of a man.

She peered at the emerging shape, trying to make out features. Not her father…

Arthur Nagy.

Blank features came alive as he recognized her. His mouth opened and closed, shoulders lifting several times before he wheezed out her name. "Bryn Haslund."

Her hands curled into fists. She wanted—she craved—to beat him into a pulpy mess. To unleash her fury at everything he'd done to her and those she loved. But she held herself still. The Overworld was a realm of mind, not substance. She could not harm him.

"Bryn Haslund," he repeated, his voice quavering. "What is this place? Am I dead? Am I in hell?"

Yes, she wanted to say. *And you deserve it.*

As she watched, he seemed to shrink in on himself. Alone, as he had always been alone. Pitiable.

Seeing him like this, she found that she did indeed pity him. The emotion surprised her. She couldn't forgive, but she could and did feel sorrow. Sorrow not only for him but for the millions of lives he had immiserated and destroyed.

"This is the Overworld," she said. "It's where you must remain now, your new home."

"No, I must return—the Alliance—that traitor—" His eyes narrowed into slits. "You are the traitor's spawn. *You* did this to me!"

He rushed at her, arms outstretched. She pivoted so that he passed her and tumbled to the gray-fog ground, although she needn't have bothered. If she lacked the power to harm him, he could not touch her, either. Glowering at her, he clambered to his feet and faced her.

"Arthur Nagy, you did this to yourself," she said, "and I am sorry for you. You will have a long, long time in which to contemplate all the wrong you have done. I don't need to punish you. You will do that to yourself."

The gray firmament trembled, and a voice spoke in her mind. The words were fragmented, fading in and out.

Bruna… Bryn… Can you—hear me?

Desiderio!

Her body softened. A smile warmed her face. Tower-trained, he was probably the only person on Terra capable of reaching her.

My father? Is he alive?

Yes—here—

—follow—my voice—

She imagined Desiderio's words as a silken rope, and it appeared before her. When she wrapped her hands around it, the strands welcomed her touch.

She turned back to Nagy, thinking of the vengeful parting words she might throw at him. Then it came to her that what she wanted was to never see him again.

The silken rope guided her toward the light.

◆◆◆

Bryn opened her eyes to the brightness of a hospital room. Her father was looking down at her and holding one of her hands in his. When he smiled, tears spilled from his eyes.

Alive, he's alive!

On the other side of the bed, Desiderio looked up from the starstone cupped in his palms. Blue radiance washed his face. She felt his relief and his weariness.

She tried to speak, but her throat was dry and raw.

"Hush," Ernst said. "Don't try to talk. You've been in an induced coma for four days."

"What—" she croaked. *What happened?*

Desiderio took her free hand. The skin-to-skin contact catalyzed their rapport.

You suffered internal damage from a blaster, he said. *The coma was necessary to repair it.*

I've been out for four days? It had seemed like only a few hours at most. Alanna had warned her, as had others, that time passed differently in the Overworld. Those who wandered too long and too deep sometimes never returned.

I'm sorry it took so long to find you, Desiderio said. *These Terranan healers wouldn't let me help at first. When it became clear you would not wake on your own, your father intervened and demanded I be allowed to try. If I had been delayed further, it might have been too late. Your father's been terribly worried.*

Arthur Nagy—I saw him in the Overworld—is he—

Slain by his own man's blaster.

And Black?

In custody, charged with murder and a host of other crimes.

"Desiderio, what is going on?" Ernst said. "Are you speaking telepathically?"

"Yes, *Mestre* Ernst. She wanted to know what happened in the fight."

"What happened," Ernst said, gently brushing back Bryn's hair, "was that my brave daughter saved me, saved us all. Desiderio has explained to me how you compelled—um, *persuaded*—Arthur Nagy to confess what he'd done, and all the world heard his disdain for the Alliance principles. When he descended to outright raving and everything was falling apart, you took the blaster fire intended for me. I cannot—I never want you to risk your life in that manner again, do you hear me?"

She sensed his thought as clearly as if he'd spoken aloud: *Parents ought to sacrifice themselves for their children, not the other way around.*

Tears stinging her eyes, she nodded.

"The patient must rest now," came a woman's voice from behind her father.

Ernst bent to place a kiss on Bryn's forehead. "More later, sweetheart. You must heal quickly, and I have a government to put together."

Desiderio lingered for a moment longer. "I don't know how you managed the truth-compulsion spell by yourself, but you did," he said in *casta*, using the intimate inflection. "My Bruna."

◆◆◆

Two days later, Bryn was feeling well enough to sit up. Her throat had recovered enough for her to talk a little, and Ernst paid her several short visits. Early intervention had repaired the damage associated with his brief loss of consciousness, although he had been advised to take it easy. As far as Bryn could tell, he was ignoring that advice. Desiderio stayed longer, sitting quietly in a chair beside her bed. She found herself drifting into half-sleep as he extended his *laran* in healing mode over her. After he left, Bryn felt considerably better.

Saralyn arrived with a bouquet. "They said you were to have only one visitor at a time. I hope it's not too much for you."

"Not at all. I'm happy to see you."

"I'm so sorry!" Saralyn burst into tears. "Oh dear, I don't know what's wrong with me. I just—we left things so horrid between us, and then you were on the run and I heard Leo had died, and matters here went from bad to worse, and no one, absolutely *no one* had heard from Father. I didn't want the last words I'd said to you to be so beastly!"

Bryn held out her arms, and Sarah bent over for a hug. "It's all history. I know how difficult the situation was for you. For us all."

"But I made that disgusting speech—"

"Sara." Bryn held her sister at arm's length and held her gaze. "It's forgiven. I understand the duress you were under. The important thing now is that you and your family are safe. Father will need our support in the days to come."

"You're right, of course." Saralyn sniffled, then managed a tentative smile. She took out a newsreader from her shoulder bag and handed it to Bryn. "So you can catch up on everything you missed. I'm sure you know Father is forming a provisional government—the Senate wanted him to assume the post of First Minister immediately, but he wouldn't hear of it. Can you imagine his response to being told he's the only one who can save the Alliance?" Saralyn rolled her eyes dramatically. "Well, you'll want to hear for yourself."

"Thank you."

"I hope..." Saralyn hesitated. "I hope you'll come to dinner again, as you used to. The children and Tomas miss you and send their love."

"Give them mine in return. I will visit when I can, but I can't promise more. I've been so focused on finding Father and getting him back here, I haven't thought what comes next for me."

"Take all the time you need." Saralyn left Bryn to rest.

Bryn propped the newsreader against her knees and opened the reports of what had happened after she'd been shot. She skimmed over the details of Nagy's death and the charges against Black, focusing instead on her father's speeches. There he was, appearing before the Senate.

"Please, Senator Haslund! You're the only one who can restore order."

Saralyn had not been joking.

"—lead us out of this chaos."

"Nagy's gone, but it isn't sufficient. The damage to our institutions—"

From the podium, Ernst raised his hands. "My friends, please be patient. Great changes are indeed upon us, but we must not rush headlong to replace one despot with another."

Then, in another address: "My friends and colleagues, from this moment we will begin to take back the dream of a fellowship of worlds. Together we will rebuild the trust on which we all depend, a trust that has been eroded over the last generation. Working cooperatively in a spirit of mutual respect, we will strive for both justice and self-determination."

Yes, that sounds exactly like him.

On the day Bryn was discharged from the hospital, Desiderio came by to walk with her to the heavily guarded mansion already occupied by her father, her sister, and her family. Two armed plainclothes bodyguards waited outside the door.

"I'm glad for the company," Bryn said as she finished packing the few personal belongings she'd accumulated in her stay. "But you really didn't need to take the time. I know you've been busy." As the representative for Darkover, the only Closed World with present ties to the Alliance, Desiderio had taken responsibility for contacting Vainwal.

"There is much to do," he admitted, holding the door open for her. "The Alliance dictator—it is not the custom in the city to speak his name—may be gone, but the status of Darkover remains unresolved."

They set off down the corridor toward the elevators that would take them to the rear entrance. The bodyguards followed at a discreet distance. "How is the panel of non-Alliance worlds progressing?"

"We've set a date to meet in closed session, without any Star Alliance presence," he said. "I expect the discussions will parallel those on Darkover while each world determines what future relationship they want with Terra, if any."

"As our two worlds move forward, that will call for an exchange of embassies."

"I expect so, if we remain in contact. That will mean appointing official ambassadors, as well. I do not seek such a position permanently, but my work is a necessary and honorable duty."

Yes, Bryn thought, he would see it as his duty, a thing Darkovans in general and Comyn in particular took very seriously. It was as much a part of him as the color of his eyes or the shape of his hands. A wave of nostalgia swept through her.

"*Preciosa*," Desiderio said, "since the time of Recontact, my people and yours have had an uneasy relationship at best. Yes, there have been moments of optimism, glimpses of a bright future together, but many more times of suspicion and misunderstanding. In the end, it may be in Darkover's best interest to go our separate way, but we will ride that colt when he is broken to saddle, as my people say. Between the smugglers and the

StarOps ship, our isolation is already at an end. Now it's up to me to make sure whatever happens next does not place my world in further peril."

My world, he'd said. Not *our world.*

It was easy to dismiss her attachment to Darkover as romantic infatuation. The truth was more complicated. Truth always was.

"You've met my father," she said, feeling her way through her complicated thoughts. "You've seen how the people here look upon him almost to the point of adulation. That's been the case all my life. I've heard Darkovans talk about Regis Hastur the same way, so I think you can understand what it was like to grow up in his shadow. Oh, I don't begrudge him their respect. He's earned every bit of it. But I wanted something in life that was just mine, work that did a little good in people's lives. In the end, I don't know how much difference I made. I helped individual children recover, but I couldn't do anything about what caused those atrocities. While I was seeing one victim at a time, a thousand more were being created. Cities bombed, families ripped apart, and biological and chemical agents loosed on civilians. And that was before Nagy started using his mind-control devices on protesters. Who knows what happened to their minds afterward?"

Desiderio gazed at her with the quiet intensity she loved about him. "In the end, though, you *did* make a difference. You made the biggest difference at all. You were the one who revealed what Arthur Nagy was doing."

"But I could not have done that had I not gone to Darkover. What I learned on your world, and who I became as a result, is what made the difference."

I'm not the same person who chose obscurity, mending one mind at a time. I've seen a world of telepaths and towers, and breathless wonder beneath the four moons.

Desiderio reached out one hand, an invitation to the immediacy of physical touch. She brushed her fingertips across his palm. The intensity was almost more than she could bear.

"You're homesick," he said in *casta*. "Even though this is your world."

You will always be in my mind, he added, *in my heart, as I am in yours.*

She moved away, but he caught her, fingers curling around her wrist. For a heartbeat she stood, irresolute, knowing she could break free and yet unable to move. Then she was in his arms, reeling on the brink of tears. There was nothing more to say.

But there was something to be done.

♦♦♦

Ernst ushered Bryn into his office with an effusive smile, although she thought his eyes looked tired. His first concern, after making sure she was comfortably seated and supplied with sparkling fruit juice since she refused coffee, was her state of health.

"Desiderio said you were well and that we should have patience. The medics don't understand how you made such a rapid recovery. I confess, I'm familiar with only a small particle of the Darkovan healing techniques, and those focused on neutralizing the theta-corticator."

"Healing and telepathy are certainly the more benign applications of *laran*." Bryn sipped her drink. "Then there is truthspell, or rather the version that served us well against Nagy. It was sheer luck, I suppose, that I happened to have a natural talent for it, and that the folk at Nevarsin Tower taught me. But not all uses of *laran* are peaceful. You may remember references to The Ages of Chaos, when mental powers were used to create weapons of mass destruction. Even today, Desiderio tells me, forced rapport with another person's mind is considered a heinous offense."

"So I gathered," Ernst said. "I admit, I was skeptical when Varzil Hastur said that contact with Terra has not always been in Darkover's best interest. At the time, I did not understand how the reverse might be true, as well. We Terrans ought not to have unbridled access to Darkovan *laran* technology. I shudder to think what use Arthur Nagy might have made of the destructive power of *laran*."

"I think we no longer have the option of isolating ourselves from one another," she said. "The way forward requires us to respect one another as equals, not one empire deigning to grant protected status to a dependent world."

"Indeed. Desiderio represents his world admirably. I wish our diplomats were as hard-working. It is to everyone's benefit that the new Alliance has someone with equal dedication and an understanding of the differences between Terra and Darkover."

They talked for a while about the preliminary changes he'd instituted, measures that would ultimately grant the member worlds a greater say in their own affairs, and forums for airing grievances and negotiating restitution.

"I see I'm being tedious," he concluded. "You're a sympathetic listener, so it's easy to forget that not everyone is as passionate about interstellar policy reform as I am."

"You know me well."

"Well enough to see that you've come here for your own purposes. I had hoped to offer you a post in my administration, but I know that you would be unhappy. Well, my excellent daughter, you certainly have earned the right to ask for any favor you desire. What would you have?"

She told him.

"I will miss you, of course, but frankly, your proposal is as fitting as it is timely. It may not bring you happiness, but it stands a better chance of allowing you to recover—and to prosper—than anything I could suggest. I'll have my aides draw up your portfolio."

They stood up, taking one another's hands in a gesture that was both formal and intimate. "I do not have to tell you how it warms my heart that you yourself have come up with this new role."

"I would never have imagined it, either. Before Darkover, I don't think it would have been possible."

Before Darkover...

EPILOGUE

And Darkover again.

Bryn descended the ramp of the shuttle that had brought her down to Thendara's newly reopened spaceport and paused to draw in the air. The wind was brisk, edged with snow, and the walls and spires of the old city glowed in the crimson sunset. Then would come the quick hush of night and the arc of a thousand glimmering points of brilliance.

Home, I'm home.

But alone, so joy had a bittersweet edge. Desiderio was back on Terra, her counterpart and ally in ensuring Darkover's survival. What might transpire over the years to come, and how their lives might be once again joined, she could not foretell. In a way, it was better that she was returning on her own. This time would be hers, hers alone, and whatever she made of it.

She turned to the waiting honor guard, uniformed in the colors of Hastur and Alton, Ardais and Elhalyn, Aldaran and Ridenow and Aillard, with her staff arrayed behind her. She recognized a few of them and noticed the warmth behind their serious expressions.

"On behalf of the Seven Domains of Darkover, I bid you welcome once more." Varzil Hastur offered her a bow, equal to equal. "It's good to have you back among us again...*Domna* Ambassador."